A

BIGFOOT

HOMECOMING

A

BIGFOOT

HOMECOMING

A NOVEL

KIM ORENDOR

HILDEBRAND BOOKS
AN IMPRINT OF W. BRAND PUBLISHING
NASHVILLE, TENNESSEE

Hildebrand Books is an imprint of W. Brand Publishing.

j.brand@wbrandpub.com

www.wbrandpub.com

Cover design by designchik | JuLee Brand

Publisher's Note: This is a work of fiction. Names, characters, places, and incidents are a product of the author's imagination. Locales and public names are sometimes used for atmospheric purposes. Any resemblance to actual people, living or dead, or to businesses, companies, events, institutions, or locales is completely coincidental.

A Bigfoot Homecoming / Kim Orendor–1st edition

Paperback ISBN: 979-8-89503-022-6

eBook ISBN: 979-8-89503-023-3

Library of Congress Number: 2025946058

CONTENTS

For my dad,
If there are libraries in heaven, check this out.

The following story is inspired by actual events,
but it's not necessarily *all* true.
Names and locations have been altered to
protect the innocent—human and creature alike.

ACKNOWLEDGEMENTS

I'm fully aware that acknowledgements typically come at the end of the book, but I'm afraid if I don't address a few issues up front, you'll just fuss and fume—maybe even toss this book—until you reach the end.

The field of cryptozoology is often debated and sometimes laughed at by many as being ridiculous and made up. But, remember the coelacanth (see-luh-kanth), a fish that was supposed to be extinct seventy to eighty billion—Billion with a B—years ago, and suddenly, it's found happy as a clam swimming off the coast of South Africa? Some things feel beyond the realm of possibility, and I'm willing to acknowledge that. All I ask is that you acknowledge that the inverse is also possible.

Now, I must also confess upfront that while I have done my very best to stay true to the Wooly-Bully story my dad told me, I have totally changed the physical landscape of part of his hometown. Lexington, Missouri, is a very real place. It has beautiful red-brick churches with white trim and is home to the Lafayette County Courthouse that does indeed have a cannonball from the Civil War lodged in a column. For the sake of storytelling, I have added buses, moved a few trees, and pushed up a little knoll to get a better view.

I acknowledge my use of artistic license, and now, sit back, relax, and enjoy.

CHAPTER ONE

LEXINGTON, MISSOURI, 1956

Only the crowns of their heads were visible as the gaggle of boys knelt in a circle on the area rug. They formed a perimeter around a random constellation of glass marbles that covered the red-hued Oriental carpet and reflected the light from the crystal chandelier.

"You can't lean over to take your shot!" shouted a blond boy opposite the brunette with a large blue marble tucked between his thumb and index finger.

"You didn't call, 'No leans-sies,' Willie. Now, let Zeke shoot." The raven-headed boy punctuated his response by sticking out his tongue. "Come on, Zeke. Knuckle down and knock his bumblebee butt." He grinned and slapped Zeke's back next to him.

Ezekiel Renick—Zeke to his friends—blew a puff of air to try to get his hair out of his eyes. He glanced up across the circle and locked eyes with Willie, who was turning beet-red. Zeke was on a hot streak, having knocked six mibs (or no-good glass marbles according to his ma) out of the circle.

Looking around at the rest of the group, Zeke was greeted with smiles and lots of head bobbing. He leaned in and sent his big blue thumper on its way. There was a soft crack as the glass orb connected with the yellow-and-black striped mini, sending it out of the circle and causing a chorus of cheers from all but Willie.

The raven-headed boy scrambled to snatch the prize. "Another one for your collection, Zeke." He handed the bumblebee to his friend.

"No. No. No, no!" Willie scurried across the carpet on hands and knees, sending the remaining marbles in various trajectories across the floor. "That's my favorite mini. He already took my red masher. He can't have that one, too, Larry."

Larry positioned himself between the two. They'd all been off-and-on friends since kindergarten. This year in fifth grade, Larry and Zeke were on and Willie was off with both of them.

"Whoa, Willie." Larry, who was a few inches taller, extended his arm to push Willie back. "You said 'for keeps' and were fine with it until Zeke started knocking your aggies out. Don't be a sore loser."

The room was quiet except for the *tick, tick, tick* of the secondhand on the grandfather clock in the next room. The boys held their breath waiting for the outcome. Willie exhaled first.

"Okay. A fella knows when he's licked." He leaned back and sat on his feet. Willie put his left arm behind his back and stuck out his right hand to Zeke.

"No hard feelings?" His eyebrows arched as they shook hands.

Zeke nodded.

"Boys! It's time for dessert," came a baritone voice from the kitchen.

All the boys but two leapt to their feet and scampered, cheering and clapping down the hall. Willie didn't let go of Zeke's hand. He pulled him close, revealing his left hand with the index and middle fingers crossed and pointed at Zeke. "Promise don't count! You're going to give me back my—"

"Hey, guys, they have chocolate cake," Larry interrupted from the doorway. "Come on. There's ice-cold milk, too."

Zeke slowly stood, keeping a fixed gaze on Willie.

Willie made a sweeping bow. "After you, winner."

Zeke put his hands in his pockets to push the treasures down as deep as he could and side-stepped to join Larry and the others in the kitchen. The boys were shoving forkfuls of cake into gaping maws and washing it down with glasses of milk.

Zeke's stomach started to growl at the sight. He couldn't remember the last time he had cake, much less fresh, ice-cold milk. His ma had been forced to switch to powdered milk when they kept losing power to their fridge. It was too costly to replace sour bottled milk.

"Here's a piece for you, Ezekiel." A tall man in black slacks, a crisp white shirt, and wide black tie handed him a plate laden with the sweet confections.

"Thank you, Mr. Lewis."

"You're very welcome. Mrs. Lewis enjoys baking for the troop."

"And we enjoy eating," Larry said between mouthfuls. "Maybe she'd be happy baking cookies for our next Cub Scout meeting."

"Larry that's rude to ask." Zeke elbowed him.

"It's alright, Ezekiel. Mrs. Lewis is fine with requests. Is there something you'd really like?"

A flood of possible desserts washed over Zeke's thoughts. The edges of his lips slowly pulled up into a smile. "Have you seen those giant caramel-covered apples at Frisco's Market?"

"Ahem." Larry cleared his throat and hitched his thumb back toward the living room. Zeke's eyes widened as he recalled his friend sticking up for him.

"But who wants fruit? Chocolate chip cookies would be great."

Mr. Lewis laughed and ruffled the boys' hair. "You two are thick as thieves. Always good to have the support of friends. Got me elected mayor four times."

A loud clamor intruded as a couple of boys jockeyed elbows for more room at the table.

"Attention, Webelos," Mr. Lewis called over the din. Samuel Lewis had been the Cubmaster of Troop 115 since long before any of his current charges were born. "It's a nice night. Let's go finish up on the porch."

The boys carried their plates and glasses to the wraparound porch to finish their desserts. The muggy Missouri summer days became bearable as the sun began to set. The Lewis home had lights along the driveway, and the city installed streetlamps on both edges of the former mayor's property. It was literally a beacon on a hill in the small Midwest town.

Cars began lining up in front of the house, and one by one, the boys were whisked away by their parents. Willie, who lived four houses down, glared one final time at Zeke and Larry and stomped across the lawn.

"You two are last, as always," Mr. Lewis smiled. "Ezekiel, would you like me to drive you home?"

"No, sir, that's okay. The walk will be good for me." Zeke wasn't fond of walking at night, but he was less fond of people seeing where he lived. Even though Mr. Lewis had been to his home many times bringing bags of groceries and cash from the church's poor fund, Zeke didn't want anyone to see his house more than necessary.

Larry came around from the side of the house pushing his bike—the Schwinn Corvette model, a gift from his parents. The most beautiful bicycle in all of Lexington. Even Willie was jealous of it. With its whitewall tires and two-tone paint job, it was the Chevy Bel Air of bikes.

"Hey, Zeke, you want me to go with you to the bridge?"

"Nah, I'd hate for you to ride back up the hill."

"It's cool. This new bike has *three* gears. It's easy as pie to go up hills."

"Still, I'll be okay. There's enough moonlight."

"Okay. See ya later, alligator."

"After 'while, crocodile." Zeke waved goodbye as his friend rode across the lawn to the road and turned left. At the end of the lawn, Zeke turned right. He was the only Cub who lived to the right down Route 224, and one of only a dozen people—most of whom he was related to—that lived on Myrick Road.

He turned and gave a final wave to Mr. Lewis, who was just shutting the front door. The Cubmaster saluted through the diamond-shaped window frame and turned out the porch light.

Zeke stood in the middle of the circle of light on the blacktop. He slowly walked to the edge of the street where the light from the lamp started to fade. He toed the imaginary line between light and darkness with his faded black Chuck Taylors and stared down the tree-lined street, lit by the waning half-moon.

Runners set! He thought to himself and leaned forward. *Go!* He was off like a rocket.

Sprinting downhill was easy; it was seeing where he was going that was tricky. Near the edge of the road, he tripped over a new pothole. Zeke tumbled and stopped himself after a few rolls. He was brushing the road bits from the palms of his hands when a noise from the woods caught his ears. He froze. *Snap!* He quickly turned toward the sound and tried to make out shapes through the trees.

"Is that you, Willie?" he shouted, braver than he felt. "You trying to steal back your masher and bumblebee?"

Zeke's voice faded, and all he heard was the buzzing of bugs. "That's what I thought," he whispered, more for his own confidence than anything else.

He started down the road at a brisk walking pace this time, when a shadow launched itself at him from the far left

5

and sent them both rolling into the trees on the other side of the road. A scream caught in his throat as he grappled with the shadow. A shadow that transformed into Larry as Zeke's eyes adjusted to the darkness of the woods.

"L-Lawrence Everett! Y-you f-fool!"

Larry was laughing so hard he couldn't hold onto Zeke to wrestle anymore. "You should have seen your face." He opened his eyes and mouth wide in imitation. "You were so scared. Did I make you pee your pants?"

"N-no!" Zeke pushed his friend. "You w-would have been s-sc-scared, too, had some shadow jumped out at you." He crawled his way back up to the road, dusting himself off for the second time that night. "I thought you w-were Willie trying to get his aggie back."

"Sorry, no, just me, making sure you get home safe."

"You have a strange idea of safe."

"Yeah, you're right. I better get home before I get grounded."

"See ya, around." Zeke watched his friend ride his bike up the hill. He was alone again.

He approached the Lewis Creek bridge that acted as the "tracks" that Zeke lived on the wrong side of according to Willie. The actual train tracks ran along the backside of his home, so either way Zeke was on the outs.

The trees on either side of the bridge had grown so tall and wide they made a tunnel that extended about fifty feet along the road. When the moon was full, it was possible to get some light through the gaps in the trees to the road. Tonight, the moon was at half-strength. There was just enough of a glow for Zeke to make out where the "tunnel" ended at the other side of the bridge. If he ran his fastest, he should be able to cover the distance in five seconds.

On your mark. Get set. He screwed the toe of his shoe into the road. *Go!*

He was focused on the light at the end of the tunnel. *One-Mississippi.*

He heard the hollow *thud* under his feet as he reached the wooden bridge. *Two-Mississippi.*

He caught the scent of something rotting. *Three-Mississippi.*

The smell overpowered his senses, and he felt as if he was going to throw up. He slowly made his way to the edge of the bridge to be sick.

Snap. Crack.

There was movement in the trees ahead on his right. The odor was so bad his eyes began to tear up. Zeke rubbed his face and tried to focus.

"La-la-Larry if this is you, it's not funny anymore!"

He spun around at the sound of heavy breathing closer on the right.

"Willard Larsen! It smells more like you." Zeke reached into his pocket. "Are these w-what you're after? I w-won these fair and square. They're m-mine."

He turned in the direction of home and listened again. There was silence. Too much of it. Even the bugs were mum. He took a deep breath, started choking again, and stumbled toward home.

On his right, a shadow grew and towered over him. The smell of rotting forest overwhelmed him. He staggered back and the shadow moved toward him. A small shaft of dappled moonlight came through the trees and lit up the top of the figure.

Zeke wet himself as the light danced off a dark brown— almost ebony—eye framed by matted hair on an otherworldly face. Frozen in place, he watched as the creature appeared to reach out for him. His fight response finally kicked in and he threw his handful of marbles at the creature. There were muffled thuds as the glass orbs hit their target. Willing his lead-filled limbs to move, Zeke ran for home. He was nearly clear of the shadowy creature when he felt something grip his shin. Once again, he found himself tumbling head over heels down the road. When both his feet found the pavement after the second roll, he scrambled and ran for home, not looking back once.

Zeke saw the small light on the edge of their property where the road made a sharp turn. The city had put it there to help the increasing traffic on the road avoid driving straight into their house. At that moment, he didn't care. He was just happy there was any light at all.

He bounded up the three steps to the front door, turned the knob—thankful that no one in Lexington locked their doors—and made it inside. He quickly locked the door, pushed a chair in front of it, grabbed a penknife off the counter, and slid himself down the wall across from the door.

CHAPTER TWO

FLORIDA PANHANDLE, PRESENT DAY

There was a slight rap at the door. Ezekiel stirred in his sleep.

"Mr. Renick, it's time to get up." A young man with light brown skin and black wavy hair slowly made his way into the room. "It's me, Nathaniel."

"I know who you are," Zeke grunted. "You're the same idiot who's been waking me up for the past three months."

"Good morning to you, too, Mr. Renick." Nathaniel winked and smiled, causing double dimples on his right cheek. The orderly crossed the room and pulled back the curtains. The brightness quickly filled the small studio room. Zeke pulled the sheet over his eyes.

"Time to get up, sleepyhead."

"I like getting up at my own pace." Zeke yawned loudly, pushed the bedding aside, and slid his legs over the edge of the hospital bed. "This damned infernal place is killing me faster than aging."

Nathaniel chuckled and shook his head. He placed a paper cup with three colorful pills on the bedside tray and poured water into a small plastic cup. "This will fight off what's ailing you."

Zeke looked into the paper cup. "Really? These will resurrect my retirement fund and allow me to get out of this place?" His gaze fell, and his shoulders slumped. "I'm sorry, Nathaniel. It's not your fault, and I didn't sleep well. I could hear someone hacking and coughing down the hall all night. Gets to a person."

"Not to worry, Mr. Renick." Nathaniel walked over to the walnut-stained dresser and pulled two shirts from the top drawer. He grabbed the collar of each in one hand and lifted them.

"Red, please." Zeke pointed to his choice. "I'll stay in these sweatpants."

"Sounds good. Now, let me see you take your pills."

Zeke sighed hard.

"Not my rules, Mr. Renick."

Zeke turned the pills over in his hand and tossed them into his mouth, followed by a swig of water. He opened his mouth wide and stuck out his tongue at Nathaniel. "Thatisfied?"

The orderly shook his head. "I have a college degree, you know?"

"Well, college boy, let's go get some breakfast."

~~~

The dining area consisted of circular industrial-grade plastic folding tables with matching folding chairs. The black, white, and gray linoleum flooring had multiple cracks and curled up at the edges in the passageway between the kitchen and the eating area. The walls were covered in colorful posters with inspirational quotes. Zeke found most of them annoying, but the dachshund puppy framed by, "Who's awesome? You're awesome!" always brought a smile to his face. The Niceville, Florida, facility's heyday was obviously in the early 1960s, and he and it had seen a lot in the past fifty-some years.

While the majority of the thirty-six residents ate in their rooms, Zeke was determined to eat in the cafeteria. In his short time at The Palms, he had seen too many people stop leaving their rooms and then stop living altogether. There seemed to be very little gumption anywhere in the facility.

He joined a table with two other men. "Hello, boys. What's good on the menu today?"

The men looked up, the pull of sleep heavy on their eyes—then back down at their bowls of pale gray slop.

Nathaniel came over with a bowl of goop and a steaming cup of coffee and set them in front of Zeke.

"Oh, yay, I was hoping it was oatmeal." Zeke pushed the bowl toward the center of the table and pulled the white mug of java toward himself.

"Good morning, Mr. Conner, Mr. Phillips." Nathaniel nodded toward the other men, who barely glanced up at him. "Such a chatty bunch this morning. Mr. Renick, I'll get my morning paperwork done while you eat—and you will eat, yes?"

"Yes." Zeke grabbed the edge of the bowl with his index finger and slowly pulled it back in front of him.

Nathaniel clapped. "Perfect. I'll check the mail room on my way back."

Zeke raised the mug toward Nathaniel and nodded.

The trio ate in silence except for the occasional slurp from Phillips or Conner. Zeke had been introduced to them weeks ago but couldn't remember their first names. Looking at the duo—one balding, the other with close-cropped salt-and-pepper hair—he wasn't even positive which one was Phillips. Zeke was hoping to be discharged soon, so he couldn't be bothered to remember who was who.

If he was honest with himself, Zeke didn't *want* to make friends with anyone there because the place and its people were depressing. Except for Nathaniel, the young orderly with the perpetual smile who intrigued him.

"Mr. Renick, mail call." Nathaniel plopped a stack of envelopes and papers on the table.

"Oh, thank God, you're back. These two were talking my ear off."

The duo looked up but said nothing.

"Oh, I'm sorry, Mr. Conner and Mr. Phillips. I didn't grab your mail. I didn't think you'd still be here."

The two men looked at each other, stood in unison, and left the room.

"Strange ducks," Zeke said. "That's okay, I don't need them knowing my business."

He gathered the envelopes into a pile "for later" and divided the papers into "junk" and "worth reading."

Nathaniel plopped down in the chair next to Zeke. The orderly interlaced his fingers, leaned back, and put his hands behind his head. "Okay, Mr. Renick, let's see what tea the *Lexington News* is spilling today."

Zeke handed the paper to Nathaniel. "My glasses are in my room. Could you read it, please?"

A soft belly laugh hit Nathaniel. He leaned forward, took the paper, and smiled. Zeke always "forgot" his glasses. The nursing attendant shook and snapped the broadsheet newspaper, and it opened fully. He lowered it until just his brown eyes showed over the top.

"You ready for this?"

"I should have just taken it to my room," Zeke grumbled. "I'd be done by now."

"Ha! You'd still be walking," Nathaniel quipped. He looked at the front page, and his eyes widened. He extended his arms to distance himself from the paper.

"Oh, Mr. Renick, this is not a good news day." He turned the paper to face Zeke so the older man could see the large color photo of two cars crumpled together. There were three student identification photos inset in the story copy.

"What happened? Are those three kids dead?"

Nathaniel turned back and started to read. "The headline says . . . what? Wait, this can't be right."

"What can't be right?"

The young man set the paper down and rubbed his eyes. He picked it up and shook his head. "Nope. Nope, my eyes are not playing tricks on me."

"Don't leave an old man to die of suspense. What does it say?" Zeke leaned forward.

"The headline says, 'Star athlete speaks out about critical injury accident allegedly caused by Bigfoot.' What kind of crazy town are you from?"

"Stifle d-down." Zeke sat up straight. His breath caught in his chest. He rubbed his forehead and slowly breathed out. "W-what does the article say? Read it!" he demanded and then repeated softer. "Read it, please."

Nathaniel leaned back and lowered the paper. "Do you want to go read it in your room?"

"N-no, no. Please, just read it." Zeke lightly patted the orderly's arm.

"Lexington High School's starting quarterback Jimmy Nixon and two others were taken to Lexington Memorial Hospital after Nixon crashed his car into an oncoming vehicle on Route 224."

Nathaniel turned the paper toward Zeke again. "Jimmy is this kid." He tapped the color picture with his index finger. "Looks like your typical high school QB. Fair-haired, nice looking."

The orderly flipped the paper around. "He tied the state single-game touchdown passing record last year with twelve. Twelve!" Nathaniel stopped reading mid-sentence and locked eyes with Zeke. "This kid threw *twelve* TDs in one game? That's insane."

Zeke raised his eyebrows, nodded his head, and pointed back at the paper.

"Right, right. Let's see, where was I?" He ran his index finger along the story. "Here we go. Nixon stated he was headed out of town when a creature jumped from the mature tree growth near the Lewis Creek bridge, causing him to lose control of his convertible and slam into the oncoming car driven by fellow Lexington High senior Ray Reynolds. Olivia Dawson, a junior cheerleader at Lexington, was in the passenger seat of Reynolds's sedan."

Nathaniel turned the newspaper around and pushed it toward Zeke. "Obviously, Olivia is the girl in the middle. Isn't she cute in her cheer sweater." He tapped the picture of a Black teenager. "This is Ray. From the looks of the sedan, he and Olivia were lucky to survive."

Zeke reached out and touched the bottom of the paper. His eyes slowly tracked the page. A slight shiver caused his body to shake.

"Are you sure you're okay, Mr. Renick?" The orderly spoke in a quieter tone.

Zeke nodded, tapped the paper, and pushed it back to the orderly. "I'm good. Just saying a little prayer. Please, keep reading."

"'One minute the road was clear, and the next a giant shadow covered it,' Nixon said. 'I thought maybe it was a deer or a bear, but when I saw it in the headlights, I knew it wasn't anything that I'd ever hunted before. It was massive . . . a beast . . . it looked like those pictures you see of Bigfoot. And it stunk, like something that's been dead for days.'

"The Lexington Police Department administered a breathalyzer at the scene of the accident. Nixon passed. The hospital performed tests for other drugs. The results were not available at the time of printing.

"Nixon, Reynolds, and Dawson were all transported to Lexington Memorial for their injuries. Nixon and Reynolds were released after exams showed minor bruises. Dawson is still in the intensive care unit after emergency surgery for a ruptured spleen and broken ribs.

"Local authorities have not ruled out an animal may have played a part in the accident, but Chief of Police Tom Denton is 'not inclined to believe in mythological creatures.'

"Whoa, that's a crazy story. What do you think, Mr. Renick?"

Zeke stared off into space. He didn't respond.

"Mr. Renick." Nathaniel reached over to touch the older man's shoulder, and the sting of ammonia hit his nose. Looking down, he noticed that Zeke had wet himself.

CHAPTER THREE

LEXINGTON, MISSOURI, 1956

A kick to his side woke Zeke. He still had a death grip on the penknife.

"Oh, my gawd, is that smell you?" Another kick, this one harder, landed on Zeke's side. "Did you roll in a steaming pile of deer guts?"

He rolled away before the offending boot could land again.

"Sh-sh-shut up, Ethan." Zeke choked out as he got to his feet and stood across from his middle brother.

"N-n-no, stupid," he mocked.

"Ethan, you know what momma says about calling Zeke stupid," came a slightly deeper voice from the hallway.

"Thanks, Eli," Zeke called over his shoulder to his oldest brother.

Eli ducked to enter the mudroom and towered over his younger siblings. A quarter-inch shy of six feet tall, he nearly scraped his head on the low ceilings and had to duck through all the doorways.

Eli's eyes watered and he grabbed for his nose. "What the hell is that smell?"

"It's Zeke. He musta stepped in some ripe sh—"

"Language, Ethan James Renick!" came a sharp woman's voice. "Just because it's not the Lord's Day doesn't mean we can cuss like sailors." She stepped into the small alcove and pulled her thin robe around her. "Oh my dear Lord, what is that horrid smell?"

"Zeke," Eli and Ethan said in unison pointing at their brother and his soiled clothes.

"It was an accident, Momma. I was trying to get away from a monster . . ."

"Now, now. No need for that. The Lord hates lying as much as cursing. Now, you two boys go fetch some water from the pump and fill up the tub out back. I'll put some water on to boil to warm it up a bit. And you, young man," she pointed at Zeke. "You go out back, strip down to the suit the Lord gave you, and toss those clothes into the barrel for burning. There is no amount of soap on God's green earth that is gonna get that stink out."

"But Momma . . ."

"Don't 'But Momma,' me. Get to goin'. And why is there a chair in front of the door?"

Zeke kept his head and voice low. "To keep the monster out."

"Don't be a baby," Ethan chimed in, pulling the chair out of the way. He went to open the door and found it bolted. "You locked the door? Dang, someone must have really scared you."

Zeke looked up at this brother and then his mother. He was hoping to find sympathetic looks, but all he saw were plugged noses and faces screwed up in disgust. He followed his brothers out the door and went around to the back to clean up.

Before tossing his pants in the barrel, he noticed a large brown smudge on his lower right pant leg. When he pulled it out straight it was just a brown blob, but when he made a bend in the material, he thought he saw the outline of a handprint. A very large hand. Zeke looked down into the cuff and found bits of road, rocks, and a tuft of matted onyx-colored hair. He ran it through his fingers. It didn't feel like any animal fur he'd handled before. He brought it up to his nose and nearly fainted.

"Step back away from the tub," Eli called out. "I don't want to have to smell you more than necessary."

Zeke fumbled the hair into the barrel. He reached down to find it.

"Whoa, you stink but we don't have to burn you, too." Eli grabbed him by the shoulder and pulled him up.

"But . . ."

"No buts; get a move on."

Zeke sighed and tossed the pants into the barrel and walked to the other side of the tub.

"Eli, if you start the garbage fire now, it may make the bath warmer," Zeke pleaded.

"Oh, Eli, please, help me. I'm so cold," mimicked Ethan as he worked the pump handle up and down. "You'd be my hero if you started the fire."

"That's a great idea, Ethan," their mother said as she rounded the house with a pot of boiling water. "Eli, please get that fire started. It will help get rid of the smell, too. Two birds, one fire."

The brothers dumped their buckets of ice-cold water into the outdoor bath. Zeke waited for his mother to add the hot water before even putting a toe into the tub. Once the boiling water was added, he jumped in and quickly started to bathe. He did his best to lather up with the slip of soap, but he could barely manage a few bubbles.

"Be quick about it," Eli said as he started the fire. "This won't last long and probably won't even heat you a little. Mom's headin' to work, and Ethan and I are goin' across town to meet some guys."

"So, I'm all alone?"

"Come on, Zeke. You're a big kid. You usually like being alone."

"I like it when Ethan's gone. You're not too bad. And then there's . . ."

"Hah, there's nothing. Come on, kiddo, the sun's out." Eli stretched his arms out wide, closed his eyes, and turned his face toward the sun. He took a deep breath and turned back to Zeke. "Nothing can hurt you. Now, clean up but don't leave until the fire is out. You don't want to stink up *and* burn the house down in the same day. We'll be home right about dark."

Zeke suddenly felt very alone and very exposed. A quick scrub behind the ears and a few handfuls of water over his head and he dubbed himself clean.

~~~

The clothes on his bed were twice-hand-me-downs. Most of the damage was done by Ethan. Eli grew too fast to leave much of a mark.

Zeke threaded a well-worn belt through the loops and pulled it tight. Eli had punched new holes in it to secure the pants on Zeke's rail-thin frame. He tiptoed into his mother's room and looked at his reflection in her mirror. He pushed his hair back with both hands and pulled a lock forward in an attempt to look like rock-and-roll singer Bill Haley.

"What time is it?" Zeke winked and awkwardly shuffled his hips. "Time to rock."

He grabbed the penknife off the counter, tucked it into his pocket, and walked out the door humming the latest tune. He did a quick check to make sure the fire was out in the barrel, tossing a bucket of bath water on it for good measure.

Zeke strutted to the highway and his courage suddenly vanished. His feet refused to move.

"Don't be a baby," he admonished himself. "Like Eli said, 'The sun's out.' Nothing bad ever happens in the daytime."

He continued to encourage himself, and slowly, without warning, his feet started to move.

"Onward!"

One step after the other, he moved slowly back toward town, back toward the bridge, back toward whatever it was that grabbed him.

Zeke was scanning the dirt shoulders of the road looking for clues when he heard the whirring of tires on the road. He looked up and saw Larry hunched over the handlebars of his bike zooming like a missile down the hill. Larry pedaled backward and continued to pick up speed as his feet wind-milled faster. His eyes widened, and a slight shriek escaped his lips.

"Look out!" He regripped the handlebars and his fingers finally found the handbrake. He relaxed his shoulders, squeezed the brake, and fishtailed to a halt in a cloud of dust.

"What are you doing?" Zeke coughed out. "You coulda killed me."

"Sorry. I'm still trying to figure out these newfangled brakes." Larry put the kickstand down on the bike. "And I had to come see if you were okay."

"You gave me a good scare last night, but I'm a big kid. I'm okay."

"I can see that. But, I'm here because I saw your brothers walking down toward Main Street..."

"They're going to the soda shop." Zeke interrupted. "I'm guessing they'll be able to con some free malteds from Curtis."

"Ethan told me you saw a monster last night and messed your pants so bad they had to burn them." There was a mix of concern and confusion in Larry's eyes.

"Oh, I'm going to kill him." Zeke's ears started to turn red.

"Is it true?"

"Yes. I m-mean, n-no. No. Yes." Zeke held up both hands and took a deep breath. He slowly lowered his hands. "Yes, I saw something. No, I didn't mess myself."

"Oh, that's good."

"But," he lowered his head, "but, I did pee my pants."

"That must have been one scary monster."

Zeke looked up and tried to determine if Larry was mocking him. "At first I thought maybe it was you, *again*, or maybe even Willie."

Larry patted Zeke's shoulder. "Tell me everything."

After recapping the events, including running, tripping, wrestling, and throwing, they started looking for clues together.

"So, you really threw all your marbles at him?"

"Yep."

"Even your big blue thumper? And the red masher and mini bumblebee you won off Willie?"

"Yes."

Both boys sighed at the loss of such treasures.

They noticed some scuff marks on the side of the road.

"Hey, Zeke, does this look like it could be a mark from your shoe?"

Zeke carefully placed his shoe next to the print. They were the same length and had the same pattern, including the spot where the sole had worn through.

"Sure looks like it. Let's keep looking for other clues. I think I threw the marbles in this direction," Zeke said as he waved his hand in an arc.

The duo moved closer to the edge of the road. Zeke noticed a smooth pattern and stepped toward it. The odd shape intrigued him. He put his shoe next to it.

"Wow, that's the biggest footprint I've ever seen." Larry whistled low.

"Huh." It was still a confusing shape to Zeke until he turned his head to see it from Larry's point of view. "Do you know what this means? I wrestled with Bigfoot."

"No way! The Wooly-Bully is back in Lexington? I've got to go tell the fellas."

"Wait, we're still gathering clues. Don't go!" Zeke pleaded as Larry raced off up the hill on his bicycle. He whispered, "I don't want to be alone."

Zeke sat on his haunches on the shoulder's edge to get a better look at the footprint. A large truck roared by, kicking up dirt and small rocks. When Zeke reached to cover his mouth, he lost his balance and tumbled down the berm into the bushes and trees.

He quickly jumped up and looked around but saw no signs of a large coal-colored creature. He let out a small sigh and brushed off his clothes. It dawned on him that the putrid odor from last night was no longer there. He took a deep breath—no gagging smell.

"Huh, maybe my imagination did get the best of me."

A glint of sunlight reflecting off something on the ground caught his eye. He meandered through the bushes and was rewarded by spotting two marbles: a green aggie and the yellow-and-black striped bumblebee.

He plucked them from the muck and did a happy little dance as he wiped them off on his T-shirt. Zeke froze when he saw another large footprint leading deeper into the tangle of trees and undergrowth.

You need to move. Come on legs, move. Zeke mentally willed his muscles to get him back up the berm and to safety. A loud *crack* from somewhere in the trees ahead of him acted as a starting gun, and he was scrambling up the berm and didn't stop running until he was back in his house with the door locked and a chair in front of it .

CHAPTER FOUR

FLORIDA PANHANDLE, PRESENT DAY

"**A**re you doing okay, Mr. Renick?" Nathaniel, the orderly asked over the sound of the shower.

"Yes. Despite evidence to the contrary, I am able to care for myself." Zeke answered from the other side of the shower curtain. "I'm too young for those adult diapers."

"No one is saying it's time for that step. And you're right, eighty is the new sixty."

"Don't mock me. Besides, I'm not eighty yet." Zeke stuck his arm outside the curtain and flexed, a slight bicep muscle popped up. "The ladies in the memory wing swear I'm a catch."

"Whoa! I'm not messing with you. I've put clean clothes on the hooks here. I'm going to run next door to check on Eunice, and I'll be right back."

Zeke held a thumbs up above the top of the curtain.

The older man walked out of the bathroom minutes later in blue sweatpants and a matching blue shirt. He rubbed a towel over his still-wet brown hair. Zeke walked to the closet and started pulling out his clothes and tossing them on the bed.

"Mr. Renick?" There was a slight rap at the door.

"Decent. Come on in."

Nathaniel walked to the bed and started folding the clothes. "Are we reorganizing?"

"Nope, and I haven't gone crazy. I'm just getting some clothes together to go away for the weekend."

"Well, that certainly does sound crazy."

"Do you know where they put my suitcase? I can't find it in here." Zeke's voice echoed from the closet.

"It's probably in bulk storage."

"Would you go get it for me, please, while I finish getting stuff together?"

"They're going to want to know why I'm getting it and what you're up to."

Zeke shut the closet door with a solid *thwack*. "Why? It's mine." He walked over and started to neatly fold his clothes on the bed. "I want it. I need to go."

Nathaniel let out a slight sigh and walked to stand by the older man. "Mr. Renick, yours or not, the administration here is going to want a good explanation of why you're leaving."

"I want to leave. That should be reason enough."

"Mr. Renick, do you know why I'm the 'idiot' who's been waking you up for the last three months?"

"You're the kid with the college degree." Zeke pointed at him.

"Because everyone in this rehab facility has an aide assigned to them."

"My memory is sharp as a tack. I don't belong here," Zeke said.

"I'm not arguing with you." Nathaniel sat on the edge of the bed. "But, Mr. Renick, you're here because you had a mini stroke while golfing with your friends, and the doctor said you shouldn't live on your own anymore."

Zeke slowly bobbed his head, refolding the shirt in his hands.

"You forgot the real kicker to the deal." Color rose along Zeke's neck as he shook his head. "Let's not forget, when I woke up here, my buddy Lloyd told me our retirement fund was gone thanks to some pyramid scheme he'd been suckered into, so while I was out of it in the hospital, he had to find a place my social security check would cover." Zeke glanced around the small room. "Thankfully, decades of hard work earned me a room in Shangri La."

"I am so very sorry, Mr. Renick."

"I'm sorry for dumping all this on you. It's not your fault." Zeke sat on the bed, rubbing his face in his hands. "I have to go. I *must* talk to that boy. I'm probably the only person who believes him."

"What boy?" Nathaniel arranged the neatly folded clothes.

"The Nixon boy."

"The kid who says he saw Bigfoot," Nathaniel's voice cracked as he started to laugh. "Why would you have to see him?"

There was a sudden pain in Zeke's eyes and his shoulders slumped.

"I'm sorry, Mr. Renick, I didn't mean to upset you. Please, tell me why you're concerned about this boy."

Zeke got up and opened the top dresser drawer. He pulled it all the way out of the slot and turned it over. There was a tin box duct taped to the underside.

"What the hell?" Nathaniel breathed out. He slowly walked to stand next to Zeke, who was peeling the tape back and carefully handling the metal tin.

"I had Lloyd grab it from my apartment after I woke up here. He brought some clothes for me, too." He glanced over at the younger man. "No offense, but I wasn't feeling too trusting early on, so I hid it to keep it safe."

"No offense taken." Nathaniel smiled and shook his head.

The small box looked fragile. It was slightly bigger than the palm of Zeke's hand. He pried off the lid and carefully arranged the contents on top of the dresser. There was an aged handkerchief with something red stitched on it, a wood-handled folding knife, a circular green canvas patch, and two colorful marbles.

"My dad gave me this knife when I was seven," Zeke opened and closed the penknife. "He died in a factory accident when I was eight."

"I'm so sorry. . ."

Zeke held up his hand. He wasn't sure he could get through all the explanation if he had to stop and accept condolences.

"I grew up okay with the help of my brothers and momma," Zeke took a deep breath. "My momma sewed the cardinal on the handkerchief and gave one to me and both my brothers. She said, 'When you boys see that bright red bird, it means a loved one is thinking of you.'" He smiled at the memory.

"But these," he pushed the canvas circle aside and picked up the green and yellow-and-black striped marbles. "Now, I'm going to tell you a story, and you're going to have lots of questions, but you're *not* going to ask any until I'm done. Yes?"

Nathaniel held up a three-finger Scout salute, nodded, and covered his mouth with both hands.

"Are you f-ing kidding me?" Nathaniel shouted and then quickly covered his mouth. "Wait, are you done?" He mumbled through his fingers.

Zeke let a smile curl on his lips. "Yes, I'm done."

"So, you really think you had an encounter with a Bigfoot?"

"I *know*." The color rose on Zeke's neck. "And I also know that my family and friends made life miserable for me after I told them. I was ten, so people cut me some slack. But the Nixon boy, he's a star quarterback. They'll make his life hell."

Sweat beads formed on Zeke's brow.

"Well, I better go find that suitcase," Nathaniel said.

Zeke wrapped the younger man in a bear hug.

"You need to let me go, so I can get it," the orderly whispered. "I'll try to come up with a cover story for us while I'm digging through storage."

"Us?" Zeke uncurled his arm and stepped back.

"Mr. Renick, there's no car stored in the lot here for you, and I'm guessing it's been a while since you last bought a bus or train ticket?"

Zeke's eyes moved left and right as he searched his memory.

"That's what I thought." Nathaniel's eyes sparked. "I'll come up with a solid story so the powers that be won't ask too many questions, and I'll drive us in my car."

"Why are you being so helpful? I've been told I can be a pain in the butt."

The orderly shrugged his shoulders. "You're the most energetic and interesting person I've met in the two years I've worked here, and this seems like a pretty fun adventure."

"Here you go," Nathaniel said as he tossed the oversized canvas suitcase onto the bed. "Also, I'm so sorry to tell you that your dear friend Catherine Anne Tullis died."

Zeke scrunched his face. "Who is Catherine Anne Tullis?"

Nathaniel pulled the newspaper from his back pocket and slapped it on Zeke's chest. "She's Lexington's soonest to be buried resident. I found her name and funeral time in the obituary section. Her service in this Saturday, so we'll drive up there for it."

"I don't know her," Zeke paced the room. "Why would I go to her funeral?"

"Because when you ask the directors to leave this weekend, they are not going to let you go visit a kid because you both claim to have seen Bigfoot."

"Point taken," Zeke walked to the bed and started filling the suitcase. "Poor Caroline Tomas, she was such a sweet girl."

"Catherine Tullis," Nathaniel corrected. "Maybe you should let me do all the talking until we get to Missouri."

~~~

Two hours later, the wooden door shook, and the glass inset stenciled "T.S. Johnston, Executive Manager" rattled when Zeke slammed it shut.

"Don't tell me what I can and can't do!" He yelled at the administrator on the other side of the closed door. "You can't keep me from my own money! I didn't authorize any trust."

"Mr. Renick, let's sit down over here." Nathaniel led him to a group of chairs. "We don't want your blood pressure to spike."

Zeke pulled his arms out of Nathaniel's grasp, but he did allow the orderly to guide him to a chair. Angry tears welled hot on his eyelids. "It's. M-my. M-money." Zeke opened and closed his fists. "I had no idea Lloyd had tied up my finances like that. We set each other up with power of attorney decades ago when we started a handyman business. I should have known from the way he handled things back in the day that anything was possible."

Nathaniel nodded his head and patted Zeke's arm.

"I don't need patronizing."

"It's empathy, Mr. Renick. I want to help."

"If you want to help, then figure out a way for me to get to Missouri without any money and help that boy."

Nathaniel pulled out his phone. He tapped icons and swiped pages faster than Zeke's eyes could focus on the screen. "You youngins and your phones."

The "youngin" held up his hand with index finger raised and tutted. "I have a way, but you may not like it."

"You planning on robbing the bank?"

"No, but if we do it right, it's almost like free money."

"Do tell?"

"Have you ever heard of crowdfunding?"

Zeke's face scrunched, and he tilted his head.

"No worries, I'll explain it."

On the way back to Zeke's room, Nathaniel explained the internet invention of raising money for various reasons, including start-up campaigns, medical bills, macaroni and cheese, travel, and entertainment.

"You can literally raise money for anything as long as you make it worth it to people. You just need a solid hook, and people will come along for the ride."

Zeke paused as he started to open the door to his room. "Why don't we take this conversation outside to the patio? I think I could use some fresh air."

The duo continued down the stark hallway and outside, where they found two wrought-iron chairs in the shade of a giant magnolia tree.

"So, you're telling me that we just ask people for money, and they give it to us? No questions asked?" Zeke raised his eyebrows.

"Mostly. They don't ask questions because part of the format is we create a webpage and tell your story, and they pay to help you complete your story."

Zeke pinched the bridge of his nose, and his eyebrows tried to touch. "You're losing me, kid."

"Okay, okay." Nathaniel tapped his thighs and sat up straight. "Here's the Mr. Ezekiel Renick version: We put your story on the website. People read the story. People donate money. We get money. Ta-da!"

"That seems too easy."

"Well, there are a few other steps, making videos, creating bonuses for supporters, and some other stuff, but I'll handle that."

"People really give money just for people to drive across the country?"

Nathaniel shifted in his chair and pulled at his shirt collar. "Nathaniel?"

"Well, you have to be very specific about what the money would be for. There was some guy who really wanted mac and cheese bad, and he started a fund for that kind of as a joke, but he got thousands of dollars donated, but it can only be used for mac and cheese.

"So, when I create your page,   I'll say that the money would be used for gas, hotels, food, all necessary road trip things as we go off . . . in search of Bigfoot."

"You'll what?" Zeke sat upright, shoulders back.

"Trust me." The orderly flashed a two-dimple smile. "People love these types of stories. We'll have loads of money by tomorrow morning to start the trip."

"Well then." Zeke jumped to his feet. "Let's finish packing and go find Bigfoot!"

CHAPTER FIVE

LEXINGTON, MISSOURI, 1956

The rattle of the door roused Zeke from his fright-induced catatonic state, causing him to drop the penknife.

"What the hell, Zeke? Open the door."

"I'm comin', I'm comin'," he called as he fumbled around looking for the wooden handle.

The door burst open, and Ethan and Eli came falling through nearly on top of each other. Zeke shuffled back toward the wall. He folded the knife and tucked it into his pocket as his brothers untangled themselves.

"You are so dead." Ethan's face flushed brick red. He reached out his arms to grab Zeke's feet. "I'm going to kill you."

Eli started to laugh and held Ethan firmly around his waist, preventing any forward movement. Zeke let out a tentative chuckle that grew as his middle brother continued to squirm.

Ethan turned his face from Zeke to Eli and back again. His squirming lessened and his face cooled to a pale pink. "I don't see what's so funny."

"You are," said Eli as he stood up, still holding Ethan at the waist. The middle brother looked like an upside-down V as he stretched to reach the floor with his fingers and toes. "You are for getting all riled up over Zeke locking the door." Eli released his grip, sending Ethan to the floor.

Zeke let out a giggle that he stifled as his middle brother locked eyes with him.

"You think it's funny, Little Man?" He pushed himself into a crawling position. Zeke shook his head, and his eyes widened. "I'll show you funny."

In a blur, Ethan leapt and turned Zeke onto his back. He started to tickle his younger brother, who giggled and squirmed.

"Help, Eli, please, make him stop."

Eli pursed his lips and rubbed his chin. "I don't know, Zeke. This seems pretty funny to me, too."

Between bursts of laughter, Zeke squeaked out additional pleas for help.

"Okay, that's enough. Let him up."

"Aw, man." Ethan started to get up and then snuck in one last tickle on Zeke's side. "What good is a little brother if you can't pick on him?"

Eli motioned with his hand for Ethan to move away. The middle brother headed down the hallway.

"Thanks, Eli," Zeke managed to get out as he caught his breath. "You're my hero."

"Stop it. I didn't bring back any candy for you today."

Zeke nodded. "It's okay. You're still my favorite brother."

"I heard that," Ethan hollered from another room.

Eli and Zeke shared a laugh.

"I guess since you're home I'll be needin' to get wood for the stove for dinner," Zeke said, pushing himself up off the floor.

"It's barely afternoon, silly."

Zeke jumped up and looked out the door. The sun was still high in the sky.

"You said you'd be back near dark."

"Well, after your buddy Larry rode his bicycle right into the middle of our group outside the soda shop screaming how it was true that the Wooly-Bully was real and you'd seen him and fought him, well, we had to come back and see for ourselves." Eli wiped sweat from his brow. "Larry and the guys are circling the blocks downtown to pick up any other boys who want to come help us."

"So, let's go have a look." Ethan came back into the room with a slingshot in his front pocket and his BB gun tucked into his belt. "Let's go get us a Bigfoot."

Zeke pulled the penknife from his pocket and unfolded it. "Ready!"

"Whoa! Hold up there, Davy Crockett and Daniel Boone," Eli took the knife from Zeke and folded it away. "We're not going hunting."

The younger brothers pouted.

"Okay, here," Eli handed the folding knife back to Zeke. "but, we're *exploring* . . . like Lewis and Clark. Not hunting."

Zeke and Ethan nodded as their smiles grew.

The trio stepped outside and headed for the bridge. Their excitement was bolstered by seeing their friends from town coming down the hill on their bicycles. It was going to be a massive search party. However, Zeke's excitement turned to dread as the town boys slid their bikes to a stop on the side of the road, kicking up a massive cloud of dust.

"No! No, no, no, nonono . . . no," he screamed as he ran toward them.

When his brothers caught up and the dust settled, the road was devoid of any tracks. The footprint on the edge of the road was gone. A fat bike tire was parked over where it had once been.

Zeke hung his head. "It's gone. All gone." He looked up to see Larry rolling up to join the group.

"Sorry, Zeke, I'm slow. I've got little legs." Larry saw Zeke's shoulders slump. "What's the matter? Look, I mustered a whole army to look for signs of Bigfoot."

"They messed up all the clues," Zeke pointed to the side of the road where both boys had seen the clear footprint earlier. "Now, it's Chuck Taylor and Schwinn tracks."

The older boys started looking around the road. One boy—Zeke thought Eli called him Morris or Moron—kept jumping out at everyone from the brush, beating his chest and roaring like King Kong. Zeke glared at the boy and decided he *was* a moron.

"I've seen *King Kong*, and it wasn't him." The youngest Renick mumbled under his breath.

Zeke was pulled from his annoyance by whoops and hollers coming from Lewis Creek. Some of the older boys had scurried down the berm and raced to check under the bridge, while a few refused to join the hunt and just leaned on their bicycles. Zeke's heart wasn't in it, but he walked into the brush area after his brothers.

Soon, some of the boys let out a loud whistle. "We found him. We found him."

Zeke's jaw dropped and his eyes nearly popped out of his head. The trio ran to join the rest of the pack on the road. One boy was holding a large swath of fabric and a pair of overalls.

"Found these here under the bridge. Your Wooly-Bully is just some hobo who decided to stick around and not catch the next train out of town."

"Phew, boy, Roger, those stink. Toss 'em back over," Eli covered his mouth and nose with his hand. "Smells like you fellas solved the mystery."

"See? I told you there was no such thing as a big-footed Wooly-Bully," Roger said to the cluster of boys. "I believe Curtis owes us all root beer floats for losing the bet."

"My pop's gonna kill me," moaned Curtis, whose dad owned the soda shop on Main Street. "You comin', Eli? I'll treat you and Ethan, but not Zeke. He wasn't there when the bet was made."

"No thanks," Eli said, putting a hand on Zeke's shoulder. "You go on without us."

"Us? I'm going to get me a root beer float," Ethan stepped forward. "Now which one of you guys is the lucky one to ride me on your bike?"

The group broke apart quickly but not before Ethan snagged the back of Larry's bike. "Oh, this is actually better. I'll pedal and you sit on the handlebars."

Zeke and Eli watched and laughed as Ethan fought to keep the bike balanced with Larry on the handlebars.

"You coulda gone. I'd be okay," Zeke told his brother.

"Nah, I don't think he really lost the bet," Eli said. "Those hobo clothes smelled horrible, but not nearly as bad as whatever you rolled in last night. And while you are not the brightest kid in your class, I'm pretty sure you can tell the difference between a drunk without his pants and some wild creature."

"Thanks, Eli. You really are my favorite." Zeke wrapped his arms around his brother.

"Why don't you show me where you found things earlier today?"

Zeke retraced his steps, pointing out where the footprint had been. He tried to draw it, but it kept looking like an hourglass instead of a footprint.

"I think I get the idea," Eli said, patting Zeke's head. "A couple years back, the paper had a story that a farmer in Jackson County saw similar tracks."

"Really?" Zeke's eyes grew wide.

"Yep. And old man Humphrey told Mr. Jenkins that he'd heard from a sheriff down in Warrensburg that he'd been called out to someone's house because a hairy man was walking through their yard at night."

"Nuh-uh." Zeke squinted and cocked his head.

"What? You don't believe me." Eli held up his hands. "Humphrey said they had pictures of huge footprints." He spread his hands shoulder-width apart. "The couple said it was so tall it just walked over their three-foot fence like it wasn't even there."

Zeke rubbed his chin. "I don't know if what I saw was *that* tall."

"I'm sure there's more than one Bigfoot anyway. Did you see anything else before the fellas messed everything up?" Eli asked.

"Oh, yeah, I found some of my marbles down here."

The two slid down the berm and were soon surrounded by high weeds, bushes, and trees. Zeke led the way, carefully pushing limbs out of the way, until they reached a small clearing.

"It was over here in the muck." Zeke took a timid step. He inhaled deeply, but the air smelled like normal. He scanned the ground. "There! It was right there."

Two small divots were still in the ground where Zeke had plucked up his marbles. He knelt beside them. "See, Eli? I wasn't lying."

Eli started to bend to get a closer look when he froze. His gaze was nearer the river's edge. Zeke held his breath and followed his brother's gaze. There by the water were two massive footprints.

"Zeke, buddy, judging by the distance between prints, your Wooly-Bully may just be *that* tall."

CHAPTER SIX

ON THE ROAD, PRESENT DAY

"Eli sounds like a great brother," Nathaniel said, keeping his eyes on the highway as he drove them north.

"He was a horrible brother," Zeke spat out.

"Huh?" Nathaniel turned his head and the wheel sharply. "Whoa. Sorry about that. But why would you say that?"

"Keep your eyes on the road," Zeke pointed forward out the window. "I don't want to be buried with Charlene."

"Catherine! Come on, Mr. Renick." Not wanting to jerk the car again, Nathaniel turned his head slightly until he could see Zeke in his peripheral vision and caught a smile growing on the older man's face.

"Gotcha," Zeke said and burst out laughing. Nathaniel joined him.

The young driver tilted his head. "Wait. Was that some sort of Freudian slip? Was there a Mrs. Charlene Renick?"

Zeke huffed. "No, there wasn't a Charlene." The older man blushed.

"Oh, but that tone means there was *some*one. Spill!"

"You should concentrate on driving."

Nathaniel regripped the wheel and leaned forward. "I can concentrate and ask questions. Let's play twenty questions so we can get to know each other."

"I'm going to regret this." Zeke took a deep breath. "But . . . fire away."

"Was there a Mrs. Renick?"

"Yes, my mother Ruth."

Nathaniel pulled the wheel slightly to the left. "Sarcasm makes it difficult for me to keep my focus on the road."

The older man smiled and raised his hands. "Okay. A man knows when his life is in danger."

"Was there a Mrs. Renick that you married?"

"Two. Or technically, maybe one."

The car swerved.

Zeke's eyes bulged. "That was an honest answer."

"I'm sorry. It caught me off guard." Nathaniel relaxed his grip on the steering wheel. "Won't happen again."

The older man held up two fingers.

"That's not two questions."

"You asked two questions. Not my fault you repeated one." A smile grew on Zeke's face, creating laugh lines around his eyes.

"Who were they? And what was the technicality?"

Zeke rubbed his face with his hands. "Do you really want to know all this ancient history?"

"Yes, please."

The older man blew a raspberry and lolled his head. "Gaylynn Hall and Claire Page. My freshman year of high school, I fell hard for Gaylynn. She was nearly as tall as me with deep auburn hair and green eyes that had those golden flecks."

"She sounds beautiful."

"She was. She was also Catholic, and her dad was against Protestant boyfriends. But, teenagers will be teens. I was walking her home one day—we'd stop walking together several blocks from her house—but this one day she says, 'You wanna kiss me, don'cha?' And, boy, I did, but I didn't want any of her five brothers to beat me up, so I just shook my head. Do you know what she did?"

Zeke shifted to face Nathaniel and tapped the seat between them.

"No, what did she do?" the orderly asked.

"She grabbed me by the T-shirt and pulled me toward her and planted her lips on mine."

Nathaniel's eyes grew wide, and a double-dimpled smile covered his face. "What did you do?"

"What could I do?" Zeke slapped his leg. "I kissed her back. Every part of my being felt tingly. It was the greatest feeling ever."

"Then what happened?"

Zeke's head fell forward, and he pursed his lips. "Her brothers found out and threatened me within an inch of my life. We were able to talk in school, but one of her brothers always walked her home the rest of the school year. I did my best to forget her—even asked Patty Macon to the fall dance—but I couldn't get Gaylynn out of my head. So, after I finished my time in the service, I decided if I could survive my brothers and boot camp, I could survive her brothers. I went back to Lexington, found her, wooed her—beat off her brothers—and married her."

"You beat up all *five* brothers?"

"No, just the biggest." Zeke flexed his skinny bicep. "I know it doesn't look it, but after the service, I was pretty fit. And it turns out her brother had a glass jaw. One hit, and down he went."

"Wow, Mr. Renick, how long were you married?"

"Two years. I think. It was annulled, so I'm not sure if it really counts."

"What?" The car jerked to the right. "I'm sorry. I'm sorry. But it's really your fault for saying such crazy things."

Zeke waved him off. "As fun as this is, digging up old dirt, I'm sure we can find something to talk about other than me for the next fourteen hours."

"If you're awake for more than half of them, I'll be impressed." Nathaniel tuned the satellite radio to Golden Oldies. "Some music will help the miles roll by."

Zeke leaned back against the headrest and closed his eyes. He hummed along with most songs, and for some he even tapped his toes to the beat with his shiny loafers. "A man needs to look sharp when he travels."

The opening chords of a popular ballad echoed through the car. Nathaniel bounced in the driver's seat and put his hands at the top of the steering wheel. "Oh, get ready, Mr. Renick, this is my jam."

Zeke's jaw dropped and he stared agog as his companion belted out "Sweet Caroline" along with Neil Diamond. The song filled his head, and Zeke was transported to his early twenties. The words returned to him, and he started to sing the chorus.

"Yes, Mr. Renick!" Nathaniel's smile grew as Zeke took the next verse.

When the song finished, the men laughed and shared high fives. Zeke held his chest and closed his eyes.

"Are you okay?" Nathaniel's voice rose in concern.

Zeke reached across and patted his arm. "Oh, I haven't felt this good in ages. I just need to catch my breath. I forgot how strenuous singing can be." He let out a deep breath and looked over at Nathaniel. "You don't even look slightly out of breath."

"All my karaoke training." Nathaniel tapped his chest area. "I've got air for days."

"Carrie Oakly?"

"Yes, karaoke. It's a Filipino tradition."

"You're Filipino?"

"Yes." Nathaniel glanced over at Zeke, who was rubbing his hands through his hair and shaking his head. "Ah, you thought I came from a different island or maybe south of a border."

Zeke's neck began to flush. "What, no. I didn't think . . . well, I wasn't sure . . . Are you sure?"

Full belly laughs escaped Nathaniel and the car drifted slightly as he reached up to wipe tears from his eyes.

"Both hands on the wheel?"

"Sorry, sorry." Nathaniel put one hand back and used the other to dab away the happy tears. "Oh, I'm sure. My mom loves to tell me how we are descendants of the Manila Men of Louisiana—my ancestors were here before the Revolutionary War. They jumped off the Spanish galleons docked near New Orleans rather than be slaves." He made a fist and shook it in the air. "Stupid Conquistadors!"

He returned his hand to the wheel with the flourish of a hand model. "They created their own community in the swampy marshes. They were amazing shrimpers who had good times but also battled a lot of suffering and destruction with prejudice and hurricanes. After a while, mom says some of our ancestors grew tired of Louisiana and moved east to Florida."

Zeke's blank stare caused Nathaniel to chuckle. "Did you have another stroke?"

The older man shook his head. "Maybe. I thought for sure you were . . . actually, I had no clue . . . I just assumed."

"Ah, your sweet, confused face reminds me of my *Tito* Efren . . . May I call you *Tito*? It's Tagalog for uncle."

Zeke pulled at the seatbelt. "That sounds better than Mr. Renick, but if we run into another Filipino, and I find out you've actually been calling me 'confused old man' . . ."

"Hah, no, cross my heart, Tito." Nathaniel traced an "X" across his chest. "And why don't you call me Nate."

Zeke nodded. "Okay, Nate. What's next on your list of things to do on a road trip?"

"Let's make a video for the crowdfunding page." Nate's eyes widened, and he pointed to the device attached to the dashboard. "You can either look into the camera or out the window, whatever is good."

Zeke looked at the small camera attached to the dashboard. "I thought it was a radar detector."

"Yep, you are just like Tito Efren." Nate reached his right arm out and tried to maneuver his index finger near the "record" button.

"Oh, my gosh, did they not teach you to drive by keeping both hands on the wheel at ten and two?"

"Ten and two?"

"Yes, like a clock." Zeke grabbed an invisible steering wheel in front of him. "You hold one hand at ten o'clock and the other at two. Like this."

Nate put his hands in a similar position and looked over at Zeke, who nodded his approval. The young man slipped his hands down the wheel to eight and four. The smile on Zeke's face faded. Nate moved his hands upward where they landed at nine and three.

"I'm sorry, Tito, but this is where I'm supposed to hold it so the airbag doesn't break my arms and pretty face."

Zeke grabbed the seat belt and started to speak.

"Tito, if your next sentence starts with, 'Back in my day,' . . ."

Both men started laughing. Nate reached out and hit the red circle on top of the camera as Zeke rubbed his chin and lolled his head around to loosen his neck muscles.

"Are you ready to tell your story, Tito?"

Zeke let out a long breath and stared at the camera lens.

CHAPTER SEVEN

LEXINGTON, MISSOURI, 1956

The house shook as the train rumbled by in the early evening.

"How is it that late already?"

"Time flies, Mom," said Zeke, "and so does the Missouri Pacific Railroad." He smiled at his own joke.

"Very funny young man. Go out back and pick some veggies. I'll make some soup for dinner."

His shoulders slumped and his smile faded as he turned toward the door.

"Zeke, some people don't have veggies in their soup."

He let out a long sigh. "Yes, ma'am."

The loud stomping of feet and a chorus of whooping and hollering beyond the door froze him in his tracks. He glanced back at his mom, whose confused gaze mirrored his own. He stepped back toward her as the door burst open and Eli and Ethan came rushing in, both holding a squirrel in one hand and a small rifle in the other.

"We got dinner," they crowed in unison. Zeke and his mother hugged each other.

"The Lord doth provide," she said. "Thank you, Lord, for boys with good aim."

Smiling from ear to ear, the boys put their bounty on the counter.

"Just what do you think you're doing? You boys take those out back and clean 'em and we'll have meat with our soup."

"Oh, boy!" Zeke clapped his hands. "I'll get those veggies."

The boisterous trio headed out the door. As they rounded the house, Eli stopped short, causing Ethan and Zeke to crash into him and each other.

"What's the holdup?" Ethan pushed him forward.

"Yeah, what's the hold—" the words caught in Zeke's throat as he could now see the man walking through the brush.

Eli put his arm out to the side to prevent his brothers from moving forward. "We don't want any trouble, mister."

"I'm not looking for any. I'm just looking for a bite to eat, and it appears you have plenty." He gestured to the squirrels. "Seems I picked the right spot to jump off the train."

"Zeke, go get Mom." Eli didn't take his eyes off the man.

"But . . ."

"No buts. Go!"

Most of the time, Eli's tone was big brotherly. But there were times when he sounded like a dad, and this was one of those times. Zeke beat a quick path into the house and found his mom in the kitchen.

"You back already?" She noticed Zeke's wide eyes and ruddy complexion. "Are your brothers causing trouble?"

He shook his head and took deep breaths. "No, ma'am. Eli sent me to tell you that there's a hobo in the yard! He wants to stay for dinner."

His mom's eyes widened, and she wiped her hands on her apron. "Well, let's go meet him."

They found Ethan, Eli, and the man in the same places where Zeke left them. The man took off his tattered cap and tipped it to the boys' mom. His overcoat was covered in brambles from the bushes and had patches on the elbows. His jeans were stained and had several tears at the knees. His shoes were held on by rope and tape.

"Hello, missus, the name's Charlie."

"I'm Mrs. Ruth Renick, and these here are my boys: Elijah, Ethan, and Ezekiel." Eli and Ethan stood perfectly still, but Zeke gave a half-hearted wave when his name was called.

"Good lookin' boys. Strong Bible names, and I can see they're good shots. I'd be mighty grateful if you could spare a bit of your meal."

"The Good Book says in Second Thessalonians Three that if a man don't work, he don't eat."

The man twisted his cap and stared at the ground. "Yes'm."

The boys stared at their mother, who never seemed so tall.

"That being said," Ruth continued, "you can split that pile of wood there and stack it against the house by the tub."

Charlie looked up and smiled a gap-toothed grin. "Yes, ma'am, I can do that. Thank you."

"Eli, get those squirrels cleaned, and Ethan, get the pail and pick a few vegetables."

"But, Ma," Zeke started. She squeezed his shoulder.

"I'll find chores for you inside."

In the kitchen, Zeke could hear the thump of the axe as it split the wood, and the chatter of his brothers' bickering. "Why can't I be outside with the others?"

"My Christian spirit means I have to be kind to others, but it don't mean I have to trust them. Eli and Ethan can look out for themselves. But you," she ruffled his hair and pulled him close. "You, you need a little more looking after."

"Ah, Momma." He pushed away and ran his fingers through his hair.

~~~

There was a waist-high stack of wood against the house when Ruth brought out a bowl of soup and a slice of bread for Charlie. Zeke trailed behind her and stopped at the edge of the house.

"Mr. Charlie. Thank you for your work. You're welcome to eat back here." She sat the meal on the splitting log. "When you're done, just leave the bowl and spoon right here."

"Thank you, ma'am."

She turned to head back to the house and locked eyes with Zeke. "And don't worry about being bothered," she added. "I'll keep the boys in the house."

Zeke let out a sigh and rolled his eyes. "I just wanted to see if he had manners."

"Get in the house, now."

Ethan and Eli were already sitting at the table when Zeke and their momma walked into the house. A steaming pot of soup and half a loaf of bread were on the table.

"Zeke, grab some bowls and spoons, so we have something to eat out of." Ruth shook her head and laughed. "Figures you two would get the food and forget the rest."

Eli flushed. "Sorry, Momma." He jumped up, grabbed glasses, and filled them from the jug.

When they were all seated, Ruth reached out her hands. The boys completed the circle somewhat reluctantly and instinctively bowed their heads. Ruth smiled.

"Thank you, Lord, for today's gift and for the bounty to share. Thank you for my boys. Thank you for the reminder from Mr. Charlie to be thankful for the home we have and to help others in need. Amen."

A chorus of "amens" came from the boys, who quickly filled their bowls. The first few bites were much too hot and all three of them were fanning open mouths.

"Do you think that hobo is using the spoon or drinking from the bowl?" Ethan asked.

"I coulda told you if Momma woulda let me stay out there."

"Don't be rude," Ruth scolded. "Mr. Charlie has fallen on hard times, but that doesn't make him crazy. I'm sure he uses a spoon."

"Oh, he just might be crazy the way he was talkin'," Ethan started. "Ouch! Whatcha kick me for, Eli?"

All eyes were on the eldest, who parted his lips as if to say something but then decided to put another spoonful of soup into his mouth.

"Eli? Is there something I should know?"

"No, ma'am. I think he's harmless. He just has some wild tales."

Ethan jumped halfway out of his seat. "He says he's seen the Wooly-Bully right here in Lafayette County just like Zeke." The middle boy sat down hard. "Oh, that felt good to get out."

Zeke's eyes darted between his brothers, and he leaned forward. "How'd he know I seen 'em?"

"I told him," Ethan said. "I was just making polite conversation."

Zeke made his hands into fists and thumped the table. Ruth put a hand on his arm. "He didn't mean no harm."

"Says who?" Zeke was tired of his brother's teasing. "May I be excused?"

"You don't want seconds?" His mother's face was pinched with concern.

He shook his head.

"Alright. Put your bowl in the sink and go to your room."

"Momma! Can't I go outside and play?"

"As soon as Mr. Charlie has finished and moved on."

Zeke squared his shoulders, put his dishes in the sink, and stomped on the wood-planked floor to his room.

~~~

From the edge of his bed, Zeke could see Mr. Charlie using the spoon to eat the stew.

I'll have to let Ethan know if I ever decide to talk to him again.

Zeke stood slowly and crept to the edge of the window. His curiosity about what the man knew about the Wooly-Bully grew with each step. Zeke hid behind the wall and tilted his head to look out the lower corner of the window.

Charlie looked up and made eye contact. Zeke's neck whiplashed as he jerked out of view.

His heart raced, but Zeke edged back to the window. The bowl and spoon sat on the log where Charlie had been. The boy craned his neck in an attempt to see more of the backyard.

"Looking for me?" Charlie popped up.

A scream caught in Zeke's throat as he jumped back and stumbled to the floor.

"Don't you be making a mess in there," came his mother's voice from down the hall.

"Yes'm," he called back as he brushed himself off and moved toward the window.

Charlie was standing there with a wide grin. He motioned for the boy to lift the window. Zeke shook his head. Charlie held up his hand with his index finger and thumb an inch apart. Zeke opened the window just a bit.

"Didn't mean to scare you," Charlie said at almost a whisper. "Forgiven?"

There was a slight nod from Zeke.

"I heard from your brother that we've both been attacked by Bigfoot."

Zeke tilted his head and raised his eyebrows.

"Quite the talker you are." Charlie smiled, and then he spit. "Of course, the horrible creature kidnapped and killed my friend, and stole my prized possession, so I guess I got it worse."

The boy's eyes widened, and he leaned toward the window. "He got my prize blue thumper, but my friends are safe. And Bigfoot didn't steal my marbles; I threw them at him."

"I understand. Encountering a creature like that can cause a *man* to do crazy things." The emphasis on "man" had the desired effect on Zeke, who didn't always like being the "baby."

"What did he steal from you?"

Charlie turned to flatten himself against the house. Zeke could see the side of his face and shoulder.

"Who you talking to?"

Ethan's voice from the hallway caused Zeke to stand up straight.

"Nobody. I'm just thinking."

"Well, I'm thinking you're going to be hungry later." And with a cackling laugh, Ethan's voice faded down the hallway.

When Zeke turned back toward the window, he saw Eli making his way toward the discarded dishware. He threw the window open with a rousing thud and leaned out to find the back of the house empty.

"You runnin' away?" Eli asked. "We were just having a laugh."

A smile spread across Zeke's face. "It's okay. I just wanted to get some air."

"Well, close it up before bugs get in, or worse, that hobo comes back and robs us."

The youngest Renick slowly shut the window and sighed. "What we got worth stealing?"

~~~

Zeke's leg muscles tightened as he crab-walked down the side of the road. He paused at the bottom of the berm to take a deep breath. There was no hint of the creature on the wind. The muddy area where he'd found his marbles was crisscrossed with prints from raccoons, opossums, and dogs. *Probably chasing all the game,* he thought.

His pulse quickened as he started toward the edge of Lewis Creek. Since one of the town boys had found some clothes there, Zeke figured hobos might like sleeping in the space between the riverbank and bridge trestles.

"Mr. Charlie," he croaked out. He cleared his throat. "Mr. Charlie, you here?"

His head was on a swivel as he glanced over his shoulders. There was no reply. The only sounds were his breathing, birds singing, and water lapping over rocks. He plotted a course through the brush, weeds, and debris to the creek.

Zeke's dry mouth prevented him from calling too loud, but the part of him that wanted to run home was okay with it. He reached the creek and let his gaze take in the embankment under the bridge. Newspapers, bottles, and charred pieces of wood were scattered about the area, but no sign of Charlie.

A sigh eased through his lips, and he put his hands on his hips. Zeke turned toward home when the snapping of a branch froze him in place.

"Hey, Little Man," came Charlie's voice from a thicket. "You looking for me?"

His dingy clothes were near-perfect camouflage against the brush. "I was hoping you'd come find me after we were so rudely interrupted yesterday."

He walked past Zeke, whose face was beading with sweat and turning a bright red.

"Better remember how to breathe, boy." Charlie popped him on the back with an open palm. A massive puff of air escaped Zeke's mouth and his skin color cooled to pink.

"Step into my parlor." Charlie doffed his hat and made a sweeping motion up the embankment.

Zeke followed him up the side to a slight cave where dirt had been dug out from under the span where it met the paved road. Charlie pointed at a small stump for Zeke to sit on as the older man pulled newspapers out of his shirt and shoved them into his bedroll that had been hidden out of sight behind another stump. "Good insulation. Keeps a fella warm at night."

Zeke nodded. He suddenly felt embarrassed about complaining to his momma about his threadbare blankets.

Charlie pulled the other stump closer to Zeke and sat down.

"The way your brothers talked made it seem you're all chicken and no pluck."

Zeke's forehead tightened, his posture straightened, and the blush grew on his cheeks.

"Easy. Easy there, Little Man. They said it, not me. I could tell from the get-go that you weren't afraid of any Bigfoot, and like me, you were a man of action."

The boy's eyes widened, and he nodded in agreement.

"And together, we'll get our treasures back."

"Yes, sir. But how are we going to find him, and how are we going to get the treasure when we find him, and how are we going to get away from him after we get it?"

"One question at a time." Charlie teetered on the stump as his belly shook with a laugh. "One at a time."

Charlie grabbed a stick and started to scratch a map in the dirt between them.

"This here squiggle is the creek right there." He pointed down the embankment. He stopped the thin line and dug deep with the stick to make a fat perpendicular line.

"That there is the Missour-uh." He pointed beyond the brush, and even though Zeke couldn't see it from where he sat, he had seen the mighty Missouri River for as long as he had memory. He nodded.

"Now, running next to the river are the train tracks." Charlie drew a parallel line next to the thick one, but then the railroad line made a sharp turn. "This here is . . ."

"Deadman's Corner!" Zeke paled.

"Huh? No, this here is Miller's swamp," Charlie continued. "The land is like quicksand, so it wasn't safe for the railroad to build over it. Instead, they had to make a sharp turn and stay closer to the riverbank where the ground was solid."

Zeke cocked his head and tossed a side-eye at the man.

"Grown folk call it 'Deadman's Corner' to keep out little kids like you." He pointed the stick at Zeke and tapped his knee. "That's right, like *you*, from trying to catch a ride on the train as it slows for the corner."

"That makes sense, I guess." Zeke's tongue slipped between his teeth and lips as he pondered the information.

"There are others who call it that because of the creature that snatches folks like me off it." Charlie bowed his head and closed his eyes. Zeke's eyes widened and he leaned toward the man.

"And that's where we'll get our revenge!" Charlie popped his eyes open, causing Zeke to jerk back with a gasp. "Easy, boy. I'll keep you alive. You're the ace up my sleeve."

Charlie went back to drawing the map in the dirt. He explained how the creature lived in a cave high up the bank that was shrouded by thick woods. The main entrance was hidden from the view of anyone on the train, but Charlie was certain he'd discovered a "back door."

"Last time I come through, I noticed a small hole about halfway up the bank. I didn't think nothing of it until I recognized that the ragged piece of cloth near the hole was the same pattern shirt my buddy was wearin' when the creature took him."

Zeke put his hand over his mouth and leaned forward, his eyes widening with every word Charlie uttered.

"Yessir, on my honor as a rail rider, my buddy Clem—God rest his soul." Charlie double tapped his head and chest with his left hand. "I was showing him the only token I have of my dear sweet Mildred, a heart-shaped locket with two rubies and one of the shiniest diamonds on the shiniest silver necklace you ever saw.

"Clem was holding it up to the sunlight when all of a sudden a mountain of a creature came crashing into us." Charlie grimaced and clutched at the space above his heart. Zeke, who had forgotten to breathe, let out a slow whistle.

"When I think back on it now, I'm thinking it was attracted by the shine of the silver, like a fishin' lure." Charlie pulled a stain-covered handkerchief from his pocket and dabbed his eyes. "The creature snatched that necklace and Clem's wrist in one massive fur-covered hand and drug them both off into the woods. I didn't expect to see either again until I spotted that shirt.

"I figure the creature hangs out at the front of the cave and shoves its waste down toward the hole I saw."

Zeke's face crinkled at the word "waste," but it also made sense with the smell.

"And that's how we get *you* in there and get our treasures back." Charlie brushed his hands and leaned back on the stump.

"What?" Zeke leaped to his feet. "You want *me* to crawl in through Bigfoot's outhouse? Ain't no way. If the creature don't kill me, the smell or my momma will if I survive and come home wreaking of filth . . . *again*."

Charlie rested the stump back on the ground. "No one is dying. Trust me. We do this right, and your momma won't even know you was gone. We'll catch the northbound train where it slows near your house after she leaves for work. We get in the cave . . ."

Zeke cleared his throat.

"You, *you* get in and get your marbles and my Mildred's bracelet, and if we've timed it all right, we'll be all set to catch the southbound train as it slows for the curve."

"I thought it was a necklace." Zeke side-squinted at the hobo. "You said bracelet."

Charlie fixed the young boy with a stare. "Millie's neck was so skinny she could wear a bracelet on it. You just look for a silver heart with a diamond."

Zeke was shaking his head. "I don't know."

"That's okay. I'll go find a kid from town who's not afraid. He can get your marbles."

Zeke puffed up his cheeks and breathed hard through his nose. "I'm not afraid. I'm just a bit nervous that's all, and I don't want no one else getting my aggies."

Charlie stood up and placed his hand on Zeke's shoulder. "Great. I'll see you tomorrow."

Zeke swallowed hard.

CHAPTER EIGHT

LEXINGTON, MISSOURI, 1956

Zeke sat on the top step and waved at his momma as she boarded the bus for work. He glanced over his shoulder to the bushes. He startled as Ethan rapped the back of his head with his cap.

"What did you do that for?" Zeke rubbed the sore spot.

"Oh, I didn't do it that hard. It can't hurt that bad." Ethan put the cap on and snugged it down.

Zeke ducked forward at the sound of the front door opening.

"Boy, you are bullfrog jumpy today," Eli said as he stepped across the porch and jumped over the three steps. "You sure you don't want to go into town with us today?"

"Nah, all those boys will tease me about wrestling Bigfoot, and I get enough of that here."

"They won't tease you about that," Ethan cut in, "but they will about peeing your pants. Such a baby."

"Am-m, n-n-not." Angry tears welled up in the youngest's eyes.

"Leave him be." Eli punched Ethan in the upper arm. The middle brother grabbed his bicep and pushed out his bottom lip.

Eli bent down in front of Zeke. "Don't listen to him," he cupped Zeke's face in his hands. "Remember, take a deep breath and then find your words. You get to stuttering again and Ma will fill your mouth with rocks again. You want that?"

Zeke shook his head and then exaggerated the motion and smiled.

"Okay, you stay close to the house. If you need anything, Mother Harris is home."

Zeke rolled his head in a circle, not sure how to acknowledge that he understood he could go to Mother Harris but would under no circumstances actually go to Mother Harris—unless he was dragged there by his own mother.

~~~

Two years earlier that's how Zeke ended up farther down Route 224 than he'd ever been before. His momma held his arm in one hand and a letter from the school in the other as she marched them all down the road to visit Mother Harris. She lived in a white clapboard house flanked by trees and nearly hidden by bushes with purple and red flowers.

Zeke tried to wriggle out of his mother's grip as she stepped onto the small porch. The door swung open before he could get away.

"Ha, Ruthie Dear, who have you brought me today?" Mother Harris's voice was high and raspy. "Is that little Ezekiel?"

"He's not so little anymore." Ruth summoned the strength to wrangle her youngest son to the door.

"I can see that. Come on in." A slight flap of skin dangled from her upper arm as Mother Harris pushed the door open wide.

Ruth pushed Zeke ahead of her into the dimly lit room. There was a small couch covered in a multi-colored crocheted blanket and two matching sitting chairs. Mother Harris pointed for them to sit on the couch.

"Would you like some mushroom tea? I just made a fresh pot; good for most anything that ails you." The old woman's smile revealed her snaggled upper teeth.

"No, thank you. Zeke brought this home from school, and I'm hoping you can help me." Ruth passed the piece of paper to the older woman.

Mother Harris's eyes swept across the page and occasionally glanced up at Zeke. He looked away quickly, unsure of this woman or the smells in her home.

"You have trouble with your words, Ezekiel?" She pointed the paper at him.

"No, m-ma'am."

"Hmm, says here you stutter over words and cause trouble in class. Seems your teachers want to keep you back a grade."

He folded his arms tight across his chest.

"You want to stay back a grade?"

He shook his head.

"Use your words." Mother Harris used a forceful tone that sat Zeke straight up.

"N-no, m-ma'am." He flushed red and rubbed his face in his hands.

Ruth put her hand on his back. "He started fumbling over words last year after his daddy passed. I thought it'd go away, but apparently, it's gotten worse."

"Do you hear him stuttering around the house?"

"Sometimes, if Ethan gets him all riled up."

"I see." The older woman walked to a hutch covered in plates, statutes, books, twigs, flowers, and small rocks and pebbles. She grabbed a handful of the smaller pebbles. "Ezekiel, have you learned about the Greeks and Romans in school?"

He shook his head and kept his eyes on the handful of little stones.

"I can't remember his name—couldn't say it right if I could remember—but some Greek guy had a similar problem with his words, and he filled his mouth with pebbles and practiced speaking."

Zeke and Ruth's eyes widened. He gripped his mother's knee.

"Don't worry, I washed 'em." She poured several into Zeke's hand. "Now, put them in your mouth and say something."

He stole a glance at his momma, who nodded for him to do it. Zeke placed the little rocks in his mouth and the taste of dirt and metal caused him to wrinkle his face.

"Wa shou uh ay?" He forced out. Zeke thought he would drown in his own saliva as he refused to swallow. "Cun uh ake em ou?" He didn't wait for an answer and spit them into his hand.

Mother Harris handed him a handkerchief. "Put them in here and take them home with you. Practice with them in the morning and before bed."

"You sure that will fix it?" Ruth's eyes mirrored the concern in her voice.

"I'm sure as the river floods."

That was pretty sure for anyone on Myrick Road.

"Thank you, Mother Harris." Ruth nudged Zeke, who added. "Yeah, thank you."

He hadn't meant it then, but it had helped some. What helped more was just being patient with words and staying calm. Zeke wasn't really good at either.

~~~

Pacing by the bushes behind the house, Zeke's anxiety grew. He couldn't remember if Charlie was meeting him at the house, or if they were supposed to get together by the tracks. He hoped it was at the house because his momma had drilled it into him to never go near the tracks without supervision. He broke a lot of rules, but never that one. Now he was about to break a lot of rules all at the same time. His mouth went dry as his heart rate increased.

The crunching of grass behind him caused Zeke to spin around.

"Good to see you're ready to go. We'd better hurry if we're going to get into position."

The mismatched duo set off through the thick brambles of the berry bushes. Charlie, being a good foot and a half taller and wider than Zeke, blazed a nice trail for him to walk through. They broke through the bushes into the open space by the train tracks. The black and gray rocks that littered the area by the tracks contrasted the greenery on the banks. Looking across the rails, Zeke saw the sprawling Missouri River. He picked up a baseball-sized rock and hurled it toward the water. It fell far short.

"Nice try, kid," said Charlie, finding a rock of his own. "Let's see if the old man's still got it." He let the rock fly, and it gave a satisfying *plop* in the muddy shore.

"Wow." Zeke kept staring in the direction the rock landed.

"Come on, we gotta hide so the engineer doesn't see us."

Sweat dripped down the duo's faces as they hid in the heavy undergrowth. Their clothes were sticking to them, and their muscles ached from sitting still. A low rumble and high-pitched grind in the distance let them know the train was slowing to make the turn.

"We won't have a lot of time, so you have to stay close. Remember, stay by me, I'll swing you up into the boxcar and then get myself inside."

Zeke nodded. His tongue was stuck to the roof of his mouth, his knees were knocking, and his courage was wavering. He took a slow, deep breath, and exhaled. The word "onward" slipped between his lips.

The rumbling of the train made it hard to hear Charlie's shouting. Zeke ran as hard as he could, but he could tell the older man was outpacing him. He imagined the creature was behind him, unlocked another gear, and closed the gap.

"Now." Charlie yelled as he reached for Zeke's arm.

"What?"

Zeke never heard the answer as Charlie lifted him off his feet and swung him into the open boxcar. He rolled a few times, moving deeper into the shadows. Zeke pushed himself up in time to see Charlie hoist himself into the car.

"That was amazing!" Zeke jumped up and soon found himself falling back onto his butt.

"Hah, you need to get your rail-riding legs."

The breeze through the open doors cooled and refreshed them. The sunlight strobing through the trees as the train sped up made him dizzy. He rested his head on his knees.

"So far, so good. You remember the plan, kid?"

Zeke went over the plan for the umpteenth time. They'd both jump off the train at Deadman's Curve—Miller's Swamp—then Zeke would climb up to the back entrance. He pinched the bridge of his nose and scrunched his face as he pictured it. Once he was inside, he would locate the creature's treasure chest.

"How do you know it has a treasure chest?" Zeke asked for the umpteenth time. "And, how do you know it's blue and on the left side?"

"I've heard rumors from other hobos who were caught and escaped."

Zeke chewed on his thumbnail and knit his eyebrows together. "I guess that makes sense." He went back to explaining the plan. "Once I have the treasure, I scurry quick as a bunny back out the way I came, and we catch the next train back home. No one knowing what we done but us."

"Perfect, partner," said Charlie sticking out his hand. Zeke took it and was suddenly flying out of the train. He landed hard on his side and bounced several times down the berm. He saw Charlie jump out, roll once, and stand up like a practiced circus performer.

"You could have warned me." Zeke brushed himself off as he stomped toward Charlie.

"Where's the fun in that?"

Standing at the bottom of the riverbank, the climb appeared higher and steeper than the view from the train. Over the hundreds of thousands of years that the Missouri River had been flowing, it carved a wide path. Very few things can stop it, and the rolling hills upon which Lexington rests have only slightly slowed and altered the course of America's longest river. In some areas, its banks are more than a hundred feet tall. Zeke was facing a climb of about half that, but he paled as he pondered his assignment.

"You'll be fine," Charlie patted him on the back. "You've got about thirty minutes until the southbound train comes through, so don't waste any time."

Zeke closed his eyes and took a deep breath, letting it out slowly through his nose. He balled his hands into fists and punched down at his sides. "Onward!"

The first few steps weren't bad, but soon he found it hard to find a solid foothold. He used tree branches to pull himself up and then rested on the trunks before moving again. The cave's backdoor entrance grew wider as he ascended.

This is probably the dumbest thing you've ever done, Zeke thought to himself, rolling his eyes and fighting off his negative thoughts.

He took another deep breath and was met with earthy scents. There was nothing foul on the wind, and his shoulders relaxed.

When Zeke was even with the backdoor entrance, he looked down for the first time. The trees appeared small, and the ground was so far away. A slight shiver ran down his spine and settled at his knees.

"Not smart," he chastised himself aloud. "Focus. Get in. Get out." He balled up his fists. "Onward," he forced out through clenched teeth, partly because he wasn't fully confident and partly because if the creature was home, he didn't want to let it know he was coming.

There was plenty of room for him to crawl through the opening. He made his way on hands and knees through discarded clothing, tin cans, glass bottles, and newspapers. He took another deep breath. The air was musty, like a wet dog and dirty socks. There was another odor Zeke couldn't quite name. It was part skunk, part rotten fruit, but it was nothing like the night he encountered the creature, so he pressed on.

He could see light streaming in from the main entrance at the far end of the cave. Glancing around, he appeared to be alone. Zeke focused his search on his left side and found more trash, piles of chicken and fish bones, and a pair of mismatched shoes. He picked one up and guessed it to be about a size ten, like the church pair Momma bought Eli. A sinking feeling settled into Zeke's stomach.

The young boy turned around and spotted a large trunk. The shadows made it tough to tell, but he figured it could be dark blue and not black. He lifted the lid and was face-to-face with a trunk load of treasure.

His eyes bounced from jewelry to silverware to coins. He reached in and pulled out a handful. Silver and gold strands dangled from his fingers as coins and rings fell back into the trunk, making a ringing sound.

"Aha! I found the treasure!" Zeke's eyes grew wide, and he started shoving handfuls of loot into his pockets. He paused and pulled it all out again. "Don't you forget the mission, silly boy." Zeke mimicked the hobo's voice.

He tried to pull the pieces apart and look for the locket as Charlie had ordered. The faint whistle of the train echoed in the cave.

Not much time now. Be quick. His thoughts spurred him to be faster.

Zeke shoveled through sections of the trunk with his hands, searching for heart shapes. He was quickly rewarded with three necklaces and two bracelets that had silver hearts with gemstones. He shoved all of them into his pockets and dug deeper to see if he could locate his treasured marbles.

Zeke was combing through a handful of coins, rings, and various baubles when a noise at the mouth of the cave froze him in place.

"Thief! How the hell did you get in here?"

Zeke turned to see a massive, shadowy figure backlit from the opening coming toward him. He held fast to what was in his hands and scrambled for the back exit. Zeke launched himself through the opening and fell head over heels down the large embankment, hitting trees and rocks along the way. When he finally stopped, Zeke had trouble standing up. There was a large gash running along his shin.

"You alright, son? What happened?" Charlie stepped out from behind a clump of trees.

Before Zeke could say anything, an angry voice called down from the trees.

"Think you can steal from me and get away with it?" The distinctive sound of rifle fire followed.

Zeke pouted and pointed toward the sound with a fistful of treasure. "*That* is what happened!"

"Well, what do you know, seems my ol' buddy, Clem, bested ol' Bigfoot. We gotta go."

The gash sent jolts of pain from Zeke's leg to his skull with each step. He could see the train. With Clem closing in fast, Charlie wasn't even looking for a place to hide before hitching a ride. The locomotive made the turn, and Charlie and Zeke were closing ground on the first open boxcar. The ground jumped up to bite Zeke as another gunshot echoed in his ears. He tumbled to the ground.

Charlie let go of the boxcar and came back to Zeke. "Get up! We gotta go," the hobo said staring into the forest. "Now!"

He grabbed Zeke by the arm and pulled him up as Clem burst through the tree line.

"Steal from me, will you?" Clem pulled the trigger, but the hammer just clicked. He tossed it into the woods.

"It's half mine, you crazy old man." Charlie yelled back. He was half dragging Zeke, who fought to stay upright. They got close to the nearest boxcar. "Ready, kid. One, two, th . . ."

As Charlie went to toss Zeke, Clem dove for the boy's leg and held fast to his foot. Zeke dug deep and found enough strength for one solid kick to the hanger-on's face. There was a sickening *thwack* as the bottom of his shoe met Clem's nose, sending him and one of Zeke's shoes tumbling. With the loss of added weight, Charlie tossed Zeke into the car and followed him inside.

"You okay?" Charlie asked with little sympathy.

Zeke looked down at his left leg. The gash down his shin was as long as the span from the tip of his pinkie to the tip of his thumb. He felt like throwing up at the sight of torn flesh and muscle. Oddly, there wasn't as much blood as he expected, but there were several small pock marks around his ankle and on his calf.

"I've b-b-been shot. How am I sup-posed to b-b-be okay?" Tears welled on his eyelids, and his face turned beet red. "You're a l-liar. You probably never saw b-b-Bigfoot. You just n-needed me to steal for you. And n-now." Zeke took a deep breath and let it out slowly. "And now, I'm shot. And he didn't have my marbles!"

A deep laugh rumbled out of Charlie. "Of course, he didn't. Who cares about your stupid marbles?" He sidled closer to Zeke. "Now, give me the goods."

Zeke tried to push himself away, but the pain caused him to stop. He had lost most of what was in his hands on the way down the hill and running after the train. He dribbled out what was left into Charlie's hand. Out the door, Zeke could see the train was nearing Lewis Creek. He reached into his left pocket and pulled out silver and gold strands that each held a heart-shaped locket. Charlie swiped them from him.

"Yes! You did great. Now, for the rest."

Zeke's heart rate quickened, and his face paled. He reached into his right-side pocket and pulled out a mix of jewelry and coins. As Charlie reached for it, Zeke launched himself up and out of the car with his good leg and tumbled into the muddy banks of Lewis Creek. He pushed his mud-covered self up in time to see Charlie leaning out of the box-car and shaking a fist. He couldn't make out all the words, but he got the gist.

As Zeke ambled through the mud and bushes and up the shoulder to the road, he tried to formulate a plan to clean up, care for his wounds, and explain how he lost a shoe; all when he wasn't supposed to have left the house. Cresting the road, his pulse quickened as he saw the sheriff's car parked in front of his house. He hopped and hobbled his way home as fast as he could.

The first people he saw were his brothers.

"Eli! Ethan! What's happened?"

The two of them turned and stopped in their tracks at the sight of their little brother. Eli took off running back to the house, and Ethan ran toward Zeke.

"You are in so much trouble," Ethan said.

"What happened?"

"Momma thinks you're dead somewhere. And she's probably gonna kill you now anyway."

"I thought she was at work."

"She was headed there, but apparently, the Pettys left for vacation and didn't bother to tell her. Their place was locked up when she got there. She saw Eli and me headed downtown on her walk home and decided we should all go home, get you, and have a picnic." Ethan looked Zeke up and down. "You are a mess."

"Ezekiel Joseph Renick! Where the hell have you been?" Ruth's voice pierced the sky.

The boys exchanged wide-eyed stares.

"Momma swore." Ethan swallowed hard. "You *are* dead."

Zeke wanted to run to his mother for comfort, but his leg was hurting something terrible, and he could see little comfort as she marched toward him. He opened his mouth to speak.

"Not a word! Not a word!" She grabbed him by the ear and hauled him toward the house, where the Sheriff was waiting with Eli. She stopped short in front of the officer. "Ezekiel, you tell this officer that you're sorry for causing trouble."

He squeaked out a barely audible, "Sorry."

Ruth yanked the ear of her youngest child.

Zeke straightened and found his voice. "I'm sorry."

"You gave your mother quite the scare. We were about to drag the river. Where did you get off to?"

He didn't want to tell the whole story, but he didn't want to lie either. He said he wandered off and found Charlie, who said he knew where the creature kept its treasures, and that together they could get their stuff back. His mother blanched and nearly fainted when he told of hopping the train, rolling down the hill, getting shot at, and, finally, escaping by jumping off at the creek.

"That's quite a fanciful tale, young man." The Sheriff arched his eyebrows.

Zeke pulled the jewelry and coins from his pocket and held them out to the officer.

The youngest Renick bent down to pull off some of the caked mud on his legs. He grabbed a dried section mid-shin near the wound that caused a surge of pain to shoot through every neuron in his body.

He fainted.

CHAPTER NINE

OUTSIDE OF MEMPHIS, TENNESSEE, PRESENT DAY

"That is one crazy story." Nate stopped his French fry-holding hand midway between the diner counter and his mouth. He pointed with the fry for emphasis. "You could have died so many different ways.

"And what was this?" Nate mimicked the older man's double taps to the head and heart when he recalled Charlie talking about Clem being dead.

"You should know. It's what your people do."

"*My* people? Filipinos?"

"No. Catholics."

Nate clicked his teeth. "*Tsk tsk*, Tito, not all . . . Never mind. *My* people are Pentecostal, but still, I know this . . ." He performed the Sign of the Cross, using his right hand to touch his forehead, chest, then left and right shoulder.

"Have you never watched a crime drama where they talk to priests?" Nate asked.

"I was a scared kid." Zeke took a giant bite of his cheeseburger and swiveled the counter stool so he faced the kitchen.

"Sure, sure. But speaking of Catholics, why don't you tell me more about Mrs. Renick the first?"

Zeke moved his head slightly back and forth.

"Please, Uncle." Nate interlaced his fingers and put his hands near his face. "Please."

"Okay, okay." Zeke took a sip of coffee. "We got married in the spring of 1968. Now, I guess I should back up a bit. While we were going steady—it was our little secret—she loved to talk about having a houseful of kids and living up on the hill in a big red-brick house. I knew this meant I needed to get a really good-paying job, but I also knew I wasn't the sharpest tack, so I knew the work I could do might not pay enough."

He pulled at his collar. "I also thought she meant the kids and big house coming along in several years, because I was still young and wanted to travel. My military service was limited, but I had been able to travel to several states and see what the country had to offer. I wanted to see more, and I was looking forward to having someone to share that with."

"But she didn't mean years, did she?" Nate asked softly.

Zeke's mouth fell open, and he tilted his head. "Nope, she did not. After our first year of marriage, we were still childless. Her younger sister had married the year before us, and she was pumping out kid number two. We hadn't even had a pregnancy scare. We were living on the hill, but only because her folks had a small house on the back end of their property. She was near tears most days, so we went to the doctors to see what could be done."

The older man took a slow sip of coffee. "And you know what?"

Nate shook his head.

"Turns out I was shooting blanks." He rested his face in his right hand and rubbed his forehead. "I felt horrible, and Gaylynn was inconsolable. She became convinced this was God's punishment for marrying a Presbyterian boy. I told her I was sorry, and that I'd convert if she thought that would help any. I even mentioned adoption."

Nate's eyebrows raised and he leaned close. "And . . ."

"And, she said she wanted her *own* children. And I guess I couldn't blame her. But then we were stuck until her dad made a few calls—and possibly a few donations—and the church officially annulled the marriage. So it happened, but it didn't."

The younger man patted Zeke on the shoulder. "I'm so sorry, Uncle."

"It worked out okay." The older man chuckled, and his face lightened. "She married a fireman from Excelsior Springs within the year. And last I heard, she had seven children—two sets of twins—so I dodged a bullet."

"How's everything?" The waitress whose name tag read Billi-Jo asked.

The duo bobbed their heads in unison. Nate gave a thumbs up.

"Okay, if that changes, let me know." Billi-Jo winked and headed toward the kitchen.

"I appreciate you sharing that with me." Nate nibbled another French fry.

"And it stays with us, right? This isn't for the crowdfunding."

Nate nodded and jumped as his phone vibrated between them. Zeke's side-eye glance reminded the young man of his disapproval of "fancy devices at the table." The orderly shrugged his shoulders and turned the phone face up.

His eyes grew wide as saucers and his mouth opened in a silent scream. Nate looked back at the phone and grabbed Zeke by the shoulder, spinning him to face him.

"Look!" He put the screen close to Zeke's face. The older man pulled back and tried to find a distance to focus his eyes.

"What am I looking at?"

"Our video went viral."

It was Zeke's turn to shrug.

"It means hundreds of thousands of people have seen the video, and they're sharing it, and then even more hundreds of thousands see it. And loads of them are joining the crowdfunding." Nate pointed to the ever-changing numbers on the screen. "Tito, if this keeps up, we could afford to look for the Yeti in Tibet."

Zeke took the phone. His jaw slackened as he stared at the screen. His focus shifted from the numbers to the words scrolling across the video: *In that moment . . . as I opened the chest . . . I really thought I'd found Bigfoot's treasure. There was so much jewelry and coins . . . I was focused on searching for my marbles when a loud noise from the front of the cave caught my attention. I turned and there was just this massive dark shape, and I just grabbed more treasure and ran.*

The video stopped and the screen prompts gave viewers the option to watch it again or see the next video.

"Where's the rest of the story?"

Nate was fully involved in eating his lunch. "Huh?" He said through a mouthful of fries.

"The video stops at the shadow. There's a lot more that I told."

Nate wiped his face and hands on a napkin and took the phone back from Zeke.

"Yeah, and we'll release that bit later. It's key to let the story out in bits to keep people interested. You know like *back in your day* when you had to wait a whole week to see the next episode of a TV show."

A smile crept up on the edges of Zeke's mouth.

"People are enjoying your video, Uncle. Check out some of these comments."

He turned the phone back to Zeke and scrolled along the screen.

@BigfootFan43 That's cra!! I'd much rather find Bigfoot than jump on and off a train. Great story! #AlwaysBelieve #TheTruthIsOutThere

@ImABeliever36 It's amazing anyone from your generation survived to today. Looking forward to the next vid #BigfootLives

@JonQPub Just take my money now! #TeamZeke #FOOT

@OuttaSync009 I HATE CLIFFHANGERS!!!! #CliffhangersSuck #YouSuck

@TheRealBigfoot01 I LLOL'd watching it all go down from my secret hiding place. You were so close that day, Z-man. If it makes you feel better, I slapped the sh!t out of that Clem. #Believe

@ZippyBB606 Pictures or it didn't happen. #BigfootLives

"You gentlemen save any room for dessert? Or want a refill on your drinks?"

Zeke jumped at the sound of Billi-Jo's voice.

"Sorry, didn't mean to scare you."

He patted his stomach and shook his head. "All good. I'm full." He glanced at Nate, who made the cut-off sign with his hand. "Just the check, please, Billi-Jo. We've still got miles to go before we sleep."

"Where you two headed?"

"North." Zeke said, folding his napkin and placing it on the counter.

"Any exciting plans?" She picked up the plates and wiped down the counter.

"If you think funerals and trials are exciting, then yes," the orderly stated matter-of-factly.

Her head shot up and the plates clattered in her arm as she looked at Nate, who greeted her shocked expression with a wink and dimple-inducing smile.

"You forgot Bigfoot hunting," Zeke added.

A slight smile appeared on Billi-Jo's face. "Okay, you got me. But remember if you don't find Sasquatch up north, there's been plenty of sightings around here." She shook her head at the duo and headed into the kitchen through the swinging double doors.

"We should probably leave her a big tip for that?" Nate said as he filled out the credit card receipt.

"She definitely earned her ten percent."

Nate choked on air. "Oh, my, *your* day was *waaay* back when. Fifteen or twenty percent is pretty common now."

It was Zeke's turn to cough. He gave Nate the "really" stare.

"Other advances we've made since *your day* are electric cars, robot doctors, and landing on the moon." He giggled and jabbed at Zeke with his elbow.

"I remember the moon landing!" He elbowed Nate back.

"What was it like?"

"I hate young people."

Nate smiled and wrapped Zeke in a giant side hug. "I love you, too, Uncle."

On their way out, Nate was sidetracked by spinning racks full of souvenirs. He gave one a turn and didn't see anything he liked.

Zeke tapped his foot and his finger on his watch.

"A minute won't kill us." Nate started twirling the other stand and startled the diners with his shout.

"Shhhh!" Zeke stepped toward Nate, his face flushing and eyes narrowing.

Nate looked around the room and saw all eyes on him. "Sorry, folks. I do love a good souvenir." He pulled a patch off the rack. "Check it out! We have to have this."

Zeke looked down at the patch. It featured a hairy creature taking a large stride, with the question "Walking in Memphis?" sewn in a cursive font.

"It didn't look at all like that." Zeke handed the patch back and walked out the front door.

Zeke stretched both arms toward the sky and then patted his stomach. He put his hands on his hips and stretched out his neck, giving a slight grimace every time there was a popping sound. He heard the diner doorbell jingle and turned to see Nate walk out holding the patch aloft between his thumb and index finger. Zeke looked at him sideways and furrowed his brows.

"It's part of my marketing plan. We'll collect Bigfoot paraphernalia along the way and make them incentives for the crowdfunding."

Zeke tapped the top of the car twice and pointed at Nate. "Now, I see the method to your madness."

CHAPTER TEN

LEXINGTON, MISSOURI, 1956

Z eke winced and a low moan escaped his lips. He tossed and turned in the bed to find a position that didn't hurt his leg or back or arms or head. He'd been confined to the bed for a week by Mother Harris, who insisted that bedrest and mud-based herbal compresses were the only way to save his leg. Even then, she wasn't sure the infection wouldn't spread.

It was Day Seven and he was eager to get out of bed and back outside. His mother hadn't said more than a handful of words to him since he stumbled home covered in mud and carrying what were now known as stolen goods. On the bright side, Zeke was happy she wasn't swearing anymore.

"Ezekiel."

He rolled over to face his mother standing in the doorway, hands on her hips. He pushed himself up into a sitting position on the edge of the bed. His lower left leg was covered in dried mud and torn cloth bandages. "Yes, ma'am."

"Get yourself cleaned up. Mr. Lewis is coming to get you this morning."

He slowly slid down the side of the bed, making sure to put the weight on his right leg. Tentatively, he tested putting weight on his left leg. The room started spinning. He shut his eyes hard and bit his lip. He steadied himself by grabbing the nightstand, which held a copy of the local newspaper edition that detailed his run-in with scandalous thieving brothers Charlie and Clement Oster.

"Yes, ma'am." He nodded and ran his fingers across the bold headline in the *Lexington News*. "Local Sheriff Lauded For Capturing Tri-County Outlaws." He tucked the paper under his arm. "How long will I work at Mr. Lewis's house today?"

"A few hours today and every other day for two weeks to earn the money to pay for the shoe you lost and the trouble you caused." Her stern stare softened and she held out her arms.

"Come here."

Zeke limped into her arms and whimpered. "I'm so sorry, Momma. I am. I am."

"I know, son. I forgive you, but you still have to pay the price for your actions."

He hung his head. "I know, but why couldn't I collect the reward money the paper said was offered from the families and pay that way?" Zeke held the paper out and looked up at his mom with puppy dog eyes. The light reflected off the green flecks in his hazel eyes as he batted his lashes.

She playfully pushed him away. "You know very well why. You can't benefit from bad behavior."

He lowered his gaze to the floor.

"Pick up that lip." She cupped his chin in her hand and lifted his head. "I've got a bite to eat on the table for you."

He pulled his biscuit apart and spooned some strawberry preserves onto each side. Zeke set the paper on the table. He swept away a few of the crumbs that fell on it.

"Momma, what's no-to-rye-ous?"

"Huh?" She turned from the sink and wiped her hands on her apron. Zeke turned the paper to face her and pointed at the troublesome word.

She sounded it out for him. "No-tor-e-us. Notorious."

He smiled up at her. He traced his finger back to the start of the sentence. "Lafayette County Sheriff Millard—boy, momma, I'm glad you didn't name me that—Millard Branson received high praise following the capture of the notorious Oster brothers, Charlie and Clement, who burgled more than twenty homes across Lafayette, Ray, and Jackson counties."

Zeke took a bite of the biscuit and chased it with some watery milk. He moved his index finger down the column of text.

"Oh, here it is." He bounced in his seat. "The Sheriff stated information he received from Lexington resident Ezekiel Renick—that's me." Zeke tapped his chest and sent crumbs flying. "Information . . . was key, *key*, to ap-pre-hend-ing, apprehending, the brothers and recovering the stolen goods."

"Your reading is getting better." Ruth placed mason jars in the cabinet.

"Thank you." He kept his eyes focused on the newspaper. "Renick told the Sheriff he was tricked by Charlie Oster into believing he was helping the older man retrieve jewelry that had been stolen from him."

Zeke pushed the last bite into his mouth and wiped his face with the back of his hand. "Momma, how come they didn't mention anything about Bigfoot?"

She stopped midstride.

"Well, my guess is they thought you were rambling from a fever dream. That gash on your leg was mighty angry. Mother Harris was worried the infection would get into the bone."

He rested his head on his hand and twisted his lips. "Was it really that bad?"

Her eyes misted over. "Yes, Little Man, it was really *that* bad. I haven't prayed that hard since your daddy died."

Zeke sat up and reached for his momma. "I'm so sorry."

"I know, baby." She kissed the top of his head. "Now, please, get outside and clean yourself up. I know Mr. and Mrs. Lewis don't want you traipsing mud and dirt through their nice house while you're there working to pay for your shoe."

Zeke slowly unwrapped the bandages and brushed at the dried mud. Most came off easily except the bit right above the wound. The fear of more pain caused him to jerk his leg before his hand ever reached it. He leaned on the tub for balance. Zeke was staring at the bathwater and trying to summon the courage to undress and get in when a sudden deluge of cold water soaked him head to toe and caused a full-body shiver.

"Ethan, you stupid . . ." he shouted and turned around to see his mother. He sighed and turned back to the tub. "Well, I'm all wet now anyway." He stepped into the tub with his shorts and T-shirt on.

"Hahaha."

Zeke turned to see his mother doubled over in laughter and rolling on the ground. After a week of near silence between them, it sounded like music to his ears.

~~~

It was strange to be at the Lewis home when there wasn't a Cub Scout meeting. It was even stranger to think he'd be working in the house because Zeke had heard several women whisper in church that Mrs. Lewis had "several colored maids who kept the dwelling spic-and-span."

Although there were some Black families living next door to white families near the center of town, most Black people lived in the opposite direction of the Lewis's two-story home on the hilltop.

When Mrs. Lewis determined she needed help maintaining her home to the standards of a former four-time mayor and the only person she could trust to do it lived more than two miles away, she dropped a bug in the current mayor's ear. Suddenly, the city approved not only the purchase of a small bus but also the creation of a bus stop with a "Colored

Only" sign on the outskirts of town just south of the Forest Grove area.

Zeke had seen several Black ladies on the bus. (It seemed Mrs. Lewis paved the way for other women on the hilltop to secure help in their homes, too.) The first Black person he talked to was Harrison Tollhouse, who lived in town next door to the Tullis family. The eldest Tullis son, Oliver, had invited Eli and several guys—including Harrison—to play baseball in the vacant field behind his house. Zeke invited himself along to play with Oliver's youngest brother, Asher, who was his friend and Cub Scout buddy.

The younger duo decided to watch the older boys play. Some of the boys were not happy to see Harrison in the mix. Oliver told them they were "welcome to leave." And they did. So instead of playing a real baseball game, everyone took turns hitting and fielding. Zeke had never seen anyone hit a ball so far and run so fast in the outfield to chase down a ball as Harrison. He could barely contain himself when the older boys huddled up for a water break.

"That was some hit." Zeke bounced with excitement. "I bet you're the best player out here."

Eli caught Zeke in a headlock and rubbed his knuckles on his head. "Why, you Benedict Arnold. My own brother turning on me." Zeke squirmed in the crook of Eli's arm.

"Don't be too hard on him, Eli." Harrison laughed. "My little brothers are still talking about last month when you made that long throw. They think you've got a stronger arm than me. Maybe we should switch brothers."

Zeke wiggled free as the older boys laughed and clapped each other on the back.

~~~

While he wasn't sure what to expect, Zeke figured Mrs. Lewis's black maid was not going to want to talk baseball with him. And he wasn't sure how he was going to be of any help, especially since he still couldn't walk well or stand long.

He followed Mr. Lewis into the kitchen, which was filled with mouthwatering, savory aromas. Zeke put his hand on his stomach and could feel the hungry rumble.

"Ezekiel, this here is Georgia. She'll be setting your chores, and you'll address her as Miss Georgia."

Zeke nodded. "Yes, sir." He smiled at Georgia and relaxed his shoulders when she smiled back.

"Alright then, Georgia, you're in charge. I'll be working downtown today, and Mrs. Lewis will be gone most of the day at a ladies' brunch in Fayette." He faced Zeke and put both hands on his shoulders.

"I know this isn't how you expected to spend your summer, but it could be worse."

"Really, how?" Zeke pointed to his leg with the bandages showing under the rolled-up hem.

"You could have to pay for two shoes." The elder statesman laughed at his own joke, patted Zeke's head, and walked out the door.

"Ha, now how are you supposed to buy just one shoe?" Georgia's voice caused Zeke to jerk his head around.

"Momma said the church has a bin full of mismatched shoes. I'm not sure why or how other folks lost one."

She nodded her head and went back to watching over the pots and pans on the stove.

"I understand you've got a bum leg." She added some sliced potatoes and carrots to a large pot, covered it, and turned to Zeke.

"Yes, ma'am, Miss Georgia." He started to hike up his pant leg.

"No need for theatrics," she laughed. "Go on into the dining room. There's some silver that needs polishing, and you can sit and do that."

He smiled and set off to begin his chore. His smile quickly faded when he saw the table covered with more silverware than he could count. In his house, there were eight forks, eight knives, and ten spoons for the table. None of them silver. His mom had special utensils for cooking, but nowhere near the number that was spread out before him.

A younger Black girl entered from the opposite hallway opening.

"Hi, I'm MayBelle, and Miss Georgia told me to come in here and show you how to properly shine the silver." Her ebony hair was braided in tight rows.

She put on a pair of white cotton gloves. In one hand, she grabbed a knife—in the other, she grabbed a cloth and dabbed it in a glass jar. MayBelle gently rubbed the silver and set it on what appeared to be a giant napkin.

"Got it?" She took off the gloves and put them in front of Zeke.

"I think so."

"Good. Georgie will be in soon to help." She started to walk out.

"Miss Georgia is going to help me?"

"Don't be silly." A smile spread across her face. "George-E will help. He's Miss Georgia's youngest boy, about your age, I'd guess."

Zeke sat down, pulled on the gloves, and followed May-Belle's lead on a spoon. He turned the piece around in his hand and attempted to see himself in the reflection. It looked cloudy, and he was afraid he'd done it wrong.

"It's not shiny until it gets a bath," came a voice from behind a small basin of water. "That's my job. I'm Georgie."

Zeke got a good look at his face as he lowered the basin onto the table.

"I'm Zeke," he said, pulling his hand out of the glove to shake.

Georgie looked at it.

"It's okay," Zeke stuck out his hand. "I've had a bath today."

Both boys laughed, and Georgie shook his hand.

"Laughing ain't working," Miss Georgia called from the kitchen.

The boys put their hands over their mouths and got to work in silence.

~~~

"Lunchtime, boys," Miss Georgia called from the kitchen.

The duo leapt from their work and raced to the kitchen. Zeke headed for the little table against the far wall where he'd eaten all the time with the Cubs. Georgie stayed by his mom's side at the stove.

Miss Georgia brought a plate with a peanut butter and jelly sandwich, carrots, and cookies to Zeke at the table. He watched and waited for her to bring Georgie's plate as well. Instead, she handed Georgie his plate and opened the back door for him to eat outside.

Zeke's mind raced, and he ran his fingers along the left side of his head. He made eye contact with Miss Georgia.

"There's a rule that Negros can't eat inside in town, not even in Mr. Lewis's home." She answered his question before he could ask.

Zeke's jaw slackened, and he glanced outside.

"What's the difference between Negro and colored?" he asked between bites.

Miss Georgia's eyes widened, and her shoulders went back.

"I'm asking because my brother Ethan said there was a special bus stop for the colored folk who work for Mrs. Lewis and the other hilltop women."

The edges of Miss Georgia's lips curled slightly up, and she stepped toward Zeke. The woman who had been towering over him stooped down and met his gaze. He swallowed hard, and his thoughts bounced around as he tried to figure out if he was about to get a whoopin' or a hug.

"Your brother is right. That's what the sign says, but I don't much like that word for describing me. Are there words people call you that you don't like much?"

Zeke bobbed his head. "Curtis—his daddy owns the soda shop—he calls me and my brothers a Peckerwood sometimes. Thinks I don't know he's calling us poor white folk." He lowered his gaze and nibbled at the sandwich.

"Makes it hurt right here, don't it?" She pointed her index finger at his heart. His eyes focused on her wrinkled black hand covered with flour. "Words have power, Ezekiel, don't you ever forget that."

"Yes'm."

"And you can call me Miss Georgia." She stood and smiled so wide the edges of her eyes closed.

"Yes, Miss Georgia." He dug back into his sandwich. As he chewed, he paused and looked out the back window and saw Georgie sitting alone on a log.

"Miss Georgia, is it okay if I eat *outside* with him?"

"Mr. Lewis got no law against that here on his property, and I think Georgie would like that."

Miss Georgia held the door open for Zeke.

"Hey, Georgie, mind if I join you?"

His choremate shook his head because his mouth was full of peanut butter and jelly.

"What are you being punished for?" Zeke took a bite of his sandwich while he waited for an answer.

"What do you mean?"

"Well, I broke loads of my mom's rules." Zeke ticked them off on his fingers. "I run off with a hobo, got shot, nearly died from infection, and I lost a shoe, which I'm earning money to pay for."

Georgie held his sandwich mid-bite. He stared unblinking at Zeke, who waved his hand back and forth in front of Georgie's face. There was still no change, so he snapped his fingers, which appeared to knock his new acquaintance out of his trance.

"Wow, my momma woulda killed me." Georgie shook his head rapidly back and forth. "That's a special mix of dumb and crazy."

Zeke laughed. "My momma wanted to kill me, but the sheriff being there probably saved my life."

"The sheriff was there?" Georgie choked on his cookie.

Zeke explained the events of that fateful day between bites of sandwich and cookies. He put the carrots in his pockets to add to his Momma's stew.

"The cut on my leg got infected, so Momma called Mother Harris—she's not my ma's mom, but everyone calls her Mother Harris. She put together some awful-smelling concoction and slapped it on my leg and wrapped it up. She told my momma to change it every day, and pray Jesus have mercy on my sinful soul."

"Whoa. Do you still put mud on it?"

"Nah, today is the first day I can just have bandages." He pulled up the pant leg to show the cloth ribbons wrapped around his shin. "You wanna see it?"

Before he could answer, Miss Georgia called, "No, he don't," from behind the screen. "You keep your bandages on. I'll give you boys five more minutes then it's back to work."

"Yes, ma'am," they answered in unison.

Zeke pulled his pant leg back down. "It's probably better that you don't see it. Makes my momma nearly faint to look at it." He smiled at his own exaggeration.

"But you know, losing my shoe and working here, that's still not as bad as losing my favorite aggies."

Georgie nodded in agreement. Zeke continued, "I was really hoping the cave was the honest-to-goodness home of Bigfoot, and . . ."

"What?" Georgie gripped Zeke's arm. "You didn't mention Bigfoot before."

"I did. I'm certain I told you the hobo tricked me by saying Bigfoot stole from him, too."

"Oh, no, because I'd remember that detail. You need to start over and hit all the details."

"Boys," Miss Georgia called from the kitchen, "time to get back to polishing."

"Darn," they sighed together.

~~~

By the second day, the boys were becoming fast friends, even if their friendship was limited to the Lewis's home and backyard.

They flew out the back door with their lunches and scrambled down the steps as the screen door slammed shut.

"Sweet thunder!" came a shout from the kitchen. "How many times do I have to tell you to mind that screen door?"

"Sorry," the duo called back between giggles.

They settled in against a log. A slight breeze rustled the leaves and kept the humidity at bay. It was a perfect summer day, except that they were working while other kids were playing.

"I told my daddy what you said, and he says you're crazy." Georgie took a bite of his apple.

Zeke couldn't respond with his mouth full of sandwich, so he shook his head to deny the accusation. He chewed faster and swallowed hard, twice, to force the poorly chewed white-bread-and-peanut-butter combo down his throat.

"Am not! I saw what I saw." Zeke's throat turned shades of red and pink.

"Oh, no, no." Georgie held up his hands in front of him. "My daddy didn't say much about Bigfoot, he said you was crazy to trust a hobo and jump a train."

"Yeah, that *was* crazy. Did he say anyone had ever seen it on your side of town?"

Georgie took a bite of his apple. "Nah, he said we have other creatures of the night to look out for, and Bigfoot is the least of our worries. So, go ahead and tell me your whole crazy story."

Zeke started back at the beginning with his big wins at marbles during the Cub Scout meeting, getting scared by Larry, encountering the creature, and throwing his marbles at it.

"Was it real ugly?" Georgie interrupted.

"More scary than ugly." Zeke took a bite and held up a finger to ask Georgie to be patient. "It was kinda like a man's face, but like those faces people carve into apples and let them dry out. You ever seen one of those?"

Georgie scrunched his face and contorted his mouth. "Like dis?"

Zeke laughed. "Yes, exactly like that . . . and its skin and hair were super dark, like the kinda dark blue in comic books. I've never seen nothing like it before, and *phew-ie*, did it stink."

"That must be some marble for you to go to all that trouble of trying to get it back."

"The best thumper you ever did see. I'm lucky I found the bumblebee, but I'm going to have a hard time winning without that big aggie."

"Boys! Time to get back to it!"

They shoveled the final bits of their apples into their mouths, juice flowing down their hands, which they wiped on their pants.

"Until next time!" Georgie said.

~~~

Over the course of several weeks, the boys had polished not only the silver tableware, but the tea set, candlesticks, and Mr. Lewis's various plaques given to him for his time as mayor. Miss Georgia was running out of things to keep them and MayBelle busy with around the house.

After spending the morning peeling potatoes and shucking peas, the boys were gathering up their lunch in the kitchen when Mr. Lewis came in through the back door.

"Hello, boys," he said, taking off his hat and putting his briefcase by the table. "Ezekiel, please stay inside."

The boys exchanged worried looks as Georgie headed outside.

"Did I do something wrong, Mr. Lewis?"

"No, in fact just the opposite." He pulled a few coins out of his pocket. "You've done your job so well that I see no reason to keep you all day. As a treat for a job well done, I'm taking you into town and you can get an ice cream cone or some candy at the five-and-dime."

Zeke's eyes were big as saucers and his jaw dropped. "No foolin'?"

"No foolin'."

"Can Georgie come? I know he can't go in, but could he ride in your car?" Zeke looked out the back window and saw his friend eating under a tree. "We worked together."

The former mayor ruffled Zeke's hair and then pushed the boy toward the door. "Sorry, not today."

Zeke's feet and heart felt heavy as he walked down the back stairs with Mr. Lewis. Conflicting feelings tied his stomach in knots. He was excited for the chance to get a treat but felt bad that his friend would be missing out. Zeke gave a half-wave to Georgie, who returned a wave with as much enthusiasm.

Mr. Lewis opened the passenger-side door for Zeke, who kept looking back to see if Georgie was still looking. He wasn't. Outside the retired mayor's home, in the rest of Lexington, their time of sharing stories was over.

It was a short drive to the store, and Zeke forgot all about his friend under the tree as he stared at boxes of candies. His first instinct was the root beer barrel hard candies. They tasted great and lasted a long time. There were also bags of candy-coated chocolate pieces. Willie was the first kid he knew to try the new candy, and true to Willie, he didn't share. It reminded Zeke why they weren't friends that summer.

"Did you decide?" Mr. Lewis looked at his watch.

"They all look so good. It's hard to decide."

Mr. Lewis handed him a bag. "Get a few of each."

"A *few* of *each*? Oh, no, sir, Momma would not abide by that."

"I believe she'll be okay with it this one time."

Zeke's mouth watered as he put a handful of root beer candies into the bag. His eyes and mouth smiled as he dropped in the special chocolate bits. He started to hand the bag to Mr. Lewis when he saw caramel squares, his mother's favorite. He grabbed a heaping handful that overflowed the bag and fell to the floor. Zeke heard a *harrumph* and turned to see Mr. Lewis standing with arms crossed. The young boy picked up the mess and added four to the bag.

The drive home was quiet except for the sounds of Zeke sucking and crunching on the hard candy. He rolled the window down and enjoyed the wind whipping at this hair. As they crested the hill, Zeke could see the bridge over the creek, the roof of his house, the railroad tracks, and the Missouri rolling on. At that moment, drunk on root beer candy, Zeke couldn't think of a prettier picture.

"Tell your mom she has credit at the church's thrift store for your shoe, or shoes, if she wants a whole pair." Mr. Lewis pulled the car into the dirt area in front of the house. "And Ezekiel . . ."

"Yes, sir."

"No more taking off with strangers."

"I've learned my lesson on that. Thanks for the candy."

Mr. Lewis grabbed the tip of his hat and gave it a little tug. He pulled the car out slowly to avoid kicking up a cloud of dust. Zeke stood outside waving until the car disappeared around the bend at the top of the hill.

"Momma! Eli! Ethan! I'm home, and I've got treats!"

CHAPTER ELEVEN

LEXINGTON, MISSOURI, PRESENT DAY

Not much had changed in the two decades since Zeke had last stepped foot in Lexington. The biggest change was a national motel chain setting up shop on the south side of town. The weary travelers checked in to adjoining rooms a little before midnight.

Despite the long drive, Zeke woke early Friday morning. He took advantage of the free continental breakfast, which consisted of stale coffee, boxed juices, individually wrapped pastries, and overly ripe bananas. It was nothing like the meal pictured on the billboard about fifty miles outside of town.

He tapped the silver call bell sitting next to the faded "Ring for service" sign. A young man with serious bed head stumbled to the desk, rubbing his eyes and yawning wide.

"How can I help you?"

Zeke looked the young man up and down. He wore a faded T-shirt that appeared to commemorate a band and pants that looked to be flannel pajamas.

"Do you have any fresh coffee and a newspaper?"

The young man stared at him, glanced at the coffee pot, and back to Zeke.

"Tyson takes care of the coffee, and he's not here today. Sorry . . ." His eyes brightened and he stood up. "Oh, but there's a coffee shop down the street. I hear they have lattes now."

"I'll give that little machine in my room a try," Zeke said. "Any chance of a paper?"

The young man glanced around again, and his eyes settled at the front door. "You're in luck. You can take that one by the front door on your way out and just drop it back in here when you're done."

Zeke tipped an imaginary hat to the kid, who awkwardly returned the gesture. He snapped up the local paper off the door mat and headed back to his room. Once inside, he put the automatic coffee maker to work and knocked on the adjoining door.

"It's odd that I'm knocking on your door, but I'm up, enjoying some gourmet coffee, and I've got the paper."

Before Zeke could sit at the bistro table in his room, Nate entered with his own coffee and joined him. He sat a little paper cup with pills on the table.

Nate rolled his eyes. "I was hoping you'd forget. Let me wash them down with some water."

The older man picked up the cup and headed to the bathroom. Setting the cup on the edge of the sink, he reached to turn on the cold water and spilled the pills into the sink. One started to dissolve and another slipped down the drain, but the opaque round gel tab was saved by the drain stopper. "Dammit." Zeke reached into the sink for the lone sphere.

"Everything okay?" Nate called from the other room.

"All good." Zeke popped the lone pill in his mouth and shoveled water to his mouth with his hand. He wiped the liquid from his chin and rubbed his hands on the front of his shirt.

"I forgot I was using the only drinking cup for my coffee." Zeke sat at the table and took a sip of the tepid liquid. "Oh, man, who knew there were things about The Palms I would miss."

"Let's not miss out on continuing to share the town gossip." Nate rubbed his palms together.

Zeke smiled and handed Nate the paper.

"That's right, we know you never have your glasses." Nate snapped open the paper and peeked over the top. "Ready?" He folded the paper.

"I swear, one day . . ." Zeke blanched after taking another sip.

"Hee-hee." Nate snickered and popped the newspaper open again. "Wow, our dearly departed friend Catherine Anne Tullis has a front-page article. She must have been a bigwig in town. You don't remember her?"

Zeke took a shallow sip of coffee, pinched his face at the bitter taste, and shook his head. "Tullis rings a bell, but not Catherine. Sorry."

"No need to apologize. There's a box with information about the funeral tomorrow. It's at Beloved Covenant Church at ten o'clock, followed by a potluck in the Fellowship Hall." His voice rose as he finished the sentence. "Oh, Tito, if white people funeral potlucks are half as amazing as Filipino potlucks . . . we'll eat like kings!"

Zeke spit out the coffee he was sipping. "Well, we're not going to get full from breakfast . . . Go on. Is there anything about the young man Jimmy Nixon or the girl and other boy who were hurt?"

"Hmm, top story says that the editorial board is supporting Thomas Lewis for mayor over Josiah Larsen."

Zeke nodded. "Good choice. The Lewis family is good folk. Wouldn't trust a Larsen as far as I could throw 'em."

"Good to know." Nathaniel folded the paper. "Also, the city council approved upgrading the sidewalks downtown and is doubling jaywalking fines to help pay for it." He dropped the paper in his lap.

"Doesn't it feel odd that these are the front-page stories along with . . ." He picked the paper up. "Hazel Tobler and her three-berry preserves will be representing Lexington at the Lafayette County Fair. Oh, wait, they *did* represent, and she came home with a silver ribbon."

Nate turned the page. "Finally, here's something. This article says a special circumstances hearing has been set for Jimmy Nixon to determine if he should stand trial for the accident . . . Mmm . . ." He glanced over the newspaper. "There's no mention of Bigfoot or any animal in this article. Do you think he changed his mind?"

Zeke bit his lower lip. "I don't know. Maybe. I need to talk to him."

"Okay, let's see how our crowdfunding page is doing this morning."

Nate's smile popped a dimple as the phone screen reflected in his eyes. "We're still gaining subscribers, and they're loving you Tito."

> **@BelieverMO1** Grew up about an hour from you, plenty of things going bump in the night in those woods. #Bigfoot #AnythingIsPossible
>
> **@CryptoZooLover** I've got goosebumps. #BigfootLives #SasquatchForever
>
> **@BoredSquidNT** OMG! Your life is a scary movie #Believe #Bigfoot
>
> **@TeamSasquatch0102** Missouri is the Show Me State, so SHOW ME some proof. #BigfootRocks #Cryptozoology #IWannaBelieve

Nate slipped the phone in his pocket. "On those happy notes, let's take a stroll down memory lane, shoot some video, and figure out how to find this kid."

The historical downtown district looked nearly identical to when Zeke was a kid. Brick storefronts, the Lafayette County Courthouse with its white colonnades—pocked with bullet and cannon holes spanning the Civil War era to Jesse James and other outlaws—and the red-brick Presbyterian church with its tall bell tower. He could almost hear the deep peals in the far back corner of his memory.

Zeke rolled down the window and rested his arm on the door ledge. This allowed him to better hear the sound he knew was coming.

Brrruuump, brrrump, brrrump. The soft rumble of tires drumming on the original hand-laid brick street brought a sweet smile to Zeke's face. Nate was less excited.

"This is going to destroy my wheel alignment." He glanced at Zeke, whose smile grew as he looked out the window. "How much farther?"

"It's just down this street a bit. We're almost there."

The houses on the streets looked like he remembered them—white clapboard siding, storm shutters, and massive trees. Although the homes needed a fresh coat of paint, the memories coming to mind were in vivid color for Zeke. He pulled on the seatbelt as they neared Willie Larsen's house. Despite their spats, Zeke was happy they'd been friends when they graduated. A friend he still didn't trust all that much, but close enough.

There was a slight incline as the road headed for the crest of the hill. Zeke shifted in his seat and sat up straight.

"Pull over just after this driveway on the right."

Nate pulled the car next to the curb just in front of a white, two-story storybook mansion with black trim. "Guessing this is your Scout leader's house, Mr. Lewis."

Zeke nodded, opened the door, and stepped out. He glanced over at the house, but he stepped to the front of the car. This was the view he'd wanted to see. He could see the mighty Missouri River rolling just as fast and wide as he remembered. His vision moved toward the railroad tracks before looping to an apparent vacant lot between the tracks and the road. Zeke swallowed hard and lowered his head. He sat on the hood of the car and braced himself with his arms.

"Are you okay, Tito?" Nate rushed to Zeke's side.

"Yeah, I didn't think it would hit me so hard." Zeke rubbed at his face and shook his head.

"Do you want to go back to the hotel?"

"No, I'm good. I'm ready for my close-up, Mr. DeMille."

Nate pulled out his cell phone and started recording. "Is this the spot where it all started?"

Zeke, who was still getting used to being filmed, stared straight into the camera lens and spoke loudly. "Yes! This is where it all started." He made a slow sweeping gesture with a ramrod straight arm. "It was right down there!" He turned to look down the road and saw the Lewis Creek bridge under its tunnel of trees. A slight sigh escaped his lips and his features softened. "This is where my world changed. Seeing it in the daylight, nearly seventy years removed, it doesn't seem quite as scary, but there's enough of that little boy still inside . . ." Zeke tapped his shirt above his heart. "In here, there's still a mighty frightened boy."

"That's perfect, Tito. You're a natural."

Zeke gave a double thumbs-up to the camera.

"Yeah, don't do that. In fact, you just stay seated on the hood, and I'll get some video from behind so people can see this amazing sight." Nate walked around the car filming at different angles.

"Okay, let's walk down together and you tell me about that first encounter."

Zeke raised his hands and furrowed his brow.

Nate cut him off before he could speak. "Not to worry, I'll run back up the hill myself and get the car."

Standing at the bottom of the hill waiting for Nate, Zeke couldn't figure out if the walk down the hill or the stroll down memory lane was taking the bigger toll on him.

"Hey, you need a ride?" the orderly asked Zeke out the passenger-side window.

The older man chuckled. "You know what, I'm going to walk the rest of the way home."

"Okay, I'll drive across and wait for you in that clearing."

Zeke had crossed that old bridge numerous times since his first Bigfoot encounter, but something felt different this time. He had time to reflect and try to comprehend what happened that fateful night. He'd come to accept the giggles he'd hear when he passed people on the street. He believed he saw Bigfoot, and it no longer mattered if no one else did.

Some of the bridge had worn away, and he could look down and see the river. He watched it flow out toward the Missouri and smiled and chuckled as he recalled jumping from the train into the muddy outlet.

On the other side of the bridge, Nate was videoing what he called B-roll. "You know, those bits in movies where they cut away from the main action and show you scenery or the cityscape."

The vacant plot of land had wooden electrical poles at either end and was covered in berry brambles, weeds, and various types of trees. The power poles and trees were being swallowed by big-leafed ivy. The vegetation was littered with bricks, wood panels, windowpanes, and metal bins.

Zeke cupped his nose, mouth, and chin in his hands. His pace slowed, and his eyes grew dark. He slowly pivoted where he was and took in the sight all over again. He dug into his pocket for his handkerchief.

"It's all gone . . ." his voice trailed off. He took a half step toward a pile of bricks. "Our porch was just about here, and I'm pretty sure I bathed in that metal tub."

He walked toward a pile of wooden boards and started picking some up. "This . . . these boards were my house . . . The last time I was here these were walls . . . leaning, but walls." He slumped forward slightly and put his hands on his knees.

"It's all gone. Like we were never here."

The sound of Nate's shoes in the gravel startled Zeke, who suddenly stood straight and shook his head. He wiped his nose with his handkerchief.

"Sorry, didn't mean to startle you."

"Nah, it's okay. I just drifted away for a moment." He returned the kerchief to his pocket, took a deep breath, and patted his chest. "I'm good. Instead of the hotel, let's head back into town and stop at the courthouse."

"Now?"

"No time like the present."

~~~

There were no parking spots open on Main Street as they neared the courthouse. The spaces were filled by customers at the boutique shops, bookstore, café, and hardware store that flanked the courthouse.

Nate turned down First Street and found a space in the parking lot shared by the courthouse, City Hall, and grocery store.

"It's like the ultimate one-stop shop." Nate said as they exited the vehicle.

They walked the concrete path along the well-manicured lawn and up the small flight of stairs, which featured massive columns, to the solid wood doors. The information desk to the left was staffed by a high school-aged girl.

"How may I help you?" The teen made full eye contact and flashed a toothy smile.

Zeke glanced at her name badge. "Hello Rayleen, I'm wondering if any counselors have openings today."

She glanced down at a piece of paper on the desk and ran her finger down the list of names. "Yes, it looks like counselors Henry and Samuel Lewis have time today. Who would you like to see?"

At the name of his old Cubmaster, Zeke's eyes widened. He knew *his* Mr. Lewis had passed away decades ago, but he'd heard several of the four-time former mayor's descendants followed in his lawyer footsteps. Zeke smiled and patted Nate on the shoulder. "Samuel, please."

"Let me call his secretary."

After a few moments of undecipherable whisperings, she hung up the phone. "You'll have five minutes. Counselor Samuel is down this hall, second door on the left."

The duo headed down the hall and entered the second door on the left. A thirty-something male sat behind a massive mahogany desk. Zeke stopped short in his tracks.

"You're Counselor Samuel Lewis?"

"Yes, and you are?" He stood up and walked around the desk.

Zeke held out his hand. "I'm Ezekiel Renick. I grew up here, and your . . . I'm guessing great-grandpa, was my Cub Scout leader."

"Always nice to meet a fellow Lexingtonian, especially one that goes back aways." He shook Zeke's hand and reached for Nate. "And you are?"

"The ord—driver. I drive for Mr. Renick."

"Very good, please have a seat. I don't have much spare time. How can I help?"

Zeke sat as straight as he could and cleared his throat. "Do you know which attorney is assigned to the hearing for the young man, Jimmy Nixon?"

Samuel Lewis put his shoulders back. "We're still working out the details for the hearing. Do you know something about the accident?"

Zeke lowered his head and took several deep breaths. Nate reached over and touched his shoulder. "It's okay, Mr. Renick."

The young lawyer shifted in his chair. "Mr. Renick? What do you know about this case?"

"I'm not sure I really know anything, but I'm curious as to why the latest article in the paper no longer mentions a . . ." He pulled at his collar. "It doesn't mention outside interference."

The lawyer brought his hand down hard on the desk and roared. "You mean that Bigfoot nonsense."

Zeke stood up, causing Samuel to shrink back in his chair. "It's not nonsense. I've not only seen Bigfoot, but I saw him right where that Nixon boy said he saw him."

The Counselor picked up his phone. "Iris, please hold my calls."

CHAPTER TWELVE

LEXINGTON, MISSOURI, 1956

The summer heat and humidity were reaching new highs, and the Renick brothers' tempers flared like the sun. They had seen *Davy Crockett and the River Pirates* and various cartoons at the theater several times thanks to Mr. Lewis, and they'd read all the good bits in the Bible. They could recount the trials and troubles of Daniel, Samson, Jonah, and David.

Even boys with the whole outdoors to play in get bored, and Ruth Renick was near her wits' end with their constant squabbling.

"Eli, why don't you and Ethan help Ezekiel get ready for his Scout camping trip?" She pointed to her youngest cutting carrots at the table. Ruth turned back to watch the pot where she was preparing potatoes just the way her eldest loved them. "He's nervous about going, and it would help him to have a practice try with you two."

Standing a foot taller than his mother, Eli peered over her into the pan and took a deep whiff. "Aw, Mom, that's not fair."

"The way to a man's heart . . ."

Eli reached out to try and steal a bit of potato. His hand was tapped with a spoon.

"Oww! Okay, okay. Brother's camping trip it is."

Zeke raised his hands and cheered.

Ruth moved the spoon, and Eli quickly snatched a morsel. He fanned his mouth as he tried to chew the hot potato. "Oh, my gosh, now I fully understand Esau selling his birthright. Do you think he was a fan of potatoes?"

"Definitely not carrots." Zeke held up a misshapen vegetable. "I wouldn't trade anything for these."

~~~

"Tell me again why we're doing this?" Ethan asked as he stuffed blankets into a green canvas duffle bag.

"Because Momma asked us to help get Zeke ready for his Cub Scout camping trip."

Zeke was folding his own blankets and having trouble shoving them into his rucksack.

"We're not miracle workers, Eli. Look at what we're working with." Ethan made a sweeping gesture toward the youngest brother, who, on cue, tumbled face first into the pile of blankets.

Eli buried his face in his hand but couldn't stifle the laugh that slipped out between his fingers. Ethan stepped closer to the first born and started to whisper.

"Hey, no secrets," Zeke said as he untangled himself from the bedding.

"Don't matter anyway." Eli pushed Ethan away and pointed at the sloppy pack. "I'm ignoring his ramblings and making sure we have a good time."

Eli unfolded a topographical map of the county and laid it on the table. His younger siblings stood on either side of him.

"How do you read that map?" Zeke tilted his wide-eyed expression toward Eli.

"I'm going to teach you, and if you learn fast, you may get another badge faster than the other Cubs."

Zeke's smile grew and his chest puffed out at the thought of having one more badge than Willie.

Ethan took off his cap and swiped it at Zeke. "Don't get all excited yet. You still have to learn to survive this weekend."

"Survive?" Zeke grabbed Eli's shirt. "What does he mean, survive, Eli?"

"He's just being stupid." Eli focused his gaze on Ethan and nudged him with his elbow.

"Eli Renick, I heard that." Ruth called from the other room. "Don't make me come in there and straighten you out with this iron."

"No, ma'am. Sorry, Ethan," he said loudly and less sincerely than necessary. He turned back to the table. "Okay, let's focus so we can plan our route."

Eli gave the map a turn so the Missouri River and Lewis Creek were lined up in the same direction as the house.

"We're here." He put his index finger on the map. "And we're going to go south—since Zeke already had a great northern adventure —and camp right here." He stretched out his thumb to span the distance they would cover.

"If all goes well, it'll take us a day to hike, then we'll spend a day fishing—hopefully catch dinner—and then come on home the next day."

"Is it a hard hike?" Zeke asked, absentmindedly rubbing the scar on his leg.

"Nope, it's damn near flat." Ethan jumped in as Ruth entered the room. "*Darn* near flat." His mother half-smiled and nodded at the middle child who breathed a sigh of relief. "The way you can tell, Zeke, is the lines. See, look close."

All three boys hunched forward to get an up-close look at the map. There were blue squiggles, brown circles, and some shapes Zeke couldn't name.

"The brown shows you mountains and valleys, and the blue shows you rivers," said Ethan.

"But how can they be mountains if they're all flat?" Zeke tilted his head toward his brothers and waited for the answer.

Eli ran his finger along the section he pointed out as their house.

"See how the rings are far apart? That means it's flat, and we know if we went outside our door that it's flat." Zeke and Ethan both nodded as Eli continued his explanation. "Now, if we go north—like our Zeke—you'll see how the lines get closer together. That means it's a steep hill."

"I can vouch for that," Zeke chimed in.

Eli pushed the map in front of Zeke. "Now, how are the lines between home and our camping spot?"

Zeke's eyebrows arched and his shoulders hunched as he hovered over the map. He looked back and forth between his brothers, who both wore blank expressions. He looked down at the map and ran his fingers along the route. "There aren't too many lines, and they don't get near as close as those other lines. So, it's like Ethan said, damn—"

"Ezekiel!"

"Sorry, Momma . . . Darn near flat."

"It's not the hike you have to worry about, anyway. It's the Wooly-Bully. *Wooooh*." Ethan continued the ghostly noises as he wriggled his fingers toward Zeke.

Eli slapped at his hands.

"Stop it. You'll scare him."

"Me? He's the one who says he saw the thing."

"I did see it!" Zeke tried to shove Eli out of the way to get to Ethan. "And I'm not afraid of it . . . I was just surprised by it."

"Well, Jon Harris said he was scared to camp in that area because he'd seen and heard something *there* last time he went." Ethan put his index finger on the map. "*Dun, dun, duun!*"

Eli stepped to Ethan and bumped him back with his chest. "I told you we are *not* doing *that*. We're just going camping."

"Not doing what?" Zeke pulled at the back of Eli's shirt. "Not doing what?"

"Nothin'. Right, Ethan?"

Ethan had grown a lot in the past year, but he had not grown enough to challenge Eli. "Right, Eli. We're just going camping."

~~~

The sky teetered between night and day as the boys scarfed down fresh biscuits their mother had gotten up extra early to make.

"I couldn't let you leave on empty stomachs." She glanced at each boy, adjusting Eli's cap, Ethan's shirt, and Zeke's scarf. "You all look presentable. Have a good time. Zeke, you listen to Eli." She bent down and gave him a kiss on the cheek, which he promptly rubbed off.

They walked in birth order alongside the road to start their journey. It was smoother than the brambles and thickets near the railroad tracks, and they had all sworn on the Bible they would stay clear of the trains.

Yellow crept across the sky, and the temperature and humidity seemed to triple in an instant. The heat didn't dampen the trio's spirits; for them, it was just part of summer. A pair of cardinals caught Zeke's attention, and he stopped to watch the birds. The bright red male was whistling a happy tune near the middle of a tree, while the brownish-hued female hopped to-and-fro on the branches.

"Hey, Zeke, keep up."

Ethan's shout startled Zeke and scared away the birds. The young ornithologist huffed and hustled to catch up to his brothers.

"You'll have plenty of time to bird-watch once we make camp," Eli said. "Just keep up while we're still on the road. Momma will kill us if something . . . else happens to you."

Eli pulled the map out and unfolded it. "Hey, Zeke, can you figure out where we are and where we should go?"

The young Cub quick-stepped to Eli's side to view the map. Zeke's eyes started to glaze over as he took in all the lines. He slowly moved his pointer finger along what he knew was the Missouri River. Zeke took a glance at this brother's faces to see if he could tell if he was hot or cold. Ethan made a mad face, and Eli's face gave away nothing.

As he moved his finger, he noticed the hard turn the river takes near Deadman's Corner. He quickly traced the river the other direction and was rewarded with a smile from Eli. Zeke continued until he saw a section with several circles far apart signaling the valley where they'd camp. "Here!" He thumped his finger in the middle of the circle.

"Great job, Zeke, you'll get that badge no problem." Eli patted his youngest brother on the shoulder.

"If we survive the trip." Ethan said in a stage whisper.

"Ethan!" The oldest Renick shouted.

The middle child shrugged his shoulders and raised his hands, palms up.

~~~

They set up camp near a clump of trees close to the lake for fishing and some bushes for relieving. Eli had borrowed a small tent, but with the rising temperature, he was pretty sure it would be too hot to sleep in. Instead, they laid it out and used it as a tarp.

Eli laid his bedroll out first and walked away to get firewood and rocks for a fire pit. Zeke set up his bedroll, following Eli's example, while Ethan seemed content to lay on the tent and use his bag for a pillow.

"That don't seem comfy, Ethan. Want me to help you unload your bag?"

"You don't touch my stuff, hear?"

Zeke held up his hands. "I hear. I hear."

"What's this? A stick-up?" Eli called as he walked out of the woods. "Hate to tell you, Ethan, but Zeke don't have anything worth stealin'."

"Oh, you're so funny." Zeke put his hands down and went to take some sticks from Eli. "It wasn't a stick up. I just asked Ethan if he wanted some help with his bag, and he got all mad and told me not to touch his stuff."

Eli dropped the firewood, brushed his hands on his hips, and stood as tall as he could. "I think I need to check your bag, Ethan."

"No!" Ethan jumped up and pulled his bag under him. Eli wrestled him free from the rucksack. He held Ethan back with one arm while holding the bag out to Zeke to untie. The youngest tipped the bag over and shook it.

"No wonder you didn't want me to get in there. I can't believe you'd do that after everything!" Zeke crumpled by the pile as Ethan leapt over to grab a bag of licorice bits.

"I was going to share." Ethan shoved the bag back into the pack.

Eli turned to him and put his hand out.

"Come on, Eli." Reluctantly, he pulled the bag out and placed it in Eli's hand.

"You're lucky this was the only surprise in your bag."

Ethan smirked.

~~~

Fishing was a bust. The only things biting were the mosquitos. The boys sat around the fire roasting slices of canned, processed pork on sticks. The night sky was full of stars that enveloped the valley in a blue light. They were happy they'd decided to sleep on the flattened tent because it was still muggy long after the sun had gone down. Originally, Zeke picked a spot on the edge, but he decided for safety he'd rather sleep between his brothers.

"You'll keep the fire going all night, right Eli?" asked Zeke.

"Oh, Eli, please keep the fire going, I'm so scared," Ethan mocked in a falsetto voice. "Please, there are monsters."

Eli leaned over Zeke to rap Ethan on the head.

"Ouch! Why'd you do that?"

"For being mean and causing trouble . . . and it felt right."

Ethan leaned back on his bedding. He huffed and crossed his arms.

Zeke glanced at Ethan, who rolled his eyes.

"How about a good tall tale—a happy one—before bed?" Eli asked, tossing another log on the fire.

The eldest swiveled around on the ground to face his brothers. They were both lying on their sides, heads propped on their hands.

"Yes, please," they chorused.

"Alright, how about Davy Crockett and the keelboat race down the O-HI-O?" Both heads nodded. Eli cleared his throat and dropped his voice an octave. As he recounted the story of the frontiersman and his pal George trying to get pelts down river on a keelboat, he raised and lowered his arms as if he were pushing the pole deep in the water to move the flatbottom barge. Zeke was enjoying the story, but he had to lay back and close his eyes because the fire gave Eli a creepy backlit glow that conjured up darker memories.

By the time Davy and George outwitted the river and the villain Mike Fink, Zeke and Ethan could barely keep their eyes open.

"The end," Eli whispered. He pulled a light blanket over Zeke and rolled over to face the fire.

~~~

Zeke woke to the sound of a twig breaking.

"Did y-you hear t-th-that?" Zeke shook Eli. "The fire's out! Add s-s-some wood."

Eli rubbed his eyes and shook his head to clear the cobwebs. He grabbed hold of Zeke's face and looked him in the eye. "Slow down. Breathe. You start stuttering again, and Mom will send you back to Mother Harris to eat more rocks. You want that?"

Zeke rubbed his tongue along the roof of his mouth and over his teeth. The metallic, earthy taste rose in his mouth. "No, sir."

"Okay, then you catch your breath, and I'll stoke the fire." Eli grabbed a couple of smaller logs and tossed them on the bright orange embers. He leaned in and gave a strong puff of air, and the embers ignited once more. Soon there was a roaring fire. He noticed Zeke's shoulders had relaxed, and he'd unclenched his fists.

"Better?"

"A little, but something is out there."

Eli looked beyond Zeke and saw that Ethan's bedroll was empty.

"I'll kill him," the oldest forced out between gritted teeth.

"We don't have to kill it." Zeke's voice went up a couple octaves. He coughed and forced his voice lower. "Uh, we don't have to kill it . . . unless . . . unless it's a bear."

"I think we're safe." Eli patted the bedroll. "Try to get some sleep."

Snap! Crack! Thump, thump, thump, thump.

The sounds of a large creature trying to make its way through the trees sent a cold tingle up Zeke's spine and set his shoulders to shivering. He looked at Eli, who wore his scrunched-up angry face instead of his open-mouthed scared one.

Eli tossed a bigger log on the fire, and there was a burst of light around the area that captured the creature in its glow. It froze midstride, its shaggy torso three-quarters exposed between the safety of trees. It stared at the brothers, shifting its weight slightly as if to get a better look at each of them.

"I told you he was huge." Zeke hid behind Eli, peeking around his shoulder to get a glimpse at the creature.

Eli shook his shoulders to try to dislodge Zeke and his dug-in fingernails.

"I'll kill him."

"No. No, no, no." Zeke crawled over Eli and put himself between his brother and the fire and the creature. "You can't kill it."

"You're right, I can't, but I can sure scare it." Eli reached for his bag, dug to the bottom, and brought out a BB gun. He brought his hand up to fire.

The creature tilted its head, and the firelight caught red in its eyes. It beat its chest and made a chuffing sound. The ting of the BB gun was followed by a crack as the pellet hit a tree about ten paces from the would-be target. The creature startled and stepped behind a bigger tree that still left it mostly exposed.

Eli fired again, and this time bark flew off the tree next to the creature.

"Careful, Eli, you almost hit it."

"We're too far for it to do any damage. I'm just trying to put the fear of God into him."

"Put the fear of God into who?"

Both brothers shrieked and jumped. They turned in unison to see Ethan.

"Did you see a coyote or bear?" Ethan dropped a roll of toilet paper onto his blanket.

"No, we saw Bigfoot! It was right over there, and Eli shot at it to scare it away." Zeke pointed to where the creature had been, but all they saw was a stand of empty trees. "Tell 'em, Eli. Tell him you saw it too."

Eli ran both his hands through his hair. He was ashen and opened his mouth as if to say something, but only "uuh" came out. The oldest Renick boy looked back at the empty woods and then to his middle brother.

"Well, come on, Eli. Cat got your tongue?" Ethan crossed his arms and stuck out his chin.

Zeke had never seen his oldest brother so frazzled. He worried that Eli's brain was broken like Mr. Benson's. They said something exploded in the old man's head, and he forgot how to walk and talk. He reached over and pushed his arm. "Eli? Eli you okay?"

Eli shoved the hand away and moved toward Ethan. "I thought it was *you*."

"You thought it was him." Zeke grabbed the back of his neck. "That's silly Eli, why would it be Ethan? Did your brain break?"

Ethan laughed. "Yeah, Eli, did you break your brain?"

"I thought you'd gone through with your stupid plan to scare him." The vein throbbed on Eli's neck as he clenched and relaxed his fists.

Zeke's eyes widened and his jaw dropped.

"You searched my bag!" Ethan put his arms out in front of him to keep Eli at a distance.

"You could haven hidden the costume when you were out looking for kindling. Heck, you could have had one of your crony friends help you."

Ethan shrugged. "I tried, but Jon Harris said his dad said he couldn't see a good reason for a son of his to be runnin' through the woods with a bear-skin rug."

Zeke stepped between his brothers. "See! It's real. I really saw Bigfoot. We, *we* really saw Bigfoot!"

Eli locked eyes with Zeke, whose head bobbed up and down beneath a Cheshire grin. "I guess we did, kiddo."

"Dang it," Ethan said. "The one time I pick to go to the bathroom is when Bigfoot shows up."

Zeke snuggled his back against Eli, who was sitting up adding wood to the fire. He'd been tasked with trying to get some sleep and was failing.

"You're wiggling a lot for a kid who's supposed to be sleeping."

"Sorry, Eli. I can't get comfortable."

"You wanna join me by the fire?"

A shiver ran through Zeke. "No, sir. I've seen enough for one night."

"Then shut your yapper and get to sleep." Ethan rolled over and put his arm over his ear. "Not all of us are afraid of the dark."

"Hush, Ethan." Eli turned back toward his youngest brother and lowered his voice. "I don't think whatever it was is coming back, but I'll keep the fire going. You can calm yourself by looking up and trying to find the dippers. Remember how?"

The youngest Renick rolled on his back and held his arm out straight. He made an "L" shape with his thumb and index finger and moved it back and forth. "I don't see it."

Eli looked up and then grabbed Zeke's hand and tweaked it to the left. "Now?"

"Oh, yeah, now I see it." Zeke's voice rose with excitement. "Thanks, Eli."

"You're my favorite." Ethan's falsetto sarcasm pierced the night.

All three brothers laughed.

~~~

116

Dawn broke and brought with it a renewed sense of adventure for Zeke and Ethan. Eli, who was drowsy and stiff, lacked the enthusiasm of his younger siblings.

"I'm going to take a quick dip in the lake to wake up."

"Sounds good." Zeke chewed on a biscuit.

"When I get back, you two can break down camp, and we'll head home."

"What? Why?" Ethan jumped to his feet. "Aren't we going to track what you and Zeke saw? What about our day of fishin'?"

"Yeah, it doesn't seem so scary during the day." Zeke's voice cracked. "And we should at least try to put the tent up once."

"Okay, okay, I was just trying to look out for my *little* brothers." Eli held up his hands. "Quick dip, and we can explore the grove for clues."

"Yes!" Ethan and Zeke shouted.

~~~

There was a mangle of tracks around the stand of trees that were part of a well-worn game trail.

"This little one here is definitely a racoon."

"How do you know, Ethan?" Zeke sat down on his haunches.

"They have creepy little fingers."

Zeke scrunched his face and nodded.

"These are either small deer or maybe hogs." Ethan pointed at a patch of crisscrossed tracks. "You see anything you recognize, Eli?"

The eldest shook his head. "These look like bear, but the claws don't look right."

Zeke scooted near the trees where Eli was standing. From there, he looked across to their camp. "It don't look right because it's not a bear. It's the Wooly-Bully. These are the trees we saw it in last night."

"But look here." Eli reached up in the tree and pulled out some black fur, rolled it in his fingers, and smelled it. "This is definitely a bear. Maybe it has a messed up paw."

Ethan put his size-nine Chuck Taylor next to the misshapen print. "I win. Either it's a big bear or a small Bigfoot."

"That don't mean nothing." Zeke bent down for a closer look. "With all these animals moving around, half the track could be erased by something else. And did you see how high Eli had to reach to get that fur? It's Bigfoot. I know it."

Eli put his hand on Zeke's shoulder. "I'm leaning a little more toward bear now."

"Eli!"

"I said leaning. Either way, let's head back, practice setting up the tent for Zeke, and fish for a bit. If we catch anything, we'll eat it here and head home. If we come up empty, we'll head home for dinner."

Ethan and Zeke sighed heavily and lowered their heads.

"Zeke, are you kidding me?" Eli put his hands on his head. "You were ready to run home last night in the dark. *Now* you want to stay?"

"I'm not afraid anymore, and I don't really want to get back to chores."

"Me neither," Ethan added.

"Well, if you two don't beat all. Okay, we'll stay no matter what. I just hope someone catches a fish because we're out of Spam."

CHAPTER THIRTEEN

LEXINGTON, MISSOURI, PRESENT DAY

T he young attorney stared at the old man and squinted. "Because you knew my great-grandpa, I'm going to cut you some slack and hear you out. But this better be good." Samuel Lewis gestured for Zeke to sit back down.

Zeke retold his story for what seemed like the millionth time. He tried to read Samuel, but the counselor had an amazing poker face. Zeke wasn't sure if he was listening or making a grocery list in his head.

"So, you can see it's nearly the same, near the Lewis Creek bridge, large unknown creature, rotten smell." Zeke counted the similarities off on his fingers. "I just want to talk to him and see why he changed his story."

"He didn't." Samuel shrugged and shuffled some papers.

"But there was nothing about it in the paper today."

"Of course not, we told the editor to keep that part out. We didn't want anything out there that might help Nixon get crazy sympathy votes, but mostly we didn't want . . ." The young attorney pointed at Zeke and Nate. ". . . Bigfoot hunters, like you two, coming in here and turning the hearing and trial into some kind of circus."

"We're not Bigfoot hunters." Zeke gestured between himself and Nate. "I've already encountered him multiple times, and really that's enough for a lifetime. Once would have been enough. I get it." Zeke moved to the front of his chair and put his hands on his knees. "I really do. I've heard it all before, but don't we owe it to the kid not to dismiss it just because we're too old to believe in fairy tales?"

"It's unorthodox, but Jimmy and his family lawyer Kendall Larsen are due in soon to go over procedures." The lawyer put his elbows on the desk and laced his fingers. He paused and then pointed at Zeke. "If Larsen agrees, you can have fifteen minutes in my office with him."

"You're defending him?"

"No, Mr. Renick, I'm a prosecutor for the county, and you have just made my case a lot more interesting."

~~~

Zeke and Nate paced the hall and learned it was fifty-three steps from the counselor's door to the back entrance and thirty-four steps from the office to the front entrance.

"You gentlemen are welcome to wait in the chairs." Rayleen, the courthouse receptionist, pointed with her pencil. "Ms. Iris will call me when you're allowed back in the room."

Nate sat down and pulled out his phone. "I'll look for a little snippet to upload this afternoon. We got a lot of good footage today."

Zeke started to sit but the creak of a door opening stopped him short. He looked down the hall and saw a woman exiting a door. He glanced over at Rayleen, who was scrolling through her phone.

He plopped hard on the chair and let out a sigh. It echoed around the entrance chamber. He heard Rayleen exhale loudly and watched her finger swipe faster.

"Relax, Tito. It's going to be okay." Nate gently pulled him back into the chair. "Let's watch the video together. You can help pick out the section for tonight."

The two men watched the video on the smart phone. Zeke's breathing eased and his face softened as he watched himself walking around parts of what used to be his home. *How could such a full childhood result in an empty lot?*

The video panned away from him and scanned the brush and trees back toward the river. A flash of red caught Zeke's eye. The video zoomed in on windowpanes in the brambles.

"Wait. Make it go back."

"What did you see?"

"I'm not sure. But can you make it go back?"

"Yep, we'll rewind, and you say when to stop."

It was a little odd watching the video in reverse, but the red jumped out at him again.

"There. Did you see that? I think it's a cardinal."

Nate stared without blinking and leaned toward Zeke.

"A cardinal, a bright red bird," Zeke explained.

"Oh, yeah, like what your mom sewed for you. We'll go forward slowly to try and catch it."

Nate started the video forward again, going a few frames at a time. At first it was just trees and brambles blowing very, very slowly in a slight breeze, and then . . .

"There! It *is* a cardinal." Zeke's gaze was fixed on the screen, and unwiped tears streamed down his face. He gently reached toward the screen and whispered, "I remember, Momma. I remember." Suddenly aware of where he was, he dug out his handkerchief to wipe his face. Nate caught a glimpse of the keepsake.

"Oh, Tito, your loved ones are thinking of you."

Both men were so transfixed by the red bird frozen on the screen they didn't hear Rayleen the first two times she called them.

"Gentlemen!" She rapped her pencil on the desktop. "You can go back in now."

They stood up, not wanting to look away from the screen.

"Okay, shake that emotion off and focus on what we came for." Nate squeezed Zeke on the shoulders. "You got this, champ."

The air felt different as they walked in and saw Counselor Lewis behind his desk, and Jimmy Nixon and his well-dressed attorney sitting on the overstuffed leather couch. Zeke and Nate took two of the three armchairs available across from them.

"Mr. Renick, I've shared with Mr. Nixon and his attorney, Kendall Larsen, what you told me earlier, and they were interested in hearing you out."

"Before we start, remember nothing said right now can be used to incriminate my client." Kendall Larsen locked eyes with Counselor Lewis.

Samuel nodded in agreement, and the defense attorney leaned back in his chair.

Zeke looked around and all eyes were looking back at him. He first zeroed in on Larsen, then Jimmy, who had bruising on his face.

"I got a chance to meet Counselor Lewis earlier, but I haven't been properly introduced to you two." The older man stood up and stepped across the well-worn carpet. "I'm Zeke Renick, and Nate here's my driver." He pointed at his traveling companion.

"Those bruises from the accident or football?" Zeke smiled as he shook Jimmy's hand.

"The airbag."

The older man held the defense attorney's hand as he asked questions. "So, you're Kendall Larsen. When I was a kid, about Jimmy's age, one of my buddies was a Willie Larsen. Lived in that massive two-story at Highland and Main. Any relation?"

"He still lives there." Larsen tugged his hand free. "He's my great uncle on my mom's side of the family."

"Well, next time you see him, please tell him Zeke says hi." The older man doffed an invisible hat and returned to his seat. He took a deep breath and smiled. "I'm sorry for holding us up. It's just been a crazy day, and I haven't been back here for twenty years. It's a bit overwhelming."

Jimmy squirmed in his chair and shuffled his feet on the carpet. "It's been a crazy time for all of us, mister. My attorney thinks you may help my case. Do *you* think you can?"

"I'm not sure." Zeke wasn't aware of all the possible charges Jimmy was facing, but there were enough for the family to hire a Larsen as an attorney. The Larsen family had a history of getting things done, not always aboveboard, but done. "I read about the accident, and something told me I had to come see and talk to you."

"Because of the creature, the Bigfoot."

Zeke nodded. "Yes. When I saw it, no one believed me. Even when other people saw it, they dismissed it as something else. It's a sucker punch when people don't believe you."

"How do you think this helps me?"

"How can it hurt? I can tell people what happened to me, and it will help them understand the creature is the cause of the accident." Zeke leaned forward and tried to close some distance between them. "Jimmy, can you tell me about that night? All the little snippets you remember, no matter how small or how unimportant you think they are."

Jimmy continued to sit back in the chair, arms crossed. He stretched his legs out and crossed them at the ankles. "We'd lost the football game the night before, and I was ticked off. I was driving fast with the music blaring, I'll admit that, but no faster than I've driven that road all my life. Usually at that time, there's nothing out there. And this *one* time, I get another car *and* a monster."

He shook his head. His lips thinned, and his eyes narrowed. "It all happened so fast. One minute there was nothing but road and then this giant creature was in front of me. I slammed on my brakes and swerved. The car got all squirrelly, and I was trying to keep it on the road. At some point, the headlights landed on . . . it . . . it was covered in dark brown, almost black matted hair, and its eyes glowed from the headlights. I still see them in my nightmares, and if I breathe too deep, I can still smell it."

He closed his eyes and rubbed his nose. A slight shiver shook his left side.

"I was so distracted that I didn't see Ray's car until it was too late, and we crashed." He paled and started to rub his temples. "I was shocked when I got out to check on him and saw Olivia in the car." Jimmy set his hands in his lap and opened his eyes. "Do you think you can help me?"

"I'll certainly try."

A small smile turned up on Jimmy's face. He stood up and reached out his hand to Zeke. "Thank you."

"Don't thank me yet."

"That's right," Samuel Lewis said. "Let's not get ahead of ourselves. I'll share a transcript of Mr. Renick's story and understanding of the creature with the judge, and we'll see if he's allowed to take the stand." The Counselor straightened the paper on his desk. "I'll get back to both parties when he's made a decision."

~~~

They exited the courthouse at what Nate called "golden hour." The orderly-turned-videographer wanted to stay downtown and video some "cover shots and filler" for the crowdsource funders, who were now being called "patrons."

Main Street looked familiar to Zeke with its single-story, red-brick storefronts featuring hand-painted metal signs hanging from the eaves. But the soda shop, five-and-dime, and Mr. Lee's dental office had been replaced by gourmet coffee, vintage clothing, and a gently used toy store.

Zeke let out a heavy sigh and leaned against the brick wall. He watched Nate continue to pan the camera down the street.

"You okay, Tito?"

"Yeah, it just feels strange, like nothing and everything has changed all at the same time." Zeke pointed across the street. "That was the soda shop on the corner, and there used to be tables outside under that tree, and the little place next to it was the dentist office. Not sorry to see that go. This place," he hiked his thumb behind him, "This was the five-and-dime where I'd get candy and a toy during the holidays if momma was able to save enough money. I'm guessing it's a bit more than a dime now, but let's see what we can find."

Nate videoed Zeke's hand opening the door. "After you, Tito."

The store smelled musty, like a child's old toy box. Some of the gently used toys were high on a shelf in their original packaging, while well-worn playthings were easy to reach. There were also new toys in the mix.

Zeke was drawn to the section featuring handmade Pinewood Derby cars. He remembered assembling and painting his own as a Scout and taking part in races. He picked up a red one with a bright yellow 115 painted on the side. He smiled as he recalled his old troop number.

"Ah, good taste," came a female voice from behind him. "That particular car won the 1972 derby."

Zeke jumped at the voice and juggled the car, securing it after a few bobbles.

"I'm sorry, I didn't mean to scare you."

He gave the car a light rub and returned it to the shelf. "No harm done to me or the car. I was getting nostalgic. My best finish was second, back in fifty-five. Lost to my best friend, Larry Everett."

"You're from here? I haven't seen you around before." The middle-aged woman's brow wrinkled.

"It's been a while. This store was the five-and-dime when I was a kid."

"Where are my manners?" She shook her head causing her salt-and-pepper ponytail to flip back and forth. "I'm Gail, Gail Wright. Welcome to my shop, and welcome home."

Zeke tipped his imaginary cap. "Nice to meet you. A few things have changed in the past few decades."

"What brings you back?"

"I'm here for the . . ."

"The funeral." Nate stepped beside Zeke. "We're here for Mrs. Tullis's funeral."

The shopkeeper stepped back and put her hand over her heart. "Look at that. It's my turn to be startled." Gail forced a laugh. "I hear a lot of people are coming back for her service. The motel is nearly full, and you two are my tenth and eleventh customers today—puts me over my quota for the day."

Zeke and Nate chuckled politely at her joke.

Gail Wright rocked on her heels and swung her arms. "I'll let you gentlemen get back to browsing."

A small glass cabinet near the back wall caught Zeke's attention. As he drew near, his eyes widened, and his heart raced. The top layer was full of a variety of marbles. There were mashers, minis, and plain ol' aggies of various colors. His features softened and glowed with the light from the case. Zeke traced his finger across the glass to help his eyes focus on the orbs.

His finger stopped, and for a second it felt like his heart did too, as his gaze fell upon a blue thumper. In his mind's eye, he was suddenly back in Mr. Lewis's living room, trying to take another marble off Willie Larsen.

"Nate. Nate!" Zeke didn't move his eyes or his finger. He could hear the footsteps running his way. "Gail. Gail, could you come here?"

Nate was next to him, already filming the case and zooming in on his finger. The marbles were out of focus. "What is it, Tito?" he said in a hushed tone.

"It's my marble." Zeke spoke just above a whisper, afraid he might disturb the magic of the moment.

Nate matched his whisper. "How do you know it's yours?"

Gail's soft steps stopped on the opposite side of the case. "Did you see something you like?"

"The thumper, where did you get it?" He looked up at her and was greeted with a blank stare.

"The what?"

He looked down and tapped the glass just above the marble. "The big blue one."

She bent down. Zeke leaned over and saw her open a drawer and take out a piece of paper. "Looks like those were brought in by Jayce Callum."

"Does it say where he found them?"

The shopkeeper glanced at the paperwork again. "No. Sorry . . . but I do have a contact number. I can reach out to him for you."

"That would be great. I'll take his number and that big blue marble."

Gail plucked the orb from the case and headed to the front of the store.

Nate cleared his throat. "You didn't say. How do you know it's yours?"

"A gut feeling."

Nate and Zeke waited for Jayce at the Veterans' Memorial Park across the street from the courthouse. The local archaeologist was running an errand across town but said he'd stop to come meet fellow treasure hunters.

Zeke sat on a bench sipping a plain black coffee while Nate wandered with his half-caf soy latte through the veterans' memorial area, which was lit by streetlights as twilight settled over the town. He trailed his hand along the smooth, black marble column topped with a sculpture featuring personnel from all five branches of the U.S. military.

Behind the column, there were several walls with the names of local service members etched into them. Zeke remembered the first time he'd seen the memorial. He knew where all the names that mattered to him were located. He watched as Nate made his way, step-by-step, across the span of the wall. Zeke brought his cup to his lips but waited to drink until Nate stopped moving. The young man looked back at Zeke, who raised his paper cup in a toast.

"That's for my brother, Eli. He died in a training accident in California, never even made it overseas." He pointed to the wall on the other side of the column. "Ethan, my other brother's name, is over there. He's alive, don't worry, and mostly well after ten or so years in the Marines. He moved about an hour away to Kansas City."

Nate walked over and traced his fingers along the wall. He craned his neck to read other tiles. "Hey, I found you, too."

Zeke gave a two-finger salute. Nate returned the gesture and joined him on the bench.

"Sorry about Eli."

"Thanks. It feels like forever ago. He joined the Army just after graduation, then Ethan joined the Marines and saw some early action in Vietnam. I thought I'd be shipped off but turns out my leg hadn't healed well enough for Uncle Sam." Zeke absentmindedly rubbed his knee.

"But your name?" Nate gestured back to the wall.

"Well, the local recruiter was ready to mark me 4-F, keep me out of any service altogether," Zeke patted Nate's knee. "But Mr. Lewis called in a few favors to some higher-ups he knew—apparently he saved some guy in World War II who went on to be a West Virginia senator—and they pulled some strings, and then I was deemed acceptable." Zeke's eyebrows arched, and he shook his head. "Me, acceptable? The powers that be got me assigned to the prairie Navy out in Olathe, Kansas. For four years, I shuffled papers and worked in the repair shops—fixing what guys with two good legs broke— and anything else they came up with for me to do. Gave me the skills to work as a handyman and start my own business."

"I'm sure your momma was happy to have you and Ethan."

Zeke lowered his eyes and turned his head.

"Tito?"

The older man's head slowly moved left and right.

"Hey, are you the guys asking about the marbles?" A teenager wearing jeans and a camouflage T-shirt walked up to them. "I'm Jayce."

Zeke took a sip of coffee to clear his throat. "Yes, I was wondering if you remember where you found this?" He pulled the blue marble out of his jacket pocket.

Jayce's eyes widened, and his smile grew until dimples showed on both cheeks. "I totally remember that day. I think between myself and every other Civil War enthusiast, all the bullets and relics in the city limits have been found, so I drove south, just out of town to see if I'd have better luck."

He opened his phone and pulled up a map of Lexington. He pinched and spread his index finger and thumb several times, finally getting the right area on screen.

"See this spot here?"

Zeke tilted his head and squinted.

Jayce pinched and spread one more time and a small green dot became a slightly bigger green shape. "Better?"

"Much."

"So, the green shape is a camping area that opened about five years ago. It's pretty nice. I parked there and planned to walk back into this valley area. I totally got turned around, stopped halfway up this hill," Jayce said. "I'd found a few old slugs, a ton of trash, and was about to call it a day when I saw a cave. Right about here." He touched the spot, and the latitude and longitude showed on the screen.

"Could you drop a pin there and send it to me?" Nate had his own phone out. He glanced at Zeke. "It will help us get there ourselves."

Zeke slumped forward a bit and stared at the screen.

Jayce threw his hands above his head. "I'll do better than a pin. I'll take you there for a small commission fee. We split anything we find sixty-forty." He pointed to himself on sixty.

"Did you find the marble in or out of the cave?"

"About six feet inside. It was pretty dark, so I used the flashlight on my phone. There wasn't much in there from what I could see. There was a massive pile of branches, looked like shredded blankets or torn-up pillows, and some random toys." He scrunched his eyes closed and tilted his head back. "There was a baseball, the marble, and a roller skate or just some metal wheels." He popped his eyes open wide. "Sorry, that's all I can remember. I didn't stay long because the place was rank."

Zeke and Nate quickly made eye contact.

"Are you available tomorrow?" Zeke's voice cracked with excitement.

"Well, my mom wants me to attend my great aunt's funeral tomorrow morning, but I'm free after that."

"That's perfect." Zeke jumped to his feet. "We're in town for the service, so we can head out from there."

Nate slowly raised his hand.

Zeke smiled. "Yes, *after* the potluck."

CHAPTER FOURTEEN

LEXINGTON, MISSOURI, 1956

A flock of boys crowded into two booths at the Maid-Rite on Main Street. As the youngest and smallest, Zeke and Larry were delegated to roost on the nearby bar stools. They were willing to sit uncomfortably all day as long as anyone else was paying for malteds.

"You really need to stop making bets," Ethan said as he put his arm around Curtis. "But I'm really hoping you don't."

All the boys raised their milkshakes in a mock toast. Shades of red rose on the neck of the soda shop owner's son. Curtis had told his friends how his dad was furious after the last poor bet cost the shop loads in lost revenue and several gallons of ice cream. There would be no more freebies at the soda shop, but Curtis "couldn't welch on a bet" his dad said. "Take that ragtag group of boys down the street and use your own money."

"Well, I'm just sorry they don't serve drinks as strong as whatever it was Eli was drinking when he saw Bigfoot." Curtis forced out.

A chorus of "*oohs*" and "*aahs*" came from the gaggle.

"Yeah," Ethan pipped up. "I missed out on both. I didn't get any whiskey or see any Wooly-Bully."

Eli put his shoulders back and sat up as tall as he could. "Now, you fellas know that I've never told you I saw Bigfoot." He pointed toward Zeke, whose eyes shot back and forth. "My little brother is the one who named them. I just shot at *them*."

"Them?" asked the skinny blond kid at the far table. Zeke knew him as Augie.

"The bear cubs," Eli said as he took a drink. "There were at least three. I didn't see the momma, but I could hear her growlin'."

Zeke inhaled wrong and had a coughing fit.

Larry gave him a few pats on the back. "I thought you said it was the Wooly-Bully?" he whispered.

"It *was* Bigfoot," Zeke said a bit louder and higher than expected.

Eli chuckled, and most of the guys laughed with him. "What we do for little brothers, right fellas?" He grinned. "I went along with Zeke because I didn't want to upset him. He was having quite a fit. But what he thought was one giant creature was actually several bear cubs crawling up and down the trees."

Zeke couldn't believe what he was hearing. Tears formed and balanced on his lower eyelid as he listened to his brother explain away everything they'd experienced on their camping trip. He caught a glance from Eli, but his brother's gaze darted to others who were listening with rapt attention to his tale.

Slurrrrrp! Larry's attempt to get every last bit of malted goodness from the bottom of the glass brought Zeke out of his despondent trance. "You gonna finish your malted, Zeke?"

"Nah, you can have it."

"Thanks." It wasn't long until Larry had reached the bottom again and patted his stomach. "Oh, boy, I think I spoiled my dinner."

"Speaking of dinner," Eli stopped beside Zeke. "We better get to moving so we can finish our chores, so we can eat."

Zeke's head hung low, and he didn't make eye contact. "Okay. Bye, Larry."

Larry half-waved and tried again to suck up more from the cup. *Slurrrrrp!*

"That wasn't your best goodbye. You and Larry have a fight?" Eli asked as the trio headed home.

"Larry and me fight? No, *he's* my friend. My fight is with *you*, you big liar!" Zeke stomped ahead. Eli and Ethan caught up and walked on either side of him.

"I'll talk to you," Zeke said, pointing to Ethan, "but not him." He wouldn't even point at Eli.

"What makes you think I want to talk to him *or* you?" Ethan was the only one who still had some of the sweet ice cream concoction left. He lifted the cup slowly to his lips and smacked the bottom of it. "I'ave better t'ings."

Eli tapped Zeke on the shoulder several times until his younger brother finally looked up.

"What? What do you want?" The youngest forced out between clinched teeth.

"You know why I said what I said back there?"

"Because you're a liar." Zeke faced forward and continued to walk.

"No. Well, I lied a bit, but those guys are my friends, and they would make life miserable for me if I said I saw Bigfoot."

"So it's okay if you make my life miserable?"

"No, that's not it. You're a kid. Kids are allowed to see Bigfoot, and no one thinks anything of it. But when grown-ups see things, it's different."

"So, you're a grown-up now?"

"Shut up." Eli pushed Zeke on his shoulder.

The youngest glanced back up at Eli, who mouthed, "Forgive me." Zeke jerked his shoulder forward and doubled his walking speed.

Not a word was spoken between the three brothers as they continued home. Their silence left room for the birds chirping, dogs barking, and insects humming. Every now and again, the cacophony of the animal kingdom was joined by a soft sniffle from Zeke. He had slowed his pace to be a half-step behind his elders. He didn't want them to hear or see him wipe his hand and forearm across his nose.

It was a rare half-day shift for their mother, who they saw tending the small garden on the side of the house as they approached. She'd pulled her hair back and tied a sky-blue gingham scarf around her head. She waved at the boys with a spade in her hand, which sent clods of dirt flying. The boys—even Zeke—laughed at her antics.

"How was town?" She stood and brushed her hands on her apron.

She was greeted by a pantomime of shrugged shoulders, semi-smiles, and a mixed chorus of "good," "okay," and "dumb."

"Ezekiel, you can't think of a better word than 'dumb'?"

He took a deep breath and exhaled hard. He pursed his lips and shook his head. "Nope. Nothing's coming to mind."

Ethan piped up. "He's just sore 'cuz Eli wouldn't admit to seeing the Wooly-Bully. Eli basically called Zeke a baby."

Eli slugged Ethan in the upper arm.

"Oww! It's the truth." Ethan walked toward the house, rubbing his arm.

"Elijah Thomas Renick, I'm very disappointed in you." Ruth pointed at him with the spade. "You know I don't abide hitting . . . or lying."

Behind her on the porch steps, Ethan turned around and stuck out his tongue.

A mix of sounds came out of Eli's mouth as he stopped and started his response multiple times. He took a deep breath, looked at his mother and little brother, and placed his hand on his hips.

"I'm sorry that I hit Ethan." He pointed to his middle brother still making faces on the porch. "But, Momma, I can't tell the fellas that I saw the Wooly-Bully. They'd tease me something awful . . . and who knows, maybe it really was a bear and her cubs."

"*I* know." Zeke stepped forward and turned to face his oldest brother. "I know it wasn't a bear and cubs. I know it was the Wooly-Bully, and I know you're a coward and a liar." He stomped his foot and started to run toward the house but was held fast by his mother.

"Ezekiel Joseph Renick! You apologize this instant." She held his arm up, causing him to try and balance on his tiptoes.

Eli stepped forward and pushed her arm down. "No, it's alright. He's right, Mom, let him go." His voice was soft and even. "If anything, I owe him an apology."

"Well, I don't forgive you." Zeke pulled his arm from his mother's grip. "I've got chores to do before dinner." He turned and walked away.

~~~

Aside from Ruth saying grace, the family ate dinner in silence. All three boys avoided eye contact with each other. The scraping of utensils on plates and the occasional *thud* of milk glasses being plopped down on the table provided background music.

"Well, if you three don't beat all. Sitting here acting like strangers, or worse—enemies. You're brothers."

"But, Ma." Eli stopped his fork midway to his mouth. "Zeke is acting like a baby."

"Am not!" Zeke pounded the table.

"Stop it! Both of you." Ruth spread her arms across the table. "It's crazy Ethan is the one behaving."

Her middle child lifted his head slightly to acknowledge his mother's comment. He smiled broadly at Eli and Zeke and went back to his meal.

"I've been working on a little something for each of you and now seems a good time to give them to you."

Ethan's head popped up at the promise of a treat.

"You boys stay here and be civil while I go get 'em."

As soon as Ruth left the kitchen, the boys started kicking each other under the table. Zeke wasn't sure whose foot connected with his scarred shin, but he knew it hurt. He fought back tears and covered his mouth with both hands to muffle a groan. He kicked out with all his might and nearly slipped out of his chair. Zeke was halfway under the table when his mother returned.

"I can't even leave you alone for a few moments."

Eli and Ethan sat ramrod straight with mini grins while Zeke pushed himself back into his seat and wiped away tears that slipped unchecked down his hot cheeks.

"Boys, you're breaking my heart." His mother grabbed a corner of her apron and wiped Zeke's cheek. He didn't pull away. "You're supposed to look out for each other. Not be the cause of each other's pain."

Zeke's tear-stained face looked back and forth between Eli and Ethan. Both refused to make eye contact.

"Alright, each of you put your right hand out on the table and close your eyes."

"Are you planning to switch us?" Ethan asked.

"It has crossed my mind, but no. This is a good thing. I promise." She smiled widely at each boy. "Now, please, put out your hands and close your eyes . . . No peeking."

Zeke scrunched his eyes tight and stretched his hand out as far as he could across the table. Eli and Ethan put out their hands and stared at their mother.

"Close them!"

They shut their eyes.

Zeke heard his mother's clothes rustle and the screech of the table sliding as she leaned over it. He was tempted to

136

open his eyes, so he covered them with his left hand. He felt a piece of soft fabric on his hand. It was cool to the touch, and he could feel the embroidery stitches as he rubbed it between his thumb and forefinger.

"Okay, open your eyes."

Zeke peeked between his fingers, afraid he would destroy the magic of the moment. The white cotton handkerchief was embroidered with a bright red cardinal perched on a branch. He lowered his hand so he could spread it apart. He noticed a small Z, J, and R in the corner opposite the bird. He traced the letters with his fingers.

"I put each of your first, middle, and last initials on them, so you could tell them apart. Ezekiel, I gave you a Z since you go by Zeke more."

"It's beautiful, momma." Eli bit his upper lip. "Thank you."

"Yes, thanks, Momma." Ethan and Zeke said simultaneously.

She reached out and grabbed the boys' hands in her own and pulled them together. Her eyes began to water, and she tilted her head back to keep the tears from overflowing.

"Family is the most important thing we have this side of heaven," she said. "You know it nearly broke me when your daddy died."

The boys nodded. Eli gently laid his hand on his mom's shoulder.

"Thank you, Eli." She patted his hand. "Now, we made it through by the grace of God, and seeing your daddy again in heaven is our greatest hope. Until then . . ." the words stuck in her throat. "Until then, we have memories and reminders, and my favorite reminder is . . ."

"A cardinal!" Zeke blurted out. The loudness caused everyone else at the table to shake and smile nervously. "Sorry." He lowered his voice and repeated in a near whisper, "a cardinal."

Laughter erupted around the table. The anger between brothers was replaced by broad smiles and belly laughs.

"Yes, yes, yes, my dear boy." Ruth tussled Zeke's hair. "When we're not together, when we see that brilliant red bird, we'll know someone we love is thinking of us."

"Even if they've died," Zeke said quietly.

"Yes, *especially* after we've died, the bird will be our personal messenger."   She kissed the top of Zeke's head, and smiled at Ethan and Eli, who were both on the verge of tears and rubbing their noses with the backs of their hands. "Seems I gave these out just in time."

Ethan put his handkerchief to his face and mimicked blowing his nose with a loud honking sound.

"Ew, you're cleaning that out yourself," their mother teased.

CHAPTER FIFTEEN

LEXINGTON, MISSOURI, PRESENT DAY

T he parking lot of the red-brick Beloved Covenant Church was full, so Nate joined the ever-growing line of cars finding spaces on the street. Mourners, dressed in everything from black dresses and suits to blue jeans and button-downs, filed toward the centuries-old building, capped with a tall white spire.

Zeke stepped out onto the sidewalk clutching a small bouquet of tri-colored carnations, white daisies, and pink roses.

"Good thinking stopping by the grocery for flowers, Tito. I'm sure Mrs. Tullis's family will appreciate the gesture."

"Huh? These?" Zeke looked over at the young man and held up the flowers. "These are to put on my momma's grave. She's with my brother and daddy in the cemetery behind the church."

Nate pulled out his cellphone. "We've got about twenty minutes before the service is scheduled to start. Do you want to go now?"

The older man had already started walking toward the massive expanse of grass. He nodded and gestured with the bouquet for Nate to keep up. Behind the church, the duo crossed the alleyway that served as a back entrance to the town's oldest cemetery.

Zeke found his bearings by counting fifteen steps from an ancient oak tree to a headstone shaped like an angel. From there, he turned left and walked twenty paces, passing tombstones of various shapes, sizes, and colors. He stopped in front of an area with three similar headstones.

"Nathaniel, I'd like you to meet my parents, Thomas and Ruth, and my oldest brother, Eli." Zeke stooped and placed the flowers in front of his mother's gravestone. He slowly ran his hand across the top of the smooth granite. "Hi, Momma. You'd never believe why I'm back in town. And I can hear Eli laughing about it."

Nate squatted near Zeke and brushed away some weeds from Eli's headstone.

"He was so young, Uncle."

Zeke bit his lower lip and nodded. "Yeah, just shy of his eighteenth birthday. He was killed on the first of March in 1958, and he would have been eighteen on the twenty-second."

As Nate adjusted the flowers in front of Ruth's headstone, a gasp escaped his lips.

"Oh, my gosh, Tito!" He ran his fingers over the date of death.

Zeke inhaled in little spurts. "Yep, Mother Harris said she died of a broken heart. The military men came in their fancy uniforms and told us Eli was killed in a training accident. Momma started crying and fell onto Ethan's shoulder."

A small tremor shook through Zeke, and he steadied himself on the headstone. "It was hard to make out what the officers were saying over her crying. The chaplain—I remember the bright, shiny crosses on his collar—he handed Momma a box with Eli's things. She sat down on the top step. She was muttering and swearing it was her fault for letting him enlist so young. She caressed the top of that box and pulled it close to her chest."

The older man drew in a jagged breath and looked at Nate. Zeke half smiled and shook his head. "If I could stop time," he continued, "I would have right then and there. Granted, I would really want to go back to before Eli even joined, but since time keeps on moving, it didn't really matter. The chaplain asked Momma if she wanted him to pray with us, and she nodded her head. He went to praying as she slipped the lid off the box. Right there on top was the handkerchief she'd sewn. Momma picked it up and slowly ran her fingers over it. Her whole body seemed to stop moving as her fingers found a reddish-brown stain covering the embroidered 'ETR.' She was frozen like a statue, staring at that stain."

Zeke stared at his empty hand and slowly moved his fingers over an invisible handkerchief. He fell silent. The wind moving through the trees was the only sound.

"Tito, are you okay? Should we go back to the hotel?"

Zeke closed his eyes and shook his head hard. "No. I'm alright. You're the first person I've told this story to in a long time." He squeezed the young man's shoulder. "Some memories are harder to remember, and I can still hear the officer telling my momma that they found his handkerchief tucked into Eli's sock. The realization of what the stain meant broke my momma. She just shut down; wouldn't eat, wouldn't drink, wouldn't talk. She just stared off into nothing. Three weeks later, she passed."

Nate put his arm around the older man and gave a little squeeze. "I'm so sorry. That must have been so hard for you and Ethan."

The church bells started to chime on the hour.

"It was." Zeke wiped his eyes on the back of his hand and patted Nate's shoulder. He stood up and reached out a hand to help the younger man up. "We better get back to the church. We'll need to find seats, and Jayce."

"Sounds good. Did you and Ethan go to live with Mother Harris?"

"Ha, no that would have made things even worse." Zeke chuckled and patted Nate on the back. "No, Mr. Lewis found a local family willing to take us. It wasn't easy, but they fed us and clothed us, so it was bearable. Ethan was eager to get away, so he figured out how to graduate early, and I finished high school then joined the Navy."

"There are a lot of painful memories here for you."

"Now you know why it's been a while since I've been back."

They fell in line with a group of stragglers and entered the church.

~~~

After the memorial service, Nate looked for signs to the Fellowship Hall while Zeke looked for Jayce.

"I bet he's enjoying the potluck," Nate said. "We should check for him in the hall."

"Okay, a man can take a hint." Zeke smiled and shook his head.

True to Nate's intuition, Jayce was in the Fellowship Hall sitting behind a plate overflowing with a cornucopia of homemade goodness. The multipurpose room was filled with the aroma of fried chicken, cornbread, barbecued ribs, and brisket.

Nate's eyes widened as he grabbed a plate for himself and handed one to Zeke. "Yes, Uncle, we eat like kings."

The men worked their way down the row of tables laden with bowls, pans, and plates full of chicken and homemade noodles, green bean casserole, corn casserole, potato casserole, baked beans, deviled eggs, hot rolls, tossed salad, and pasta salad. Next to the rolls was a jar of Hazel Tobler's three-berry preserves with a silver ribbon leaning against it.

Zeke kept one eye on his plate as he loaded up and occasionally glanced up to see if he could catch Jayce's attention. After adding a spoonful of chicken and noodles, he looked up in time to see Jayce looking his way. He waved, and the young treasure hunter gestured at two seats across the table from him.

"It was a nice service," Zeke said as he sat down.

"Yeah, seemed like everyone came out to say their good-byes." Jayce took a bite of greens. "I don't remember how you knew her."

"To Catherine," Zeke raised his glass of sweet tea and those at the table followed suit.

"To Catherine," they echoed.

"To be honest, Jayce, I can't remember much." Zeke bit a chunk from a fried chicken leg. "Oh, man, I even forgot how good Missouri cookin' is." He closed his eyes and chewed slowly. "Nothing makes a man feel more at home than a home-cooked meal."

Jayce shrugged his shoulders and went back to eating.

Nate finished his plate and went back for seconds.

"What?" He took in Zeke's raised eyebrows. "I'm carbo loading for today's trek. Jayce made it seem like quite the trip."

"Totally is," Jayce cut in. "You should eat up, too, Grandpa. And make sure to grab a bottle of water when we leave. It could be pretty warm out there."

Nate gave a thumbs up as he dug back into his meal.

An older man who had been sitting at the front of the church walked toward Zeke, whose eyes darted back and forth as he searched his memory to match the face.

"Zeke? Ezekiel Renick is that really you?" The man stuck out his hand. "It's me, Asher. Asher Tullis."

"Well, I'll be." Zeke's eyes widened as he stood to shake hands. "I thought you looked familiar."

Nate cleared his throat.

"Oh, where are my manners." Zeke pointed at Asher. "Nate, this is Asher. We were in Scouts together. Boy, we got in some trouble."

"*You* got in trouble."

Zeke nodded.

"Wow, it's so amazing to see you here. And I see you've met my great-nephew, Jayce, but I didn't know you and Catherine were close. She was a couple grades behind us in school."

Zeke stood still and his mouth fell open. "Catherine was your wife." His voice went up at the end.

"Yep, fifty-five years."

Shouts of "Hey, Asher," came from a faraway table.

He raised his hand and held up one finger. "I've gotta go, but it's great to see you, Zeke. Thanks again for coming. If you're going to be around for a few days, maybe we could try to catch up. Sorry to hurry off."

"No worries, and my deepest condolences."

They shook hands again, and Asher headed away.

"You okay, Uncle?"

Zeke nodded and slowly sat down.

"Uncle?" Jayce queried.

"It's complicated." Zeke nodded at the treasure hunter. The older man smiled at Nate. "I'm fine. Really. Just a lot of old memories that I thought I'd forgotten seem to be popping up." He went back to eating.

After two trips to the dessert table by Jayce and Nate for slices of apple pie, chocolate cream pie, pecan pie, chocolate layer cake, and a brownie, the trio decided they'd better get started on their expedition.

~~~

After dismissing carpooling because of heading separate directions after the hike, the trio arrived in two cars at the park. Zeke knew where he was within moments. He recognized the small hills that served as markers for the brothers' camping trip. They seemed smaller now that he was grown.

"It was off this direction." Jayce pointed toward the hill on the right and then looked down at his phone. "Good signal today; we should be there in no time."

Much of the smaller brush and trees had been cleared away to make room for a swath of grass the city turned into a dog park. There was a concrete path from the parking lot that ran alongside the dog park and ended about a football field away from the entrance. Concrete gave way to a hard-packed earth trail for people, dogs, and horses, according to the brown sign. There was another brown sign with the word "danger" in yellow capital letters. It warned of plants and animals to avoid while walking.

"You ever see any of the things on this list?" Nate paled as he stared at the sign.

"I've seen a few snakes, found a tick or two in my socks, and had my share of poison ivy." Jayce absently scratched at his forearm.

"Anything bigger?"

Zeke shoved Nate's shoulder. "Hey!"

"Bigger?" Jayce's eyebrows knit together. "Like a deer or bear or something?"

"Or something." Nate touched his nose.

Jayce's eyes widened and he shook his head. "You're acting weird. I'm not sure I feel comfortable taking you hiking."

Zeke stepped forward. "It's okay, kid. My friend is a little 'weird.' He's heard all sorts of stories about creatures, like the Wooly-Bully and other things that go bump in the night."

"Hah, that's awesome." Jayce slapped his thigh and ran his hand through his hair. "That makes sense now. Don't worry mister, I won't let Bigfoot get you . . . I'll keep an eye out for the Easter Bunny, too . . . Oh, man, oh, man."

He continued to giggle as he led them down the trail.

~~~

Cresting the bluff, Zeke was glad he'd grabbed a bottle of water from the reception hall. The swig of now-tepid water refreshed him, and he covered the short distance between himself and the younger hikers.

"There it is." Jayce pointed at a cave opening about a hundred yards off the main trail. They'd have to walk the final distance through low brambles.

The trio stood at the entrance. It was about seven feet high and four feet wide. The sun gave light to the first five feet inside the cave. Jayce used the flashlight on his phone to allow them to go deeper.

Zeke inhaled deeply. There was no tell-tale stench to say the Wooly-Bully was home, if it had ever been his home. The cave walls curved to the left and there was a small area out of view. The flashlight beam fell on dirty, tattered clothes, old tin cans, shredded newspaper and magazines, and other bits of trash.

"I don't see anything of value in here." Jayce moved the light beam back and forth and kicked at items on the floor. "Someone even beat me back here to get those old skates. Bummer. You see anything you want to take back?"

Zeke squeezed his eyes shut and instinctively put up his hand as the flashlight shone in his face. "Nah. I'm not really sure what I was hoping to find."

As they exited the cave, the small lake caught Zeke's attention. On the other side of it is where he'd camped as a kid with his brothers. If this was Bigfoot's cave, the creature could have sat there and watched the boys set up camp and waited for the fire to die down before going out for the night.

"You ready to head back?"

Zeke nodded. "Yep. Sorry the trip was a bust."

"No worries. That's how treasure hunting goes." Jayce took a drink of water.

"Do you mind if we head back along the lake?" Zeke wiped his brow and cooled his throat with a drink as well.

Jayce turned his hands up and lifted his shoulders. "Sure. That trail's a bit steeper, which is why we came up the other way, but hey, if you're game, we'll get back faster."

The trio started down the trail. They had to turn sideways in a few steeper sections to avoid tumbling down the side of the hill. A small section of rocks gave way and sent Nate sliding into Zeke, who put his hands out to brace himself as he tumbled forward. When the dust settled, all three of the men were tangled in the weeds with various cuts and scrapes.

"Oh, Tito, I am so sorry. I slipped." Nate brushed the dust and rocks from his hands and knees and crawled over to check on Zeke.

"It's okay. I'm alright." He brushed himself off and noticed a tear in his pant leg. "I can't say the same for my clothes."

Jayce jumped up and brushed himself off. "I'm not much about luck, but you two have been nothing but bad luck for me today. I say we part company right here. The parking lot is about a five-minute walk down this path."

"Wait, wait." Zeke rolled to his knees to get into a better position to stand up. Nate helped him to his feet. "Wait, Jayce. Let me pay you for your time."

"Sure. Let's say fifty."

"Fifty!" Zeke's jaw dropped. "That seems excessive. I didn't even pay that much for the marble."

"Well, as I see it, it's ten for gas, ten for my time, ten for lost treasure, and twenty for keeping you safe from Bigfoot." A Cheshire grin spread on Jayce's face as he held out his hand.

"*Harrumph.*" Zeke cleared his throat and rolled his eyes. "I don't think I've ever paid to be mocked before, but I guess there's always a first time."

"I'll text you my username and you can transfer the money to my account," said the local treasure hunter turned extortionist.

Nate and Zeke shook their heads as Jayce flashed a toothy smile and headed to the parking lot.

Zeke exhaled loudly before taking a deep breath, holding it, and letting it out slowly. He repeated this three times and looked at Nate, who was agog.

"What?" The older man asked. "You're the one who's always telling me to breathe, take it easy, watch out for my blood pressure."

"Who knew you were listening?" The orderly smiled and gave two thumbs up.

"Shut up." The older man smiled back and patted Nate on the upper arm. "I'd like to meander through those trees down by the lake."

"Is it the lake where you and Eli saw the Bigfoot?"

Zeke nodded and pointed across the water. "We camped right about there. This grove of trees is where we saw it . . . I'm not sure what I was hoping to find after all these years."

"We should come back tonight and recreate the campout for one of our videos." Nate snorted and covered his mouth and nose.

"Yes! Great idea."

"No, Tito. I was just kidding. It was a joke." He ran his fingers through his hair. "I've never camped in my life. I've never wanted to camp in my life."

"It'll be fun." Zeke smiled. "What's the worst that could happen?"

"We get lost or get eaten alive by mosquitos or bears." The young man rubbed his face and shook his head.

"Or, we could see the Wooly-Bully." Nate's eyes crinkled as his smile grew.

CHAPTER SIXTEEN

LEXINGTON, MISSOURI, 1956

Two Cub Scouts pulled tents, poles, stakes, rucksacks, and fishing tackle from the trunk of Mr. Lewis's car and set them on the ground while the rest of the Den picked up the items and transported them along the well-worn path like ants.

The members of Troop 115 worked in pairs to set up the pup tents eighty steps from the shoreline of the lake. Mr. Lewis had marked off the steps and drawn a line in the dirt. He assigned Willie to extend the line parallel to the shore and told the troop to pitch their tents behind the line.

"Seems like an awful long way from the water." Zeke spread out the Army green tent. "When I came with Eli and Ethan, we were way up there." He pointed to the grove of trees about half the distance to the water.

Larry shrugged his shoulders. "If we wanna get our badges, we need to follow Mr. Lewis's instructions."

The best friends arranged the tent poles at the front and rear of the tent and placed the stakes near the corners. They mirrored each other as they put the three metal sections together to create the longer supports. Each one put the pointed end of the pole through the gromets and hoisted the canvas, which draped straight down.

"Okay, Larry, you have longer arms, so you keep ahold of yours and grab this one, too."

Larry's eyebrows arched. "I don't know, Zeke."

"Trust me. This is how Eli showed me."

"Eli's arms are twice as long as mine." Larry stretched out his arms and nearly dropped the tent pole.

"Trust me." Zeke gestured with his free hand for Larry to take the support pole.

Stepping on one side of the tent, Larry stretched his arms as far as they could go. His eyes bugged out when he was able to span the distance. "What do ya know?"

Zeke smirked and held back an "I told you so." He pulled the front guideline taut and staked it into the ground. He quickly ran to the back of the tent and did the same thing. Zeke was staking the front left corner when he noticed the guideline wiggling in the air.

Both boys turned to see Willie standing on the other end of the line laughing.

"What are you laughing at?" they queried in unison.

"It's too close to the water." Willie ran his shoe along the mark he'd made and then pointed to the stake on the wrong side of it. "You need to back up."

"Don't be a drip." Larry struggled to keep his balance and temper. "You know Mr. Lewis meant tents behind the line. Our tent is behind the line."

"We'll see about that." Willie headed toward the Cubmaster's tent, passing several other Cubs with the same perceived violation and leaving them all alone.

"Oh, he drives me crazy."

"Calm down, Larry, we don't want to have to start all over." Zeke easily reattached the guide rope and went back to securing the corners. "I really thought he'd stop being sore by now."

Once the front two corners were secure, Larry let go and the duo anchored the back corners. After inserting the spikes for the sides and the front door flap, the boys stood in front of their tent. Looking down the row, they saw they were the first ones finished.

"I guess you do know what you're talking about." Larry clapped Zeke on the back. "Looks good enough to be on the cover of *Boys' Life*."

They were putting their bedrolls inside the tent when they heard Mr. Lewis outside.

"Great job, boys!"

They crawled out to see their leader accompanied by Willie.

"Thank you, sir." They stood ramrod straight and saluted.

Mr. Lewis returned the salute. "That is some mighty fine work, and so fast. Reminds me of another Cub of mine." He winked at Zeke. "Has Eli been giving lessons?"

Zeke flushed and rubbed his jaw. "Yessir. We borrowed a tent and practiced putting it together and taking it down."

The leader saluted again. "Carry on."

"But, Mr. Lewis," pleaded Willie. "Their guide rope is over the line."

"As long as the tent is behind it, they're okay." He walked away and started talking with other troopers.

"Ha! That'll teach you to be a tattletale." Larry stuck out his tongue, put his thumb on his nose, and wiggled the other four fingers. Zeke followed suit. The pair laughed as Willie stomped off.

"It's going to be a long six days if he keeps that up." Larry ducked back into the tent.

"Yeah, but it will be nice to have another patch."

Larry peeked out. "Sure, but it's still five less than Asher. We could be in Scouts forever and never have as many badges as him."

~~~

After a group lunch of peanut butter and jelly sandwiches and homemade chocolate chip cookies, courtesy of Mrs.

Lewis's Ladies Group, the Cubs were free to explore the area. The largest group went off hiking with Mr. Tullis, whose son Asher wore a badge sash that was the envy of the entire troop. Zeke and Larry decided that sitting and fishing sounded much better than walking and sweating.

"It was sure nice of Mr. Lewis to bring all these new rods and reels." Larry was getting his hook ready with a worm. He glanced over and saw Zeke staring blankly at the rod and reel. "Eli didn't teach you how to fish?"

"Not with something like this." Zeke pushed the reel toward his friend. "I'm good with poles and hooks and stuff ."

"It's easy. Watch." Larry went through the casting motion several times, explaining when to push and release the button.

After a few snags, including hooking his own jeans, Zeke finally got a hook in the water.

The two of them plopped down on the beach and sat cross-legged. Moments passed in silence as they watched their lines and listened to birds and the wind through the trees. The sounds of nature were occasionally interrupted by the cacophony of other campers' shouts and laughter.

"Man, sometimes I wish summer could last forever." Zeke inhaled deeply and breathed out slowly through his nose.

"Yeah, this is the life. I've pretty much learned all the geography and history I need, and my dad hired an accountant to do all the math. I figure I'll do the same," Larry said.

"You want to sit in an office all day like your dad?"

Larry made a raspberry. "No, not what he does now. Before he was the big boss, he got to design buildings. It was neat seeing all the lines he made on the blueprint turn into houses or offices. I'd like to build things. Get dirty and no one tell you to clean up."

"Oh, that makes more sense." Zeke jiggled the fishing pole to see the bobber dance. "Eli said he's thinking of joining the Army, make some money, and learn a trade. He's not much better at math and stuff than me, so maybe I'll join the Navy. Then I can be by the water and fish all day."

The fishing line in front of Larry stretched out and there was a whirring sound from the reel.

"You got one. You got one!" Zeke cheered.

Larry leapt to his feet and started to reel in the catch. "It feels like a big one."

Zeke's eyes bulged as his gaze swung between his friend and the line. The ripples turned to splashes as the fish was pulled up the bank. The friends whooped and hollered as the fish floundered on the beach. Larry bent to pick up his prize by the gills and held it aloft. The tail hit his elbow.

"Wow! That's bigger than any fish me *or* my brothers ever caught." Zeke congratulated his friend.

"Maybe that's why Bigfoot was here."

Zeke gave his friend the side-eye.

"No, wait, a monster fish for a monster dinner."

Zeke bit his lip and shook his head. "I don't know. It doesn't really seem possible. How would he catch them? I think somebody would have seen it sitting on the bank."

"Not at night . . . You saw him at night." Larry's eyes grew wide, and he tapped the top of Zeke's shoulders like a drum. "Oh, I have an idea. Let's set a trap for it. We'll leave the fish on the far shore and see if it comes to get it."

"I guess we get sandwiches for dinner."

~~~

The glow from the bonfire bounced off the row of make-shift structures. After an hour of songs and stories, the Cubs retired to their tents. Mr. Lewis and the other chaperones walked the row, shining their flashlights into each shelter for a head count.

"Fourteen," came a shout from the far end.

"I've got fourteen, too." Mr. Lewis confirmed. "Good night, boys."

From their hiding place, Zeke and Larry giggled as they watched the flashlight beams swoop across the ground as the adults made their way to their own tents.

"I told you it would work." Larry punched Zeke's shoulder.

"Ouch!" Zeke sucked in his lips and covered his mouth. "Ow," he whispered as he rubbed his arm. "Whatcha do that for?"

"You said my plan to stuff our caps with our extra underwear and socks wouldn't fool 'em. Actually, you said it was dumb."

"This whole plan is starting to feel dumb. We're laying in the weeds with a dead fish hoping to trap Bigfoot."

Larry smiled and pushed himself up. "So let's get going."

They crawled along the bank and crouched in a group of bushes to get their bearings. Zeke pointed to the stand of trees where he'd seen the creature with his brothers. Larry took the lead as they made their way single file to the small grove.

Larry dropped the fish in the grass and pulled a folding knife from his back pocket. "Zeke, you got the flashlight?"

A small ray of light circled the fish.

"Perfect." Larry cut the fish open and pulled out the innards. "This should catch us a creature." He put the splayed bass near a well-worn animal trail. "Now we'll wait back there in those bushes."

As the duo turned, they were caught in the beam of a flashlight. They put their arms up to shield their eyes.

"What are you two up to? I'm telling Mr. Lewis."

Willie's voice was unmistakable. They couldn't see him behind the glaring light, but they knew it was him.

"Shhh! Put that thing down, Willie!" Larry moved toward the light and pushed the flashlight down. "If you tell, you'll miss all the fun."

"Fun? What are you up to?"

"Let's move back to these bushes, and we'll tell you." Zeke grabbed Willie by the elbow and led him to the proposed hideout.

"You have to swear not to tell." Larry took the flashlight and held it under his chin causing a ghostly glow across his face.

"I swear," Willie said half-heartedly.

"On your Cub Scout badges." Larry held up two fingers.

"And keep your other hand in front, too!" Zeke quickly added. "No take-backs."

"Fine." Willie breathed out hard and put up two fingers. "I swear."

A commotion in the small grove caught the boys' attention and their flashlight beams. A large black form was plodding through the trees near the bait. The trio held its breath and froze. The massive black outline suddenly rose from four feet to two. The black bear bared its teeth in the glare of the flashlight.

Screams filled the night as the boys turned and ran for the camp.

"I told you this was a bad idea," Zeke said, breathing heavily as he glanced over his shoulder.

"Shut up and run." Larry grabbed his friend to try to speed him up.

They stumbled near the glowing remains of the fire and looked up to see Mr. Lewis and the other adults. They looked to their left and saw the rest of the Den members peeking their heads out of their tents.

The low roar of the bear caught everyone's attention. Mr. Lewis raised his revolver and fired high toward the trees in the direction of the bear. The report of the gun echoed across the small lake. The bear turned away and raced off into the darkness.

"What on earth were you boys thinking going off in the dark?" The Cubmaster helped them off the ground.

"We were hunt . . ."

Zeke elbowed his best friend in the ribs. Larry rubbed his side and continued. "We were hunting . . . frogs."

There was a sigh of relief from his friend.

"You know how they freeze when you shine a light on them? We were trying to make up for not catching any fish."

"They why did I find you in the trees?" Willie piped up.

"Frogs can hop from the lake to the trees." Zeke's eyes darted back and forth between the grown-ups. "We were looking everywhere."

"We'll discuss this further in the morning. Now, all of you get back in your tents." Mr. Lewis showed the flashlight down the row of tents with boys hanging outside trying to listen. "All means *all*."

Zeke and Larry crawled into their tent. They stared wide-eyed at the roof.

"You think you'll be able to sleep?" Larry inquired.

"Nope."

"Me neither."

The sound of snores from other tents let them know the other boys had no trouble getting back to sleep.

"Larry?"

"Yeah."

"Do you think this means Eli was right? That it was a bear and cubs we saw?" Zeke's voice was soft.

"I don't know, but I do know he's going to hear about *this* bear and *think* he was right."

"That's what I was thinking."

"But you know what?"

"What?"

"Now, we know Willie not only screams like a girl. He runs like one too."

Laughter erupted from their tent.

"Ezekiel! Lawrence! Go to sleep!"

"Yes Mr. Lewis." They stifled their laughs in their pillows.

~~~

Tooo-too-tooot, brrrrup, too-tooo-tooot

The breathy and sour notes of the troop's bugler's attempt at *Reveille* rattled the Cubs awake.

Zeke pulled the thin pillow over his head and squeezed his elbows tight against his ears. "It's no use. I can still hear it."

"People in Jeff City hear it." Larry stuck his index fingers in his ears. "He's horrible."

The duo crawled out of their tent as the final notes drifted over the hills. They followed the throng of campers to the morning meeting around the ash-covered fire pit. The Den members jostled elbows to be near the front—not to hear their leader, but to be closer to the breakfast layout.

Mr. Lewis raised his arms, and the chatter quieted to a murmur. The lone voice in the back was silenced as the troop leader cleared his throat. After a quick prayer, he dismissed the Cubs to eat.

"Mr. Renick and Mr. Everett, not so fast." Mr. Lewis gently held them by their shoulders. "We need to talk."

Zeke and Larry exchanged glances. They were used to Mr. Lewis calling them Ezekiel and Lawrence when they were in trouble. "Mister" was new and unnerving.

"Gentlemen, this morning I discussed your actions with the other chaperones."

The boys looked up. Mr. Lewis was rubbing his temples and letting out long breaths through skewed lips. The boys stole a glimpse at each other. Their slack-jawed expressions mirrored each other.

"It pains me, boys, it really does . . ."

"Hey, Samuel, I've got the car ready." The boys turned to see Danny Martin's dad waving toward them.

Mr. Lewis held up a full palm and then just his index finger. The boys were still staring at Mr. Martin.

"Lawrence. Ezekiel." They shook their heads and looked at their leader. "Boys, this was not an easy decision. But after your actions last night, we feel you can no longer participate in the campout."

"What? But . . ." Larry's voice rose several octaves. He looked at Zeke, whose eyes were downcast and filling with tears. Larry cleared his throat. "Is Willie being kicked out, too?"

"No."

"That's not fair! Tell him that's not fair, Zeke."

Zeke took a breath that shook his body. He blinked back tears and emptied his lungs slowly. "But it is fair, kinda."

"Kinda? Are you kidding me? Zeke back me up on this." Larry's eyes bulged and his neck grew red.

"We came up with the plan. We kinda tricked him into coming with us." He looked up at Mr. Lewis. "I'm sorry."

The Cubmaster nodded and patted Zeke on the head. Larry's eyes were zeroed in on Zeke.

"But Larry is also kinda right. Willie was also out of his tent."

Larry relaxed his shoulders and crossed his arms.

"Yes, Willie was up because he was going to the bathroom. He said he was headed back to his tent when he saw you. His intention was not to break any rule."

"His *intention* was to get us in trouble," Larry barked.

"Gentlemen, regardless of Willie's actions, you set out to deceive. Your trap could have resulted in serious physical harm, and then you lied about what you were doing." He waved Mr. Martin over to them. "Mr. Martin will take you both home and explain to your parents what happened."

"I'm dead." Larry rubbed his face with both hands.

"Are we still in the troop?" Zeke stared straight ahead and spoke in a near-whisper.

"Yes. Yes, you're both still part of one-one-five." The Troop Leader reached out and mussed their hair. "But there is one more thing: Since you won't be here for the entire campout, you won't be able to earn your camping badge this year."

Zeke didn't even try to hold back the tears this time.

CHAPTER SEVENTEEN

LEXINGTON, MISSOURI, PRESENT DAY

"I would like the record to show I think this is a bad idea." Nate pulled camping equipment from the trunk of the car and loaded it into a large foldable wagon.

"It was *your* idea." Zeke clapped his fellow traveler on the back.

"I was joking. I didn't think you'd really want to spend the night out here when we have a perfectly good hotel room."

"Where's your sense of adventure?" Zeke started for the camping area. "And what about all the patrons?"

Nate nodded. "True. True. We've got to keep the viewers happy." He shut the trunk with a thud and followed Zeke.

Several upgrades had been made to the area since the last time Zeke camped there. He hadn't had time to check out the camping area the previous day with Jayce, so he was pleasantly surprised to see the addition of firepits and toilet facilities. The key to a successful camping experience was to find a site close enough to the bathroom for nighttime visits but far enough away to avoid any unpleasant smells.

Zeke walked down to the edge of the lake and paced off eighteen steps. He looked toward the outhouses, took a deep breath, smelled nothing but clean air, and declared, "This is the perfect spot."

Nate rolled the wagon next to him and started unloading.

"I still can't believe you woke me up so early to drive to the recreation outfitters in the city." The young man yawned and let out a long sigh.

"Oh, come on, Nate, it will be a great adventure. Besides, it's Sunday, and the front desk clerk said the outdoor store in town is closed. It's kinda nice hearing some stores still close on Sundays." Zeke shut his eyes and drew in a deep breath. He rubbed his stomach as he held his breath for several seconds and then slowly let it out. Tilting his head back, he opened his eyes wide. Zeke's face was barely big enough to hold his grin. "I haven't felt this alive in a long time."

"Okay, then it was worth it." Nate pulled a rectangular bag from the wagon and plopped it in the middle of a wide flat space.

"What's that?"

"It's the tent. I got us a four-man self-constructing one. I think the guys said it had hydraulics. If we're camping, we're doing it in style." He pulled the tent from the bag and started to unfold it.

"That's huge! Last time I was here, it took Larry and me forever to put up a little pup tent."

Nate's dimples highlighted his smile. He grabbed the center of the tent area that resembled an umbrella top. With a quick wink, Nate pulled up on it, and the tent took shape. "You might want to pick up your jaw, Tito. Wouldn't want you to catch any flies." He laughed and started taking more pieces from the wagon.

"Well, I'll be. A tent that makes itself."

"Right! I told you. Only the best for us." He handed Zeke bedrolls and pillows. "Once I put the cots up, you can roll out the sleeping bags."

Zeke put the bedrolls with the opening facing the back of the tent. A beach-ball-sized fluff of blond fur flew by his head and landed on the sleeping bag. "What the heck was that?"

Nate laughed and stepped inside. "Wow, you can jump. It's going to be part of a giveaway to a patron. Isn't it cute?"

The young man picked up the stuffed Bigfoot doll with oversized feet, a well-defined six-pack, and super soft fur. Nate snuggled his face into its tummy. "It's the cutest."

Zeke grabbed its foot. "It's not even the same color."

"If we're going to nitpick, it's about six feet too short." Nate held the toy aloft.

"Other than those two things . . ." Zeke let a smile curl on the edges of his lips.

After the tent was fully furnished, Nate set up the cooler and grill. "I also picked up a can of Spam in case we don't catch any fish."

"I haven't had fried Spam in ages." Zeke stepped out of the tent and came to sit by the fire pit. "I may not even try fishin'."

Now it was Nate's turn for his jaw to drop. Zeke reached over and gave him a tap under his chin. "May want to close this." The older man chuckled. "Son, I've had Spam for breakfast, lunch, and dinner more times than I can count thanks to being poor and in the military."

The younger man continued to shake his head as a goofy grin spread on his face. "Well, Uncle, one day, I'll fix it for you the island way—musubi—with rice and seaweed wraps . . ."

"Whoa!" Zeke held up his hand. "There is a better chance of us seeing the Wooly-Bully again before I eat anything with the word 'weed' in it."

"Sounds like a good bet to me."

The duo sat in the folding chairs with their feet propped up on the firepit. Nate folded his arms behind his head and gazed out over the lake and up toward the rolling hills they'd walked the day before.

"Does it feel weird getting ready to camp here again?" The younger man glanced at Zeke.

"A bit. Things always seem different when you're older. Memory is a tricky thing."

"How so?" Nate leaned forward in the chair.

"Well, most of my memories of this place are from child-hood, so back then every hill looked like a mountain, the lake like an ocean," he sighed. "And now I see it through grown-up eyes, and it seems ordinary. But, boy, when I was a kid, it was everything."

"You and Larry were a great team. What happened with him? And what about that horrible kid?"

"Willie?" Zeke chuckled.

"Yeah, him."

A smile eased on Zeke's face as he closed his eyes to picture his friends.

"Like most boys, we forgot why we were annoyed with each other and considered ourselves friends." The older man slapped his thigh. "I even got an invite to Willie's first wedding. I couldn't go because I was still in the service, but Larry was his best man." Zeke's eyes softened and his voice trailed off. "I was supposed to be Larry's best man, and I put in for a weekend pass. Originally, it was a go, but then my superior officer told me they needed me to stay and help with some top-secret project, so I couldn't go."

"What was the project?"

"Top secret." Zeke raised his eyebrows.

"Even now?" Nate turned his palms up. "Come on, it's been a long time."

"It's easier just not to say than to try to remember if it's okay to say." The older man leaned back and rolled his head, winching with each popping sound. "I haven't told Larry, and I guess if anyone deserves to know it's him. Stupid project put a knot in our friendship."

"Sorry, Uncle."

"It's not your fault." Zeke tapped the younger man on the knee. "Besides, we worked out the best we could. He kinda forgave me, and I kinda kept in touch. Strange how people you think will always be a part of your life slip out of the edges."

Zeke's gaze drifted off as he rested his chin on his hand. He looked like an elderly version of The Thinker if Rodin had set his model in a folding chair.

Nate shifted in his chair and cleared his throat. "You know something, it sure looks different from here to me."

"I'm sorry. What looks different?" Zeke sat up and pushed his feet on the fire ring so the front legs of the chair were off the ground.

"They just look like little rolling hills like you were saying. But when we were walking up and down them earlier, they seemed steeper, like little mountains."

"Yep. Apparently, there are loads of things out here to fool your eyes." Zeke swept his eyes across the expanse of the valley. He picked his feet up, and the front of the chair plopped back down to earth. "Sitting here, it feels both like yesterday and a thousand years ago since I was here."

"Well, Tito, technically, it *was* yesterday."

"Oh, shut up." He made a half-hearted swing at his young companion. Nate feigned being hit and toppled out of the chair.

"You're ridiculous." Zeke shook his head.

Nate stood and brushed himself off. "Fine, I'll be quiet, and you can do some talking for our next video."

The noonday sun eliminated most shadows, but made it tricky to find the right angle for the bucket hat that Zeke insisted on wearing. He *tsked* and *chuffed* as Nate tilted the hat back to remove the shadow from his face. Zeke complained about the sun in his eyes and threatened to sue Nate for increasing his skin cancer risk.

"If the hat has to stay down, let's moved closer to the lake where the reflection off the water will lighten your face."

Zeke let out a slow sigh as the duo walked to the shoreline.

"Perfection." Nate mocked a chef's kiss. "Okay, Tito, for this video let's remind the viewers of your previous encounters at this spot."

Zeke made a sloppy smile and flashed two thumbs up. Nate started filming at the campsite and panned down to Zeke. When the older man was in frame, he pointed at him.

"Welcome back. And thank you all. So very much. For your support." Zeke spoke in a staccato manner. Nate didn't call cut. He flashed a dimpled grin, gave an okay sign, and then pointed to his own smile.

A grin slowly spread on Zeke's face as he mirrored the expression of his cameraman.

"It's been a few moons since I've been back to this camping spot. This is where my brothers brought me to help me prepare for my camping badge. This is also where I encountered Bigfoot for the second time. It was in the middle of the night when Eli and I saw the figure in that grove of trees right over there." As he pointed toward the group of trees, Nate slowly moved his arms that direction.

"Later, Eli would say that it was just a bunch of bear cubs climbing up and down the trees. I was so angry . . . and hurt, when he told that story." Zeke looked down at the ground and took several deep breaths. He shook his head and straightened his shoulders. "But I felt like I owed him an apology when I came back out weeks later for the Cub Scout trip and encountered an honest-to-goodness angry bear. I even started to doubt if I'd really seen a Wooly-Bully back on the bridge.

"Yesterday, we came out here with a local treasure hunter named Jayce. He normally finds old bits and bullets from the Civil War battles around here, but he'd also found this." Zeke put his hand in his pocket and pulled out the blue thumper. Holding it between his thumb and index finger, he thrust his arm forward toward the camera. Nate quickly stepped back and focused on the blue orb. He framed the shot, so it eclipsed Zeke's eye.

"That's right. He found my favorite aggie that I'd thrown at the Wooly-Bully all those nights ago." He lowered his hand and kept turning the marble in his fingers. "You're probably asking, 'Zeke, how do you know that's *your* thumper? All marbles look alike.' Well, they may look alike, but they don't feel alike. When I saw it in the case in town and then held it, I knew. Like you know a favorite baseball mitt, or how you fit in your favorite recliner seat just so, you just know.

"Jayce took us to the spot where he'd found it." Zeke turned to look toward the rounded hills. "You can make out the trail we took up that hill—some may say a small mountain." He winked, and Nate's chuckle caused the phone to bobble and the picture to bounce. "He'd found the marble in a cave with some other odd trinkets, and we went to check it out."

Nate zoomed in toward the path and panned the shot up the trail.

"When we got there, we sadly couldn't find any other marbles or treasures or honestly, any sign of Bigfoot. The cave looked lived in, but it didn't stink . . ." His voice trailed off as he noticed Nate's eyes widen and veins pop out on his neck. The young man was beginning to hyperventilate.

"Nate? Nate!" Zeke blanched and hurried to Nate.

The young man took a deep breath to calm himself and then put his index finger to his mouth. "Shh, Tito, be very quiet. I see it."

Zeke jerked around to face the hill and quickly scanned up the trail line. He froze and held his breath as the all-too-familiar outline took shape between the trees. "Got you now, you son of a gun," he whispered.

The figure started moving quickly deeper into the woods in the direction of the cave. A blur brushed by Zeke heading toward the trail.

"What are you doing?" he yelled after the orderly-turned-chauffeur-turned-Bigfoot hunter.

"Making history," Nate yelled, without turning back. He lifted his phone high into the air. "We're going to go viral!"

"Kids these days." Zeke shook his head and started off after him.

"Hurry, Uncle, hurry!"

Zeke jogged as fast as his septuagenarian legs could carry him up the trail. Perspiration marks grew on his faded blue polo shirt. He pulled several times on the front of it to get some air moving inside to cool him off.

"Uncle!"

"I'm coming. Hold your horses!" Zeke yelled in the direction of Nate's voice. He hadn't been able to see the young man since Nate crested the hill in hot pursuit of Bigfoot. "Why is it this beast wears me out every time we meet?"

Zeke rested his hands on his knees and stretched his head back, causing popping noises along his spine. "Oh, that feels much better."

With a renewed vigor, Zeke started up the hill again. As he reached the crest, he saw Nate slumped against a tree. "Nate! Nathaniel! Nate, are you okay?" He raced over to the young man, who was drenched in sweat.

"Took you long enough."

"Sorry, I'm old, and you were moving like a bat outta hell."

"Forgiven." Nate gestured for Zeke to sit on a nearby boulder in the shade. "Take a load off those well-worn knees."

Zeke doffed his bucket hat and took a seat. "So, Speedy, tell me what you saw."

"I'll do better. I'll show you."

The two sat side by side and watched the video footage. The early video by the lake was steady as it zoomed up the trail. Movement stopped and a sudden inhale by Nate could be heard on the playback. It wasn't hard to see what caused him to gasp as the outline emerged. Suddenly, the video became a swirl of sky and forest and grass and lake as Nate took off running.

He fast-forwarded the video to when he reached the top of the hill. The picture slowly steadied as Nate's breathing returned to normal. He scanned the trees slowly looking for any movement. *Snap!* The camera swung to the left, and a large shadowy creature disappeared behind a clump of trees. "Hurry, Uncle, hurry!" Nate's plea replayed softly on the video.

"I was moving as fast as I could." Zeke sat back.

"I know. I know. I was just so excited." Nate tapped the screen to pause the video. "I didn't see anything after that. I was waiting for you so we could check out where I lost him together."

"Let's go." Zeke tapped him on the shoulder. Nate jumped up and reached out a hand to help Zeke up off the boulder.

They walked slowly and took deliberate steps to avoid ruining any tracks. Most of the area was hard-packed ground, and they had a hard time finding any sort of evidence that even they'd been there. As they neared the trees where the creature was last seen, Zeke noticed a clump of hair on a branch above his head.

"Look at that! If that's from its shoulder, it's gotta be close to seven, seven-and-a-half feet tall." The older man reached high up the tree.

"And look here." Nate pointed at a patch of broken soil near the base of a tree. "It looks like a partial footprint. See these? They look like toes, and this smudge like the beginning of a sole, maybe."

Zeke crouched down to get a better look. He tilted his head, and a flashback of sitting on his haunches on the side of the road near his house flooded his thoughts. His body wriggled, and a whistle slowly escaped his lips.

"We need to film this, too." Zeke jumped up and ran his fingers through his hair. "Tell me when you're ready."

Nate took a few steps back. He mouthed "three, two, one," and pointed at Zeke.

"Yahoo! Boy howdy, was that something." Zeke's eyes shone like a kid seeing presents under the tree Christmas morning. "Did you see what we saw? We couldn't believe our eyes either, which is why we ran . . ."

Nate cleared his throat.

"Why one of us ran and the other jogged quickly up the trail to see if we could catch a better glimpse of the creature. Nate caught it again on camera before it disappeared through this section of trees. But look what it left behind." He pointed, and Nate tilted the phone and zoomed in to the clump of dark hair on the branch. "And down here, too." The phone was tilted down to reveal the partial footprint.

"These markings are similar to the ones I saw as a kid. Now, I'm not saying this is the same Bigfoot." Zeke turned back toward the camera. "It could be the same one. I don't know. But I know I've got the same chills. It's definitely going to make for an uneasy night of camping."

"Wait, we're still camping?" Nate touched the stop icon. "I thought maybe we'd go back to the hotel now and edit some video."

"Don't be silly. We spent money on the equipment, and you made a great camp. Plus, we've got a can of Spam to fry up." Zeke smiled so wide his eyes crinkled. He slapped Nate on his shoulder. "Besides, I know you can work magic on that phone of yours no matter where you are."

The glow from the fire lit up Zeke's face. His eyes were closed, and a slight smile turned up the corners of his lips as he wandered back through time in his mind's eye. He could hear his brothers bickering and the rustling of leaves in the wind.

"I'm a genius," Nate said.

Zeke shook out of his memory and rubbed his face. "You don't say."

"I do say, Uncle. We may be the next Patterson and Gimlin."

"Who's the gremlin?" Zeke scratched his head.

"No, no, Patterson and *Gimlin*. I searched online for other Bigfoot videos, and theirs is the most famous. They took it in Northern California in the sixties."

"Oh, I think I remember that." Zeke leaned forward in the seat.

"The sixties?" Nate winked.

"Don't disrespect your elders," he said with a laugh. "Don't just stand there gloating. Sit down and show me how Renick and . . . um . . . This is embarrassing. I don't know your last name."

Nate pulled the chair next to Zeke. "It's okay. After I post this video, everyone will remember Renick and Villanueva."

"Nathaniel Villanueva. That's got a nice ring to it."

Nate started to laugh. "Technically, it's Nathaniel Francisco Abayon Villanueva."

"That is quite a mouthful. And speaking of mouthfuls," he grabbed a blue tin with large yellow letters out of a bag. "Let's eat!"

Nate took the can of Spam. "It's no church potluck, but it's still tasty."

The sizzling of the processed pork joined the nightly songs of insects and frogs. Zeke looked up into the night sky and tried to find constellations he'd learned from Eli. The only ones he could remember were the Big and Little Dipper and Orion's Belt. There were thousands of twinkling lights above, but he couldn't seem to find any familiar ones.

"What are we looking for, Uncle?"

Zeke turned to see Nate staring straight up into the night sky.

"I was trying to see if I could find the Big and Little Dipper. Eli was really good at finding all the constellations."

"Oh, I got you. First we find the bowl of the big one. There it is." Nate pointed toward the vast expanse of space. "And then we follow it to find the North Star. Right there, and now we have the Little Dipper. See, Tito?" He pointed and slowly moved the angle to shift from one bowl to the next.

Zeke squinted and rubbed his eyes. "I'm not sure."

"To your left just a bit and up."

"Oh, yes. I see it." Zeke's voice rose several octaves.

Nate smiled at the joy in Zeke's voice. "I can show you . . ."

Zeke held up his hand and barely shook his head. "This one's good for now."

The young man went to work dishing out dinner.

The men enjoyed their meal in the quiet of nature. They'd had enough excitement for one day and relived it each time they watched the video. There was something to be said about enjoying a meal in peace.

After they finished off the last of dinner, Nate gathered up the compostable plates and cutlery and took them to the massive animal-resistant trash receptacles across from the bathrooms.

"Better safe than sorry." He brushed his hands against each other.

"Sure, but now you've got me second-guessing the need to pee in the nighttime."

"Don't worry, I picked up a can of bear spray with the tent."

"Do you plan on coming with me and standing guard?" Zeke tilted his head.

Nate laughed. "No. I trust you can do it."

"Really?"

"Mmmm." Nate rubbed his chin. "Okay, if you need to use the bathroom in the night, wake me up. Of course, we could avoid all this . . ."

"I'm *not* wearing a diaper." Zeke sat up straight. "I'll be eaten by a bear first."

"Okay. Okay." Nate threw up his hands. "Buddy system to the bathroom it is."

"Thank you."

Nate tossed another log on the fire, causing sparks to fly. "Better be softer on my next toss. Don't want to burn down the forest."

"How much wood do we have left?"

"Enough for about an hour more of campfire enjoyment and the morning's cup of coffee."

Zeke's eyes slowly moved left and right. His eyes reflected the flames as they strained to see into the darkness beyond the glow. He tightened his grip on his chair.

"I'm a very light sleeper, Uncle." Nate used his soothing nursing voice. "I promise if I hear anything, I'll get the fire cranking again. Or we can stay up telling ghost stories because we can always get coffee from the café on our way back to town."

"Eli was really good at telling not-scary stories around the fire. I'm not even sure what story I'd tell."

"Why don't you tell me the story about the second Mrs. Renick."

Zeke relaxed his grip on the chair and laughed. "You are like a dog with a bone. I guess out here under the stars is the best place to talk about Claire."

"Yes!" Nate sat cross-legged and rubbed his hands together.

"I felt pretty silly after the annulment, and with Lexington being a small town, everyone knew everything. I mean *every*thing, so getting out on my own seemed like a good idea.

Mother Harris sold me her Chevy Nomad for cheap. Said she was done drivin.' I think the whole town breathed a sigh of relief when they saw me drive away in it."

Zeke paused and stared off in the distance. "That was a great car. It got me all the way to California. I'd spent time near San Diego at the end of my service, so I drove north to San Francisco. A beautiful city full of very interesting people, that's for sure. That's where I met Claire in '72. She told me she'd been a Beatnik but was embracing the Hippie movement. Did they teach you about them in school?"

Nate pursed his lips. "Kinda, it was like an anti-government movement that was pro-love, drugs, tie-dye, and anti-war in Vietnam."

"That fits the Hippies." Zeke leaned forward. "The Beatniks were more about poetry and deep books that hurt your head and living a more natural life. So when I met Claire, she was this amazing angel with flowing golden locks and baby blue eyes, high as a kite, and quoting Kerouac. How could a boy not fall in love?"

Nate raised his palms to the sky and shrugged his shoulders.

"That's right." Zeke pointed at the younger man. "I couldn't. We stayed in San Francisco for several months, bunking with different friends of hers. We drove up the coast, sometimes sleeping under the stars, sometimes in the back of the Nomad. It felt so perfect. She didn't want kids. She didn't want a house. There was no pressure."

The older man gazed up at the night sky. "She would have loved it here."

"Did she die?" Nate asked in his lower orderly voice.

"Huh?" Zeke saw the younger man's big eyes start to water. "Oh, no son, she's fine. When we get back to Florida, I'll introduce you to her."

"Phew." Nate rubbed his face and tossed a log on the fire. "But if she's in Florida . . ."

"I'm getting there, Sherlock." Zeke smiled. "After about a year of traveling, all those Sunday School lessons flooded my head and I was suddenly worried about fire and brimstone, so I asked her to marry me. She said, 'Seems like ruining a good thing, but sure.' I might have taken her response as a clue." He chuckled and slapped his leg. "Eventually, the Nomad was more costly than classic, and the idea of four walls and a soft bed was sounding better and better. I was not ready to go home, and she had people she knew in the Florida panhandle, so we moved there and settled outside of Pensacola."

Zeke leaned forward and warmed his hands by the fire. "Looking back, that was likely the beginning of the end. Who knew the end would start with the beginning of opening a business with Lloyd? We were both handymen. I did everything but electric, and he did it all but plumbing, so we combined our services and had all the bases covered.

"We built a very successful business." The older man leaned back in the chair and sighed heavily. "Claire went from needing nothing fancy to needing the latest of everything. I wanted to make her happy, so I worked extra nights and even took jobs several towns away. On one of the away jobs, I realized when I was about an hour from home that I'd forgotten to toss the extra parts I'd ordered special for the job in the truck. I whipped a U-ey and headed back. When I got home, I saw Lloyd's truck in the driveway and all the curtains closed."

Nate gasped and covered his mouth with both hands. His eyes were wide as saucers.

"Pretty much my reaction." Zeke shook his head. "Part of me wanted to run inside and catch them in the act, and part of me really didn't want to see that. I got my parts from the garage through the side door, put a note under the windshield wiper of his truck, and drove away."

"What did the note say?" Nate leaned forward.

"I'm divorcing her and you." A hint of a smile curled on Zeke's lips. "In the long run, I only ended up divorcing her. Lloyd and I worked out an arrangement. He married Claire a couple of months after the divorce was final."

"Wow, you've obviously forgiven them if he's got power of attorney for you."

"Yeah, but now I'm not sure I can forgive him for making bad investment decisions and losing our retirement funds to a pyramid scheme," Zeke huffed.

"FYI, that's a horrible bedtime story." Nate laughed.

"Well, you asked for it." The older man yawned and stretched his arms. "I'm feeling like I could nod off right here, so I should head to bed." Zeke stepped inside the tent and then did a quick turn. He headed off in the direction of the bathrooms. "Better safe than sorry."

Nate snorted. "I'll get the bear spray."

CHAPTER EIGHTEEN

LEXINGTON, MISSOURI, 1956

"Good morning, Miss Georgia." Zeke waved as he entered the kitchen. "I've got my buddy Larry today. Is Georgie here?"

"Good morning to you both. Nope, he's helping his sisters at the house." She clicked her tongue and put two bowls on the table. "Mr. Lewis told me I'd have two for breakfast, but he didn't say anything about lunch. Did you bring something to eat?"

"No, ma'am." Larry sat across from Zeke. "Mr. Lewis has a job lined up for us at the V-F-dubuh-ya."

Zeke sat up straight and his eyes widened. "And he said if we do a good job, he'll treat us to a Maid-Rite burger."

Both boys rubbed their hands together.

"Well, all I got to give you this morning is some oatmeal, made all right by me." Her smile caused her eyes to close. "It'll give you strength to do the job and stick to your ribs so you won't get hungry."

"Thank you, Miss Georgia."

The boys were spooning the last oats from the bowl when Mr. Lewis came in through the back door. "Perfect timing. Thank you for seeing to the boys' breakfast." He turned to the duo at the table. "Gentlemen, please put your spoons and bowls in the sink, and meet me in the car."

He headed back out as fast as he came in. Larry dropped his dishes in the sink with a loud clang. Zeke saw Miss Georgia's shoulders shudder and he carefully placed the bowl into the sink. "Thank you again, Miss Georgia. Please tell Georgie I said hi."

"I will. Now you go on and get before Mr. Lewis has to honk at you."

Zeke bounded out the back door and down the steps. He sighed when he saw Larry hanging out the front passenger side window of the pale green 1953 Cadillac.

"You can sit up front, too, in the middle if you like." Larry reached over to open the door from the outside.

"Nah, I'll sit in the back so I can have a window, too."

"Suit yourself."

Mr. Lewis harrumphed. "Gentlemen, let's get a move on."

Zeke slid into the massive backseat of The Jolly Green Giant, as the car was dubbed by the troop. Riding in any car was exciting for boys who were used to walking most places, but there was an extra sense of excitement being in Mr. Lewis's shiny Caddy.

"Mr. Lewis, your car always smells so nice." Zeke laid his head back on the seat and put his arm on the door.

"I'll pass your comment on to Mr. Hart, since he cleaned it last."

Zeke marveled over how it felt like forever walking just part way across town to get to the soda shop, but they zipped *all* the way across town in the car in minutes. Didn't even break a sweat. They pulled into the parking lot of the Veterans of Foreign Wars Post 4052. There were a few cars and pickup trucks scattered across the lot.

"Hey, Mr. Carson is here. I'd recognize that old Ford truck anywhere." Larry pointed at the dark red vehicle. "It could use a bath, but you can tell it's his from the whitewall tires."

"Mr. Carson should probably bathe with it." Zeke giggled.

"Boys!" They covered their mouths and stood straight at Mr. Lewis's rebuke. "Johann Carson has been through a lot. He's a decorated veteran, and you shouldn't make fun of him."

"Yes, sir." Zeke lowered his gaze. "I'm sorry."

"That's a good boy." Mr. Lewis patted Zeke on his shoulder. "Come along, Larry."

The boys had been to several community functions at the VFW Hall. They'd eaten, danced, played games, and celebrated various holidays, from serving the veterans during Thanksgiving week to receiving presents during Christmas.

But today would be no holiday.

Mr. Lewis walked them into the kitchen.

"Mrs. Florin, here are your two helpers for the morning." He pushed each boy slightly forward. "They're good, hard workers. I already okayed it with Jolly for them to have lunch with the vets today."

Zeke let out a slight sigh and whispered to Larry. "So much for Maid-Rite."

"Well then, I better get as much work out of them as I can before lunch." Mrs. Florin pushed back her unruly, gray-flecked hair that had slipped out of the bun on top of her head. "I'll get them some aprons and get 'em started."

"Great." The Cubmaster bent down to be at eye level with the young duo. "Okay, gentlemen, listen to Mrs. Florin and do your best. This will count as your community service requirement to make up for your bad behavior at camp."

Zeke and Larry lowered their gaze and turned their heads away. It had been a week since they were expelled from the camping trip for baiting a trap for Bigfoot, catching a bear, and nearly getting Willie killed. Zeke often forgot about that last part, but he reasoned it was probably the biggest reason they were in trouble.

"Look at me, gentlemen." They met Mr. Lewis's gaze. "Good. We live and we learn." He smiled and received smiles back from the young duo. "Excellent. Work hard, enjoy lunch, and I'll be back to pick you up. Later this week, we'll meet with a fish and game agent to talk about bear safety."

They nodded and gave two-finger salutes. Mr. Lewis returned the salute.

"All yours, Edith."

She waved as he left and tossed tan aprons with various stains on them to the boys.

"You can start by washing, rinsing, and drying that stack of dishes. After that, unfold a few more tables and set chairs around them for lunch."

The boys stood at attention and gave a hand-to-the-forehead salute. "Ma'am. Yes, ma'am." She shook her head and laughed.

~~~

Zeke, Larry, and their aprons were soaked through by the time all the plates, glasses, and utensils were washed, rinsed, dried, and put away.

"Look at my fingers." Larry shoved all ten digits in Zeke's face. "They're all pruney."

"Yeah, we shouldn't have to wash our hands for days after this."

"For weeks." Larry's voice rose an octave.

"I'm pretty sure my momma would catch on after a few days."

"Yeah, you're right." Larry turned his hands back and forth. "I don't think they'll be this clean again."

Zeke tugged on his friend's shoulder. "Well, they'll get a little dirty putting the tables and chairs out."

A group of four veterans sat playing cards at one of the tables already set for lunch. The boys recognized Mr. Carson right away. His white hair was in stark contrast to the dark green garrison cap emblazoned with VFW 4052 in gold. The fancy red and gold cross on the side always impressed Zeke. The duo had seen the other men around town but couldn't remember any names.

"How many tables did she say?" Larry tapped on the stack of flattened tables.

"I don't think she did. Maybe three." Zeke shrugged.

"Sounds good." Larry pointed. "You get that end, and we'll take it up there next to Mr. Carson."

The tables were heavier than they expected, but the boys grunted their way across the floor and set them up. They found the stacks of chairs and put four around each table to match the first.

Zeke plopped hard into the last chair he placed. "Boy, that was hard work. I worked up an appetite."

"Me too." Larry leaned back in the chair.

"You boys look beat." The dark-haired man lifted a glass. "Edith makes a mean sweet tea to refresh a weary soul."

They exchanged wide-eyed glances and jumped up with newfound energy.

"Since you're going that way, I'd like a refill." The red-headed man took off his cap and ran his hand from his forehead to the nape of his neck.

"Me too," Mr. Carson and the man with a burn scar across his cheek and ear said at the same time.

The boys returned carrying all the drinks on a tray.

"Pull up a chair if you'd like." Mr. Carson scooted his chair over to make room. The red-headed man did as well.

Zeke and Larry exchanged nods and joined the grown-up table.

"You boys play poker?" The man with the scar asked.

"No, sir. My mom doesn't like me gambling. Says it's a sin." Zeke took a drink of the sweet tea and smiled.

"Ha, that's funny, because the way Jonesy plays cards is a sin." The red-headed man laughed at his own joke.

"You're no better, Red. You're just on a lucky streak." Mr. Carson shuffled the deck. "Are you in this round, Billy Boy?" He nodded at the dark-haired man.

"I'm in."

All the men tossed a blue chip into the middle of the table. Red had the most chips in front of him, followed by Mr. Carson, Billy Boy, and Jonesy. Despite his mother's wish that he not know how to play poker, Zeke had learned the basics from Ethan—who, according to several of the boys who lived in town, was a card shark.

Even with the slight primer from his middle brother, Zeke found it difficult to follow the game and the conversation.

"Whatcha thinking, Red?" Mr. Carson tapped his finger on the table.

"I raise." Red tossed two white chips into the middle.

"Oh boy, big spender." Jonesy tossed in three white chips. "I'll see ya and raise myself."

"Your pile is going quick, Jonesy, you may want to slow your roll." Mr. Carson added three chips.

Billy Boy tossed in three.

"I call." Red tossed in another chip. "You still planning to go to the Lake next week, Johann?"

"Yep, the missus was a bit nervous, but we've always enjoyed our time in the Ozarks."

"Why was she nervous?" Red put his cards on the table. "Three of a kind, gents."

"Aargh! I hate this game." Jonesy threw his cards down on the table.

"Beats my pair of queens." Johann tossed his cards face up in the middle. "She heard from her cousin that lives there about some creature. They're calling it the Ozark Howler."

The grown men chuckled while the youngest set at the table exchanged worried looks.

Red reached both arms on the table and pulled all the chips his direction. "Wonder if the Howler is just the Wooly-Bully taking a vacation to the Lake himself."

"From how she described it, it sounds terrifying." Johann gathered the cards and passed them to Red. "Your deal."

"Terrifying?" Jonesy leaned forward.

"Apparently it's like a massive shaggy bear with a high-pitched bugle that can sound like a woman screaming."

Zeke's jaw dropped, and he held his breath.

"Ha, probably some guy's wife screaming at him to get out of the hunting blind and get home." Billy Boy chuckled and collected the cards dealt to him.

"I don't know," Johann anted up. "There's some strange things out there in the woods."

"Wait, I heard of that Howler last month but forgot what it was called until you sparked a memory." Red bit his chip. "But they said it was like a leopard, and one guys said it had a horn. Sounds more like boys down there been drinking a bit too much of their own hooch."

Zeke inhaled sharply and then covered his mouth. He stole a glance at Larry.

"You okay there, boy?" Johann patted him on the back.

"Yes, sir." Zeke's eyes were glassy from choking on air. "So you don't think there's anything to the Howler or the Wooly-Bully?"

"Whoa, Bigfoot is real, and my uncle has seen him." Jonesy put his hand on the table and focused on Zeke. "Who knows what those folk down south are seeing and hearing?"

"I believe in Bigfoot, too." A slight smile spread on Zeke's face. "And I've—"

"Jonesy, was that the same uncle who talks to *wee little people* in the garden?" Billy Boy slipped into an Irish accent. "Didn't he end up in the asylum?"

There was a jagged white area on Jonesy's face as he flushed at the verbal assault on his family. He tugged his cap off and pointed at Billy Boy. "You know better than to say something like that about a man who fought in the Great War. Take it back."

Billy Boy held up both hands. "Sorry. Sorry. I take it back. It was all in fun."

Zeke shrunk back in the chair. He glanced at Larry, who ran pinched fingers across his lips like a zipper. Zeke nodded and pinched his lips shut.

Jonesy blew out a strong puff of air and replaced his cap. "Sorry, guys, I'm just a little protective of him. Poor guy saw way too much over there."

The veterans lowered their eyes to the chips in the middle of the table and nodded.

"No need to apologize." Johann patted Jonesy on the shoulder. "A man's gotta stick up for blood."

"Even blood who sees things that don't exist . . ."

Jonesy bored a hole through Billy Boy with his stare.

"Oh, come on, fellas, am I the only one here that refuses to believe in the Wooly-Bully?"

Three sets of eyes looked at Billy Boy with conviction, while the youngest sets of eyes bounced around the table to see if they were friends or foes.

"Zeke, Larry, come help me get the trays ready for lunch," Edith called from the kitchen, startling the boys.

"Well, get to gettin'. The rest of the bunch will be arriving any moment now." Billy Boy shooed the boys away like puppies with his hand.

As they headed into the kitchen, the doors opened and men—all wearing their VFW hats—poured through the opening. The echo of hellos and how-do-you-dos around the hall made the boys cover their ears.

"Did you hear that?" Zeke leaned over to his friend once they were in the kitchen.

"Yeah, how creepy does that Howler sound?"

"Not that! Those vets believe in the Wooly-Bully, too." Zeke's eyes shone.

"Sure, he seems harmless enough." Larry shuddered. "But my family is headed to the Ozarks next week, and I don't want to run into any Howler."

"Next week? You'll miss the Cub Scout ceremony," Zeke whined. "I'll be the only one not getting a badge."

CHAPTER NINETEEN

LEXINGTON, MISSOURI, PRESENT DAY

T he shrill call of morning birds caused Zeke to stir. His back cracked as he arched and rolled his shoulders. He started to panic when he couldn't move his arms and then remembered he was zipped up in a sleeping bag.

"Camping is a young man's adventure." He wiggled until his arm was able to bend just the right way for his hand to reach the zipper. Zeke flipped back the bag, and the coolness of the morning sent a shiver throughout his body. "Oh, no way." He reached over the cot in an attempt to pull the warmth of the sleeping bag back over him.

Nate stuck his head through the tent flap.

"Good morning, Tito. Are you ready to head back to the hotel for breakfast?"

Zeke tried to wrap himself back in the bag. "Five more minutes."

"I'll give you three."

"I move faster with coffee."

"Sorry, I ended up using all the wood to keep the fire going last night. We can get coffee and breakfast at the hotel."

Zeke tossed the sleeping bag aside and sat up.

"Whatever it is they provide at that place, it is *not* breakfast *or* coffee. Let's stop at the diner in town, and we can check in at the courthouse as well."

"Sounds like a plan. Plus, after posting the video, we've had a massive spike in patrons and funds."

"I may get the super-sized scramble with fresh-squeezed OJ then."

It took longer than expected to get packed up and back on the road. The self-expanding tent was not self-folding, and it took several attempts to figure out how to get it to fit back into its bag. While Nate wrestled everything into the car, Zeke hauled water from the lake to make sure the campfire was properly drowned.

"Whew, I worked up another level of appetite. How about you, Tito?"

"Agreed. I may skip the senior-size menu and go for the young'uns' portions."

~~~

The drive back to town was clogged with traffic. It cleared up slightly after the four-way stop near the top of the hill.

"Monday morning traffic." Zeke rolled down the window. "Who knew so many people here commuted to work? Times have changed."

The downtown area was jam-packed with cars. Nate was glad to see not everyone knew about the little parking lot near the courthouse.

Zeke slapped the dashboard. "I know what it is!"

"What what is?"

"Why there's so much traffic. The answer is right in front of us." Zeke gestured toward the courthouse. "They're here for the trial."

Nate nodded. "Could be. But you know why I'm here?"

"Food," they said in unison.

There were several men in camouflage sitting on the benches in front of the diner. The main street parking area resembled a monster truck sales lot.

Zeke and Nate slipped by the men and entered the eatery. The aromas of coffee, bacon, ham, and biscuits wafted through the air. Both men closed their eyes and took a deep breath. The place was nearly full, and between the chatter, tables being cleared, and the cooks hitting the ready bell, it was noisy.

"Oh, it's you two."

The waitress's voice knocked the duo out of their trance.

"Us two?" Nate hadn't seen the woman before, but her name tag claimed she was Clara.

"From the video. That's all anyone's been talking about in here." She let out a long sigh. "There was a line of people waiting when I got here to start my shift at seven. Seems like every crazy Bigfoot believer saw it, and they're here to find it first."

"Oh my gosh, do you know what this means Tito? We're famous." Nate grabbed Zeke by his shoulders and gave a little shake. "This is amazing."

Zeke's eyebrows arched, and he gently grabbed Nate's wrists and slowly pushed them away. He turned to the non-smiling waitress.

"Ma'am, my young friend and I are sorry for any trouble we've caused you. Is there any chance we could get a table and make it up to you with a nice tip?"

Her eyes lit up, and her shoulders relaxed.

"Uncle?" Nate's head tilted to the side.

Zeke put his finger to his lips. "Food is part of what the crowd is funding, right?"

"Yes." Nate's eyes lit up. "I see now."

Clara led them to the table next to the kitchen. "No one wanted to sit here. Said it was too noisy."

"We'll be fine. Thank you, Clara."

They were looking at the menus when someone came up to the table. Without looking up, Zeke noted the brown camo pants, a military-style canvas belt, and a dark green T-shirt. As he looked up, he noticed a tattoo of two hairy legs in full stride walking out from under the short sleeve. His gaze continued up and up and stopped when he was looking into the brown eyes of a thirty-something man with a well-kept beard.

"The name's Danny." The camo-clad man stuck his hand out. "Saw your video last night, and I had to come see for myself."

Zeke shook his hand. "I'm Zeke. This is my partner, Nate."

"Nice to meet you. It would be great if you could show me where you saw Bigfoot."

"Well, we're here to get some breakfast, and then we have some things we need to do—"

"We'll have a new post up soon with more details," Nate interrupted.

Danny looked back and forth between the men and tapped his index finger on the table. "Sure. Don't want to give away your secrets for free."

The tension dispersed as the front door swung open and hit the wall with a bang. A man in his forties wearing a plaid shirt and jeans, burst into the diner.

"A kid just ID'd the spot the video was made, not far from here!"

The diner erupted into a cacophony of sliding chairs, clanging silverware, and thumping boots as the Bigfoot hunters stood and fought to exit first. After the door closed, Zeke, Nate, and Clara were a lonesome trio in the dining area. The stillness was interrupted by the *ding, ding* of the order up bell.

Clara's arms hung by her side and her chin fell to her chest. "All that food," she whispered.

Zeke reached up and lightly put a hand on her shoulder. She stirred slightly, not making eye contact. "Don't worry. We'll cover it."

Nate blanched.

Zeke *tsked* and held up his hand. "We caused this mess. We'll clean it up."

Nate inhaled deeply and nodded.

"Clara. Clara?" Zeke took his voice up an octave.

She took in a deep breath and looked at him with a fragile smile.

"Okay, Clara, do you know of anyone nearby who may want a free breakfast, or can we put some in to-go boxes and hand them out?"

"I'll check with Frankie. He's the boss today."

"Sounds great. And instead of ordering, we'll take the next dishes that are ready."

Nate continued his bobblehead impression as she left to get their plates. "I admit at first the idea was terrifying, but I see it's a good idea."

Zeke tapped his temple. "I told you everything's all right up here."

~~~

The town felt abandoned after the pickup trucks and their camo-clad drivers left and were nowhere to be found. Nate and Zeke enjoyed the quiet as they walked out onto Main Street rubbing their bellies after downing plates of biscuits and gravy, thick-cut bacon, nearly burnt hash browns, and sausage links. Clara assured them Frankie would make sure the extra food was delivered to the senior living center down the road.

The KCTV5 and FOX4KC television news vans were parked in front of the courthouse. The side panel doors were open, letting Nate and Zeke catch a glimpse of the inner workings of live field reporting.

A man with his back to them toggled switches and turned knobs. Over his shoulder, a small black-and-white monitor showed a female reporter scrolling on her phone in front of the courthouse. The duo turned around and saw her in living color.

"Testing. Testing. Live from the Lafayette County Courthouse. Testing."

They saw her lips moving but the sound rattled them as it came from behind. They glanced back at the van.

"Sounds great, Jaime." The van tech adjusted a few more toggles. "We're live in five minutes."

"We'd better get a move on." Zeke headed toward the door. "I don't mind being on your phone, but I don't want to be on local TV."

"Uncle, you know the internet is kinda bigger than local TV, right?"

"Sure."

Rayleen let out a heavy sigh as Nate and Zeke entered the courthouse. She reached for a stack of papers and started to shuffle through them.

"Good morning, Ray . . ."

She stopped Zeke's pleasantries with a raised hand. "I'm not sure if you'll think the same after reading this."

His face paled as he read the slip of paper. The receptionist drummed the desktop with her nails.

"What is it, Tito?"

"It's a gag order. I'm forbidden from talking about Bigfoot outside the courtroom until I testify."

"What? Why?"

Rayleen slapped her hands on the desktop. "Because, his . . . yous . . . *your* video has the town crawling with Bigfoot hunters and news vans. It's tainting the jury pool."

"Huh?"

"No, she's right, Nate. It says it on this paper, right under 'Confidential.'"

The young receptionist's neck turned crimson. "It does not."

"No. No it doesn't. I'm sorry for insinuating you were being nosy."

She relaxed her shoulders and blew out a sharp breath between closed lips. "Apology accepted. Also, Counselor Lewis told me to send you to his office the moment you got here."

Zeke tipped an imaginary hat. "Thank you."

~~~

The lawyer's office was filled with extra people in suits. The addition of Zeke and Nate not only upped the temperature of the room but also amped up the tension. Jimmy Nixon was surrounded by Kendal Larsen *and Associates* today, and a couple in their early forties with similar jawline and hair color to Jimmy's sat behind him. There were three twentysomethings in ill-fitting suits on the opposite side of the room.

"Thank you for joining us this morning." Counselor Lewis motioned toward two chairs. "We're also joined by Mr. Nixon's parents and this term's college interns. Seems after your latest revelation, we're going to need all-hands-on-deck for this case."

"My revelation?" Zeke put his hand on his chest and looked back and forth at all the faces in the room.

"The video, Mr. Renick. The video you and your driver took of something running through the woods outside of town. You've stirred up a hornet's nest of complications."

Zeke noted the vein bulging on the counselor's neck and the slight smiles creeping on Jimmy and his legal team's faces. Mrs. Nixon sat ramrod straight, her hair pulled up in a librarian bun. With one hand, she clutched her purse, and with the other, she covered her mouth. Zeke wondered if she, too, wore a Mona Lisa smile beneath her handkerchief.

"I beg your pardon. I don't see how this is my fault. It's not like we planned to see Bigfoot while . . ." Zeke stopped abruptly. Counselor Lewis's eyes were burning into his, and the interns were leaning forward. "Damn," he whispered.

"Uncle?" Nate touched his arm.

Zeke's shoulders straightened, and his eyes locked on the counselor. "They think we made it up. They think we created some elaborate ruse to sway the jury and get young Mr. Jimmy outta here."

"No! That's crazy! You can test the video. It hasn't been tampered with. Check it!" Nate's voice cracked, and his cheeks flushed.

"Oh, we will." Counselor Lewis pointed to the intern closest to him. "Mr. Kellogg, please relieve Mr. . . . We weren't formally introduced before."

Nate pulled his phone out and handed it to the brown-haired intern. "Can I just go by The Driver?"

The counselor shook his head.

"Nate. Nathaniel Francisco Abayon Villanueva."

The intern taking notes stopped his pen above the paper. "'The Driver' sounds good."

"Mr. Davis, no shortcuts here."

"Could you please spell all that?"

After several attempts, Nathaniel was officially in the proceedings.

"To make my life easier—and to keep this case from getting any further out of hand," Counselor Lewis said, interlocking his fingers and steepling his thumbs, "we've issued Mr. Renick a gag order; he may not discuss Bigfoot or the Wooly-Bully outside of this courthouse. And we'll cross our fingers the horde of creature stalkers will dissipate when they learn it was a hoax."

"It wasn't a hoax." Nate stood and took a step toward the massive desk.

The upstart counselor slid his chair back and stood at the same time. "Be careful, Mr. Villanueva."

Zeke put a hand on his young friend's forearm and gently pulled him back down to the chair.

"It's okay. We know. It's okay." He looked from the interns to the counselor. "Yes, I came here to help the boy, but not to help him get away with a crime. I came here because I believe Bigfoot is real, and I didn't want people to dismiss his encounter with the creature. That's why I'm here. I didn't come to interfere with justice."

He shifted his focus to Jimmy, his team of lawyers, and his parents. "Make no mistake, I am not on your side. If it turns out you lied about what you saw and you go to jail, I won't lose a wink of sleep. And if it turns out you're behind what we saw yesterday at the lake," Zeke fixed Larsen with a glare, "I'll happily see to it you all are disbarred and you, young man, in jail."

Mrs. Nixon gasped, clutched the front of her blouse, and buried her face in her husband's shoulder. He gave her a half-hearted pat on the back.

"If you're through with your theatrics, Mr. Renick, we'll take a break and reconvene this afternoon in the courtroom where Mr. Jimmy Nixon will tell his story to Judge Henderson, who will determine what charges, if any, will be filed and if we move forward with a trial."

Zeke and Nate stood to leave.

"One more thing, Mr. Renick. The gag order extends to your videos."

Nate sucked in a gasp, and Zeke patted his back. "It's okay."

The young man grumbled under his breath the entire way out of the courthouse.

"This is so unfair."

Zeke nodded and kept walking. He stopped on the other side of the news vans. "Okay, here, take my phone."

Nate held the older man's phone between two fingers like it was a dead rat. "When was this last updated?"

"I don't know what that means, but let's make a video." Zeke adjusted his collar.

"Oooo, I see where you're going with this." After a few quick swipes and downloads, Nate had the app loaded on the flip phone. "Are you sure you want to go to jail, Tito?"

"No one is going to jail." He ran his fingers through his hair. "Just make sure you can see the news trucks and courthouse."

Nate gave him a thumbs up and then counted down from five.

"Four . . . three . . . two . . . one." He pointed at Zeke.

"Good morning, I'm here in front of the Lafayette County Courthouse where I've just received a gag order." He pulled out the paper and unfolded it. "It says Mr. Renick—that's me—is prohibited from speaking about, mmm, I'm not allowed to say his name, so let's call him Bruce. Mr. Renick is prohibited from speaking about . . . Bruce." Zeke guffawed and rubbed his chin. "Except in the courthouse during court proceedings. And since I'm too old for jail, I won't be able to tell you more about our recent Bruce encounter. Thank you for your patience. Until next time, keep believing."

"Great job, Uncle." Nate gave him a high five.

"Well, let's get back to the hotel and upload it."

"No need. I went live with it."

"Live?"

"Welcome to the twenty-first century."

~~~

Despite feeling more energized than he had since his mini-stroke, Zeke finally agreed with Nate to head back to the hotel for a little cat nap. Refreshed, the duo arrived at the courthouse to hear Jimmy Nixon's testimony before the judge.

The walk from the air-conditioned car to the courthouse in the ever-rising humidity zapped some vim but not the vigor from Zeke's step. He wasn't sure if it was being back in Lexington or just being out of the retirement home that supplied his surging pep. He reached the courthouse door first.

"After you," he said, stepping back for Nate to enter.

"No, Uncle. I insist." Nate reached over Zeke's shoulder to grab the door with one hand and gestured for him to enter with the other.

Zeke gave a thumbs up and ducked under the younger man's arm to enter the air-conditioned foyer. They both closed their eyes and tilted back their heads.

"God bless the man who invented AC." Zeke pulled at the buttons on his shirt.

"Amen to that!"

"It's weird weather this fall, a lot hotter than normal." Rayleen shuffled some papers. "Counselor Lewis wants you to meet them in Courtroom Two."

Zeke raised his eyebrows and pointed down the hall.

"Yes, all the way down the hall and turn right at the double doors." Rayleen accentuated the directions with her pencil.

"Thank you." Zeke tipped his invisible hat, and he and Nate headed to the courtroom.

Courtroom Two, as expected, was much larger than the counselor's office. The massive room featured wall-to-wall deep burgundy carpet and an ornate judge's bench of dark oak. The public seating area featured four rows of wooden chairs, and the rail separating them from the lawyers was a deep cherrywood.

Jimmy Nixon and his lawyers were seated at a table on the right, and Jimmy's parents sat behind them in the public area. Counselor Lewis was at the opposite table with the interns, who were shuffling papers and making small talk.

The hand-carved wooden doors creaked as Zeke and Nate pushed them open to enter the room.

"Great, you're finally here." Counselor Lewis tapped the nearest intern. "Find the bailiff and tell him to tell Judge Henderson we're all here."

The twentysomething jumped to his feet. He practically skipped out of the courtroom.

Counselor Lewis shifted his focus. "Mr. Renick and Mr. Villanueva, you can have a seat there in the front row. The judge will hear Mr. Nixon's testimony this afternoon and get your statement tomorrow."

Zeke and Nate were about to sit when the intern returned through the main doors and the bailiff entered from the side. "All rise. The honorable Judge Morton Henderson is presiding."

Judge Henderson entered, motioning with his hands for everyone to sit down. "Thomas, I told you we don't need all the formalities today. We'll save that for when we have a packed house."

The bailiff smiled and shrugged his shoulders. "It's a hard habit to break."

There were light chuckles around the room. Zeke noticed Mrs. Nixon didn't crack even the smallest of smiles. She sat with perfect posture, hands folded in her lap.

"Alright, Samuel and Kendall, remember you promised you'd play nice today." Judge Henderson pointed a finger at each of the lawyers.

"Yes, Your Honor," they chimed in unison.

"Perfect. Then this shouldn't take long, and I shouldn't need this." He adjusted the gavel on the edge of the bench. "But I'm going to keep it handy because these proceedings are venturing into new territory, and I enjoy order."

A young woman entered through the side door. She hunched her shoulders as she tried to duck under the judge's view and quickly step to a chair in front of the bench. He raised an eyebrow.

"So sorry Judge Henderson. Marilyn just got a call from Joey's daycare that he's running a fever, so she had to step out and get him." She uncovered the stenotype machine and massaged her fingers. "I'm not as fast as she is, but I promise I can keep up."

"Your Honor, I object." Kendall Larsen turned his hands upward.

"On what grounds?"

"On the grounds that she's a kid." He pointed at the young woman, who shook her head.

"Overruled on account Miss Greely is nineteen and has successfully earned the necessary court stenographer certificates. Isn't that right, Katie?"

A smile turned up on the edges of Katie's lips as she looked at Nixon's attorney.

Judge Henderson adjusted the collar of his robe. "Samuel, you have any objections?"

"Not to Katie."

The judge's left eyebrow shot up. "You object to something else then?"

"Your Honor, this is not how we normally do things."

"We don't normally have Bigfoot involved in our cases, Counselor Lewis. So, I'm going to proceed as planned, and we won't make any decisions until I'm certain things are clear. Sound good?"

The lawyer slumped back and nodded.

"Perfect. Let the record show that Counselor Samuel Lewis and his summer interns are here for the county, and Counselor Kendall Larsen is seated with his client, Mr. Jimmy Nixon. In the gallery, we have James and Joyce Nixon, and I'm guessing the other two are the infamous Bigfoot believers who have brought the crazies to our doorstep."

All lawyers turned around to stare at the duo. Nate gave a half wave, but Zeke looked at him sideways and reached out to pull his hand down.

"Gentlemen, can you please recite you names for the record."

"Ezekiel Joseph Renick, Your Honor."

"Nathaniel Francisco Abayon Villanueva, Your Honor."

Katie Greely lifted her head and started to open her mouth.

"Most people call me Nate Villanueva."

The stenographer smiled and resumed tapping on the keys.

"That'll work. Are you ready, Katie?"

She nodded.

"Okay, Mr. Larsen, let's have your client take the stand. After hearing his testimony, we'll adjourn so I can check his testimony. I was hoping to finish up today, but I have to push Mr. Renick's testimony to tomorrow. After I've heard it all, I'll decide if this is something to take to trial or just a tragic accident."

Joyce Nixon gasped and quickly covered her mouth. James put his arm around her and patted her shoulder. Zeke noted Jimmy rolling his eyes at his parents' actions. The teen shook his head and headed for the witness stand.

After swearing to tell the truth and nothing but the truth, Jimmy stepped up into the witness box. He dropped his swagger. His shoulders slumped forward, and he lowered his gaze.

"Okay, Jimmy, take a deep breath. I know we've gone over this a million times, but I need you to tell the judge exactly what you told me and Counselor Lewis on Friday." The boy's attorney smiled and nodded at him.

Jimmy bit his lip and let out a long, slow breath.

"Yes, sir," he said. Even his voice had lost the bravado Zeke heard on Friday.

"Doesn't even seem like the same kid, does it?" Zeke whispered to Nate, who shook his head.

The teen shifted in the seat, rocking side to side.

"Before I start, Your Honor, I want to say that I am so very sorry that Ray and Olivia were hurt in this accident. And I swear—not just on the Bible, but on my football scholarship to State—that it was an accident."

"Yes, Mr. Nixon, the whole town is aware of your records and recruitment," the judge said. "Just tell me what happened, step by step. No need for more swearing."

"Yes, sir, Your Honor." Jimmy closed his eyes and took a deep breath and held it. He exhaled through tight lips and leaned his head back. He clenched his eyes tight and shook his head. "Sometimes I think if I concentrate hard enough I can stop things from happening in my head and turn back the clock to undo it all. But I can't."

He opened his eyes and focused in the direction of his lawyer. "I can't even count the number of times I've driven that road. I've driven it in rain and snow and never had an accident." He turned in his seat to look up at the judge. "You can even check with the county clerk. I've never had accident or even a ticket."

Jimmy lowered his head and then looked back up at the judge. "No, that's a lie."

Judge Henderson's eyebrows shot up, but Zeke noticed Counselor Larsen didn't react at all, as if he knew this statement was coming.

"Sorry, Your Honor, I did get a parking ticket last year in Kansas City."

The judge smiled. "Noted. Thank you for taking this 'whole truth' seriously."

"Yes, sir." He turned back toward his lawyer and a hint of mischievous smile crept around his eyes. "I've admitted to my lawyer and Counselor Lewis that I was mad and driving over the speed limit, but it was a clear night, so I didn't think much of it. I was trying to get the pain of losing everything out of my head.

"I was coming up to the top of the hill. The music was blaring. I was pounding the steering wheel to the beat, when all of a sudden—I know you may think I'm crazy or making stuff up—but I swear this massive creature just reared up out of nowhere. I've never seen anything like it before, and I hope to God I never seen it again."

"Jimmy?"

The teen jumped at the sound of his name and looked up at the judge.

"Yes, sir."

"Could you please describe this encounter in more detail?"

Jimmy closed his eyes and bit his lip. Small cracking sounds echoed in the chamber as he tilted his head right and left.

"Yes, sir. At first, I wasn't sure I saw anything because I was driving pretty fast, but then it caught my eye again, and I thought it was a bear. It looked like it was down on four legs when my headlights caught it, but then it stood up on its back legs and I knew it wasn't a bear—or anything I'd ever seen. It was covered in fur that resembled matted hair—like a sheep that goes too long before being sheared.

"I'm really not sure what the car was doing because I was staring at the creature—this Bigfoot—thinking, this can't be real," Jimmy said. "The headlights seemed to bother it because it lifted an arm to block its eyes, but not before I got a look at his face. If you could call it a face. It was like part man, part ape, part monster—and its eyes, they were reflecting white back at me, like a deer caught in headlights. I slammed on the breaks to avoid hitting it, and the car went sideways on me. That's when I saw Ray's car, and I couldn't stop." He buried his head in his hands.

"Do you need a break, Jimmy?" The judge reached over and patted the edge of the bench.

"No, sir. I'm okay. It's just so crazy to think about. Sometimes I don't believe it happened either, except Olivia is still in the hospital, so I know it happened. I'm truly sorry."

"Sorry my ass," Zeke mumbled.

"Tito!" Nate chastised, elbowing him.

The crack of the gavel hitting the bench jolted every eye to look at the judge.

"That's enough of that." Judge Henderson pointed with the gavel in Zeke's direction. "Before I hear any more from you, Mr. Renick, I'm going to adjourn this proceeding so I can check Mr. Nixon's statement. Let's meet back here tomorrow morning. How's ten for you, Samuel and Kendall?"

Both counselors nodded.

Judge Henderson rapped the gavel twice.

"All rise," called the bailiff.

Nate leaned toward Zeke and whispered. "Uncle, another day? I'm going to have to check in with administration at The Palms to tell them we're going to be longer and get them to call in an emergency order of your meds or we won't have enough to get home."

"Great, then we can kill two birds with one trip to the hospital."

The lawyers and the Nixon family filed by the duo. The pained look on Joyce's face derailed Zeke's train of thought.

He stopped talking until the doors were closing behind both parties.

"I think the judge has the same suspicion I do." Zeke cupped his hand and whispered.

Nate arched his eyebrows and tilted his head.

"The kid's lying through his perfectly straight teeth."

CHAPTER TWENTY

LEXINGTON, MISSOURI, PRESENT DAY

"How do you know he's lying?" Nate speedwalked to keep up with Zeke as he rushed to the car.

"The eyes."

"What in his eyes told you he was lying?" he asked as they got in the car.

"Not *his* eyes, Bigfoot's. He said the eyes he saw that night glowed white, like a deer. The eyes I saw glowed red—like a person's."

Nate slowly shifted his torso and reached over to place his hand on Zeke's arm. "And bears?"

Zeke brushed his hand away. "Are you switching sides?"

Nate—the orderly turned chauffeur turned friend—wiggled his body until it faced forward and placed his hands on the steering wheel at nine and three. "Nope, nope, nope. I'm Team Tito!"

"Good choice." He patted the young man on the shoulder. "I'd like to go the hospital to see if I can talk with the young lady who was hurt in the accident."

"That could be tricky." Nate held out his hand. "I'll need to borrow your phone until the court gives mine back."

"Tricky seems to be what we do best." Zeke scrolled through and found The Palms number, pressed it, and handed over his phone.

"Good afternoon, it's Nathaniel." His voice was high and cheery. "Yes, I know we were originally scheduled to be back today . . . Yes, I'm aware of the liability . . . Yes, I'm keeping a close eye on Mr. Renick."

Zeke feigned unlocking the car door and jumping out.

"Mr. Renick is doing great." Nate rolled his eyes. "He wants to see as many old friends as he can before it's *their* memorial he's attending."

Zeke shook his head and arched his eyebrows. He opened his mouth, but Nate raised a hand with an upheld index finger and pursed his lips.

"Yes, sir, I totally understand, but it should be just one more day, two at the most." Nate gave a thumbs up. "Thank you. Thank you so very much. If you send in the emergency prescription to the hospital pharmacy, I'll pick it up, and we'll be all set. Thank you again."

He tapped the red icon on the phone. "Okay, Uncle, I bought us a couple days."

"Would missing one or two days of pills really be that bad?" Zeke asked remembering those he'd lost in the sink.

Nate handed the older man back his phone. "Missing your vitamin D—that's the big round one—wouldn't do too much besides maybe make you less cheerful."

"Oh, we wouldn't want that." He patted the younger man on the back. "And possible side effects of missing the others."

Nate's demeanor turned serious, and his voice was even. "The little one keeps your cholesterol down, but the main one is the blood thinner to avoid future strokes—mini or otherwise."

"Hmm, those do seem important."

~~~

In the hospital parking lot, Nate popped the trunk and started sorting through a pile of laundry. Zeke watched as he matched the tops and bottoms of hospital scrubs. Nate held up an orange shirt with cartoon tigers, giraffes, and orangutans at play.

"Perfect! Put this on while I find the pants."

"I'm not a huge fan of orange," Zeke mumbled.

"Too bad, it's a cheery color and makes most patients smile."

Zeke pulled it over his head, but it was a couple of inches short of his waistline. He tried pulling it down.

"This isn't going to work."

"Yes, it will." Nate pulled on a yellow top with suns, lemons, and butterflies. "Here are your pants."

Zeke pulled the scrubs over his slacks. He looked down at his high-water scrubs that left several inches of his black slacks exposed. He gestured down with both hands at his waist and then pointed with both index fingers to his ankles.

"It's not my fault you're taller than me." Nate adjusted his scrubs and grabbed a couple of new surgical masks from his first-aid kit. "People have bigger things to think about than whether or not an orderly's scrubs reach their ankles." He handed Zeke a mask. "Let's just be happy that I hadn't gotten around to going to the laundromat before our trip."

Zeke pulled the scrub up to his nose and inhaled. He curled his lip and shrugged his shoulders. "It's not that bad. I don't think I'll need a mask."

"The mask is to hide our faces and help us blend in better."

They donned the blue surgical masks and headed inside. Zeke trailed slightly behind; aware he was entering a world more familiar to Nate. The reception area was filled with a handful of people waiting patiently—all but a Black teenager who was pacing the floor.

Nate spotted the sign directing them toward the ICU and made a quick right. "I think that kid is Ray." His voice carried in the sterile halls as he pointed at the teen.

The teen looked up and jogged toward them. "Yeah, I'm Ray. Do you have news on Olivia? I've been asking every doctor, nurse, orderly, security guard, and they all say they'll get back to me. But no one has. I heard you say my name, so I was hoping you'd have news."

Zeke and Nate exchanged glances. The older man stepped forward and put a hand on Ray's shoulder. "How's the head?"

"It's okay. Smacked it on the window." Ray reached up to rub his forehead and winced when his fingers hit the sutures. "The doctor said I have a concussion. He keeps telling me to go home, but I can't until I know Olivia's going to be okay."

"Have you been here the whole time?" Nate asked.

"Yes, how could I not?"

"Has Jimmy been here?" Zeke tugged at his shirt.

"No. At least I haven't seen him. Off the football field, we don't talk much."

Zeke tilted his head. "Really? Why's that?"

Ray stepped back. "Hold up. I thought you were calling me to update me on Olivia, not to cross-examine me."

"Sorry, that's my fault." Nate used his calm orderly voice that Zeke knew from The Palms. "I'm training Ezekiel here how to be a volunteer. I forgot how much he loves town gossip."

The teen relaxed and smiled. "Well, this is the town for it."

"Ray, we need to get back to training, but if we run into Olivia, we'll make sure to tell her you're here and wish her the best."

"That would be great. Thank you." Ray reached out and shook hands with Nate and Zeke.

The duo regrouped after Ray returned to pacing the reception area.

Nate said the key was "acting like you belonged there," and so far, no one was the wiser. The pair continued down the hall and entered the ICU area. They tried to do a quick walk-around and peek in the rooms without attracting attention.

"You two lost?" a nurse in hot pink flamingo-covered scrubs asked.

"No, it looks like another doctor got his paperwork wrong." The nurse relaxed as Nate cast blame on the doctors. "They told us to come check Olivia's vitals."

The nurse rolled her eyes and picked up a chart. "Isn't that just like them. She was stable this morning and moved into her own room on the second floor." The nurse glanced at the chart again. "Room two-oh-four."

"You're the best!" Nate tapped the counter. "Thank you so very much."

The pair headed back down the hall toward the elevator. Nate grabbed a clipboard from a plastic tray on the wall.

"You were laying it on a bit thick, don't you think?" Zeke asked as the giant silver doors closed. "And what's that for?"

"This is to help sell the con." He placed the clipboard under his arm. "And to your first question. If there's one thing I've learned, it's that nurses aren't told often enough they're doing a good job." He stared at Zeke and raised his eyebrows.

Zeke held his gaze and then smiled. "Okay, okay, you're doing a good job."

"Thank you, Tito."

The elevator beeped and opened to the second floor. The sign on the opposite wall noted that even-numbered rooms were to the right and odd-numbered rooms to the left. They turned right.

As they entered Room 204, Olivia Dawson appeared to be asleep. There were several wires running in and out from the neck of her nightgown to various monitors. An older brunette woman was reading a magazine in the chair beside the bed. The woman looked up when the brightly clad duo entered the room.

"Oh, you two are literally a ray of sunshine."

The men nodded.

"They just checked in on her about an hour ago. Has something changed?" The woman set the magazine down and sat up straight on the edge of the chair.

"No, it's okay. No cause for alarm." Nate spoke in a calm manner and a lower tone that Zeke recognized. He'd used it several times to reassure Zeke things were going to be alright. So far, he was always right.

"More tests?" The words stuck in Olivia's throat. She pushed her hair back, revealing a three-inch-wide, deep purple bruise with stitches running along it.

"So good to see you awake." Nate pulled the clipboard out and ran his finger down the list. "Nothing to worry about. There were a few numbers missing from the earlier check." He turned to the brunette. "We'll just be a few minutes. This may be a good time to walk to the cafeteria and get a snack and drink."

The women rose and crossed to the bed. She gave Olivia a soft kiss on her forehead. "I'll be right back sweetie."

As soon as she was out of the room, Nate took the girl's hands and asked her to squeeze.

"What are you doing?" Zeke raised his eyebrows, which creased his forehead.

"I'm doing a wellness check . . . in case people walking by look in."

"Oh, good call."

Olivia's eyes ping-ponged between the men who flanked her bed. "Are you guys really nurses?"

Zeke pulled down his mask and put his index finger to his lips. "He's a nurse, technically an orderly, but I have some questions that only you can answer."

Her nose wrinkled.

Nate leaned forward. "He's harmless, and also, there is a very handsome young man pacing in the lobby."

"Ray is here?" Her eyes brightened. "I'm so glad he's okay."

Zeke rubbed his chin. "You seemed to know it was Ray and not Jimmy."

She blushed slightly.

"Aha, your heart rate just skyrocketed." Nate held the girl's wrist. "How long have you two been dating?"

Zeke cocked his head. "How do you know they're dating? And why are you stealing my question time?"

"Tito, the way her heart rate jumped, she's either crushing hard or they're dating."

The older man looked at Olivia, who smiled and nodded.

"You don't look like a Tito," she said.

"My name is Zeke. He swears 'Tito' means uncle in Filipino."

"Tagalog," Nate interjected.

Zeke pinched his fingers and ran them across his lips.

"*Zzzziiiip.*" Nate mimicked the action.

The older man spoke quickly and quietly. "I grew up here in Lexington, down by Myrick Road. I'm back because when I was a kid, I saw Bigfoot, and I wanted to see if it came back."

She opened her mouth.

"Don't yell. I promise I'm not here to hurt you." He glanced over at Nate, who was looking at machines and writing on the paper. "I talked with Jimmy last week, and his story felt true, but today when he was talking to the judge, it felt different. And I don't want to jump to any conclusions, but I think he's lying about what happened."

Her eyes clouded with tears, and she cupped both hands over her mouth.

"You think he's lying, too?"

She nodded and blinked away the tears.

"Do you know why?"

She continued to nod in small movements.

"Will you tell me?"

She lowered her hands and tried to form the words. Her voice cracked, and she couldn't speak too loud or for too long. Zeke leaned in to hear her better.

"Were you dating Jimmy at the start of the school year?"

Olivia's lips moved, but it was the slight head nod that spoke volumes.

"Really?" Zeke raised an eyebrow.

"A love triangle?" Nate's voice rose.

Olivia shook her head and cleared her throat. "Ray asked me out last year. I wanted to go out with him, but I was already dating Jimmy. People talk if a girl is going out with two guys. So we stayed just friends."

"Just friends," Nate air-quoted.

She nodded. "I didn't want people talking about me. Plus, it felt like as the head cheerleader, I was expected to be with Jimmy."

"How did Jimmy take the news?" Zeke asked.

"Oh, we never told him." She shook her head, then winced and grabbed her neck.

"Are you okay?" Nate asked.

"Yeah, it's not as bad today." She forced a crooked smile. "Ray and I have done our best to keep it between us. I'm pretty sure a few football or baseball guys know, but we don't even go on dates in town. We were coming back from seeing a movie in Wellington the night of the crash."

"Thank you. You've been very helpful . . . and brave."

The brunette returned to the room with a bag of chips and a canned drink. "That's what I tell her every day."

"Everything looks great." Nate tapped the clipboard. "Keep up the great work, miss."

The duo found their way back to the elevator.

"Were you able to get the information you needed?" Nate asked.

"Yes. My grandfatherly look and this amazing orange out-fit seemed to work magic."

The elevator doors opened, and as they turned to leave, Nate put the clipboard back in the tray.

"Some habits die hard." The young orderly flashed a double-dimpled smile. "Before we go to the pharmacy, let's check in with Ray, tell him the good news, and put these scrubs back in the trunk."

~~~

There was a long line at the pharmacy, so Zeke found two blue plastic seats together among a sea of patients in the waiting area. Nate snagged a slip of paper from the take-a-number machine.

"We're fifty-two." The young man showed Zeke the ticket.

Zeke glanced from the ticket to the "Now Serving" dis-play on the wall showing number forty-one. "We may be here a while."

"If only I had my phone, I could work on the crowdfund-ing page."

"I'm wounded you think so lowly of my phone." Zeke put his hand on his heart.

"Sorry, it's good for calling and Googling and texting, but it doesn't have the *oomph* I need for the site."

"Let's Google the Nixon boy." The older man sat up straight.

Nate twisted his lips and cocked his head.

"Look, if I've got questions about him, and if what she just told me is true, other people have probably had trouble with the boy before, too." He turned his palms up. In the hand closest to Nate rested the flip phone. "Sooo."

With a groan and half a smile, Nate snatched the phone and did the best he could to research James "Jimmy" Nixon, star quarterback for the Lexington Minutemen. He reworked the search parameters to narrow the articles several times. After the fourth time, Nate slid down in the seat. "Damn, Uncle, you were right."

"What? Don't leave an old man in suspense. And I'm not even going to pretend I can read that itty-bitty type."

Nate turned toward Zeke and lowered his voice. "Seems he doesn't have many traffic run-ins, but he's in the middle of a lot of fights—and his dad's a piece of work, too."

"How so?" Nate's eyes widened and he leaned toward the phone.

"Last year after a game at South Callaway, Jimmy got in a shoving match with a Latinx kid on the way to the bus."

"Latin X?"

"Sorry, Uncle, in Florida, the Hispanics I know like to be called Latinx. I'm used to translating the paper for you."

"Wait, are you saying you haven't been reading the paper verbatim?"

Both dimples appeared with Nate's smile. "No. I edit as I go, but you get the gist of the story."

"This is how hometown journalism dies."

"You're cracking me up, Uncle." Nate shook his head and looked back at the phone screen. "Anyway, the coach and the Callaway kid's parents worked out a deal . . . says Jimmy had to write an apology."

The young man scrolled more. "Here's a story on his dad suing for the right to bulldoze some low-income housing outside of Kansas City and replace it with condos. His company is also under investigation for discriminating against tenants."

"The start of a pattern between them. Maybe." Zeke looked up at the counter. "They're on forty-nine. See if there's anything else."

"Oh, this may help the puzzle." Nate's voice went up. "Their sophomore year, Jimmy and Ray were on the baseball team. The article mentions Ray being named shortstop and ends with Jimmy saying he quit to concentrate on football."

"Fifty," Zeke chimed in.

"Okay, okay, let me check one thing." Nate was laser-focused as his fingers flew across the keypad. "Yep. When I look up Ray, there's an article on his car being vandalized with the N-word."

"Does it say who did it?"

Nate scrolled through the story. "Nope. No one was ever charged."

"I've got a sinking feeling we both know who it was."

The younger man flipped the phone shut and handed it to Zeke. "My work here is done."

"Nope, still going." Zeke pointed at the display that was flashing a red fifty-two.

~~~

"How may I help you?" the thirtyish-year-old pharmacist with auburn hair asked, barely looking away from her computer screen.

"Hi, we're here to pick up a prescription for Ezekiel Renick." Nate handed the woman the paper stub. "It would have been called in from The Palms Retirement Village in Niceville, Florida."

She moved the computer mouse. "Oh, yes, it was called in a bit ago. They're working on it now. But we don't have the Vitamin D brand they requested."

Nate tapped his hand. "Do you have a generic?"

"The facility said no substitutes. We called the pharmacy in Richmond, and they can get it here in about an hour."

Nate nodded. "Sounds good."

She turned to Zeke. "I need to see a photo ID. What are the last four digits of your Social?"

He dug into his pocket and pulled out his identification card and slid it toward her. Zeke leaned in as close as he felt was appropriate and whispered his numbers.

"Thank you. It all matches up. The should the two ready soon. I'll call you back."

The duo reclined in the blue chairs with their heads resting against the wall. Zeke crossed his arms and closed his eyes. His breathing was even, and Nate was sure he was about to fall asleep.

"Mr. Renick," called the lady from the counter.

Zeke shook awake. His arms flailed for a second before he steadied himself.

Nate put a hand on his shoulder and knee. "It's okay, Tito, you fell asleep. You stay here and recover, and I'll get the meds."

"Nah, I'm alright."

The pharmacist put a small white bag on the counter as they approached. "My son has horrible allergies, too. It's that time of year. We'll text the number on file when the Vitamin D arrives."

"Sounds good. Thank you." Zeke handed the bag to Nate.

~~~

"What do you think she meant by that?" Zeke asked as they got into the car. "Why would she tell us about her kid's allergies?"

"I don't know. Maybe the guy in front of us had an allergy medication, and she got confused." Nate reached into the bag and pulled out the presorted daily pill packs. "They look like the ones you always get."

Zeke lowered his head and peered under his brow. "That's a great vote of confidence. Should I take them now, just to get it over with?"

Nate snorted. "Ever the Drama Queen. That won't be necessary."

"You know what is necessary?"

"Lunch!" They said at the same time.

CHAPTER TWENTY-ONE

LEXINGTON, MISSOURI, 1956

T he Renick boys were skipping rocks across the lake while they waited for Mr. Lewis, Larry, and the fish and game warden.

"I can't lie, Little Brother, I'm kinda glad you got into trouble because we can meet an honest-to-goodness game warden." Ethan's rock skipped four times.

"I've thought about becoming a warden." Eli flicked his wrist, sending the stone tumbling over the water.

"Really?" Zeke juggled the stone in his hand.

"Sure, how neat would it be to get paid to be in the woods?"

The youngest Renick nodded and tossed his stone, which skipped twice. "It would be pretty neat, and you'd be closer to home than if you joined the Army."

"And you could help me avoid trouble during hunting season." Ethan laughed.

Eli swatted the back of his middle brother's head. "I'd have to be extra hard on you so people didn't think I played favorites."

"Well, then you oughta just join the service." Ethan rubbed the back of his head.

The sound of tires rolling over gravel and the low *honk* of a car horn caught Zeke's attention. "They're here. They're here!" He ran toward the car.

Honk! Honkhonkhonk!

"That's enough, Lawrence." Mr. Lewis's voice carried over the noise as he stepped out of the car.

Larry ducked under his outstretched arm and scrambled to Zeke.

"Boy howdy, is that a great car to ride in." Larry grinned from ear to ear. "How come you didn't have Mr. Lewis pick you up?"

"My momma said the walk would do me good, and my brothers came, too." Zeke pointed back toward the lake. Eli and Ethan jogged toward them.

"Good morning, Ezekiel." Mr. Lewis waved at the older boys. "Glad to have you two join us today. I've missed having you at Scouting events."

"Really?" Zeke squinted and scratched his forehead. "Even Ethan?"

"Yes, even Ethan." The Cubmaster patted the top of Zeke's head.

"Gentlemen, let me introduce Fish and Game Warden, Bailey Price."

The thirtysomething warden was decked out in his khaki uniform, topped with a broad-brimmed ranger hat. He stood a few inches taller than Eli, which made him seem like a giant to the youngest Cubs.

"You can call me Warden Price." He grabbed the edge of the brim with his left hand. "I work at Big Springs down in the Ozarks, but I grew up nearby in Richmond."

He stuck out his hand, and all the boys stepped up to shake with him.

"I've known Warden Price since he was little." Mr. Lewis put one hand about thigh high. "His great uncle Davis and I met at a mayor's council. When I heard he was coming home to visit, I checked to see if he'd be willing to lead our bear safety session today."

"And here I am." Warden Price adjusted his shirt and hat. "I enjoy teaching young people how to be safe and enjoy the amazing outdoors of Missouri."

"Well, this punishment is way better than the other ones I had to do." Zeke put his hands on his hips.

"If I do my job right, it shouldn't feel like punishment." The warden winked. "Before we take off on our hike, let's make sure we have the essentials. Everyone have their canteens full of water?"

The boys nodded. Zeke and Larry held out their canteens for inspection.

"They look perfect, fellas." He took each and shook them. "It's also important to have a knife, flashlight, and compass."

Each boy pulled out their folding knives. Eli pulled a compass from his back pocket, and Ethan pointed to the small flashlight tied to his belt.

Warden Price turned to Mr. Lewis. "You've trained these guys very well."

The former mayor's chest puffed. "They're good boys. They just need a little extra guidance."

Eli and Ethan pointed at the youngest boys. "They need a little extra."

"Oh, stop it." Zeke playfully swatted at his brothers' hands.

"Well, that's what I'm here for, so let's go over some basics, and then we'll go for a hike and see if we can find and identify some tracks."

They stood in a circle and listened as Warden Price read through his list of wildlife safety.

"Number one, avoid feeding or harassing the wildlife."

Zeke and Larry dropped their gaze.

"You two broke the first rule." Ethan shook his head. "And it's not like we haven't been told it before."

"We weren't *feeding* or *harassing*, we were trying to trap." Zeke let out a sigh and rubbed his face.

"Well, no matter what word you use, it's too early to be trapping or hunting bear." The warden tapped his little notebook.

"It weren't . . . *oof* . . . ow."

Larry elbowed Zeke.

"It wasn't what?" Warden Price asked.

Larry shook his head.

"Nothing." Zeke looked at his friend sideways. "Sorry to interrupt."

All the boys exchanged glances.

"Am I missing something, Mr. Lewis?"

The older man smiled kindly at Zeke. "I don't think it's my place to tell, Bailey. I'll leave that story up to Ezekiel."

"Okay, then, let's talk about what to do if you see a bear." He flipped a page in his notebook. "In Missouri, we have black bears, which oddly enough can come in colors black, brown, reddish, and blonde."

He walked them toward a berry bramble. "It's important to know where you are and what's around you—especially, if it's a source of food for a bear, like these berries." He pointed toward the lake. "Or even fish from the lake."

"What about our food?" Eli inquired. "Some fellas like to tie their stuff in a bag and hang it in a tree, and some say to bury it."

"It really depends on where you are." The warden took his hat off and ran his fingers through his hair. "Different bears seem to behave differently in different parts. You can ask local wardens what they recommend, or if what you're doing is keeping you safe, keep that up."

Eli and Ethan nodded at each other and smiled.

"What you don't want to do is leave food or innards when you clean your fish near your camp. Bears are opportunistic and love a free meal." The warden took a swig from his canteen. "Why don't we start our hike? The trees will give us shade and keep things a bit cooler."

They stopped by the small stand of trees where Eli and Zeke saw Bigfoot, the same ones where Zeke and Larry fed a bear. Smirks and crooked smiles appeared on almost every-one's faces.

"Is there something about this spot?" Warden Price asked.

"This is where Ezekiel and Lawrence splayed the fish that attracted the bear." Mr. Lewis pulled at his collar and unbuttoned the second button.

"Here?" The warden looked back and forth. "This is a major game trail. See how the area is worn? You boys are very lucky no one was hurt."

"Yes, sir." Zeke nodded. "I'd forgot about all the other critter tracks I'd seen the first time. I wasn't thinking."

"This was your second try to catch a bear?" The warden's eyebrows rose. "Mr. Lewis maybe I should reconsider my 'good boys' assessment."

"No, no, they are good boys." Mr. Lewis put his hands on Zeke and Larry's shoulders. "They just can't seem to think when they get excited."

The warden nodded. "What tracks did you see?"

"Raccoon, deer, and a gnarled bear track." Eli counted on his fingers.

"Gnarled?"

"Yeah, it was shaped weird and didn't have claw marks."

"That's because it wasn't a bear. It was Bigfoot." Zeke puffed out his cheeks and felt the weight of five sets of eyes. "Everyone's told me not to talk about it to you because you'll think I'm crazy, but I saw what I saw—and so did Eli, but now he's saying it was a bear."

The warden cocked his head and rubbed his chin. "Well, you're not the first, nor—I'm guessin'—the last, to see Bigfoot in Missouri. We get all sorts of reports about some massive unknown creature."

"Have you seen the Howler down in the Ozarks?" Larry's eyes were wide.

"Ha, no." Warden Price chuckled. "Thankfully, that thing sounds like something from your worst nightmare. But I've taken plenty of calls about Bigfoot, and I've even gone out to campsites to see tracks."

"What'd they look like?" Zeke leaned toward the Warden.

"Similar to what you described seeing." He bent down and drew in the dirt. "Something like this."

Eli drew in a sharp breath and his eyes widened.

"Damn, that is just like what we saw." Ethan smacked Eli in the middle of the back. "You really saw the Wooly-Bully."

A satisfied Cheshire smile spread on Zeke's face.

"Or there's more than one bear with a gnarled paw out there." Eli slowly let out his breath.

The warden nodded. "True. For now, let's stay focused on bear safety."

He led the group toward the trail at the base of the hill. "Keep an eye out for any tracks, and we can practice identifying them. If we see a bear, freeze, and wait to see if it sees us. If it doesn't, we'll back up out of its space. Never want to surprise a bear."

"What if it sees us?" Zeke tucked behind Eli.

"Then we stay calm and look as big as we can." Warden Price widened his stance and raised his hands about his head. "Speak calmly and in a lower tone. It's not easy to do because bears will sometimes stand on their hind legs, and they can snap and growl and drool and be otherwise terrifying."

The boys and Mr. Lewis were frozen in their tracks, all eyes glued on the warden.

"But that doesn't mean it's going to attack. Learning to read body language can help you, just like reading people— if their arms are crossed or their chin is set, for example." The warden spoke directly to the youngest two. "It's very important that no matter what the bear does, that you don't scream or make sudden movements. You know how with dogs if you move quickly, they want to chase you? The same type of sudden movements can trigger a bear to attack."

"We were too scared not to move, and none of us could help screaming." Larry ducked behind Ethan, who pushed him back in front.

"Well, if you encounter another bear, try to make your scream deeper and not high-pitched." The warden demonstrated a low- and high-pitched scream. Zeke and Larry burst out laughing.

"Oh my goodness, that's why that bear was after Willie. He screams like a girl." The duo doubled over with laughter.

"Boys, pull yourselves together." Mr. Lewis covered his mouth to hide the smile that showed in his eyes.

"Yes, Mr. Lewis," they said in unison as giggles continued to rack their bodies.

"High-pitched scream plus a splayed fish? Your friend Willie was a very lucky boy." The warden shook his head. "You were all lucky that Mr. Lewis was able to scare it off. Bears are very fast, and it could have caught all three of you."

Zeke and Larry paled at the realization they all could have been injured or worse.

"How fast is fast?" Ethan asked.

"Black bears can outrun any man, and don't think about climbing a tree. They're some of the best climbers, too."

"That's fast." Ethan let out a slow whistle.

"As hunters, you typically don't encounter bears close up, but it's good to know in case one surprises you." Warden Price pointed out different bushes and trees. "It's good to scope out the whole area to avoid unwanted encounters."

The trail opened to a clearing, and they could look back down the hill toward the lake. They rested on a rock outcropping. Mr. Lewis pulled out a bag of beef jerky to share. It was the perfect moment—the boys were quiet as they sipped from their canteens and chewed the dried meat.

"Did you fellas ever hear about the Bigfoot sighting in Rayville?" Warden Price wiped his forehead with a handkerchief.

The boys' eyebrows shot up and their eyes widened.

"Would you like to hear it?"

All heads nodded.

Warden Price chuckled. "Okay. It was about ten years ago, so you guys might not've even been old enough for school."

"We were." Eli pointed at Ethan and himself. "But those two were just babies."

"Gotcha. I was just starting out in fish and game, and they sent me to loads of places to learn the ropes." He shook his head. "Boy, I traveled a lot. This one time, I was heading up north, and I got a call about something messing with some farmers' chickens on Road C."

The boys inched closer to each other.

"The farm was back off the road a bit, tucked away in trees with a lake, similar to this." He gestured toward the lake. "When I got there, the coop was a mess—blood and feathers everywhere."

Zeke's jaw dropped. "Bigfoot killed the chickens."

"Oh, no, it was several foxes. The tracks were clear as day. But . . ."

He leaned forward and the boys mirrored his action. "There were other tracks. Tracks too big to be a man, and if it was a bear, it was missing its claws."

"Bigfoot tracks," Zeke and Larry whispered.

"That's what the man told me. He said he heard a commotion in the chicken coop and grabbed his shotgun to show those foxes who was boss, but when he poked his head out, there was a tall, furry creature, shooing away the foxes. He said the creature saved him from losing all his chickens."

"Whoa."

"Wow."

The boys were limited to one-word phrases as they thought about what they'd heard.

"You really think Bigfoot is real?" Eli fixed Warden Price with his gaze.

The warden held his stare. "I think there are a lot of things out there in these woods that we can't explain. And I sleep okay at night with the idea that one of those things is Bigfoot."

Zeke sat up and pulled his hands together over his chest. He bit his lower lip. "Do you think he could live here?"

"I don't see why not—plenty of places to hide and loads to eat." Warden Price leaned close to Zeke. "But there is no Bigfoot hunting, trapping, or whatever-else-you-think-of season. Promise me you'll both be safe out here."

Zeke and Larry both held up a two-finger salute. "I promise," they said together.

"Check to make sure they haven't crossed their fingers behind their backs." Eli leaned back to see behind the young duo. Zeke and Larry showed their hands with uncrossed fingers.

"This has been very interesting and informative." Mr. Lewis stood and brushed off his pants. "We should head on back so Bailey can get some family time."

They brushed off their clothes and took one last look around the area.

"Hey, it looks like there's a cave over here," Larry called to the group.

"Lawrence, have you learned nothing?" Mr. Lewis waved him back. "Don't go exploring on your own and possibly surprise a bear in their den."

Larry hopped and skipped back to the group.

"Can we go see it?" Zeke asked.

"Sorry, Ezekiel, not today, we need to get back."

The younger boys were positioned behind Eli and Ethan and in front of Mr. Lewis and Warden Price to keep them from wandering off.

"Did you see inside the cave?" Zeke asked.

Larry scratched the top of his head. "No. I'm not even sure it was a cave. I didn't get chance to see."

"Next time, just whistle and I'll come running, and the grown-ups won't be able to stop us."

"That sounds like a good plan." Larry bit the inside of his cheek. "But what if it is a bear's house? I'm not sure how big I could make myself look."

"And I'm not so sure I wouldn't scream."

"Yeah, and I'd really want to run." Larry patted Zeke's shoulder. "And we know I'm faster than you."

"Not by much." Zeke pushed his hand away. "I wonder if this means we're getting grown up."

"How so?"

"Well, we're thinking about things before we do them, and we're thinking they might not be so smart."

Larry nodded. "Yeah, that does sound like some grown-up thinking."

"I agree." Mr. Lewis patted the boys on the head.

~~~

When they reached the car, all their canteens were empty, and the boys were covered in sweat.

"Are you boys sure you don't want a ride home?"

The Renick trio exchanged glances.

"It's no trouble." Mr. Lewis held open the door. "Lawrence can sit up front with Bailey and I, and you three will fit easily in the back."

"There's even air conditioning!" Larry pulled at his T-shirt.

Zeke pushed his sweaty hair back out of his face. "Air conditioning, Eli. I think Momma would be okay with us not dying from the heat."

The oldest Renick grabbed Zeke's lower face and squeezed it. The younger's smile became a twisted squiggle.

"Pweeze. Pwetty pweeze." Zeke squeezed out of his misshapen grin.

"How can I say no to that face?"

"Yes!" Ethan jumped into the car. "I was thinking of going by myself, but I'll make room for you two."

Eli pushed Zeke into the middle. "Thank you, Mr. Lewis. It's very kind of you."

"Thank you, Mr. Lewis." Zeke and Ethan echoed.

"Warden Price," Zeke scooted forward and rested his arms on the front seat. The slight breeze from the air-conditioning vent cooled him. "Can I ask you another question?"

"Sure. Shoot."

Ethan grabbed his younger brother's shoulder and pulled back slightly. "Please, don't embarrass us with more Bigfoot questions."

Zeke shook his shoulder loose.

"It's okay, Ezekiel, you can ask me about anything."

"Thank you." The youngest turned and stuck his tongue out at Ethan. "We agree that Bigfoot is real, but I'm a bit nervous about the Ozark Howler. See my buddy Larry here is headed to the lake soon." He patted his friend's shoulder.

"I'd almost forgotten about that. Thanks for the reminder." Larry shook his whole body. "How am I supposed to have a fun vacation now?"

"You'll be fine." The warden turned slightly to face Larry. "I've been working down in the Ozarks for years now, and I've never seen or heard the Howler. You remember what you learned today, stay with your group, don't leave food around, and you'll have a great time."

Larry took a deep breath and let it out slowly. He nodded quickly. "You're right. You're right."

The car turned onto Myrick Road and was in front of the boys' house in a matter of minutes. None of them wanted to leave the cool car. Eli led the way, opening his door first.

"Thanks for letting us come along and for the ride home." The oldest tapped the roof of the car.

"Yeah, thanks." Ethan slowly slipped out of the back seat.

"Oh, wait a minute." Warden Price reached over the seat to stop Zeke. "I totally forgot I have something for you fellas."

The warden opened the glove box and pulled out two gold-colored tin Fish and Game badges. He handed one to Zeke and the other to Larry. The boys turned them over in their hands.

"Wow, this is neat." Zeke pinned it on his T-shirt. "Thanks," they echoed.

"Remember to be safe."

Zeke held up the Cub Scout salute.

CHAPTER TWENTY-TWO

LEXINGTON, MISSOURI, PRESENT DAY

T he monster truck driving, camo wearing brigade returned from its morning outing hunting Bigfoot and was refueling at the diner.

Zeke and Nate entered the fray. They saw Clara, who waved with her free hand as she balanced a tray of dirty dishes on the other. She pointed to a booth in the back corner away from the kitchen. Zeke tipped an invisible cap, and the duo headed toward the table.

"Sorry, gents, it's a madhouse again, so enjoy this complimentary snack until I can get back to you." She dropped the menus and some saltines, then darted behind the counter, poured two cups of coffee, and then spun around to dish up two slices of pie, and set them beside the steaming mugs at the counter.

Nate and Zeke tried to hear the conversations coming from other tables to garner any news on the day's "hunt." They weren't sure what they were hoping to hear.

"If someone else saw something today, that should put us in the clear with the court." Nate leaned back in his chair to be closer to the group at the counter.

"I don't know, Nate. That counselor doesn't seem to like us much."

"It's not us. It's *this*." He leaned forward and waved his arms pointing around the diner. "He's not happy with the circus that's come to town. Did this happen when you were a kid?"

"No, thank goodness. There wasn't *this*." He tapped his phone. "What happened to folks on the other side of Lewis Bridge didn't make the papers. I made the papers because the Oster brothers robbed some fancy people over three counties, not because I saw Bigfoot."

Clara returned with a coffee for Zeke and a glass of water for Nate.

"You gents need some more time?"

They shook their heads.

"I'll have the fried catfish with fries, please." Nate handed her the menu.

"Hmm, I was going for the club, but fried catfish is calling my name, too. Can I get some slaw and any gossip you've heard from this bunch on the side?"

"Coming right up."

Two men walked up to the table, pulled out the chairs, and sat down.

"Mind if we join you?" the taller of the two men asked. His sandy blond hair curled around the back of his baseball cap that sported the logo of a large outdoor supply company.

Nate leaned back and folded his arms, while Zeke placed his forearms on the table.

"Seems you've answered your own question." Zeke turned his palms up.

"I'm sorry, where have my manners gone," the outdoor fan reached out a hand. "I'm Curt, and this is my friend Gabe."

Zeke and Nate cautiously shook hands and exchanged names.

"We watched your video like a hundred times before we got here today." Gabe wore his hat backwards. "We've had some close calls ourselves but never caught Bigfoot on camera."

"We're *this* close to getting a show with a streaming network." Curt put his thumb and index finger millimeters apart. "We work together, and this could be big money for all four of us."

Zeke and Nate exchanged glances with each other and then with the men across the table. The older man leaned back and crossed his arms to create a united front.

"Nate and I are doing pretty good on our own. We're not looking to bring on any partners, and we've already got a virus . . ."

"Gone viral." Nate corrected. He smiled and reached over to tap Zeke's elbow.

"Oh, right, we've already gone viral, but thank you for stopping by to say hello."

Clara set the plates on the table. "Are these guys joining the party?"

Zeke dug into his coleslaw. "Nope. They were just leaving."

The duo scowled as they got up and left the table.

"Can I bring you anything else, hon?"

"No, thank you, we're all set."

Nate smacked the bottom of the ketchup bottle and swirled a crinkle fry through the bright red blob.

"What are you thinking about?" Zeke took a sip of coffee.

"Nothing."

"I've seen you plow through a basket of fries in seconds. When you dawdle, something's up. Spill!"

Nate held up the ketchup-covered fry. "I was just wondering if those guys were for real about a streaming deal. That could mean a lot of money and real production equipment."

"We seem to be doing more than fine with our patrons funding us. I don't want more, and I definitely don't want to work with other people. Look how long it's taken me to stand you." He tapped Nate's forearm.

"You're right, Uncle. We need to stick to the task at hand."

Clara stopped at the table with pitchers of coffee and ice water. "Refills? Rumors?"

"Both, please."

"Most of these guys are upset that they drove so far and can't find anything." She spoke slightly above a whisper. "Apparently, Jayce tried to make some quick cash by leading several groups to the camp site and cave, but most refused to pay him once they got there." She glanced quickly over her shoulder. "A few of them are saying you two are frauds and made it all up."

Nate and Zeke sat up straight and darted their eyes around the room.

"Easy, fellas." She set the water pitcher on the table and started wiping an open space with a rag. "So far, all the evidence points to the guys who arrived this morning. A crowd came in earlier bragging about how they taught some size-eleven, would-be Bigfoot a lesson for laying down fake footprints."

"I'm so sorry to drop this mess on the town." Zeke rubbed his chin. "After I talk to the judge tomorrow morning, I'm pretty sure they'll all head home."

"You don't think it's real?" Her voice went up an octave and several heads turned toward the table.

Zeke motioned for her to lower her voice. "No. I mean yes."

Her eyebrows raised.

"He believes Bigfoot is real, he doesn't believe . . ." Nate stop talking when he caught the glare from Zeke.

Clara fixed Zeke with a stare of her own. "Well, mister, what is it?"

He ran his fingers through his hair. "It's complicated."

"Isn't everything." She affixed the rag to her apron and grabbed the pitcher.

"I feel the judge should be the first person I tell, that's all." He held up a two-finger salute. "Right after I'm done with him, you're the first I tell. Cub Scout's honor."

She brushed invisible crumbs from her apron. "Sounds good. I'll get your bill."

"Sorry, Uncle, I didn't mean to let that slip."

"It's okay. Everyone will know soon enough." He put his face into his hands. "I feel like a fool all over again."

"No, you're not." Nate leaned over the table and lowered his voice. "You saw what you saw as a kid. You know how that impacted you, and you didn't want the same for this kid. Besides, I believe *we* really saw Bigfoot on that trail. Just because Jimmy lied doesn't mean you did."

Zeke put his hand on the younger man's shoulder. "That's kind of you to say, but I don't think they'll separate him from me."

"Here you go, hon. I look forward to seeing you tomorrow." She set the bill on the table. Zeke picked it up and waved it at her.

"Let's pay this and head back to the hotel. I'd like to lay down."

"Are you feeling okay? You tell me naps are for old people."

"Today, I feel old." Zeke jumped as his phone vibrated. "Looks like we can run by the pharmacy on the way. My vitamins have arrived just in time to keep up my sunny disposition."

~~~

The waiting room was empty when they arrived at the pharmacy.

The lady behind the desk waved them over.

"We just got these sorted for you, Mr. Renick."

"Thanks." Nate reached for the package. "I was worried he'd fall asleep if we had to wait too long."

"Haha." She laughed loudly and covered her mouth. "It's true though. Those allergy meds can really knock a person out. Drink more water, that should help. It may make me a bad mom, but I actually like allergy season because my kid stays so calm."

"Allergy meds?" Nate tilted his head.

Zeke leaned on the partition. "I don't have allergies."

An uneasy look crept across her face. "I can show you the order from the facility." Her fingers punched the keyboard at a fevered pace. She turned the screen to face them. "See, right there? It's one of the stronger allergy meds on the market."

Nate pinched the bridge of his nose and squinted at the screen. "That doesn't make sense. The doctors all told me he was taking a blood thinner, a cholesterol med, and the Vit D."

"What's the name on the box when you prepare them?"

The young orderly looked at her and his face fell. "I don't take them from the box. The facility doctor puts the meds in the cups for us."

"For what it's worth, the other pill is a statin used for cholesterol patients. And the allergy pill looks similar to a top-selling blood thinner. It's close enough it could fool some RNs."

Nate shook his head and rubbed his face. "It doesn't make any sense."

"It finally does to me." Zeke's eyes widened. "Like she said, it's what keeps her kid calm. The Palms is drugging us to keep us quiet and easier to manage."

Nate's eyes widened to match Zeke's.

~~~

"I knew there was something screwy about that place." Zeke tossed the bag of medicine on the bistro table in the hotel room. "Didn't I tell you I was okay?" He plopped down hard on the bed.

"Yes, you did, but I'm still having trouble making sense of it all." Nate crossed into his adjoining room. Zeke heard the *clink* of keys and *thunk* of a wallet hitting a dresser.

"Come on, kiddo, it makes perfect sense." Zeke placed his hands on the edge of the bed. "How do you run a senior facility with minimal staff and make maximum profit? I'll tell you how. You drug the seniors."

Nate stepped into the doorframe. He had on a different shirt and was combing his hair. "It just goes against what we're taught."

"My guess is that nurses—orderlies—even the cooks and bottle washers aren't behind it." Zeke jumped up and grabbed a bottle of water from the mini fridge. "It's the administrators. The fat cats with deep pockets and wallets to fill them. All they need is to find one doctor willing to look the other way for a slice of the pie."

Nate crossed the room and sat at the little table. "My head hurts."

Zeke grabbed an extra water and put it in front of the young man. "I'd offer you a beer, but this is all I've got."

"Thanks." Nate smiled. "I'll pop a few ibuprofens and it should help. I guess we need to call the police."

"What? No, not yet." Zeke joined him at the table. "What if it's just my pills? Or what if they learn we're on to them and give me something worse than allergy pills?"

"I hadn't thought of that."

"That's probably because you've never seen Kojak or Mannix, or any of the great detectives." Zeke tilted his head back and closed his eyes. "No, we just keep doing what we're doing until we have all the information to *book 'em, Danno*."

"Danno?"

Zeke shook his head. "Forget it. Right now, folks at The Palms are basically sleepy. Let's concentrate on what we need to wrap up here, and then we can figure out what to do there."

"It feels risky, but I'll go with you on this one."

"Thanks, Nate. There's one other thing I need you to go with me on."

"What's that?"

"I'm not taking that pill anymore."

"Uncle!"

Zeke held his hand up. "The lady at the pharmacy said the prescription was for allergy pills. I'll sneeze if it comes to that but no more foggy brain." The older man didn't want to admit he'd already missed doses.

"But . . ." Nate pointed at the older man. "You have to take the cholesterol and vitamin D."

"Deal."

"Deal."

~~~

A mix of excitement and anxiety filled Zeke's thoughts the next morning.

There were only two pills to take, and he was champing at the bit to see how different he'd feel—if at all—minus the one pill for more than a day or two.

"Down the hatch." He tossed the pills into his mouth and followed with a couple swigs from the bottle of water. "So far so good."

There was a light rap on the adjoining door. "May I come in?"

"Yep. I'm dressed, drugged, and ready to go. I'd like to get breakfast at the diner before meeting with the judge."

"Sounds good to me. I'm not a fan of the continental breakfast here either."

A few pickup trucks with out-of-state license plates still dotted the downtown area, but there was only one news van by the courthouse. The diner was halfway full, but it was library-quiet compared to the previous days.

An auburn-haired woman in her mid-forties greeted Zeke and Nate as they walked in.

"Good morning, gentlemen, table for two or would you like to sit at the counter?"

"Can we have a table in Clara's section?" Nate asked.

"She took the morning off. She'll be in this afternoon. Said those crazy Bigfoot hunters finally pushed her over the edge."

Zeke's eyebrows shot up and his mouth made an O shape. He looked at Nate.

"Oh no." The waitress blushed. "Are you two Bigfoot hunters?"

"No, it's alright, we're more like Bigfoot enthusiasts." Nate's bright smile put her at ease.

"Ah, you're the big tippers!"

Nate choked on air.

Zeke chuckled. "Yep, we're the big tippers." He patted Nate on the back. "How about that booth in the back corner?"

"Sure." She grabbed two menus and led them to the table. "My name is Cheryl, and I'll be serving you today."

"Thank you, Cheryl. We'll need just a few minutes."

Once she was out of earshot, Nate leaned toward Zeke. "She could be our last big tip ever. I'm a bit worried the patrons will cancel their support after hearing what you have to say after meeting with the judge."

"If they do, it's been a heck of a ride, and I'm thankful you helped me get this far."

Zeke looked out the window at the courthouse's tall white columns and white-washed walls. It looked so small compared to when he was a kid.

"Ok, fellas, you know what you want?"

Cheryl's return knocked him from Memory Lane.

They ordered and ate slowly, killing time until they were needed at the courthouse.

"The biscuits seem lighter." Nate added some preserves. "Could be a different cook today."

"It's not necessary to fill all the quiet," Zeke said, looking up from his plate.

"Sorry, I'm just a little nervous. And when I get nervous, I get chatty."

"Have you been nervous this whole time?" A sly smile turned up on Zeke's face.

"Oh, feeling extra funny are we, Tito? Don't make me add your allergy pill back into the mix."

Zeke held up his hands in surrender.

Cheryl brought the bill, and as promised, they left a big tip.

~~~

"Good morning, Rayleen, how are you doing?" Zeke gave a wink with his smile as he addressed the courthouse receptionist.

"Much better this morning. There's only the one news crew, and they've stayed outside so far."

"Has Judge Henderson arrived?"

"He's here, but Marilyn is running a bit late, so you might as well take a seat. He'll let me know when he's ready for you."

"Oh, no, is Joey still sick?"

Rayleen tapped her pencil and cocked her head toward Zeke. "He's better. How did you know he was sick?"

"The young girl, Katie, who took her place, had mentioned it."

"Oh, okay. Well, he's better today. She's just running behind. Please, take a seat."

Zeke and Nate felt like regular visitors with their own special seats as they waited to be called into the courtroom. Nate pulled up the crowdfunding page on Zeke's phone.

"Patrons are getting restless, Uncle. Look at these comments."

The younger man swiped his finger up the screen. The messages scrolled by with emojis, capital letters, vulgar photos, and fluffy kittens. Zeke moved his face back and forth from the screen.

"I should have brought my reading glasses."

The younger man chuckled. "I've got it."

Nate read out a few:

> **@CryptoCarl** Did you find Bruce? Odd name for a Sasquatch. #Believer #BigfootBigheart #MissouriMadness
>
> **@TheBigfootFanPage** FAKE NEWS!! I should have known this would turn out bad when a "Florida Man" is involved. Several reputable cryptozoology sites have received reports saying multiple people were seen creating footprints and planting hair high in trees. I'M CANCELLING MY PATRONAGE. #FAKENEWS #SCAM
>
> **@JBRO123123** Drove overnight from Jackson, MISS. What a mess! Trackers making and destroying tracks. If Bigfoot was here, that crazy crowd drove him to Iowa. What a sh!t show. #ShowMeTheMonkey

"It's worse than I thought." Zeke mopped his forehead with his handkerchief. "Let's hope we have enough funds to get back."

"We'll just stock up on Spam for the drive home."

"And we can cook it on the roadside and sleep in the car." Zeke winked.

"Now that's just crazy talk, Uncle. We have all the glamping equipment we need."

Their laughter was interrupted by Rayleen's throat-clearing "ahem."

"Judge Henderson is ready to see you now." She directed them down the hallway with a flair of her pencil.

The duo walked to the back of the courthouse to Courtroom One. Zeke took a deep breath and pushed the door open. The scene was similar to the day prior except the stenographer was an older woman with dark brown hair and two of the interns were missing. James and Joyce Nixon were seated behind their son's counsel, and Zeke and Nate took seats behind Counselor Lewis. The door to the judge's chamber opened.

"All rise!"

The squeal and thumps of heavy wooden chairs being shoved back from the lawyer's tables jarred most in the room. Jimmy Nixon snickered seeing involuntary shakes and shivers convulse the stenographer's shoulders.

"Be seated." Judge Henderson sat and rapped the gavel. "Good to see you back, Marilyn."

She nodded but kept her eyes straight ahead and fingers on the keys of the steno machine.

"Good morning, all. Let the record reflect we have Counselors Lewis and Larsen, Mr. Jimmy Nixon, and his parents. Ah yes, and our out-of-town visitors, Mr. Renick and Mr. Villanueva." The judge ran two fingers along his collar and tugged. "Same rules as last time Counselors, we'll hear Mr. Renick and then I'll make my ruling. Marilyn, let the record reflect both counselors have acknowledged. Wait, amend that to acknowledged unenthusiastically."

Both lawyers' tables were full of mummers and head shaking.

Zeke chuckled. "I like this guy."

"Let's hope you feel the same way after you're done telling him your story."

"Mr. Renick could you please join me up here?" Judge Henderson motioned with the gavel to the witness box.

After swearing to tell the whole truth, Zeke sat in the witness seat. A cold sweat broke out on his upper lip and his stomach did a couple of turns. He closed his eyes and let out a long, slow breath.

"Are you alright?" Judge Henderson asked, cocking his head.

"Yes, sir, just a little nervous. This is my first time here." Zeke stretched out his arms and patted the railings around the box. "It's a bit unnerving on this side of the rails."

The judge smiled. "There's nothing to worry about. We'll get your sworn statement, which I understand is pretty exciting, and then I'll determine if or how this impacts Mr. Nixon's case. Since this is more for me than the counselors, I'll be asking the questions."

Zeke inhaled deeply. He moved his hands from the top of his thighs toward his knees and slowly breathed out. "Ready."

"Mr. Renick, do you believe you encountered Bigfoot as a child?"

"Yes," Zeke answered without hesitation.

The stenographer and defense attorney failed to stifle giggles. Judge Henderson tapped the gavel. "We'll have none of that."

"Mr. Renick, do you believe you and Mr. Villanueva encountered Bigfoot on Sunday?"

Zeke made eye contact with Nate, who nodded. "Yes." Zeke's answer was strong, but he started to squirm in the seat anticipating the next question.

"Mr. Renick, based on Jimmy Nixon's testimony yesterday, do you believe Mr. Nixon encountered Bigfoot the night of his accident?"

Both lead counsels leaned forward, while Jimmy continued to lean back in his chair with arms and feet crossed. His mother had her head bowed like she was praying. Nate flashed two thumbs up.

"Mr. Renick, did you hear and understand the question?"

"Yes, Your Honor."

"Well, then do you believe Mr. Nixon encountered Bigfoot?"

"No. No, I don't."

CHAPTER TWENTY-THREE

LEXINGTON, MISSOURI, PRESENT DAY

"Order! Order in this court! I will have order!"

"Objection!" Counselors Larsen and Lewis shouted over each other.

Jimmy Nixon's eyes and mouth dropped open, and his arms fell limp at his sides. His dad continued to be stoic, but his mother's face was ashen.

"Mr. Renick, my understanding from Counselor Lewis was that you believed Mr. Nixon when you first heard him on Friday. What happened to change your mind?"

"When he told the story on Friday, he . . ."

"Excuse me, Mr. Renick, but can you please clarify who 'he' is for the record?"

"Yes, I'm sorry. On Friday, when I met Jimmy the story he told didn't have a lot of details. The area of the accident isn't too far from where I first saw the creature by the Lewis Creek Bridge, and Jimmy mentioned the horrible smell." Zeke shifted in the chair. "However, when he was describing Bigfoot yesterday, the hair, the face, the size all felt right, but the eyes were wrong. He, Jimmy, said the eyes glowed like a deer in headlights. Now, we've all been driving at night, and we've seen those bright white reflections. But both times I've seen Bigfoot at night, his eyes were red. Gave me the heebie-jeebies."

"Your Honor." Counselor Larsen stood. "This is ridiculous. Are you going to let some scared old man jeopardize the future of my client?"

"Sit down, Kendall. Your client is the one who came up with this ridiculous defense in the first place. Mr. Renick is entitled to his opinion."

"But Your Honor. It's an opinion solely based on eye color."

Zeke hesitantly raised his hand.

"Yes, Mr. Renick."

"It's not based *solely* on the eyes, Your Honor." Zeke pulled at his collar and swallowed. "I talked to an eyewitness."

"Objection! Now he's talked to Bigfoot." Counselor Larsen put his hand on the top of his head.

Jimmy's eyes bulged. He leaned forward so fast the table shook. "Who? There was no one else out there."

Judge Henderson rapped the gavel. "Mr. Larsen, control your client."

Larsen put his hand on Jimmy's shoulder and pushed him back into the chair.

"It's a great question though, Mr. Renick." Judge Henderson leaned over the bench. "Who is your eyewitness?"

"Olivia Dawson."

Both counselors were on their feet, loudly voicing their objections again.

"Order! Order!" The banging of the gavel echoed through the courtroom. "Mr. Renick, it is highly irregular when the counselors in my courtroom gang up on the same witness. You seem to have a special talent for finding and getting into trouble with the law."

"I'm sorry but I just had to follow my hunch after hearing Jimmy's testimony."

"Your Honor, I haven't had a chance to interview Miss Dawson." Counselor Larsen waved his arms. "I didn't even know she was allowed visitors. Did you?" Larsen turned to Counselor Lewis, whose forehead was a series of deep furrows.

"No. The doctors said they saw improvement, but they didn't say anything about visitors. How did you get to talk to her?" Counselor Lewis glared and pointed at Zeke.

"I wore hospital scrubs and just walked on in."

"Do I even want to know where you got the scrubs?" Judge Henderson rubbed the back of his neck.

"I didn't steal them if that's what you're thinking." Zeke's gaze shifted from the judge to Nate. The younger man gave a slight nod and a thumbs up. "I got them from the trunk of Nate's car. He's an orderly."

"Mr. Renick, are you telling the court that you impersonated a doctor to talk to a victim of this accident, a potential witness?"

"No, sir. We . . . I was acting like an orderly. I just needed to know."

"What did Miss Dawson tell you?"

"Your Honor! Objection! Hearsay."

"Sit down, Counselor Larsen. There is no jury to impress here. Just like Mr. Nixon's statement, I'll have my staff check everything Mr. Renick says unless . . ." The judge shifted the weight of his gaze to Jimmy. "Mr. Nixon, do you have any idea what Miss Dawson may have told Mr. Renick? If you do, it may go better for you if you tell me yourself."

Jimmy slumped back in the chair and crossed his arms. He sucked in his lower lip and shook his head.

The smack of James Nixon's hand on the rail behind his son shot Jimmy straight up in his chair. Joyce Nixon tucked her chin to her chest and covered her face with a lace-edged handkerchief.

"Son, don't you sit there pouting." A vein bulged on James's forehead. "If you know something . . ."

Jimmy sat on the edge of his chair and leaned against the table. "No. Ray said he didn't see it, so I wouldn't expect Olivia to see it either."

"Well, then, we're back to you, Mr. Renick." Judge Henderson pointed at Zeke with the gavel. "Did Miss Dawson tell you she saw Bigfoot?"

"No, Your Honor. I didn't ask her."

"Ah, ah, ah." The judge pointed at Counselor Larsen. "Before you object again, I'm going to exercise my right to ask questions and ignore you."

"All this will go into an appeal if that's necessary," the boy's lawyer huffed.

"I would expect nothing less from you, Kendall. Now, Mr. Renick, what did you ask her?"

"Again, Jimmy's testimony yesterday felt different. On Friday with just the attorneys, he said he was upset because *they* lost the game. Monday with you, he said *he'd* lost everything, but he didn't mention the game. I started thinking about other things a fella could lose, and I thought of the girls that got away in my life. That got me to thinking of the young lady involved here, Olivia. That's how I ended up at the hospital. I asked her if she thought Jimmy was lying, and she said yes."

"Did she give you any more information?"

Zeke shifted in the chair. He looked at Jimmy. The young man's eyes filled with hot tears. The older man raised his eyebrows. "Jimmy?"

The star quarterback's jaw was set, and he shook his head hard, causing a few tears to slip down his cheeks.

"She started to cry." Zeke's eyes welled a bit. "Olivia said she and Jimmy had stopped seeing each other after the Lathrop game." He looked up at the judge. "I don't know when that was."

"Thomas," Judge Henderson said, looking at the bailiff. "Would you please pull up the football schedule for this season on that cell phone I know you snuck in inside your back pocket?"

248

A nervous smile made its way across the bailiff's face.

"Okay Mr. Renick, while he tracks that down, please continue."

"She said he was really upset about the loss. Angrier than she'd ever seen, and it scared her. She said she ended it."

Thomas held up his phone. "It was the second game of the season. They lost thirty-six to nothin'."

"Your Honor." Counselor Larsen remained seated and spoke in a measured tone. "I'm still not connecting any dots or seeing how this disproves my client's statement."

"Mr. Renick, can you help the defense counselor connect any dots?"

"She said that not long after that, she started going out with Ray. That they tried to keep it a secret because they were worried about Jimmy and his temper."

Jimmy's face was beet red, and he slammed his fist on the table. "I knew they were dating. Like the whole school wasn't talking about it. She made me look like a fool, dating a Black guy. What was she thinking?"

"Mr. Larsen, control your client."

Larsen reached over to push Jimmy back, and James Nixon grabbed both of his son's shoulders over the rail. He yanked Jimmy so hard the chair jumped backward, screeching until it collided with the rail.

Jimmy shimmied his shoulders loose and leapt to his feet.

"You want to know what happened?" His eyes bulged as he spun around pointing at everyone. "You want to know? She dumped me. ME. For him. I thought she was trying to make me jealous. But then she was just making me look bad."

He stopped spinning and rested his hands on the table. "Jimmy Nixon, star quarterback. My teammates were laughing *at* me. Saying I wasn't man enough to keep a girl, that I couldn't keep a girl satisfied." He slapped both hands on the table. "After our last loss, I was beyond mad. We were on the verge of losing three in a row, after making the playoffs last year." The vein in his neck started pulsing. "And then, and *then*, I hear Ray talking about how he's going to take 'his girl' to Wellington for a good time. His girl! Something in me snapped."

He turned to look at his mother. "You've got to believe me. If Ray was out of the picture, I knew she'd come back to me. I didn't think the car would roll. I didn't mean to hurt her."

Joyce's body rocked with sobs. Jimmy turned to look at his father, who reared back and slapped his son across the face. The *smack* reverberated around the room.

"Bailiff, escort that man out of my courtroom." Judge Henderson tapped the gavel several times. "Jimmy. Jimmy."

The young man turned toward the bench. A bright red welt in the shape of hand slowly rose on the side of his face.

"Are you okay, son?" Judge Henderson spoke softly.

Angry tears rolled down Jimmy's cheeks as he stood with his arms at his sides.

"In light of this new information, Counselor Larsen, I'm going to give you some time with your client. And Counselor Lewis, my guess is you'll be writing up new charges."

The lawyers nodded. Both appeared numbed by the outburst.

"Mr. Renick, thank you for your testimony. Part of me wants to fine and detain you, and the other part of me wants this behind us as quickly as possible."

"Me too. I appreciate you not putting me in jail, and I am truly sorry for going outside the rules."

"My parting gift to you, Mr. Renick, will be to remove the gag order Counselor Lewis put on you and your Bigfoot videos. However, you may not discuss anything Mr. Nixon said here today in any capacity. Understood?"

"Yes Your Honor, thank you."

"Ahem." Nate cleared his throat.

Zeke held up his hand. "And could we get Nate's phone back?"

~~~

Zeke and Nate said goodbye to Rayleen on their way out of the courthouse for what they hoped would be their last time. As they descended the steps, a reporter with a KCTV5 microphone raced over to them.

"Mr. Renick, Mr. Ezekiel Renick, I recognize you from your videos. I understand you spoke before Judge Henderson today regarding the Jimmy Nixon versus Bigfoot case. What did you tell the judge? Was any decision made about Jimmy going to trial?"

Zeke paused and gave a slight smile to the reporter. "I have no comment, but I'm sure someone will later today."

The two men walked over to the diner and took a seat at the counter. Clara brought over two mugs and menus.

"From your long faces, I'm guessing it was a rough morning at the courthouse."

"Yeah, I may skip lunch and jump to a slice of pie with a glass of milk." Nate handed back the menu.

"And for you?"

"That actually sounds good. I'll take the same but with coffee."

"Two slices coming right up."

Zeke put his elbows on the counter and rested his head in his hands. He stared at his misshapen reflection in the napkin dispenser. Zeke barely moved when a purple-hued triangular reflection slid next to his.

"Wow, it must have been bad. What happened?" Clara asked.

"I feel horrible." Zeke poked at his berry pie with his fork. "I can't tell you everything that went on, but I can tell you it had nothing to do with Bigfoot."

Clara arched her right eyebrow.

Nate nearly choked on his bite. "I don't think Clara thought it did in the first place."

"You're the brains of this outfit, aren't you?" She winked at the younger man.

"He's pretty clever." Zeke took a sip from the steaming mug. "But I don't think even he knew what was going to come out today."

"What did you say?" Clara asked.

"Oh, it wasn't me." Zeke bobbled his head.

"Wasn't me, either." Nate held his hands up and a little bit of jam dripped from the fork onto his hand. He quickly licked it off.

Clara glanced between the two men. "You promised you'd tell me."

"Yes, I'm telling you what the judge will let me." Zeke lifted the white porcelain mug to his lips. "After listing to Jimmy yesterday, I suspected he was lying about Bigfoot. And I was right. The rest will have to come from there." Zeke spun around on the barstool to see the courtroom through the diner's side windows. "My guess," he spun back to face Clara, "is Counselor Lewis will be making a statement on those steps in the very near future."

She leaned across the counter and whispered. "So I'm guessing you're saying it wasn't an accident."

There were slight nods from Zeke and Nate as they went through the motions of eating their pie.

"And all this Bigfoot chaos it caused?" She spread her arms wide. "Were you two part of the plan?"

"No!" Zeke's voice boomed and heads turned. "Sorry everyone," he said, then mouthed *I'm sorry* to Clara. "No," he repeated. "Scout's honor, I came here thinking what he said was true, and I saw—we saw—what we saw."

Nate nodded. "I even told them they could check to see if I altered the video."

"Okay, calm down, I believe you." Clara cleared away Nate's empty plate. "But will your followers?"

"Let's hope so." Zeke crossed his fingers and licked the crumbs off his fork.

CHAPTER TWENTY-FOUR

LEXINGTON, MISSOURI, 1956

The final Cub Scout meeting of the summer was typically the highlight of the season for Zeke. Mrs. Lewis made some of the best fried chicken—though he knew now that Miss Georgia was the real cook in the kitchen. There were sides of coleslaw, corn on the cob, biscuits, and baked beans. The dessert table was always his favorite, covered with berry pie, cookies, and a variety of hard candies.

But this year, Zeke felt sick. He didn't even want to go, but his mom made him.

"You march yourself up that hill and to that ceremony." She tossed his tennis shoes toward him and pointed at the door.

"Aw, Momma, I don't feel well." He put his head in his hands.

"What you're feeling is sorry for yourself. You and Larry had your fun, nearly got Willie killed by a bear, and you're lucky the only punishment was not getting to earn your patch."

His shoulder shook, and his head bobbed back and forth. The slamming of the front door caused him to look up.

"Sorry, Mom." Eli had his hands in the air. He had announced earlier in the week that since he was starting his final year of high school, he'd was too mature to say Momma anymore. "Just came back to get that old baseball glove. The fellas want to have one more game before school starts Monday."

"That sounds like fun. Will you do me one favor?"

"Yes'm." He reached up to the top shelf and pulled down the well-worn glove. "What do you need?"

"I need you to walk Zeke to the Lewis home for the troop celebration."

He looked over at his younger brother sitting on the couch with his shoes in his hands. A dirt-covered face looked back at him. Eli took a deep breath and glanced at his mom. She raised her eyebrows and smiled.

"Okay, sure. I'll wait outside. Make sure you wash your face." He tucked the glove under his arm and headed for the front.

"Sometimes it's hard to remember who the mom is around here." Their mother chuckled and straightened her apron. "But I'm pretty sure it's still me. What do you think?"

A slight smile crept up on the corners of Zeke's mouth. "You're the mom. He's just bossy." He pulled his shoes on and double-knotted the laces.

"Have fun." She tussled his hair.

"Oh, Momma." He ducked away from her and skipped to the door.

Eli was pacing at the edge of the road as Zeke bounded down the steps.

"I'm surprised you're not already up the hill and enjoying some fresh-squeezed lemonade in Mr. Lewis's backyard," Eli teased. He tossed the glove up in the air and caught it as they walked. "And you know it will be one of the best meals you get all year. You can't pass that up. I'd still be Scouting if I could just for that."

"I know. I know. But they'll be passing out the badges, and I don't get any. It's not fair." His voice went up an octave.

"Really, from what I overheard Mr. Lewis telling Mom, you're lucky to still be a in the Den."

Zeke's jaw fell. He reached up to grab Eli's elbow and turn his older brother toward him.

"I c-coulda b-been . . ."

"Slow down. Breathe in. Breathe out."

Zeke followed his brother's instructions.

"Okay, I'm good. Thanks Eli." He exhaled and shoved his fists down at his side. "Onward!"

Zeke looked up at Eli. "So you're saying that I could've been kicked out of the Cub Scouts?"

"That's what it sounded like." Eli put his hand on Zeke's shoulder, and they started walking. "It's not easy to overhear grown-ups whispering in the front from the kitchen, but the gist was sneaking out of your tent wasn't that bad, but gutting the fish and hunting for bears was too far for a couple of the parents."

"We weren't hunting for bears." Zeke huffed through his nose. "We were hoping to catch Bigfoot."

"I'm not sure that would have made the parents feel any better." He chuckled and pushed Zeke's arm.

"Probably right," he said, joining in on the laughter.

"And remember, you're not the only one missing out on getting a badge."

"Yeah, I am. Larry and his family went fishing down to Lake of the Ozarks."

"Sorry, bud." He patted the top of Zeke's head. "It won't be easy or fun, but remember your manners, and eat an extra piece of chicken for me."

"Deal." Zeke put out his hand and Eli shook it.

"This is your stop, little brother." Eli swatted him on the tail with the baseball glove. "Get to going."

Zeke plodded up the walkway. "Thanks, Eli. I hope your team wins." He stopped to turn and wave. Eli was already jogging, and he lifted and waved an arm without looking back.

The house sounded like every other troop meeting: boys talking loudly over each other and heavy furniture being moved around. However, it didn't smell like normal. The aroma of a homemade meal wafted from the kitchen and filled the home. Zeke breathed deeply and held it for as long as he could.

"There you are, Ezekiel." The Cubmaster's voice roused Zeke from his food dream. "I was starting to think you weren't coming. I figured you may still be upset about the camping trip."

Zeke's shoulders slumped. "Yeah, a bit, I guess."

"Well, maybe some fried chicken will make you feel better."

The Cub's mouth began to water, and his eyes lit up. "Yeah, that could do it."

Following the meal, members of Troop 115 filed out of the kitchen to the Lewis living room for the ceremony. Zeke held back a moment. For the first time in a long while, his stomach was full, but he still contemplated enjoying another chicken leg before joining his friends.

"Hey, Zeke, come on," several boys called at him from the other room.

Hearing his name broke the spell the fried fowl held over him, and he reluctantly joined the troop. Zeke stayed toward the back of the pack, knowing his name wouldn't be called out during the ceremony.

Mr. Lewis took his place in front of his charges like he'd done for decades. Zeke had witnessed numerous ceremonies when Eli was in Scouting. His older brother earned every patch available. It was a magical memory for Zeke, who couldn't wait to follow in Eli's footsteps.

There was no magic tonight. Zeke's thoughts drowned out the Cubmaster's introduction. He saw Mr. Lewis's lips moving, but he didn't hear anything. He drifted back to a night earlier in the summer when he played his best round of marbles ever and then lost them when he threw them at a creature that he was sure was Bigfoot.

A slight smile crept across his lips as he imagined being handed a patch embroidered with a silhouette of Bigfoot and the Lewis Creek bridge embroidered in dark brown and black. He'd shake hands with Mr. Lewis, who'd smile and pat him on the back. "Such a brave boy."

Zeke squirmed and tucked his hand quickly to his side as he realized the sporadic clapping and cheers were not in his daydream, but for Mr. Lewis's opening remarks. He shuffled his feet and glanced around to make sure no one was looking at him. The heat on the tips of his ears cooled as he realized all eyes were on the Cubmaster.

He watched Mr. Lewis call the Cubs up one by one and place the circular green cloth in their hands. Zeke put on a brave face, biting the inside of his lip to keep from pouting. Turns out, he was still sore at not being able to complete the week-long camping trip. Seeing everyone but himself receiving a badge was like lemonade in a paper cut. Larry was extra lucky not only to miss the embarrassing moment, but to also have a dad, a fishing boat, and the means to stay at the lake for weeks.

Zeke's stomach turned, either from eating too much or from jealousy. He gulped air to force a burp. If that didn't work, he'd excuse himself and head home.

Buuurrrrp.

The Den erupted in laughter and shouts of "amazing." Zeke held his stomach and let out a sigh of relief.

"Ezekiel Renick." Mr. Lewis's voice cut through the laughing.

"Sorry. Excuse me."

Mr. Lewis nodded.

Willie Larsen reached out and patted Zeke on the back. "That was an amazing burp. Too bad there's not a badge for that." He caressed his camping patch and then held it in front Zeke. "Maybe you'll get this next year. My dad said you're lucky to still be in the Den, so we'll see."

Zeke slowly curled his fingers into fists and gritted his teeth. He opened his mouth to say something, but a strong puff of air came out instead. Zeke's eyes narrowed, and his chest heaved.

"What's the matter, Zeke? Stutter got your tongue?" Willie laughed at his own joke and looked around to see if anyone else heard and wanted to join in on the joke.

Crimson rose up Zeke's neck as his fists clenched. He leaned toward Willie, whose eyes widened and jaw went slack.

"Not cool, Willie." The sound of Asher Tullis's voice from behind him caused Zeke to jerk. Asher not only had the most badges in the troop, but he was also the tallest Cub by several inches, which he demonstrated when he stepped between Zeke and Willie.

"You're right. I'm sorry." Willie's chin trembled and he raised his hands in surrender. "On my honor."

Asher grabbed Zeke's and Willie's right hands and brought them together in a forced shake. "Truce?"

"Truce," they said half-heartedly.

"Great." Asher slapped both of their backs. "Let's get some cookies."

The dessert area was surrounded by boys grabbing sweets. Mr. Lewis stepped in and organized a line. "Once you have your treats, head out to the porch to enjoy them."

Zeke caught movement in the kitchen in the corner of his eye. Hope rose in his chest that Georgie was here and that he'd stayed out of the way until the group went outside.

Once in the kitchen, he saw Georgia trying to clean up the mess they'd left.

"Good afternoon, Miss Georgia." He leaned against the doorway. "Is Georgie here today?"

She smiled at the familiar voice. "No, he's home today."

"Could you tell him I said 'Hi'?"

"I could." She stacked plates and glasses to carry to the sink.

"Would you like some help?"

"Ezekiel, that's nice of you, but you know you don't work here no more. Why aren't you with your friends eating sweets?"

"My tummy's been sour."

"You saying my cookin' is sour?" She stood straight and pointed at him with a dish towel.

"No, ma'am." He lowered his shoulders and stumbled back a step.

A warm, toothy smile spread across Georgia's face. "I'm just teasing you. Didn't mean to scare you." She turned back to the sink. "If it's not my cooking, what else is upsettin' your stomach?"

He stepped next to her and whispered, "I'm guessing it's because I'm jealous."

Georgia raised her left eyebrow and tilted her head.

"I *am* jealous." He exhaled hard. "I didn't get to earn a badge. And my best friend is off fishing with his dad."

"You know what I hear fixes all that?"

He shook his head. She walked to the pantry and pulled out the box of waxed paper. Georgia uncovered the leftover chicken and picked out four legs.

"My momma likes thighs." Zeke's eyes were wide.

Georgia pursed her lips and nodded. She exchanged one leg for a thigh. Zeke smiled and rubbed his hands together. "Thank you, Miss Georgia."

She wrapped two legs together and a leg and the thigh in another piece of wax paper.

"Now, you tuck one each into your back pockets, and you can put some candy in your front pockets."

His smile stretched across his face. "Yes'm."

The dessert table and living room were nearly empty when he returned. He could hear the others playing outside. Zeke decided the butterscotch and root beer hard candies were the best choices to fill his pockets. He also grabbed a chocolate chip cookie to fill his mouth.

He joined the raucous scene outside. The sadness of missing his friend and not getting the coveted patch waned as he savored the cookie and thought of the look on his momma's face when he brought home the chicken.

Zeke's jaw dropped and his eyes widened when he saw Eli talking with Mr. Lewis near the street. He ran to join the duo.

"Eli! What are you doing here? I thought you were playing baseball?" He pulled up short of the sidewalk and wiped the cookie crumbs from his mouth.

"I was just telling my old Cubmaster how Roger launched a ball deep and we lost it in the duck pond. We all went in looking for it but couldn't find it and called it a day." Eli's jeans were covered in mud from the knees down. Zeke scrunched up his face and pointed at his older brother's dry shoes.

"Oh, I took my shoes off before going near the water." Eli laughed. "I wasn't going to lose a shoe and end up doing work to earn another one."

"You shoulda because Miss Georgia makes an amazing lunch." Zeke's smile touched his eyes as his hand touched his belly.

"I'll remember that. I figured I'd swing by to see if I could walk you home."

"Sounds good to me. See ya, Mr. Lewis."

The Cubmaster reached out and shook Eli's hand. "It was great to see you, young man. Keep a close eye on this one." He patted the top of Zeke's head.

"Yes, sir, will do."

Eli put his arm on Zeke's shoulder as they started off toward home.

"How was lunch? Did you eat an extra piece of chicken for me?"

"Better!" Zeke reached into a back pocket and pulled out the drumsticks wrapped in waxed paper. "Miss Georgia gave me one piece for each of us. She even gave me a thigh for Momma."

Eli gasped, and he wrapped his younger brother in a bear hug and swung him around. "Boy howdy!"

"I'm getting dizzy."

"Sorry, Little Man." He put him down. "You want me to hold onto them?"

"I got it." Zeke threw his shoulders back.

"But if we run into the Wooly-Bully, I don't want you throwing our dinner at him." A grin spread on Eli's face as he watched Zeke's cheeks pinken.

"Why you . . . I oughtta." The youngest Renick pulled back his arm and made a fist, but his smile betrayed him. "I'm thinking of giving your piece to Ethan."

"Oh no you don't." Eli made a half-hearted attempt of a swing to grab the wax paper-wrapped treasure. Zeke ducked under his arm and started running down the hill. Their laughter echoed along the river as they raced home, and Eli kept himself a full stride behind.

"I win!" Zeke slapped the stair post. Between deep breaths, he flashed a full-toothed smile at Eli. "I'm super-fast downhill."

"Yes. Yes, you are." Eli breathed normally but bent over to rest his hands on his knees. "I must be getting old."

"Oh, stop, I know you let me win so I wouldn't give Ethan your leg."

"Why would I want his old leg?" Ethan called from the kitchen window. "I've been waiting and watching for you clowns to come home."

"Well, if you hadn't woken up with that cough, Mom would have let you come play baseball with me instead of going to Mother Harris for a cure."

"Was it a disgusting cure?" Zeke curled his nose.

"I'm surprised you don't smell it out there. Come on in and get a whiff."

The brothers met inside at the table. Zeke pulled the wrapped chicken from his back pockets and then reached into his front pockets and pulled out handfuls of sweet treats.

"Jackpot!" Ethan raised both arms high above his head. "Great job, little brother."

"You're welcome, and you do stink a bit."

Ethan raised his T-shirt to show off the plaster of herbs and whatnot adhered to his chest. "It's supposed to clear up my lungs and my attitude."

"My money's on you breathing better only," said Eli. "And put your shirt down. Where's Mom?"

"She should be back any time." Ethan pulled his shirt down and grabbed a butterscotch candy. "Mrs. Hudson stopped by to see if she could help set up the Sunday School room for tomorrow's potluck after church."

"Okay, then we'll get everything ready to eat when Mom comes home." Eli swept the candies into his hand and put them in his pocket. "And no more sweets until after dinner."

"Hey, no fair. Ethan got one." Zeke pouted and glared at his older brother.

"Who was wiping cookie crumbs off his face at the top of the hill?"

Zeke sighed and forced a crooked smile.

"Okay, Zeke, you go out back to pick some flowers and then put them in a mason jar with some water."

The youngest boy gave a two-finger salute and headed to the front door. He returned moments later with a brilliant bouquet of red, purple, and yellow flowers with stems and roots. A trail of soil led from the door to where he stopped at the kitchen sink to put water in the glass.

"Damn it, Zeke, now I gotta sweep the kitchen, *again*." Ethan's face flushed red. He emphasized "again" by pointing at the dirt trail with the broom. "I swear."

"Yes, you did." Eli slapped the middle child on the back of the head. "Don't do it again."

Zeke held the half-full mason jar in one hand and the up-rooted flowers in the other. "I'm sorry."

"It's okay. He can sweep again. He probably missed something the first time anyway."

A low growl escaped Ethan's scrunched mouth.

Eli crossed to the sink and pulled out his pocketknife. "Let's trim these a little." He cut the flowers, tossed the extra stems and roots out the window, and placed the trimmed bunch in the jar.

"Zeke, set the table and put these in the middle."

"Aside from bossing and trimming, what are you doing?" Ethan leaned on the broom.

"I'm *supervising*. Someone has to assign the work and make sure it gets done."

"Bossing." Ethan nodded.

Zeke joined him. "Yep. Bossin'."

"Let's just work together so Mom can have a special meal."

"Yes sir, Boss." Zeke and Ethan stood at attention.

Eli saluted, and they all laughed.

~~~

After they'd swept three more times and rearranged the utensils twice, Eli decided they should change into their nicest clothes and sit at the table to wait for their mother. It felt like they'd been waiting hours, but the clock on the wall said it had been a mere ten minutes.

"Eli, please let us change." Ethan pulled at the shirt collar.

"No. It will make it extra special."

The munching sound of tires on gravel alerted the boys that their mom was being dropped off.

"Okay. Sit up straight." Eli got up from the table to open the door. "Welcome home, Mom."

"What are you boys up to?" Tears welled in her eyes, and she covered her mouth with her hands. She shook her head. "Oh my goodness. This looks amazing."

She put a hand around the nape of Eli's neck. His eyes started to water.

"Miss Georgia sent me home with a piece of fried chicken for each of us." Zeke nearly leapt from the seat. "And Eli decided we should have a proper meal."

"I still don't know why I have to wear this itchy shirt though." Ethan furrowed his brow. Ruth reached over and caressed the top of his head.

"You look *very* handsome, and I *am* very grateful for this." She met the gaze of each of her sons. "I'm so very, very blessed."

"Let's eat." Zeke motioned for his momma and Eli to sit down. "Look Momma, I picked some flowers, too."

"Wow, you've had quite the busy day." She reached out and pulled the jar of flowers close to smell them. "Very nice."

She turned to Ethan. "Are you feeling any better? That plaster working?"

His features softened. "Maybe. I'm definitely hungry."

"A good appetite is a good sign." She reached out, and they joined hands. "We thank you, Lord, for this day. We are thankful for Miss Georgia's cookin', Mother Harris's medicine, and your colorful creation. Amen."

"Amen," echoed the boys.

~~~

Eli pushed himself away from the table and started clearing the rest of the dishes.

"Thank you boys for such a great meal. I feel like a queen." She started to slide her chair backward.

"Wait, Momma, there's dessert." Zeke put his hand on hers. "Really?"

"Yep, there were loads of candies at the ceremony." He pointed at Eli. "He took 'em and put 'em in his pocket."

Eli pulled his pockets inside out. They were empty.

"You ate them!" Zeke accused.

"Ezekiel." Ruth placed her hand on her youngest's arm. "I'm sure there's another explanation. Eli?"

A mischievous grin curled up on Eli's lips. He opened a cabinet, went on his tippy toes, and reached to the back of the top shelf. He pulled out a closed fist and slowly opened each finger, revealing the dark brown and caramel-colored treats.

"I was just keeping them safe." Eli nodded toward Ethan, who was sucking the marrow from the chicken leg bone.

"Probly a smar idea," Ethan mumbled with his mouth full.

Eli put the hard candies on the table in front of their mother.

"My, oh my, Ezekiel, you've provided quite the meal for us today." Her eyes smiled and she pinched his cheek.

"Oh Momma, cut that out." He blushed and playfully pushed her hand away. "That's why mommas are not allowed at meetings. We'd die from embarrassment."

She reached across the table and enveloped him in a hug and covered the top of his head with kisses. Zeke squirmed and squealed. Ruth slowly let go of his racked frame. She held him at arm's length. His face was bright red and sweat beaded on his brow and lip.

"Good thing it's bath night, especially for you, Little Man."

"Aw, man, fancy clothes *and* a bath? I thought watching Willie get that camping badge was going to be the worst part of my day."

"Oh, Zeke, with being pulled away to help at the church, I totally forgot I have a surprise for you." She got up from the table.

"No bath!" He shot both arms straight up in the air.

"No."

His arms and face fell.

"Pick up your lip." She disappeared down the hall.

"What do you think it is?" He asked his older brothers. Both shrugged.

"We start school on Monday. I'm guessing she sewed a new shirt." Eli moved the clean dishes from the sink to the counter.

"Nah, with Momma it's more likely some kid's Bible." Ethan threw the bone at Eli. "Thanks for tossing that out the window for me."

Zeke rested his head in his left hand and let out a slow, heavy sigh. Eli and Ethan tried to stifle laughs. "It's not funny." The youngest brought up his right hand and set his chin against his palms.

"Why such a sad face for a surprise?" She returned with a folded paper in her hands.

"A shirt and Bible are not fun surprises," he forced out through pouty lips.

"Who said it was one of those?"

He sat up and pointed at his brothers.

"Well, you should know by now that they are more likely to tease you than tell the truth." She pushed the small package across the table. "Do you think a shirt or Bible could fit in there?"

He shook his head. Zeke's brow furrowed with concentration as he unfolded the paper to discover a green disc about the size of a quarter. It looked like a jumble of threads. He glanced at his mother.

"Turn it over." She mimicked the motion.

Zeke turned the disc over. The dark green canvas featured a bright green embroidered circle around the edges, and three colorful orbs in the middle. The larger of the trio was blue, but it was the smaller yellow-and-black striped sphere that sparked recognition in his mind.

"It's my marbles. You made me a badge for my marbles?"

She nodded. "At first, I thought you not getting a badge was fair, but your brothers argued for you."

Zeke's eyes widened as he looked at his brothers, their heads bobbing like a fish was on a line.

"Eli said you'd done everything right when you boys went that weekend, but Mr. Lewis is the leader, and I didn't want to make a camping badge if he said you couldn't have one."

"I understand. Thank you, Eli." He ran his fingers along the stitches. "But how did you come up with this idea?"

"That was me." Ethan raised his hand. "I wanted a Bigfoot hunter badge . . ."

"What?" Zeke leaned against the table. His voice rose as his neck reddened.

"Goodness gracious, calm down. Obviously Momma said no. She asked what's something you do really well, and . . ." He made a sweeping motion at the homemade badge. "Well, *tada*, marbles."

"Thank you!" Zeke leapt from his seat and ran around the kitchen hugging everyone.

Eli grabbed his shoulders and pushed him back. "You do know that you can't put it on the sash with your other badges."

Zeke pulled at his ear and his eyebrows came together. He opened his mouth, but Eli tapped his lower jaw back up.

"You know why."

"Because it's not official." Zeke lowered his head.

Eli gently grabbed his youngest brother's nose and pulled his face up to see him eye to eye.

"Yeah, but mostly because if the other Cubbies see what amazing badges Mom can make, they'll all want one."

Zeke smiled and rubbed his thumb across his one-of-a-kind patch.

"You keep that with your prized treasures. Deal?" Eli stuck out his hand.

"Deal." They shook on it.

"Can we have some candy now?" Ethan's hand was inching toward the pile of treats.

"Yes. Yes. Yes." Their mother tossed a piece to each of her sons.

CHAPTER TWENTY-FIVE

LEXINGTON, MISSOURI, 1956

"I can't believe I'm wearing dress shoes two days in a row," Ethan groused, forcing his feet into the faded leather shoes. "I don't think God would care if I wore tennis shoes."

"God may not, but Momma sure does." Zeke wiggled his toes in his oversized shoes. "It's not so bad."

"My toes are like this." Ethan curled his fingers under. "It *is* so bad."

Heavy steps echoed in the hall, and Eli stuck his head through the doorway.

"Hurry up! Mom is waiting outside. If you two stop arguing, we could catch a ride to church instead of walking in these horrible shoes."

"Coming!" The younger siblings nearly knocked Eli down as they raced past him to get to their mom outside. They bent over out of breath next to her.

"I've never seen you boys so excited to go to church." She licked her fingers and tried to slick down some of Ethan's wayward hairs. "Or is it the potluck that has you moving so fast?"

"Eli has us moving fast. He said we were going to get a ride to church." Zeke's eyes were wide as he looked up at his momma.

"Elijah! Lying is not a good way to start the Lord's Day."

Ethan and Zeke's heads fell to their chests. They both let out heavy sighs. Ethan bent down to start untying his shoes.

"What are you doing?" Ruth asked.

"I'm not walking in these all the way to church. My toes will be raw."

A familiar rumble caught the boys' ears and they all looked right. They kept staring down the road as the familiar shape of Mother Harris's Chevy Nomad came into view. They started jumping and waving. Ethan still had his shoe in one hand. Ruth pointed at it, and he begrudgingly shoved his foot back into it.

Mother Harris pulled the car off the road in front of the house.

"I call the very back." Zeke ran to the rear of the car and unlatched the window. Eli lifted him up and over the tailgate and shut the window.

Ruth joined Mother Harris in the front while Eli and Ethan sat on opposite sides in the middle row. Their mother often told the boys she'd love to have an automobile big enough to take them on trips around the country.

"Thank you, Mother Harris, for giving us a ride this morning." Ruth reached over and patted the older woman on the shoulder.

"Oh, it's my pleasure." The eighty-year-old gripped the steering wheel tightly at ten and two with her white-gloved hands. "Just adding on to my heavenly home by helping my earthly neighbors."

Ruth looked over her shoulder and cleared her throat.

A chorus of "Thank you, Mother Harris," came from the boys.

Zeke sat with his back against the seat as he stared out the rear window. His house grew smaller as they moved up the road. He felt the rumble of the Gypsy-red Chevy as Mother Harris gave it some extra gas to crest the hill. A toothy grin spread across his face as his small frame bounced with the car over the brick-lined street.

The trip from their house to the First Presbyterian Church typically took five minutes when Mr. Lewis or anyone else drove them. However, despite the powerful Chevy engine under the hood, a ride with Mother Harris took at least fifteen minutes. When Ethan complained about it taking so long the first time she gave them a ride, she'd pulled the car off to the side of the road.

"You're welcome to walk the rest of the way," she said. There was no smile on her lips or twinkle in her eye. Mother Harris was all business.

"No, ma'am. I'm sorry." Ethan ran his hand over the seat. "It's just that this car can go faster. It's red with *chrome*. It should go faster."

"My brother, Merritt, God rest his soul, bought this car off the showroom floor. He was all about showing off. You know what happened to him?"

Ethan shook his head.

"He dropped dead one day. Just like that." She snapped her fingers, and everyone jumped.

The boys' mother let out a little gasp and a "Dear Lord, Mother, no need to frighten the children . . . and me."

"Well, I miss my brother, and I'm thankful that I have a car to get to where I need to get, but I'm not about to show off and tempt any type of judgment falling on me."

Since then, the boys quietly enjoyed their leisurely drive to church.

Every church in the city center was built from red brick and featured white trim and shutters, and most of them had bell towers. The First Presbyterian Church wasn't even the oldest in town—just over a hundred years old—but what it did have, unlike any other church, was Ada Yost Wright on the pipe organ. She'd learned to play in Boston and was traveling west with her family at the turn of the century. While her father wanted to continue to California, her mother felt Missouri was far enough, and they settled in the small hill-top community.

The other churches had lovely pianos, and one even saved up to buy a Steinway. Zeke heard there was a church outside the city limits that didn't have a piano or even allow music, which he thought was sad because music was often the only thing that kept him from falling asleep.

Climbing out the back of the station wagon, Zeke heard the rich chords Ada was playing inside. He started humming along to the ancient hymn as he jumped to the ground. He reached out and took Ruth's hand. "This was Daddy's favorite."

She looked down at him and tears rimmed her eyes. "Yes it was." She closed her eyes and started humming and then softly singing. "Lift up your heads, ye heavenly gates." She opened her eyes and moved her hand like the choir director. She pointed at Zeke.

"Behold the King of glory waits." His eyes shone bright.

Ruth pointed at Eli.

"Oh, Mom." He glanced around quickly and spoke just above a whisper. "The King of kings is drawing near."

She beamed and pointed at Ethan, who dropped his voice as low as he could.

"The Savior of the world is here!"

Ethan tucked his arm in the crook of Mother Harris.

"I'll sing inside." She pulled her arm close to her side—and Ethan along with it. "Where other voices can drown mine out a bit."

The group was met by a throng of others inside the church. Zeke wasn't fond of dressing up and wearing shoes, but he did appreciate the calm that came with "being in the house of the Lord." The stained-glass windows cast colorful arrays around the room, creating a sense of magic and wonder. He kept track of time by watching the light move across the walls. Depending on the time of year, when the purple hue hit the wooden attendance plaque, the children would be dismissed to continue their studies in the Sunday School room.

"Dang it!" Zeke put his hand on his head.

"Ezekiel! I've a good mind to take you outside and put a switch to you. Swearing in God's house like that."

He covered his mouth, and his eyes were wide. "I'm so sorry." Zeke spread his fingers. "I just remembered there's no Sunday School because of the potluck."

Ethan and Eli wore wide smiles as they laughed at him over their mother's shoulder. Her expression softened. "Well, food can make a boy crazy, so instead of a whippin' I'll come up with some extra chores for you when we get home."

"Yes, ma'am." She led her boys down the center aisle to the middle row of pews. The Ladies Group had reupholstered the pews the year before, adding firmer padding and a longer-wearing textile. They were still too hard for Zeke's liking, but he did appreciate the fuzzy feel of the fabric.

Ada broke into "Good Christian Friends, Rejoice," and those still mingling in the foyer knew it was their cue to sit down. There were no assigned seats, unlike school, but Zeke noticed most people sat in the same place every time. He knew before even turning around that the Trigg family was behind them. Earl and Mabel Trigg had seven stair-stepped-aged children ranging from seven to sixteen. They made up nearly half of the Sunday School class.

Zeke turned around and smiled at Caleb, Deborah, and Benjamin, the three youngest Triggs. They waved at him, and he returned the gesture. Eli's strong hand plopped on Zeke's head and turned him back toward the front where Pastor Woodbridge was at the pulpit.

"It's good to be in the house of the Lord today." The pastor's booming baritone voice filled the sanctuary. "Let us turn to Hymn 165, 'Nearer, My God, to Thee.'"

Zeke enjoyed Pastor Woodbridge's voice, but he pouted when he realized there wasn't a choir on the platform with the preacher. The young man not only liked listening to the choir but also appreciated that it usually took up five to ten minutes where he didn't have to hear a sermon.

The choir was on vacation this week on account of Martha Chaucer—the sweetest soprano this side of the Mississippi, according to her husband—was in Arkansas taking care of her oldest sister. This all came back to Zeke as he remembered overhearing his momma talking to Mrs. Miller when she dropped her off after work in the middle of the week. Apparently, Mrs. Chaucer's sister, Katherine or Katarina—Zeke's eavesdropping skills were not as good as they could be—had fallen ill from consumption.

"Consumption of too much of that vile spirit," Mrs. Miller spat.

Momma had put her hand on Mrs. Miller's arm and tapped it several times. "Mrs. Miller, we shouldn't speak ill of those who can't control themselves. Besides, she really could have consumption."

Zeke had to spring from his hiding place when the women headed to the door, so he never was sure what was consuming Mrs. Chaucer's sister, but he was sure that he missed the choir. He wasn't as sure that he missed her warbly high-pitched voice or not.

His thoughts were interrupted as Eli thrust an open hymnal at him. He smiled up at his oldest brother. Zeke recalled his first attempt to sing along being a disaster as he read the hymnal like he'd been taught to read a book. He belted out: "A-maz-ing grace, how sweet the sound, that 'twas grace that taught my heart to fear, and thro' man-y dan-gers, toils, and snares . . ."

Ruth had noticed that while the rest of the congregation was singing about how precious grace was, Zeke was singing about encountering dangers, toils, and snares. She'd sat beside him and explained how to sing along. She took his index finger in her hand and dragged it along the lyrics and jumped down to the proper line below. Zeke's mouth made a little O, and his eyebrows shot up. He'd been keeping up ever since.

Zeke looked down and realized he'd already missed the first two verses. If the choir were here, choir director Mr. Milton would have them sing all four verses, but Pastor Woodbridge tended to skip the third stanza and jump right to four. BillyJo told Zeke several years back in Sunday School the Baptist church always skipped the third verse. Zeke thought it might be nice to skip it most of the time because it was typically his least popular wording. Today, he was more focused on what would happen after church, but he joined in for the final verse.

"What a wonderful way to start our day together." The pastor closed his hymnal. "Before taking your seat, please greet your neighbors and let them know what you've brought for the potluck. I've seen some of the desserts already, and let me say, it is a good day to be here."

A cacophony of laughter, chatter, and hymnals dropping filled the room. Zeke shook hands with the Trigg children and waved across the aisle to Mr. and Mrs. Lewis. He knew they would have a plate of Miss Georgia's fried chicken and a platter of cookies "made" by Mrs. Lewis. The written Word wasn't the only gospel in the church on Potluck Sundays. Working at the Lewis home, it became clear to Zeke that there wasn't a hint of difference in the taste of Mrs.

Lewis's potluck items and what Miss Georgia made for him. He wasn't going to tell because there were times that he'd passed off Larry's answers as his own for his homework.

"Now that I've got you ready to feed your stomachs, let's feed your souls." The pastor smiled and opened the over-sized Bible on the pulpit. "Today's lesson is taken from Matthew chapter fourteen, verses fifteen to twenty-one. The miracle of feeding the 5,000. It seemed appropriate on this day as we share what we have with one another." The pastor cleared his throat. "Remember, a great crowd was following Jesus, it came up on supper time, and his disciples were worried because there were lots of people and none of them had brought any food. They told Jesus to send the people away so they could get their own victuals."

Zeke giggled thinking that the disciples said "vittles." He slouched in the pew trying to find a comfortable spot to endure the adult-size sermon that his child-size brain was about to hear. He leaned his head on the back of the bench. If he could turn his head a tad to the right and force his eyes as far right as they could go, he could take a census of those in attendance.

The sound of the sermon muffled in the back of his head as his pondered what victuals he may encounter after the pastor finished his preaching.

He smiled when he noticed Mrs. Doris Ryland two rows over. Her homemade apple cobbler was not only famous in Lafayette County but also across the river. Some restaurant owner in Kansas City heard of it and tried to buy the recipe. She declined his offer and gave him directions back to the highway. Her fried rabbit with biscuits and gravy was Zeke's favorite dish, but he knew she saved that meal for dinner at her house.

Zeke squinted to try and focus on the third pew back. It was either Mrs. Morgan—the mother of fellow Cub Scout

Carter Morgan—or it was her twin sister, who was a spinster. Zeke prayed it was Carter's mom because her baked bread typically brought home blue ribbons from every fair. On the other hand, the town agreed it was the lack of baking skills that kept Mrs. Morgan's sister single.

Somewhere between Pastor Woodbridge's mention of Jesus's disciples finding a boy willing to give up his food and asking to stand for the Benediction, Zeke enjoyed a nap. He rubbed sleep from his eyes as the parting words were spoken over the congregation. Ada played "It Is Well with My Soul" as adults filed out orderly and children raced around them to get to the Sunday School area.

Before Zeke could make it to the aisle, his mother grabbed his collar and turned him around. She corralled the boys around her and spoke softly. "Remember your manners, and don't overfill your plates." She pointed at Ethan. "One dessert each."

"Momma!" Zeke pleaded, his puppy-dog eyes and falsetto voice forcing her surrender.

"Oh, my goodness, how can I deny that?" She held his face in her hands. "Okay, two desserts each."

Eli and Ethan patted Zeke on the back. "Great job, Little Man." The oldest ruffled the youngest's hair.

The Sunday School room featured two rows of tables covered in fried chicken, fried catfish, homemade noodles, potato salad, green beans, corn on the cob, homemade rolls with jams and jellies, along with chocolate cake, triple-berry pie, chocolate chip cookies, brownies, and sliced fruit. There were tables and chairs in the corners for adults, and the children took their plates outside to eat.

Most of the children left their plates half-full, choosing to play tag instead of eating. Zeke was left alone under the shade tree. He noticed an untouched piece of chicken on an abandoned plate. Zeke slowly reached over, grabbed it, and put it on his own plate. He smiled and glanced around to see if anyone noticed. With no sign of protest, he chomped into the leg.

Eli came from behind the tree and sat next to him. "You don't want to play with your friends?"

"School starts tomorrow. I can play with them then." He took another bite. "This is my last chance to enjoy Miss Georgia's fried chicken for a while."

"I'm with you." Eli took a bite out of the fried catfish. "Man, is there anything better than food fried in lard?"

The boys shook their heads in agreement and continued to fill their stomachs.

"I had my eye on Miss Palmer's chocolate cake. You want me to get you a slice?" Eli stood up.

"No, but I'd love a piece of that berry pie and a cookie."

Eli returned with the desserts and their middle brother, who had a plate piled with cookies and cake.

"Ethan!" Zeke pointed at the topping tower. "Momma said."

"Oh, stop your whining." Ethan plopped down cross-legged and took off his shoes. "*I* only took two, but all the old church ladies kept saying 'how sad' and that I was 'nothing but skin and bones,' and *they* piled all this on here."

"Sometimes it pays to be poor, I guess." Eli reached over and took a cookie from Ethan's plate.

"Hey, knock it off."

"Were you not listening to the sermon? It's important to share." Eli reached for the plate again. "If you're not careful, I'll really help you learn that lesson."

"I got it." Ethan handed Zeke a cookie. "I got it."

The youngest brother smiled as he started his own cookie pile.

~~~

The Renick brothers were catnapping against the tree with their hands on full bellies. Their mother nudged Eli's foot. He stirred and roused his younger brothers.

"You boys look like you had your fill and then some." She smiled. "Mother Harris is ready to head on home. Are you boys joining us or walking?"

Ethan grabbed his shoes. "Shotgun!"

Their mother put her hands on her hips and tilted her head. The middle child blushed. "Middle seat?"

She nodded and lightly tapped the back of his head. "Eli? Ezekiel?"

"Curtis said some of the fellas are going to play catch at the pond. I was hoping to join them." Eli held up crossed fingers.

"You don't have your glove," Zeke piped up.

"I've got pretty tough hands." Eli turned his well-calloused hands over for Zeke to inspect.

"Okay, but be home before dark. School starts tomorrow, and I want you to have a full night's sleep." She looked at Zeke. "And what about you?"

"I think it's safer for me to walk on this full belly than ride with Mother Harris."

"Alright. Don't dawdle." She kissed his forehead.

"Aww, Momma." He rubbed off the kiss with the back of his hand.

Zeke walked down Main Street. With all the stores closed on Sunday, he took time to window shop at the five-and-dime store. He'd had enough candy and cookies in the past twenty-four hours, so his eyes barely registered the barrels of hard candies. Zeke's gaze stopped on the transistor radio kit. He knew his momma really loved listening to music. He'd seen her tap her toes and dance at the community barbeque. As much as he'd love to build the radio with Eli, he knew his momma would budget the money elsewhere. Zeke pondered asking Mr. Lewis for work, but he figured he'd have to work twice as long to make enough money for the kit.

His breath fogged the glass in front of him as he leaned on the window. Stepping back, he absentmindedly rubbed his jaw when he noticed the dentist sign across the street. Zeke skipped along the sidewalk. The uneven pavement tripped him and sent him sprawling to the ground. He popped up and brushed off his hands and pants. There was a slight fray by the knee patch and a quarter-sized scuff on the toe of his right shoe.

"Dagnabbit!" He sat on the edge of the sidewalk. Zeke slipped off the right shoe and spat on the toe. He vigorously rubbed it against his pants. He turned it over and grimaced. "Oh, man, Momma just got me this shoe." He spat on it again and then rubbed it with his thumb. Zeke felt the roughness of the scuff, but the color was shinier. He could see Willie's house and knew the Lewis residence was just a bit farther—then the crest of the road, after which it was all downhill from there—literally.

He took off the other shoe, tucked his socks inside, and started for home. Once he passed the last downtown business, he moved from the sidewalk to the front edge of the lawns. A sigh escaped his lips as the coolness of the grass soothed his feet. Zeke sprinted when he crossed in front of the Larsen house. He didn't want Willie to see him and charge him with trespassing.

He paused in front of the Lewis's home. The well-manicured grass and hedges set it apart even from the other fancy homes on the hilltop. In his mind's eye, he could see himself winning marble after marble from Willie. He remembered polishing the silver with Georgie. Zeke's eyes fell as he thought back a couple of days to the badge ceremony. It had been quite a summer.

He started down the hill. It was his first time down Myrick Road alone since he'd encountered Bigfoot months ago.

"Nothing bad happens in the daytime." He shoved his arms down by his side. "Onward!"

He kept to the dusty shoulder to avoid cars and the hot asphalt. He squinted and shielded his eyes from the glare bouncing off the Missouri. It was running well within its banks, heading east to join up with the Mississippi River.

Zeke peeked between the planks as he crossed the Lewis Creek bridge. He didn't see anything that made him think Charlie or another hobo had moved in under the bridge. Granted, Zeke couldn't see the secret cave tucked under the span. He stopped on the other end of the bridge. He was minutes from home, minutes from chores, minutes from the end of summer. He left his shoes on the side of the road and slid down the bank.

There were more weeds and less mud than he remembered. He made his way carefully to the edge of Lewis Creek. The bridge cast a massive shadow that kept his side of the creek cool. Zeke looked to the other side of the creek, which was choked with weeds, bushes, and small trees. He climbed up the berm to make sure a hobo wasn't hiding in the alcove under the bridge. It was all clear, so he scooted on his backside down the embankment. Zeke found a small log to sit on and listened to the creek.

A strangely shaped shadow caught his attention on the opposite bank. Zeke took a deep breath. There was no wretched odor. He threw a rock to the right of the shadow and several small game birds flew out of the bushes.

He laughed and nearly fell off the log.

"Great job." Zeke spoke aloud in an attempt to bolster his confidence. "Way to scare yourself. If nothing else, you'd think I'd be braver by now. How many other kids have fought Bigfoot and a bear in the same summer? Buck up, buddy!"

As he continued his pep talk, a dark shadow grew behind a tall brush. It looked smaller than the previous creature he'd encountered. "Are you a lost baby Bigfoot?" Zeke spoke low and his voice was barely audible.

It definitely looked like a head. Zeke could make out shoulders, too. He inhaled. Still no horrid smell. Zeke's pulse beat loudly in his ear as he continued to hold his breath. The shadow raised its arms and waved them wildly. Zeke furrowed his brow, and his heartbeat sounded louder in his ears.

"Zeke! Zeke! Up here. It's me, Larry."

"Huh?" Zeke gulped air and twisted his neck to look up at the bridge. Larry was standing on the edge waving both arms high over his head. Zeke glanced across the creek and knew he'd mistaken Larry's shadow for Bigfoot. "Eli's right. Nothing bad happens in the daytime."

"What?" Larry's voice boomed and echoed under the bridge.

"Nothing! How was Lake of the Ozarks? Catch any fish?"

"Yeah, it was nice. I'll meet you at the end of the bridge and tell you all about it."

"Okay. Wait by my shoes. I'll be quick."

Zeke watched Larry wave and head for the end of the bridge. When the youngest Renick child turned for one last glimpse of the opposite bank, he saw his friend's shadow move to the left. Which is why he was shocked to see a dark, furry creature move to the right. Zeke froze.

Bigfoot stopped midstride and looked at Zeke. The massive body was covered in matted ebony fur. Its face seemed softer in the light of day. Its eyes were a dark brown, rather than the soulless black Zeke glimpsed at his first encounter.

Zeke stood as tall as he could and waved with a half-raised arm. The creature slowed and tilted its head. The breeze switched directions, and a stomach-turning smell hit Zeke's nose.

"Oh my God!" His eyes watered as he covered his nose and mouth.

Bigfoot startled at Zeke's voice and moved into the shadow under the bridge.

"Wait, come back!" Zeke's foot slipped as he neared the edge of the berm. He glanced down to look for a solid foothold.

"Make up your mind!" Larry called from above. He was bent over at the waist. "First you say wait at the shoes. Then you scream at me to come back. What do you want?"

Zeke stared at the shadows across the creek. All he saw were bushes, weeds, and trees. He shook his head and rubbed his face with both hands.

"You okay, Zeke?"

"Yeah, I'm okay." He turned and jogged down the path toward his shoes and home, collecting Larry on the way.

CHAPTER TWENTY-SIX

LEXINGTON, MISSOURI, PRESENT DAY

"Back to the hotel to rest and regroup?" Nate started the car.

"No, physically I'm feeling okay." Zeke rolled down the window and put his forearm on the car door. "Let's drive over to my old house. I'd like to walk around and clear my head."

"Sounds good."

Zeke reclined the seat slightly. "How about some music?"

"It would be my pleasure." Nate pulled out his phone, tapped the musical note icon and scrolled to the "Tito's Tunes" playlist. "I made a playlist based on the artists you tend to sing along with the most. So let's start things off with Bill Haley & His Comets."

The older man smiled and tapped with the beat. The song's pace and lyrics matched his feeling of the passing of time.

The Main Street storefronts looked like he remembered them from his youth. The red brick alongside stone, with the occasional wood Victorian gingerbread, brought him back to childhood—running down the sidewalks and window shopping.

While the buildings were historically the same, the current businesses felt foreign to Zeke. There were antique stores, clothing boutiques, and artisan pubs. There was a national pharmaceutical chain where the movie theater used to be.

As they drove west down Main Street toward the river, the storefronts were skinnier and painted in bright colors.

"This part of town feels like they ripped up everything I knew and dropped in random things."

Nate turned the music down. "Is that a good or bad thing?"

"I guess that depends." Zeke stuck his arm out the window and pointed at the buildings. "If you need a chiropractor, oven-fired pizza, phone case, or gently worn clothes, it's probably a good thing." He rolled his head to face Nate. "Ha, I'm starting to sound like that cranky old guy in Room Seven."

The younger man snorted. "Aw, poor Mister Turner. He is a cranky one."

Zeke lolled his head to look back out the window. Empty lots signaled the end of Main Street. As Nate turned the car left onto the residential street, the older man recalled the families who lived in the two-story homes. He shook his head, and a slight smile curled on his lips as they passed Willie Larsen's house. The two-story antebellum brick house was typical of the Larsen family: pompous.

The music and drive down memory lane made Zeke nostalgic. He sat up and pointed across Nate's side. "My best friend, Larry. So many adventures with him. He lived down that street."

"Do you want to go see his house?"

"Nah, but thanks for the offer."

"You said 'lived.' Where does he live now?"

"Before he got married, he planned to go to school in St. Louis to be an architect." Zeke kept his eyes focused on the road ahead. "But then with the marriage and a kid, he ended up going to Richmond to be near her family. Last I heard, he'd moved up to running one of his in-law's car dealerships."

"Good for him."

"Yep, good for him." Zeke nodded.

The melancholy from missing his friend lifted as they hit the brick section of the road.

"It is nice that some things never change." Zeke exaggerated the bumpiness of the road by shaking his arms and head.

"I can tell you did not have your allergy meds." Nate's massive smile triggered both dimples. "It is going to be a long drive home."

"Probably." Zeke stopped shaking and reached for his seatbelt. "Let's stop here in front of Mr. Lewis's house. I don't know when—or if—I'll see this view again."

A smattering of high clouds provided hit-and-miss shade for the duo as they looked out over the river below. Zeke appreciated that no matter how people or buildings changed, the river stayed its course. Sure, sometimes it overflowed its banks and flooded their house, but it was still flowing east toward St. Louis and the Mississippi River.

Zeke tapped the hood of the car. "No use putting off the inevitable. Might as well tell our patrons the news right now."

"Are you sure?"

"Yep. Plus, look at the view. You'll have a hard time finding a prettier view."

"Alright. You're the boss."

"And let's do this live." Zeke clapped his hands.

"Are you sure?"

"Very sure. I finally feel like I know what I want to say."

Nate moved in front of Zeke. "This is perfect, I've got you, the bridge, the tracks, and the river. Looks great." The young man held up five fingers. "Five. Four." He lowered a finger as he counted down to one and pointed at Zeke.

"Hi everyone, I've been reading the comments, and I know you've been waiting for an update . . . and some of you would like a refund." Zeke looked down and let out a cleansing breath.

"If after this update, you still want to walk away, no hard feelings—and thank you for supporting our journey so far." He nodded quickly. "I—Nate and I—started this journey back in Florida, hoping to help a young man whose life had been impacted by Bigfoot. Reading his story, it reminded me of when I encountered the Wooly-Bully when I was kid, not far from where I'm standing right now. That night, my life was turned upside down. I really felt like I needed to get here and support that young man because I didn't feel like I had much support when I was a kid. And when I shared that with you, you supported me, and I'm forever grateful for that."

Nate's eyebrows started to rise as his eyes widened. He gave Zeke a thumbs up.

"Now, as you're painfully aware, I'm *not* a natural in front of a camera." The older man chuckled. "But I've always been honest with you. And that continues now, even if some or all of you may decide you've had enough. Trust me, there were moments these past few days when I had nearly enough and wanted to call it quits.

"This morning, I went to the courthouse to share my thoughts with the judge about the accident. I'm not allowed to talk about everything that happened, but I can tell you after listening to Jimmy Nixon's story that I do not believe Bigfoot, a bear, a deer, or any other animal was involved in his accident. Also, it's true after our video showing the Wooly-Bully running up the hill, a group of people descended on the spot looking for—and some even going so low as to create—evidence. But . . ." Zeke stepped toward Nate and pointed at the camera on the phone. The screen blurred as the finger pulled the shot out of focus. The younger man held up a hand and motioned for Zeke to move back. He stepped back and retracted his arm but kept pointing.

". . . But!" Zeke continued. "But I still believe that all those years ago, on this road, by that bridge, I had a face-to-face encounter with Bigfoot . . . twice."

Nate's jaw dropped and his hand fell, sweeping the shot from Zeke to the road to the sky and finally, back to Zeke.

"The last Sunday of that summer, I walked down this road by myself. My oldest brother, Eli, would tell me nothing bad happens in the daytime." He smiled, looked up toward heaven, and reminisced about the past. "I climbed down the berm and made my way back to Lewis Creek. That's when I saw it again. In the day, the Wooly-Bully didn't seem as scary. Don't get me wrong, my heart was pounding so hard I thought it would jump out of my chest. But in the light of day, there was something in the way he looked at me. You know, kinda like when a dog tilts their head at you."

Zeke tilted his head to the left, and Nate angled the phone to mirror the move.

The older man continued: "And you kinda feel you have to do the same. In that moment, it's like you and the dog make some sort of connection. Real or imagined. There's a little bubble of joy that floats up into your heart and you have a little laugh."

Zeke shook his head and ran his hands through his hair.

"That's the feeling that I had when I met Bigfoot that last Sunday before school started up again. It was like we'd both had more than we bargained for that summer. I wasn't scared of Bigfoot after that. Granted, until a few days ago, I hadn't really thought about it."

Zeke looked straight into the camera. Sunlight danced in his hazel eyes. "No matter what happens, it's been a pretty exciting few days. Thank you." He waved until he heard Nate call "cut."

Nate rushed to him and showed him the screen. "Look at all the love, Uncle!"

Zeke moved the younger man's hand back and forth to find a distance in focus. Happy faces, hearts, and thumbs-up emojis exploded from the bottom of the phone and floated up the screen. There were the occasional red mad faces and middle fingers, but the vast majority of emojis and comments were positive.

> **@TheRealBigfoot** I remember that day. You wore blue. I wore black. Good times. #Believe
>
> **@SamCarr23** I appreciate your honesty. I'm not going anywhere. I love following you and Nate. Where are you going next? Did you see that report of Bigfoot in Colorado? #BigfootBeliever #TeamZeke
>
> **@TheBigfootFanPage** Too little too late #FakeNews
>
> **@BoredSquidNT** LLOL my dog just tilted his head #Bigfoot #OnlyBelieve
>
> **@CyrptoZooLover** I'm with @SamCarr23 where are you going next? Oregon is nice this time of year, and Bigfoot is seen here a lot. #TeamZeke

"Wow. I didn't expect that." Zeke rubbed his eyes. "I thought we'd be eating Spam all the way home."

"Not unless you want to enjoy a few days of glamping."

"No, I've got more energy, but these old bones still enjoy a nice bed."

"Well, get your old bag of bones in the car, and we'll roll down to say goodbye to your house."

Seeing the empty lot this time felt less jarring to Zeke but just as empty. Nate pulled the car off the road, and Zeke took a deep breath before opening the door and swinging his legs around. He sat there, unmoving.

"Uncle, are you okay?"

He nodded and grabbed his folded bucket hat from the glove compartment. "It's still shocking to see. When you're a kid, you never think one day your house will be gone."

Zeke stood up and stretched his arms wide. "Shoot, all of this would flood pretty much every year. We'd have inches of mud in the house along with various creatures brought in with the rising water. And the house still stood." He shook his head and pinched the bridge of his nose. "But now, it's gone. It's only real in here." He tapped his head.

"While you say your final goodbyes, I'm going to walk back up along the river and get some video to put in future posts."

"Don't let the Wooly-Bully get ya." Zeke winked.

Nate let out a worried laugh and cleared his throat. "Nothing bad ever happens in the daytime, right?"

"Sure." With a slight nod, Zeke waved as the younger man walked back toward Lewis Creek. He loved repeating what his older brother had told him, but Zeke never told anyone that the training mission Eli died in was during the day. Zeke knew bad things could happen whenever, but at least during the day, you usually saw them coming.

Zeke walked to the back edge of the property, still lined with bushes. He pushed his way through the thorn-covered branches and stepped on to the rocks covering the railroad berm. Zeke picked up a silvery stone and ambled up to the tracks. He tossed the rock in his hand a few times before throwing it with a "*harrrr*" toward the river. It landed far short of the water.

"I still stink at throwing. Even as a grown-up I can't throw." Zeke chuckled at his lack of athleticism. He turned and saw Nate slowly making his way toward Lewis Creek. "I think I might be a little more sporty than *him*, though," Zeke mumbled as he watched Nate stumble through the bushes. A warm smile turned up the older man's lips and he pulled on the front of his hat to block the sun.

~~~

Nate was cursing himself for not wearing walking shoes to go walking and cursing Mother Nature for creating flora that scratched, clung, and caused itching. The one thing he was thankful for was having the foresight to film the destination, not the journey.

He walked to the top of the bank of Lewis Creek. The sun was high overhead. He brought the camera up and back toward the bridge. The sunbursts through the bridge spans caused him to shut his eyes. Nate moved his arm in a sweeping motion to pan the bridge and continue down the other side of the creek.

Sunspots danced in his vision, creating white and blue spots as he blinked to help his sight return. A few of the blue dots mixed with dark shadows on the other side of the creek. Nate thought it looked like a snowman, then a deer, then a giraffe. With each blink, the spots jumped to new locations.

Nate rubbed his eyes and rolled his head. There were loads of *cracks* and *pops*, followed by a *thump*. He froze in place. The last sound was not from his neck but across the river. Nate squinted in the direction he thought the sound came from, and a cold tingle ran down his spine. There was a dark outline of the creature. Its head appeared rounder than the one they saw at the park. Nate tilted his head, and the creature mirrored the motion. He was reaching for his camera when the creature's arms shot into the air and waved like crazy.

"What the . . ."

Laughter exploded above him as he turned to see Zeke jumping and waving his hands on the bridge.

"I would have given anything to see your face," the older man called down.

"Oh, you think you're so funny." Nate raised a fist to the sky. "You're lucky I've been raised to respect my elders."

Zeke held his midsection. "I couldn't resist. I saw you taking a long time to get over here, so I thought if I could beat you to the spot, it'd be funny. Come on, it's at least a little bit funny."

Nate's smile said he found it at least a little funny.

~~~

Back on the road, Nate turned to Zeke. "Was *that* the same Wooly-Bully you saw?"

"At first, yes." Zeke explained Larry's surprise visit. "But after Larry left the bridge, I saw the real Bigfoot. The way it looked at me was like it knew I was the kid who threw marbles at it, but he didn't seem upset about it."

"You got all that from one look?"

"You sound like my brothers." He pulled the bucket hat off and stuck it in the glove box. "I don't know how to explain it. It's like the way a stray dog looks at you. You know it's not going to hurt you, but at the same time, it could. But the way it tilts its head tells you you'll be friends from afar."

Zeke looked over at Nate, who continued to watch the road with his hands at nine and three. "It's silly and crazy. I know. This whole thing feels silly and crazy."

"You're being a little hard on yourself, Tito." Nate pointed out the driver's side window with his right hand and swept it across the windshield. "Even today, this place looks like the perfect hiding place for Bigfoot. There are some parts of this country that are left feeling wild, and who knows what's out there?"

"You think Bigfoot is out there?" Zeke waved his arm out the window.

"I don't know if it's *right* there, but we *definitely* saw something. And look at all the other people who came through after your video. There are loads of people who believe."

"And we have a boatload of them as patrons." Zeke's eyes got big as saucers. "What if we kept them?"

"Kept them?"

"The patrons. What if we kept checking out Bigfoot reports?"

CHAPTER TWENTY-SEVEN

LEXINGTON, MISSOURI, PRESENT DAY

"You want to become Bigfoot hunters?" Nate's eyes were wide.

"Kinda. I haven't had so much fun in a long time." Zeke's smile stretched from ear to ear as he stepped into the hotel parking lot. "We could just do it on our way back to Florida. Couldn't hurt could it?"

Nate rubbed the back of his neck. "I'm all for adventure, but . . ."

"What? Have I been keeping you from a Mrs. Francisco Abayon Villanueva?"

"Huh? No."

"A Mr. or Them Francisco?" Zeke winked. "Are you blushing?"

"No, no, and no." Nate bit his lower lip. "I mean I do have a girlfriend, but she's studying in Tampa, so she's not missing me."

"Aw, that's sad." Zeke patted the young man's shoulder. "I wonder if I'd miss you if given the chance?"

Nate pushed him away and laughed. "You are so mean."

"I'm taking that as a yes." The older man's eyebrows shot up. "Hey, ask the patrons where they think we should go, and then we'll pick a winner. Oh, the person we pick could get all the goodies you've been buying."

"Not a bad idea. I'll get that sent out." Nate opened his room door and Zeke followed him inside.

"Sounds great." The older man took a seat at the small table. "While we wait, you can tell me about Angel."

"Who's Angel?"

"Your girlfriend." Zeke smiled.

"Her name is Reyna."

"Gotcha." Zeke clicked his tongue and pointed to the chair opposite him. "Do tell me more."

"Only if you tell me more about how you stayed friends with your business partner and ex-wife Claire after their affair."

Zeke gave two thumbs up to accept the deal. "But you first."

"I met Reyna when we were in elementary school in Pensacola. Her family moved to the Tampa area, but our families kept in touch." Nate got up and went to the mini fridge for a bottle of water. "Her family came to my college graduation. It was nice to see her again. My family plans to go to her graduation." He sat and took a long drink.

Zeke stared at him as he chugged the water.

After a long *aaaaahhh* from Nate, the older man drummed his fingers.

"That's it?"

"That's it."

"You've seen her once since sixth grade, and she's your girlfriend? Do your families expect you'll marry?"

"Yes, and probably. She's a great person. She's also Filipino, so it's a good match."

Zeke shook his head and rubbed his face with both hands. "Wow, that's somethin'."

"My parents' story is similar, and they've been married nearly fifty years. My grandparents were married for seventy."

"Better track record than me."

"Speaking of . . ." Nate's phone vibrated.

"Saved by the bell." Zeke brushed the back of his hand across his forehead. *"Phew."*

"Hello, Mr. Johnston." Nate muted the phone and mouthed "The Palms" to Zeke. "Yes, Mr. Renick is doing okay. Yes, we were able to get his additional medication, and we're heading back tomorrow. Yes, sir, we'll be careful."

"Did they seem like they were on to us?" Zeke asked.

"He sounded like he usually does, though there may have been a hint of worry."

"Good, any feedback from the patrons?"

Nate opened the app and pulled up his latest post. The replies flew by on his screen. "This could take a while, Uncle."

"I've got nothing but time." Zeke joined him on the small couch.

@TheRealBigfoot01 Oh, feels great to have you still on the hunt. But ditch the middle of the country, and come play hide-and-seek with me in Oregon. #Bigfoot #Sasquatch #CatchMeIfYouCan #TeamZeke

Nate looked up from the screen. "Is just me, or does sometimes it feel like @TheRealBigfoot01 *is* The Real Bigfoot? I mean I know the Wooly-Bully doesn't have a phone, but this guy."

Zeke closed his eyes and shook his head. "And *I'm* the one under observation."

@BiggerFooted33 There was a sighting in Jonesboro AK. Lady said something came out from the trees nearly scared her & her dog to death. #Bigfootsightings #TeamZeke

@BelieverMO1 IMO keep looking in MO. Loads of reports up and down the state. Teens reported seeing massive reddish-brown ape-man outside of Branson. Take in a show while you're there. #Bigfoot #cryptid

@TheBigfootFanPage Not ready to totally say you're legit, but I'll give you another chance. Three different people reported chuffing sounds and wood knocks in Snohomish County. #BigfootBeliever #Sasquatch

@CanucksBGr8 It's cold this time of year, but last week there was a report of a rust-colored #Bigfoot crossing HWY 3 outside of Elko. BC not NV.

@PetiteDancer24 Hikers spotted something in the woods around Cumberland Caverns in Tenn. #BigfootSighting #TeamNate #Team Zeke #TeamZete

@BawdyGoddess00 Looking for Bigfoot and a good time, head to Grass Lake, Illinois, boys

@BoredSquid . . .

"Wait, go back to that last one." Zeke reached over to stop Nate from scrolling.

"You can read without your glasses!" Nate made an exaggerated O with his mouth and covered it with his hand. "Color me shocked."

"Oh, hush." The older man chuckled.

"Let's look for sightings that take us south. How's that?"

"Doesn't sound as exciting as Illinois, but you're the driver." Nate started scrolling again.

@BoredSquidNT 3 sighting in 3 days Bigfoot's Tennessee triangle Smithville, Sparta, McMinnville; dark brown Bigfoot seen by 2 couples near cave and I saw a dark red Bigfoot while hiking

@ChiefBakerCandleMaker Reports of loud roars, chest beating, & wood knocking near Natchez.

"Hold up a sec. Did the Squid say they *saw* it?" Zeke blinked.

Nate reversed his scrolling. "Yeah, 'I saw a dark red Bigfoot.' Let's Google Smithville, Sparta, and McMinnville . . . it's just a little east of Nashville. And another person mentioned activity near Cumberland Caverns, not far from there. Shall I put a pin in it?"

Zeke raised his eyebrows.

"Should I mark it on the map?"

"Yes, please." Zeke rubbed his hands together. "Maybe we can stop in Nashville and take in a few honkytonks."

Nate gave a thumbs up. "And a karaoke bar."

"And a karaoke bar."

Nate dropped his phone on his lap and threw his head back and sighed.

"What's the matter? I said yes to karaoke."

"No, no, I appreciate that, that's not it." Nate rubbed his face. "I forgot about your medicine. We can't spend several days in Tennessee and show up late to the facility without them being suspicious."

Zeke's eyes swept back and forth and then a slight smile formed. "*Aaa-choo! Cough, cough*!" He pretended to sneeze, then coughed into his hand.

The younger man rolled his shoulders. "Bless you?"

"Oh my gosh, did you never fake sick to avoid going to school? Or church?"

"Ah, you are very clever, Tito."

"Thank you."

The next morning, Zeke rose early and headed to the lobby for a lackluster continental breakfast for the last time.

"Oh, my sainted aunt." The aroma of a perfect cup of coffee, thick-sliced applewood smoked bacon, and fresh-baked pastries hit Zeke's nose before his eyes could comprehend what they were seeing. This was the breakfast promised on the freeway billboard.

The front doorbell was still ringing when a tall, blond twentysomething came out of the office.

"Good morning, I'm Tyson. Let me know if you need any help."

"Tyson, I need a time machine to go back and have you here for each day of my stay."

The young man smiled. "Yeah, I heard things were a bit rough. Hopefully today will make up for it."

Zeke held up a steaming disposable cup of java. "So far, so good, young man."

The older man piled his plate with bacon, scrambled eggs, and a pastry. "If you don't mind, I'll pick up the paper at the door and bring it back when we leave later this morning."

"Wow, things were really lax while I was gone." Tyson disappeared behind the door marked "Employees Only" and came back with a newspaper and a tray. "We keep extra papers here for guests. The tray will help you get it all back to your room safely."

Zeke's jaw dropped. "Figures that the day I leave, this place turns into paradise."

Tyson chuckled. "You can leave all the dishes in the room. Just drop your key cards in the jar when you're ready to check out."

"Sounds like a plan."

The younger man headed back to the office, and Zeke loaded the tray, adding a couple of oranges, an apple, a small plate of bacon, and a banana nut muffin for Nate.

~~~

Zeke knocked on the adjoining room door. "Breakfast is served, Sleeping Beauty."

A minute later, Nate stumbled sleepy-eyed through the door. His eyes widened as the sights and smells of Zeke's haul hit his senses.

"Where has this been our whole stay?" He quick-stepped to the table.

"Apparently, Tyson is the only one who knows how to make breakfast."

"Who?"

"The kid running the lobby today."

"They let a kid run the lobby?"

"Well, I guess he's twenty-five. Tops."

Nate laughed. "We probably graduated the same year."

Zeke blew a raspberry.

The younger man laughed. "Yes, *we* are the kids."

"Don't you have a phone call to make?" Zeke took a piece of bacon and followed it with a gulp of coffee.

Nate grabbed his phone and dialed The Palms. He tapped the speaker mode button. Zeke toasted him with his coffee cup. The phone rang twice before the automated system answered. The orderly turned Bigfoot hunter didn't need to listen to the menu—he punched in the extension for administration.

"Good morning, this is The Palms, senior living at its finest. How may I help you?"

"Terri, is that you? It's Nate."

"Oh, hey, Nate. Mr. Johnston said you and Mr. Renick would be heading back today. Everything going okay? Was it a nice service?"

"It was a nice service."

Zeke pinched his hand like a sock puppet, opening and closing the "mouth." With his other hand, he made circular motions, urging Nate to hurry up.

Nate furrowed his brow and covered his mouth with his hand and mimed sneezing. The older man's eyebrows shot up.

"But," Nate lowered his voice and used his serious orderly tone.

"But what, Nate?" Terri's voice went up two octaves.

"I should probably tell Mr. Johnston first." Nate pointed at Zeke, who started coughing and sneezing.

"Is that Mr. Renick?" Terri's voice continued to climb the register. "He sounds horrible."

"Yeah, it's him." Nate held out a hand and lowered it. Zeke's coughing and wheezing sounds slowed. "He was fine yesterday, but he has a fever this morning. I'm afraid he may have caught something. We're going to need some more time before we get back."

"Sure, sure. He needs to rest."

"That's what I told him. He still wanted to come back today because of his meds, but I told him he needs to rest."

"Aw, how sweet, he wants to come back."

Zeke rolled his eyes and cleared his throat hard.

"Oh my god, Nate. That sounds like he's got fluid buildup in his lungs. Should I call the local hospital there to have him checked out?"

Nate shot Zeke a sideways glance. "Oh, I'm sure it won't come to that."

"Okay, but keep me in the loop." The sound of papers shuffling filled the air. "And I'll send a scrip to the pharmacy you used the other day and let Mr. Johnston know you'll be needing a few more days."

"Thank you, Terri. That's a big help."

"It's too bad Mr. Renick got sick. I know the administrators didn't want him to go in the first place, and this will probably mean he won't get out again."

Zeke choked on his fake cough. He opened his mouth to speak, but Nate held up a hand with a raised finger.

"Yeah. It's too bad."

"Tell Mr. Renick I hope he's feeling better soon."

Zeke made a pouty face at the phone.

"Will do. Thanks, Terri."

Nate had barely ended the call when Zeke jumped to his feet and started pacing the room.

"I won't get *out* again? Hah! At this point, I'm betting I'll never go *in* again."

"Remember your blood pressure." Nate patted a chair. "Sit down and let's look at the paper."

The older man let out a long sigh and plopped down into the chair. "At least, there's good food to go with today's reading."

"Cheers to that." Nate raised his coffee mug and took a sip. "Oh, man, that's good. Now let's see if we made the paper. Yep, here we are, nice big headline, 'Judge Mulls Charges Against Star Quarterback; Bigfoot Ruled Hoax.'"

"Does it say what charges?" Zeke asked between bites.

"No specifics, really." Nate shook his head. "It mentions conflicting testimony but doesn't list any possible charges. They're probably wait for us to leave town."

Zeke and Nate laughed.

~~~

The duo headed to the hospital pharmacy to pick up the prescription. Nate added the vitamin D and cholesterol meds to the medical travel bag and put the allergy pills in his backpack.

"If I'm not taking those, why not just toss them?" Zeke asked before getting into the car.

"They're evidence at this point." Nate started the car. "That's how I see it. If we say the pharmacist said they were allergy meds, not blood thinners, but we don't have any physical proof, it becomes a classic he-said-she-said situation. And you know how it goes—when they talk, they win."

The older man nodded. "You got that right."

"Next stop, Tennessee."

Zeke made loose fists and tapped his legs. "Onward!"

SHOW ME STATE POTLUCK RECIPES

There are few things as key to memory as food. The sights, smells, and tastes can take a person back to an exact moment in time.

Growing up in Southern California, I enjoyed pretty standard Americana fare: Sunday roast with potatoes and carrots, bologna on white bread with a single slice of American cheese, fried chicken and mashed potatoes. Of course, there was the occasional international flare—pepperoni pizza, taquitos, and French fries tossed in for good measure.

When we visited my dad's family in Missouri, I knew I'd been missing out on a whole other level of cuisine. I remember the first time I had my uncle Wayne's fried catfish, mainly because I can't remember eating any type of fish before his (unless you count cafeteria fish sticks and canned tuna). Also, we'd all gone out fishing and caught the slippery bottom-feeders ourselves.

I have very few memories of my aunt Doris outside of the kitchen. If she wasn't cooking something when we arrived, she'd jump in there to fix us up something. While I understand her fried rabbit is amazing, I didn't get to try it. However, I had some of her fried frog legs, and they were amazing. (My dad and cousins would go out giggin' overnight to catch the hoppers. One morning on their return, a few frogs tried to escape the pickups and go through the yard. This story only ends well for the humans.)

When writing a book inspired by my dad's childhood, there was no way I could do it without acknowledging the food and, sometimes, lack thereof. My dad talked about going hungry, but never with sadness or anger—it just was what it was. He also talked about potlucks and gatherings where he'd eat like a king. Based on photographic evidence, his life was more the former than the latter.

Instead of complaining, he would talk about food and meals like they were long-lost friends. He'd close his eyes, and a slight smile would curl on his lips as he talked about eating squirrel and gravy or mashed potatoes and fried chicken. My dad never met a chicken he didn't like.

In honor of him, his hometown, and home cooks everywhere, I asked my Missouri family to share some of their recipes for this book. I got hungry just talking to them, and I'm planning a trip back to the Show Me State to enjoy some potluck fare myself.

Bear in mind, many recipes were handed down through word of mouth. There were some jotted down on recipe cards, but time and various food splatters have not been kind to things written in the 1900s.

My cousins and I have done our best to get these recipes as close as possible to having a shot at being recreated. Granted, it may be hard to find lard or Crisco these days, and for general health, substitutions may be sought out.

Many recipe ingredients are "to taste" because no one remembers how much actually gets added. Again, we've done our best to figure out pinches, dashes, teaspoons, tablespoons, and cups.

And finally—to keep the lawyers smiling—please, check the Department of Health's recommended temperatures for all meats.

Happy eating!

SHOW ME STATE POTLUCK RECIPES

Mains and Sides
Uncle Wayne's Fried Catfish
Gertie Mom's Frozen Coleslaw
Aunt Doris's Fried Rabbit and Gravy
Uncle R.B.'s Loose-Meat Burgers
Aunt Nancy's Chicken and Dumplings
Cousin Jonna's BBQed Fried Chicken
Cousin Sue's Chicken Supreme Casserole

Desserts
Aunt Margie's Chocolate Supreme
Aunt Doris's Apple Cobbler
Aunt Geraldine's Fruit Cocktail Cake
Cousin Shelley's Strawberry Dump Cake
Grandma Lula's Angel Food Cake
Great-Aunt Grace's Chocolate Sauce

Uncle Wayne's Fried Catfish
Ingredients
Catfish filets
* 1 C flour
* 1 C cornmeal
Salt, to taste
Pepper, to taste
Garlic salt, to taste
Lard
Directions
In a large Ziploc bag, combine dry ingredients.

Put filets in bag, no more than two at a time. Squeeze the bag to make sure each filet is coated.

In a large skillet, melt enough lard to fry catfish. Make sure the lard is very hot before adding filet.

Fry in lard until crisp and golden brown.

Remove and dry on paper towels.

* Depending on the number of filets, you can increase or decrease this amount. Make sure it's always equal parts flour to cornmeal.

Gertie Mom's Frozen Coleslaw

Ingredients

1 head cabbage, shredded

1 C vinegar

¼ C water

2 C sugar

Directions

Put cabbage in a 9x13 tray*

In a small saucepan, combine vinegar, water, and sugar, and bring to a boil for 1 minute.

Let mixture cool to room temperature, pour over cabbage, stir, cover with foil, put in freezer.

The longer it's in the freezer, the better the flavor.

Before serving, let thaw in fridge for several hours.

* Gertie Mom would often make large sheet trays of the frozen coleslaw that she stored in a deep freezer and later serve during a fish fry. Today's chef may want to use a food storage container.

Aunt Doris's Fried Rabbit and Gravy
Ingredients
Crisco or lard
Rabbit, cut into legs, thighs, breast
Flour, some to cover rabbit, 2 tbs for gravy
Salt, to taste
Pepper, to taste
Directions
In a heavy skillet, melt enough shortening for shallow frying of rabbit on medium-high heat.

In a bowl, mix flour, salt, and pepper.

Roll rabbit in dry ingredients, add to hot liquid in skillet until golden brown. Cover with lid to finish.

Remove rabbit from skillet, do not drain pan.

Gravy
Add about 2 tablespoons of flour to remnants in skillet, stir until brown. Add milk for desired consistency.

* If rabbit is still tough, put in baking pan with onions and water in 325° oven until tender.

Uncle R.B.'s Loose-Meat Burgers

Ingredients

1 package fresh med. size buns

5 lbs of hamburger

2-3 beef bouillon cubes

1 tbsp seasoned salt

1 tbsp garlic salt

1 tbsp ground black pepper

1 tbsp minced onions

1/2 package onion soup mix

Directions

Cook your hamburger slowly, chopping into very small (tiny *tiny*) pieces as it cooks. Do not drain once cooked.

Place in a large soup-type pot.

Mix all other ingredients together in a bowl and pour over the hamburger meat.

Cook this slowly for at least four to five hours.

*You can put into a Crock-Pot if you don't want to watch it, but the taste is better if you stick with it.

Aunt Nancy's Chicken and Dumplings
(This recipe requires chicken to be cooked the night before.)

Ingredients
Chicken thighs (as many as you think four people eat)
2 cans of buttermilk biscuits
1 package frozen noodles
Water
Chicken bouillon cube
Galic powder, to taste
Salt, to taste
Pepper, to taste

Directions
The night before, boil chicken thighs. After thighs have cooled, place in refrigerator.

Debone and shred chicken.

Put water on to boil.

Open can of biscuits.

When water boils, add shredded chicken thighs and bouillon cube.

Pinch off pieces of biscuit dough (the size depends on how big you like your dumplings).

Add noodles to pot.

Add garlic, salt, and pepper.

When biscuits and noodles are cooked, it's done.

Cousin Jonna's BBQed Fried Chicken

Ingredients

Chicken, whole, or just your favorite parts

BBQ sauce* (your favorite)

Directions

Preheat oven to 325 degrees.

Fry chicken as usual.

Cover the bottom of a 9x13 casserole dish with some of the BBQ sauce.

Arrange fried chicken on top of sauce.

Cover chicken with remaining sauce.

Cover dish with aluminum foil, poke a few holes for venting.

Put in oven for 20 minutes or until sauce is bubbly.

Cousin Jonna highly encourages eaters to take extra sauce for dipping.

*Cousin Jonna's favorite is KC Masterpiece.

Cousin Sue's Chicken Supreme Casserole

Ingredients

1 (3 lbs) chicken, baked

3 to 4 C chicken pan drippings/chicken broth

1 ½ stalks celery, diced

½ onion, chopped

2 to 3 tbsp butter

½ lb grated American or Cheddar cheese

1 can mushroom soup

2 sleeves or 3 C crushed Ritz crackers

4 eggs, unbeaten

Salt, to taste

Pepper, to taste

Directions

Preheat oven to 350 degrees.

Bake chicken in oven, save drippings, let chicken cool.

Pull chicken off the bones, chop it up.

If less than 3 C of drippings, add chicken broth to reach at least 3 C of liquid.

In large bowl, combine chopped chicken and drippings/broth. Set aside.

Sauté onions, celery, and butter until tender.

Add onions and celery to chicken and mix.

Add cheese, soup, crackers, eggs, salt, and pepper to chicken. Mix well.

Pour into greased 9x13 casserole dish.

Bake 45 minutes to an hour.

Aunt Margie's Chocolate Supreme
Ingredients
First layer
1 C flour
½ C oleo
½ C chopped pecans
Second layer
8 oz package cream cheese
1 C powdered sugar
1 C cool whip
Third layer
2 packages instant pudding*
3 C milk
Top layer
Cool whip
Pecan, chopped (optional)

Directions
Preheat oven to 350 degrees.
Mix **first layer** ingredients in a bowl.
Press mixture into bottom of 9x13 baking pan**
Bake for 15 minutes.
Remove from oven and let cool.

For **second layer**, mix cream cheese and powdered sugar until smooth.
Fold in cool whip.
Gently spread on cool crust.

(continued)

Mix **third layer** ingredients and pour over second layer.
Top with cool whip, as much as you like.
Sprinkle with chopped pecan (optional).
Refrigerate at least 12 hours.
* Margie uses one box of chocolate and one box of vanilla.
** Margie uses a 9x13 glass pan.

Aunt Doris's Apple Cobbler
Ingredients
Crust
1 C Crisco or lard
2 C flour
3-4 tbsp cold water
1 tsp vinegar
Filling
Apples, sliced
½ C sugar (Less if the apples are sweet)
1 tsp cinnamon
½ tsp nutmeg
½ tsp cloves*
Directions
Mix filling ingredients until apples are well coated.

Mix topping ingredients together. Roll out crust into two large rectangles. Put one in the bottom and fold up the sides of the pan. Put in filling. Cover with remaining crust.

Brush top with butter and sprinkle with sugar.

Bake at 350 degrees for about an hour or until crumble is golden brown.

*Original recipe called for whole cloves. It's been altered to avoid having to spit out cloves.

Aunt Geraldine's Fruit Cocktail Cake
Ingredients
Cake
2 C flour
2 C sugar
2 tsp baking soda
1 tsp salt
2 eggs, slightly beaten
1 tsp vanilla
1 can fruit cocktail with syrup
Directions
Stir ingredients together.
Bake at 325 degrees for 45 minutes.

Icing
1 stick of butter
1 C sugar
½ can evaporated milk
½ C coconut
½ C chopped pecans
1 tsp vanilla
Directions
Combine first three ingredients in a saucepan and bring to a boil over medium heat. Continue to boil, stirring occasionally, for two minutes.

Add remaining three ingredients, stir, pour over hot cake, and smooth evenly.

Garnish with whipped cream.

* This cake is best kept on the counter for a few days. If stored in the fridge, the cold air changes the texture of the icing.

Cousin Shelley's Strawberry Dump Cake

Ingredients

1 box strawberry cake mix

1 can strawberry pie filling

Small bag frozen strawberries

8 oz cream cheese

½ C powdered sugar

1 stick of butter

Directions

Preheat oven to 350 degrees.

Spray bottom of 9x13 cake pan.

Dump frozen strawberries and pie filling into the bottom of the cake pan.

In a mixing bowl, beat softened cream cheese and powdered sugar until smooth.

Drop spoon-sized blobs of cream cheese mixture over strawberry topping.

With a spatula or butter knife, spread the mixtures.

Sprinkle cake mix over the mixture. DO NOT STIR. Lightly and evenly spread mixture.

Cut butter into several pats and place like a checkerboard on top of cake mix.

Bake 25 to 30 minutes.

* Serve warm with fresh strawberries, ice cream, or whipped cream.

Grandma Lula's Angel Food Cake

Ingredients

1 C cake flour

1 ½ C sugar, divided in half

12 large egg whites (Important: NO yolk bits)

½ tsp salt

1 ½ tsp vanilla

1 ½ tsp cream of tartar

Directions

Preheat oven to 375 degrees.

In a medium bowl, sift flour and ¾ C sugar, set aside.

In a large bowl, whip egg whites, vanilla, cream of tartar, and salt to medium stiff peaks.

Slowly add remaining ¾ C sugar and beat to stiff peaks.

Slowly fold in dry ingredients. Be careful not to overmix or the cake won't be fluffy.

Pour batter into non-greased tube pan.

Bake 40 to 45 minutes.

Cool upside down on a glass bottle or wire rack.

Great-Aunt Grace's Chocolate Sauce
Ingredients
1/3 C unsweetened cocoa powder
3 tbsp all-purpose flour
1 C sugar
1 pinch salt
1 ½ C milk
3 tbsp butter
1 tsp vanilla
Directions
In a medium saucepan, whisk together the cocoa powder, flour, sugar, and salt.

Pour in milk and whisk until all lumps are gone.

Place pan over medium heat and cook 5 to 7 minutes, stirring constantly, until it just beings to boil and thicken.

Once thick, remove from heat, and stir in butter and vanilla. Stir until butter is melted.

Cool slightly before spooning over slices of angel food cake (or hot over ice cream).

ACKNOWLEDGEMENTS II

There are so many people to thank for helping this story come to life in the best way possible.

Beta readers Debbie Davis, Matthew Johnson, Katelyn Rowland, Maddy Ryen, and Ryan Whitesitt—your critiques and kind words were the perfect blend of butt-whooping and hugs to help tighten the story and keep my ego intact.

Special shoutout to my cousin Amy Caccamo who dispensed medical information, which I promptly ignored. Any inaccuracies are totally mine. Thanks to Laura Jensen Walker for early reads and edits. Any grammar errors are all mine.

There were several times when my brain fogged and my fingers faltered, and I wasn't sure how to stay consistent with my writing at times. Thanks to #1000WordsofSummer and Inkers 10K Words in 5 Days Writing Challenge for coming along at the right time and helping me reach my word count.

My Missouri family showed me so much love during this project. I received recipes from Wayne, Frank, Margie, Sherilyn, Jonna, Donna, Shelley, Ryan, Nancy, Stevie, Allison, Robin, Sandra, and Shelly.   Extra love to Uncle Wayne for always answering the phone and chatting about life in 1956 Lexington and his beloved Darlene. Special thanks to my cousin Ronnie Sims for the literal drive down memory lane.

Thank you to JuLee Brand of W. Brand Publishing for bringing this story to print. I am continually thankful to be an author in the community you have built.

I couldn't have done this without the love and support of my mom, Nickie. She is my biggest fan and critic. I knew this story was solid when I could make her laugh out loud and then cry two pages later.

Finally, to my dad, who passed away too soon. His childhood stories were as rich as any book I've ever read. The book you're holding came from a story he told my cousins and I numerous times. He *did* walk home alone following a Cub Scout meeting. He *did* encounter something that scared him witless. He *did* throw his marbles at it. He said that something was the Wooly-Bully. And according to "credible" websites, he's not alone. More than 160 sightings of Bigfoot/Sasquatch have been reported in the Show Me State.

I've tweaked a few other childhood memories he shared to add excitement to Zeke's life. My dad talked about jumping on trains to go between towns—what's a guy to do without a car? He had a gnarly scar from the arch of his foot to halfway up his lower leg from the time he jumped shoeless into a ditch and landed on a shattered soda bottle. Instead of going to the doctor, a family member familiar with various remedies wrapped his foot with mud and herbs. It worked, but man, what a scar.

Lastly, the only two books my dad read cover to cover were his Bible and the inches-thick exhaustive concordance that went with it. He was a man of faith and strong beliefs, and he encouraged me in my faith and creativity. I like to think the God who created the platypus and okapi gifted me with a creative side to invent my own worlds. I think my dad would have really liked this one—and the ones that follow.

ABOUT THE AUTHOR

K im Orendor is an award-winning author and jour-
nalist. Her second book, *To Whom It May Concern*
(Idun), won the 2024 NextGen INDIE Awards gold
medal for youth adult fiction.

A Bigfoot Homecoming is her third book.

Before writing books, Kim honed her writing craft as a
sports reporter and editor at *The Sacramento Bee* and *The Davis
Enterprise*. At *The Enterprise*, she won state and national awards
during her twenty-year tenure.

Kim's career path took a dramatic turn in 2006 when she
began a five-year teaching stint at Sias International Univer-
sity in China's Henan Province. The administration took advantage of her newspaper experience, and she taught news-

paper and reading classes. She also taught American Culture Through Film where she learned the universal secrets behind storytelling. This led to her first book, a memoir *Unbound Feet: Finding Freedom in Communist China*, also with W. Brand Publishing.

Kim returned to the Sacramento area in 2018 to be a caretaker for her parents. Her dad, a Navy veteran, was diagnosed with a rare neurological disease and passed in 2022. Kim continues to live in Northern California with her mom.